THE WATCHERS AT WAR

THE WATCHERS AT WAR

The Watchers of Moniah

BARBARA V. EVERS

Cameleopard Press

Contents

VL Publishing/Cameleopard Press
Greer, SC
Cover Art by Miblart.

The Watchers at War/Barbara V. Evers – 2nd ed.
Print ISBN: 978-1-959859-13-0
Ebook ISBN: 978-1-959859-12-3

To Bruce, my rock, my hero, my Kiffen.

Acknowledgments

I can't begin to tell you how humbling it is that people choose to read my books. From the bottom of my heart, I thank each and every one of you who picked up and read Adana's story and decided to share it with others.

Writing is never a solitary endeavor, and if you had any part in my journey, you have my gratitude. Still, there are several whom I must mention. To Rowe and Beau, my sounding boards as I struggled through the process of getting this story right, thank you for letting me bounce ideas off of you. Also, to Rowe, for always believing in this series and forgiving me for some of the events that had to happen in this book.

My journey to tell this story began many years ago, and my faithful writing tribe, the Greenville SCWA chapter, gave me encouragement, support, and advise when I needed it. Thanks go to Marcia, John, Bob, Phil, Adrienne, Jim, Roiselyn, Larry, Gill, Alexa, Vyki, Allen, and Jane. Every book needs an editor or two, and I've been blessed with Rowe, who knows these characters almost as well as I do, and Mia, who has an incredible knack for suggesting the right adjustment to enhance the reader's experience.

Several others contributed in their own ways. David B. Coe receives the honor—as I promised at the time—of naming the newest giraffe in this book, and Darin Kennedy has my undying thanks for his quick response to medical questions while I struggled through a difficult scene.

A special thanks to Miblart for creating new book covers for this series You take my suggestions and what you come back with always amazes me. Thanks for putting up with all of my tweaks and suggestions, especially with this cover.

I've said this many times on social media, but I must thank the people who encouraged me to pursue writing in my early years: Mary P. Seamon, the best English teacher a high school student could want, and Vivian Gladden, my early transcriber. In my later years, I must add Faith Hunter, my encourager when things got tough.

And always, my undying love and gratitude for my husband, Bruce, who believes I can do anything.

I

The giraffes came to them in towers, groups of three or four at first. Then they arrived in larger towers with as many as ten.

Adana, exiled queen of Moniah, knew of their arrival first through her bond with Am'brosia, her royal giraffe. A ripple of excitement along their connection drew her away from the displaced leaders and soldiers gathered around the map table dominating the room in the Border Keep's Central Tower. It had been four days since her kingdom fell to the traitor. Four days putting their dead to rest and arguing strategy.

She strayed to the window, relieved Am'brosia's emotional pull gave her a distraction. Below, throngs of refugees and soldiers rushed to the outermost gates, energy and excitement in their actions obvious even at this distance—evident to all, not just a visually-gifted Watcher.

"Did Am'brosia alert you?" A warm hand on her shoulder accompanied Kiffen's breath on her neck.

She nodded, taking comfort in his closeness. The one constant in her life right now, her betrothed. Did her presence do the same for him? With Kiffen's throne seized by his stepmother and Kiffen declared outlaw for the crime of agreeing to marry her, a savage queen, did he find solace with her?

I

"Bai'dish did, too." He leaned in closer. "Do you know why?"

"I got a glimpse of giraffes through the bond."

She had, but what did it mean?

A stir outside the keep's gates drew her attention, the slight shift visible to her through her Watcher's gift, but not yet visible to a man not blessed with this sight. She gasped and tried to stifle her shout of glee, but a little squeak erupted from her mouth. Grabbing Kiffen's hand, she said, "Do you see him?"

He shook his head.

She pointed. "There. Look over there, across the lake."

A large giraffe stood on the edge of the lake, his head and neck visible beyond the walls as he moved toward the makeshift bridge set up for refugees to cross the lake and enter the keep. Behind him came two more giraffes. No, three. A calf, almost hidden among the mother's legs, ambled along.

A quick squeeze to her shoulder told her Kiffen saw them.

The door to the map room burst open, startling the leaders and advisors gathered there. They frowned in consternation as Glume, Moniah's giraffe keeper, rushed into the room, panting. Eyes bright, his cheeks rounded by a grin, he sought out Adana's gaze. "Your Majesty, they've come." Without waiting for a response, he turned and sprinted from the room, his agility hard to fathom for a man of his bulk.

The other commanders turned to Adana and Kiffen, their faces registering confusion and curiosity.

"Who's come?" Montee, the First Vision, left the table and came to the window.

"Giraffes." Adana couldn't hold back the grin that erupted with her announcement.

The six other people in the room crowded around the east-facing windows in the tower.

Adana grabbed Kiffen's arm and pulled him past their advisors toward the door. "Come. Glume wants us."

A lightness came to her limbs as they rushed down the tower's stairs. The keep's layout forced them to travel through the halls of the central tower to the gate leading into the West Tower. The stairs and corridors echoed with their hurried footsteps, the silence profound except for their passage. No one roamed the corridors or clogged the stairwells. Everyone must have gone outside or were in the outer rim of the keep.

Circling the middle part of the keep, they headed to the gate that opened into the outer, walled section. With no one around to see, Adana dropped her royal demeanor and ran. The pure joy and freedom of movement added to her excitement. No woman in Elwar could do this, not wearing the mandatory heavy skirts of their society. After spending nine seasons in that kingdom, she would never take something as simple as clothing styles for granted. No matter if Elwarian women frowned over her Watcher's leggings and tunic.

Behind her, Kiffen, the one good thing she'd found in Elwar, laughed and raced to catch up.

A large mass of people crowded the gate to the outer wall. Adana, blessed by the height of a Watcher, peered over their heads trying to determine the delay. Nothing moved.

But even this didn't destroy her excitement. Giraffes, here, at the keep, far from the plains of Moniah where they lived.

A quick touch to her link with Am'brosia sent a new spurt of energy through the connection. Her giraffe reveled with joy over the arrival of her kind. That's all Adana could learn from the bond, though. Am'brosia moved somewhere in the keep as she did, anxious to greet these newcomers. Bai'dish followed her, the two giraffes able to navigate the gathering crowds due to their size. The keep's inhabitants gave them wide berths, still unsure how to react to noble giraffes living among them.

Montee, who had followed closely behind Adana and Kiffen, pushed through the crowd. "Make way for the queen. Make way for the king."

A narrow gap appeared, and their small band rushed through the Eastern Gate. People had spread out along the shores of the lake encircling the keep's island. An excited babble of voices grew in volume as the first giraffes stepped off the temporary bridge. The animals stood on the small jut of land beyond the wooden dock, unable to come farther.

Seven more giraffes stood on the opposite shore of the lake, hesitant to cross the bridge. Hopefully, they would not attempt it. That four of them managed without it collapsing said more for the quality of the makeshift bridge than anyone expected.

In the midst of the four who had crossed, Glume stood offering carrots and patting their flanks. He looked up in delight as Adana approached, the people stepping back to give her room. "Mistress, they have come."

The joy on the man's face washed over her, and she laughed with delight as she drew near the tower of giraffes.

At the sound of her laughter, the animals turned and eyed her. The tallest one spread his legs and bowed, dropping his neck and head low to the ground. The ones behind him, with no room to properly bow, lowered their necks.

A murmur of awe raced through the crowd. Adana accepted this homage, the warmth of love for her kingdom's most sacred animal spreading through her chest. At a nudge from Kiffen, she looked across the lake in time to see the seven on the other side of the bridge bowing, too.

She sensed the approach of Am'brosia before her bonded giraffe reached her. Now eight years old, Am'brosia stood over twice as tall as Adana. All the giraffes remained bowed until Am'brosia and

Bai'dish came to a stop behind Adana and Kiffen. Then, as one, they raised their heads and gazed toward the royal giraffes.

Adana placed a tentative hand on the elongated face of the one closest to her, amazed the unknown animal allowed the contact. These weren't the giraffes who lived inside Adana's View, her fortress and Seat of Authority.

Why had they come? She sent the question to Am'brosia.

An image of the Border Keep, perched on its island at the center of a large lake, swam into view. A circle of giraffes stood around the entire outer wall. Another circle surrounded the opposite shore of the lake. With these images came a surge of pride from Am'brosia.

Unsure what to make of this, Adana wandered between the giraffes and followed Glume across the bridge to the other shore. When she caught up to the man, he already stood in their midst.

"Glume, why are they here? Where are they from?"

"Mistress, these giraffes traveled from the wild. From the plains beyond your fortress. They come to serve you and their queen."

"Isn't she their queen?" Kiffen asked.

Adana turned to find him behind her again, unfazed by the animals towering over them. Yes, he shared a bond with his own giraffe, Bai'dish, but that bond was fresh and untested.

Kiffen, raised in Elwar, a land of mountains and forests, still worked to understand his bonded connection with Bai'dish. Most people preferred observing the tall beasts from a distance, where the sheer size of them did not overwhelm them. Kiffen, once more, found a way to surprise and thrill her with his willingness to venture among the towering animals.

Glume nodded at Kiffen. "Queen Adana is their queen, yes, but Am'brosia is their queen, too. And Bai'dish their king, as well as you."

A brief, curious "huh" escaped Kiffen's mouth as he reached a tentative hand out to touch the flank of the nearest giraffe. He opened his mouth to speak, but excited murmurs from the crowd stopped him. From the edge of the forest, another tower of giraffes emerged. At least ten more.

Before Adana could finish counting this tower, more emerged near the southern edge of the lake. These giraffe looked familiar. She turned to Glume, hoping for some hint as to why.

Unaware of her questioning glance, the keeper wandered through the trees of giraffe legs heading for the edge of the lake. She'd never seen him so content. The stiffness in his shoulders, present ever since the Battle for Adana's View, no longer shoved his neck forward, hunching his back. His face had relaxed into gentle rapture.

The stoic man had spent his life among the giraffes in Adana's View. Until now. Ever since Maligon seized her Seat of Authority, Glume's charges had dropped to two, Am'brosia and Bai'dish. It never occurred to her the absence of other giraffes might cause him stress. Yet the proof stood before her.

At this, a horrific thought struck her. What of the giraffes inside Adana's View? Those chosen to serve the queen living within the vast estate. She would feel their distress through Am'brosia, wouldn't she? Or Glume would say something. At least, she thought he would. No one understood the depth of his ability to communicate with giraffes, a life's secret kept until Am'brosia had revealed it a few weeks before.

A hazy image wavered along Am'brosia's bond; more giraffes gathered at the edge of the pastures within her estate. They stood among the trees at the edge of the High Field, far from the traitors who had captured the fortress. Relief rushed through her limbs. Brief lived, though, followed by a different concern. Maligon knew the giraffes' powers. So far, it appeared he hadn't concerned himself over their presence, but at some point, he would remember them. What then?

Before this worry could drive her deeper from the joy of the moment, a giraffe's soft nose caressed her hair. She looked up in time to see the last of the familiar giraffes emerge from the trees. An old bull came last, the knobby ossicones on his head large and rubbed free of fur. He stretched his neck toward the sun now that he was clear of the forest's overlapping branches.

With a start of recognition, she gasped. "He's alive."

The dizzying journey on the day her mother died swelled into her memory. An incredible and rare experience, Am'brosia had controlled their bond, pulling their sight beyond the walls of the fortress. Their combined vision had traveled across her kingdom, jumping from one giraffe's sight to the next and the next and the next.

When the dizzying journey halted at the edge of her kingdom, she and Am'brosia had shared the sight of an old bull giraffe, the same giraffe coming out of the forest now.

From a distant hill, she and Am'brosia had witnessed the return of Maligon using this giraffe's sight. The traitor somehow sensed her presence that day and ordered one of his archers to shoot the giraffe. She had always thought the giraffe had died. Died because of her.

A lightness of thanks eased some of the guilt in her gut. The giraffe lived.

Glume stood next to her, nodding as if he knew her thoughts. Knowing the giraffes, he probably did. "The arrow grazed him, but he survived. He bears a scar on his left hindquarter."

Scarred, but alive.

The injury had thrown her out of the vision on that horrible day. The day her mother died. The same day Serrin, Kiffen's younger brother and her first betrothed, died, leaving her with no one in the world to lean on.

Glume patted her hand in reassurance. "He's honored you re-member him, mistress. He's summoned these towers to serve you. He wishes me to share his name with you. He is known as Tog."

A name with a singular sound. How odd. "It's unusual."

"Not for wild giraffes, mistress. People give them fancy names. Animals in the wild have simple ones."

Kiffen cleared his throat. She'd forgotten he was standing behind her. "But why are they here?"

"To guard the keep, Sir Kiffen."

"But we don't have room..." Adana began.

"Not inside the keep. They will remain out here. Guarding outside the walls and around the lake."

Am'brosia's earlier image made sense, now, but doubt crept into Adana's thoughts. In the wide-open spaces of the savanna, the giraffe's height and great vision gave anyone near them an advantage. Called the watch towers, giraffes saw and responded to danger first. Other animals followed their lead. The Watchers, women gifted with enhanced sight, based their existence and training on this protective trait of the giraffes.

The Border Keep sat on the border between Elwar to the north and Moniah to the south. Trees and rolling hills obstructed most of the view. What could giraffes see here?

Even her Watchers struggled, their gifts of enhanced sight blocked by the closer quarters, forests, and hills. Only in a small area south of the keep could they breathe with relief and seek the horizon.

"Their help is welcome news," Kiffen said. "We can reduce the watch and give our soldiers rest and time to prepare for battle."

She glanced up at him in surprise. His lack of familiarity with giraffes allowed him to see something she had missed.

"What is it?" he asked, a frown replacing his pleased expression.

Instead of answering, she studied the current guards. The giraffes would see as well as any guard, probably better. Their connection through the royal giraffes meant she and Kiffen would know the instant one of them detected danger.

She smiled. "Do we have enough armor for all of them?"

2

The flurry of excitement over the giraffes' arrival disrupted the rest of the day's strategizing. Kiffen remained near Adana and the giraffes, but he worried over the delay.

They needed to plan a counterattack against Maligon before he came after them in the last place they held. The man waged war on everyone in the four kingdoms, seizing Elwar, Belwyn, and Teletia before heading to Moniah, Adana's kingdom and his true goal. The rest of the coups forced the victims to divide their forces while he swept into Moniah with his traitorous army.

Adana still wandered between the gathering giants. She looked small and delicate among them, an observation she might find amusing considering her height, almost even with Kiffen's.

Another tower arrived, and she rushed to greet them. According to Glume, this tower traveled the farthest, out of the desert south of Moniah.

"Not from Moniah?" Kiffen asked Glume.

"No. From beyond." Glume observed the beasts strolling on the lake's shore. "All giraffes share homage to Moniah."

Kiffen stopped calculating the number of giraffes needed to guard the perimeter of the lake and the keep. "Why would giraffes from outside Moniah serve us?"

The older man leaned against a stone pillar marking the entrance to the bridge. "When the first queen—Queen Moniah—found and nursed the injured giraffe calf, she became the first person to ever bond with one. She sensed sadness in the animal. The connection overwhelmed her." He smiled at Kiffen, signaling his awareness of his own struggle to adapt to the bond with Bai'dish. "She didn't know how to respond or manage it."

"Not hard to imagine." Kiffen felt sudden kinship with the ancient Matriarch. A presence hovered in the back of his mind, always there until he or Bai'dish sought a deeper connection. Even thinking about it drew the giraffe deeper in his awareness.

Glume watched him, head tilted to the side for a moment, then continued his story. "She refused to ignore the giraffe's emotions and finally learned the animal grieved over the death of his tower, that's what we call several giraffes together. Giraffes were dying out. Queen Moniah spent endless hours working out a way to communicate with the giraffe. When she succeeded, she proposed forming a special relationship between them. The giraffes would share the bond with each generation of rulers descended from her. In turn, she promised to protect them. All of them."

Along the unusual connection, Bai'dish's contentment radiated with satisfaction. The animal's serenity stemmed from having just eaten or re-eaten as giraffes do. Kiffen wasn't sure which. Or how he knew this.

It felt like the giraffe shook his head over that last thought. Never groomed as Adana's betrothed, Kiffen had half-listened when his younger brother rambled about the bond. Until Serrin died and Bai'dish survived to select Kiffen as Adana's betrothed, the bond never mattered to him.

Aware Glume watched him with curious eyes, Kiffen faced the man. "So, they are here. All the giraffes from the savanna and desert?"

Sixty of them wandered the lakeshore, now.

"Mercy no." Glume laughed. "Thanks to Queen Moniah's agreement, they've had centuries to recover their numbers. Hundreds upon thousands of giraffes roam the plains, now."

"If they're to guard us, how can we protect them? That's the agreement, isn't it?"

"You can't," Glume said. "These giraffes have chosen to endanger their lives to protect you."

An army of giraffes. He should feel remorse over their potential deaths, but memories of fighting the last battle with Bai'dish in his mind made him appreciate the sacrifice. Throughout the battle, Bai'dish warned him of danger, his and Adana's. He even knew when a soldier would strike from behind. They both survived unharmed.

Could they bond all the soldiers to giraffes?

Glume snorted at the same time Bai'dish's emotions spiraled in alarm. A raised eyebrow from the round, older man confirmed his suspicion. Sometimes Bai'dish shared too much of Kiffen's thoughts with the keeper.

"Why can't we connect an entire troop to the giraffes?" Kiffen asked.

"Disaster," Glume said. "Plus, there's not enough of the potion. It's rare. It took me years to adjust to all the giraffes' attention. You're still learning your own way through the bond, and you're only bonded to one." He sighed. "Remember, when you're connected to Bai'dish, sometimes you feel Am'brosia through him."

"Which links me to Adana somehow."

"Yes. A whole army connected to giraffes?" Glume shook his head. "Chaos."

Agreement sizzled from Bai'dish. How he knew the meaning of the giraffe's thought, Kiffen didn't understand, but he did. At least this time.

A swish of leather preceded the arrival of the intoxicating scents he associated with Adana, sunshine and fresh air and berries. Every time she drew near, his heart raced. He was surprised no one could see it pulsing beneath his tunic.

Unaware of his thoughts, she addressed him in the tone of a queen, not his betrothed. "We may have lost our councilors as they cope with our new arrivals, but I would speak with you." She gestured for him to follow her. "We must determine our next step without their constant bickering."

He turned and followed. When he drew up beside her, he entwined his hand with hers, and warmth curled up his palm at the touch. She slanted a smile up at him, and the pounding in his chest rocketed.

* * *

The next morning, Adana and Kiffen gathered with their advisors. Ten of them circled the large map in the tower room: the First Vision Montee; Simeon, Kiffen's advisor; Kassa, the former First Vision; the Watchers Sinti and Nuala; Halar, Commander of Moniah's Soldiers of the First Sight; Sergeant Markel, the highest-ranking officer of the loyal members of Elwar's army; and Prince Jerold of the Kingdom of Belwyn. The only kingdom missing was Teletia.

The discussions went as Adana anticipated. She and Kiffen bided their time, letting the others argue their points. They'd learned before the last battle that the more experienced warriors often negated their suggestions due to their youth.

"Shouldn't we retake Elwar or Teletia first?" Simeon circled the map of the four kingdoms, fingers drumming on the surface.

"No," Prince Jerold countered. "We should send forces to Belwyn to rescue my mother from the dungeons." Jerold's mother, Empress Gabriella, had refused to marry Maligon when he first returned from his exile. He infiltrated her guard and imprisoned her for it.

"King Ariff is weeks ahead of us in that regard," Montee said. "For all we know, he's overtaken the kingdom for Empress Gabriella already. We should retake Adana's View before Maligon gains strength."

King Ariff's kingdom of Teletia fell first to Maligon. Thanks to quick thinking on his son's part, the royal family had escaped through a secret passageway. Once assured of his family's safety, Ariff had volunteered to join a squad of Watchers in an attempt to rescue Empress Gabriella. Rumors of Watchers imprisoned in the same dungeons persuaded several Watchers to make the rescue attempt, and they had accepted Ariff's addition to their mission.

Adana had sent one of her fleetest Watchers, the fastest messenger available since the carrier pigeons had disappeared from the Border Keep, to locate Ariff and alert him to the news of the fall of Elwar and Moniah.

The bickering at the table continued until Kiffen caught Adana's gaze, eyebrows raised. She nodded.

He rose and interrupted Halar's rant about the First Soldiers' duty to Queen Adana and her Seat of Authority.

"Silence." He spoke the word in a normal voice, not loud or soft.

Startled, everyone turned to Kiffen. Adana scanned the group, noting the tiny quirks on their faces, an entire language to Watchers.

Kassa's hawk-like gaze zeroed in on Kiffen, her face a stony blank, thoughts hidden except for Adana's awareness of the impatience this particular gaze implied.

Halar, Kassa's husband but not a Watcher, dropped his mouth open in confusion then snapped it shut.

Simeon drummed his fingers on the table, only glancing up for a moment before returning to his study of the map.

Montee smiled. Had she known? In her years of training under Montee, the First Vision never missed the minute clues alerting her to Adana's plans. Somehow, she picked up on ideas and thoughts Adana barely considered.

Once he had everyone's attention, Kiffen began the speech they had crafted the night before. "Three years ago, the four kingdoms gathered to discuss our concerns about Maligon's rumored return. At that time, I suggested he sought to divide us and spread our forces too far to aid each other. Even though we knew this, we still fell prey to his plan. Our armies responded to the needs of our people and were sent in many directions. This weakened each of the kingdoms.

"If we continue to argue, he will continue to triumph. Your discussions delay us too long. We must act, and Adana and I have decided on our next steps."

Prince Jerold glared between the two of them, probably concerned that they hadn't included him in their discussions. Yes. He was Belwyn's prince, but he wasn't the ranking ruler in the room, and his identity as Gabriella's son remained a secret to most people. Adana knew from her discussions with him that his training in leading armies fell short, even though his enthusiasm hid it well.

Kiffen continued, "I'd like to know what Maligon is doing while we argue."

"And how would you do that, sire?" Simeon asked.

Adana sat forward, thankful to finally share their plan. "We should send Suru and Nuala back into Adana's View. Through the aqueducts."

The two Watchers had escaped the fortress just before Maligon breached the gates. Unlike most of the inhabitants in the estate, Suru knew how to get in and out through the aqueducts. The only source of water this close to the desert, the location and access of the waterways remained a guarded secret.

Adana turned her persuasive powers on Montee, ignoring the rest of them. "At the least, we can find out if anyone has discovered the passages. If not, we can use them to our advantage."

The room grew quiet as the others considered her words. In the silence, Father Tonch, the Keeper of the Faith, entered the room. He nodded in her direction. "I concur with the queen."

It still felt odd to be called queen, especially without a crown or coronation to reinforce the title. Glancing around the room, she found acceptance and acknowledgement of a good idea. After three years of fighting for a voice in her own kingdom, had she gained it, or did they defer to Tonch?

Kiffen stood taller, his shoulders thrown back in a measure of confidence she'd seen only once. On the night of their betrothal. He had grown into his role in the short period of time following that startling announcement. His confidence faltered only once. That same night when an armed gang attacked the gates of Elwar's castle protesting the planned marriage.

Adana turned to Nuala when no one spoke in opposition to this plan. "Can you manage this? Slip in undetected and gather information?"

"We will do so, Your Majesty. With pleasure."

"Good." She turned to the others. "I must ask for a private audience with Nuala and Suru to discuss these plans."

Simeon and Jerold lurched forward; mouths open to object.

Their acceptance fell short of full belief in her capabilities, it appeared. Arching a brow at them, Adana said, "I prefer to keep the location of our aqueducts secret. The fewer who know, the less likely the wrong people find them."

"If you're to use them for an attack," Jerold said, "we will need to know."

"And you will if that time comes. But not yet. Montee and Simeon, please stay. The rest of you, please leave our presence."

It was a royal order. They left, faces sour with displeasure, although Kassa cast a sharp glance over her shoulder as she went through the door. A rare smile of approval shimmered across her face and disappeared.

Adana nodded toward Nuala. "Call Suru in, please."

Nuala summoned the Watcher from the hallway where she and two others stood guard. A lean and muscular woman, Suru entered the room and bowed her head in Adana's and Kiffen's direction. "Your Majesties."

"Where is the aqueduct access in the fortress?" Adana asked the moment the door closed.

One half-blink gave the only indication of Suru's surprise. Like any Watcher, she regained control of her expression before most would note the shock, a lesson learned in their first season of training. "The access, Your Majesty? You wish me to disclose this information?" She glanced between Montee, Kiffen, and Simeon.

Good. She wasn't willing to reveal the secret without cause. The Watchers and glimmer makers who knew the passages beneath Adana's View endured years of warnings and lessons on how to protect the fortress' secret to fresh water. The Watchers for obvious reasons of protection; the glimmer makers to hide the secrets of the valuable, iridescent substance responsible for Moniah's wealth. Were those people still at work below the fortress or had they been discovered by the invading army?

Adana glanced at Montee. "Flame and Sword, correct?"

Suru answered instead of Montee. "Yes. That is the password."

The Watcher approached the huge map table in the center of the room. She leaned over the area devoted to Moniah's royal fortress and circled the table. With one last glance at Adana, she laid her finger on an area beyond the southernmost wing of Moniah's fortress, behind the horse stables. "The easiest way to gain access without detection will be behind the stables, near the pigeon coops. There are two others. Does the queen wish me to share those?"

The question encouraged confidence in Suru's loyalty and honor. As queen, she should have known all three, the information shared with her the night before her coronation. A night yet to come. "Yes. I believe we can trust this gathering."

"One is beneath your Seat of Authority in the Great Hall. It's meant for a quick escape if you're threatened while holding court. The other is in the queen's chambers, the access triggered from within the queen's chest. That one's purpose, I believe, needs no explanation."

The chest at the foot of her mother's—no, *her* sleeping chaise, if she ever managed to take her home back from Maligon. Opening it required knowledge of a secret clasp, its location still not shared with her, either. Escape from the queen's chambers required extra time to trigger a second secret within. Clever or foolhardy?

Adana took a deep breath, let it flood her chest, then released it in a slow breath through her lips. She breathed again, using the exercise to awaken memories of her home. On the edge of her focus, Am'brosia's presence floated, the giraffe's gentling influence drawing her deeper into the trance.

Tapping her fingers together, one by one, she explored the routes. The Great Hall, too open and risky. Her chambers provided access to Maligon and Shana, a tavern maid turned spy who happened to resemble Adana enough to be her decoy. Could she trust her? Was Shana still loyal to Adana, who opened her awareness to her gift of Listening, or had they handed the wench over to her true masters as a queen replacement?

Adana shook her hand, releasing those thoughts, and tapped her ring finger to her thumb. The access behind the stables provided the safest route into the fortress, but it left a lot of open ground to cover without detection. From there, Suru and Nuala would have to navigate the Watcher's barracks and still cross the Great Hall to reach the royal wing. A gentle nudge from the bond with Am'brosia opened her sight to a vision of the fortress at night. She saw the queen's chambers in the moonlight, and the sleeping form of a woman who looked so much like Adana it choked her for a moment. Am'brosia trusted Shana.

Warmth spread within her shoulder. The puncture wound from her recognition ceremony in Elwar casting endorsement of Shana? It had flared hot and uncomfortable over the last few days. The warmth eased the pain considerably. It must mean approval.

The bond surged again. Images of Suru and Nuala floated between her and Am'brosia. They could trust these two Watchers to choose well.

"Suru. Nuala. I need you to gain access to the royal chambers and learn what Maligon is planning. I would also like to know how Shana—the decoy queen—fares. If you judge it wise, try and speak to her. I believe you should go at night, but I leave the choice of access to the two of you. You're well-trained Watchers. You managed to escape without detection. I believe you can return safely, too."

Before either could reply, Montee said, "If at all possible, try to gauge the numbers of Watchers and soldiers in the fortress and for signs of their loyalties. Maybe some still remain loyal to our queen."

Kiffen stepped forward and studied the map. "It's been six years since I saw the inside of Adana's View. I remember its expansiveness, nothing more. We need information on the troops, but the barracks are nowhere near the royal wing. Where are the kitchens and laundry? Gossiping servants might be a better source."

Adana sighed. They managed to oust from the room those who delayed decisions and still couldn't agree. "I believe we need to leave the choice up to Nuala and Suru. We have no idea what they'll find. They're trained to shift plans when necessary." She eyed Kiffen before returning her gaze to Nuala and Suru. "I give my blessing on your ability to make the best choice."

Relief flooded over her when Kiffen nodded in agreement. So far, they agreed on everything. The time would come when they didn't. At least it was not today.

3

⸎

The night air brushed over Shana's uncovered legs as she reclined on the chaise in the Monian queen's chambers. Restless, she sat up and wandered out onto her private courtyard. A fountain gurgled in the night's silence; the sound of refreshing coolness still surprising in this hot, dry land.

In the distance, she heard Maligon's agitated voice in discussion with Brother Honest's calm one. "A teacher presumes to advise me at war?"

How long before Maligon realized she and Honest served Adana and not him?

Honest's voice, though soft, still sounded clear in her ears. "It's been six days. You must act soon while they still try to recover."

The idea of striking the Border Keep made her stomach clench. What if Adana died in the attack? Or Kiffen? An outcome Maligon desired so no one could deny her false claim to the throne. Some nights she lay awake, troubled over the idea that she, Shana the tavern maid, masqueraded as queen of this huge kingdom. So many would laugh until they cried and soiled their pants over that one.

Just last night, during her prescribed time of religious guidance, Honest told her of his plan to pressure Maligon to act. "The sooner we attack, the better. Maligon's soldiers have no formal training. I doubt all of them truly support him. Many plundered the fortress and left the next day."

"But we don't know what's happened to Adana and Kiffen." She hadn't mentioned her closest friend, Joannu. She'd seen the Watcher taken down in the battle. Cold shame threatened to drive her to her knees every time she recalled what happened. The plan, one of Honest's again, was for Pultarch's men to grab Shana instead of Adana. When they did, Joannu came after her anyway. She knew the plan. Why had she thrown away her life over a tavern maid?

"Adana and Kiffen live." Brother Honest's voice radiated strength and conviction. "All our sources say so."

That news—that Queen Adana resided at the Border Keep with her betrothed King Kiffen of Elwar—wreaked havoc with Maligon's plans. He'd bellowed and complained for an entire day before bothering to listen to Samantha's advice—send out official notices stating the woman at the keep was a pretender. Proclaim Shana the true queen.

A bit shorter and lighter-skinned, Shana resembled Adana enough to convince the Watchers who remained in the fortress. They hadn't seen their queen in three years because she had lived in Elwar until she was of age to reign.

Wrapping her arms around herself to ward off the night's chill, she tuned in to the voices of Honest and Maligon rumbling in the night.

"The soldiers aren't prepared," Maligon said.

"Is anyone ever prepared for battle?" Honest countered.

She stopped listening and wandered across the sandstone floor to sit on the edge of the fountain. The stones still held warmth from the day's unyielding sun, but the night air cooled quickly this close to the desert.

From this perfect—but not rightfully hers—seat, the courtyard provided a peaceful scene and escape from the realities of pretending to be queen. Not that pretension challenged her abilities. She'd survived the tavern and she would survive this new role, thanks to her ability to adopt the manner of others. A talent Adana and Joannu told her came from her gifts as a Listener, the same gift that helped her eavesdrop on the two men.

A tiny splash on the far side of the fountain snatched her from her reverie. Circling the huge stone structure, Shana searched the water's surface in the moonlight. A tiny blob no bigger than her fist bobbed in the fountain squeaking with fright. Kneeling on the stone edge, she scooped the floundering creature from the water. Its body writhed in her hands, and the yellow eyes of an odd-looking rodent locked on her. Its large ears made her giggle as it clawed at the air, scrambling to escape.

"There, there," she said. "You're safe." Setting the unusual mouse down on the stone floor, she waited for it to streak away. If she saw where it went, she could alert her maid to its presence. A mouse in the fortress meant more.

Instead of running away, it rose on its hind legs, whiskers twitching, and regarded her.

With a shrug, she started back to her favorite spot on the fountain's side. "Suit yourself, but if someone gave me a chance of escape, I'd take it."

The mouse scampered after her using short hops. When she sat, it jumped onto the wall beside her, hesitated a moment, then leapt onto her leg.

Stifling a squeal of surprise, Shana stared at it. She held her breath in amazement. When it didn't move, only looked up at her with its tiny eyes, she placed a tentative finger on its still damp back and stroked it. The mouse leaned into her hand. No Elwarian mouse hopped or had large ears. "How odd. What are you little guy?"

The voices of Honest and Maligon returned to her ears, strong and easy to understand.

"Do you really trust her?" Maligon's sharp voice carried an edge of sarcasm. "I know Sarx groomed her, but she spent time with Adana. Is she truly ours?"

Her heart pounding loud enough to block her hearing, Shana strained for Honest's answer. In her imagination, his thumb and forefinger pulled at his lower lip as he considered. After a long pause, he said, "I don't think Adana endeared herself to Shana. The queen is an untrusting girl. Difficult to warm up to. Probably something learned from her father."

"Right, right. Micah. Thank the Creator we're done with that usurper finally. Such a pompous bore he was."

Even Shana knew of the hatred between the two men. Thank goodness Honest had a knack for saying the right thing to appease Maligon. At least, so far. Was that part of his Empathic abilities? She wished she knew more about his gifts. And hers. The night Adana figured out she was a Listener still came to her in the quiet hours. The thrill and rush of realizing she heard things others didn't. Of course, she'd known about her amazing hearing, but to have it affirmed, and by a queen? She felt lightheaded just remembering it.

The recumbent mouse shuddered in her hands. Its whiskers twitched. The voices had faded for a moment but now returned to her.

"She needs training," Maligon said. "Not enough to cause harm, but questions will come if she doesn't behave like a Watcher. She uses their mannerisms, that blazing stoicism that hides all thoughts, and she appears to read people well. Still, we need her to fool everyone. You believe she can keep this up?"

A tiny squeak of protest from the mouse made Shana realize she'd tightened her hold while leaning forward, waiting for Honest's reply. "Sorry." She set the mouse down on the fountain.

Watcher training. Could she handle a bow? Or a sword? A knife posed no issues. Nor a hatchet. All tavern maids knew how to use them. Necessity was a strong teacher.

The voices faded from hearing. She sighed. How did Honest answer?

"Your Majesty?" The young, round-faced Watcher assigned as one of her honor guard called from within the chambers. Almost as tall as Shana, Malay's outline in the doorway blended with the darkness of the room, her skin as dark as the night. "I thought you had retired."

The mouse on the fountain bounded away in one impressive jump. In two more, it disappeared into the night.

As fast as the tiny rodent hopped, Malay flung her knife at the creature but missed. "Jerboa in the fortress. They carry the pox. I'll need to alert the kitchens."

The woman retrieved her knife and peered in the shadows where the animal disappeared. "No surprise with armies coming and going these days. They always bring vermin."

Annoyed at Malay frightening the creature away, Shana pushed the emotion down in order to speak with curiosity not annoyance. "You think there are more?"

"Maybe. They're hard to catch. Takes poison. No worries. We'll clean any out before they do damage." She gazed at Shana, head cocked to the side. "Trouble sleeping?"

"It's been a long time since I've seen the night sky." Honest had drilled her on things Adana might say. Even she understood this one. She'd missed seeing the huge expanse of sky above her while working in Elwar's capital. The stars shone so bright here. Even when Queen Adana sought refuge in the village of Roshar, the many cookfires in the army's camp and the refugees' camp hid the splendor of the night.

Malay tilted her head upward and smiled, her teeth flashing in the light. "I can't imagine how you managed for so long. I love the stars, especially here, close to the desert."

"Yes." She gave a not-so-fake shudder. "You can't see the sky for the buildings, except in the country. Not much opportunity for that, though." She rose and headed for her chambers. "Thank you for checking on me. I'm tired now."

* * *

Nuala and Suru approached the fortress after midnight. It took almost two days instead of four to reach Adana's View thanks to the underground tunnel network below the Border Keep.

The moon had cooperated with their journey as they drew closer. The small crescent moon ducked in and out from behind a few wispy clouds. Its dim, shadowed light bathed the landscape with just enough to see by but not enough to be seen. A blessing from the Creator? Nuala hoped so.

Suru raised her hand in warning. Lower ranked than Nuala, the Watcher's position as a Water Watcher gave her advanced knowledge of this area outside the fortress, so Nuala accepted her guidance.

They huddled behind a small area of bushes, ones that cropped up after the rainy season. With the dry season coming to an end soon, Nuala couldn't believe this one remained from the last year. Most growth like this disappeared as the drought parched the land.

The massive cliff wall, a natural border, formed the southern and western edges of the fortress. It loomed above them, the walls sparse and flat, impossible to scale. A dense growth of thorny bushes, kept alive by Moniah's gardeners, thwarted any rash attempts to scale the cliff. The thick accumulation of long, spiked thorns stopped any thought of trying to cut through the bushes, too. Fire would destroy the growth in a short span of time, but only if one dared start a blaze in this dry land. Even invaders weren't that foolish.

A few lengths from the bushes grew a huge acacia tree, one of the many food sources for the giraffes. Thorns prevented climbing it, too, but they sought to go down, not up.

Suru walked to the trunk of the tree, turned west, and paced three steps. She stopped at a large bed of rocks tumbled over each other. Within these rocks, a hidden chasm led to the aqueducts. Even if someone discovered and entered the chasm, they might not realize it went anywhere. The access to the tunnels remained hidden beneath a cluster of stones larger than the ones outside.

Suru led Nuala into the chasm and down a rocky path. She lifted a chiseled section off a stone halfway to the end of the small cavern and dug her fingers into a groove. Stone ground against stone.

Nuala flinched at the loud sound.

Seeing her reaction, Suru said, "You can't hear it from outside. I've tried."

A narrow slit opened in the opposite wall, deeper within the cave. The two women slipped through, Suru activating its closure behind her.

The first thing Nuala noticed was the overwhelming moisture in the air. Even a few days earlier during their flight from Maligon's invasion, she'd noticed the humidity. Who wouldn't? She'd even dreamed about it.

A steady drip of water on stone farther down the path drew her forward like an antelope desperate for drink. She had never expected to see this place again, and its simple but valuable treasures rippled a chill that had nothing to do with the temperature across her arms and neck. The narrow passageway closed in around them, solid rock just a finger's width above her head and brushing her arms as she passed.

Unable to tolerate small spaces for long, Nuala inhaled and focused on her breathing, reminding herself that the chambers supported many who lived here.

Suru walked ahead of her, at ease with the confined space. At last, they reached the heavy entrance door to the aqueducts. Made of layer upon layer of cedar trunks, the scent mingled with the moisture, clearing Nuala's mind. She inhaled again, using the wood's perfume to aid in her focused breathing.

Suru knocked three times, paused, and knocked four more.

They waited. As the time extended, it ramped up the patter of Nuala's heart. Place her in the midst of battle or as a spy in enemy territory, and she thrived. Send her underground with close walls, and she fought to keep her breathing steady.

Many Watchers and glimmer makers worked in the aqueducts. She'd encouraged them to escape with her when Suru led them out of the fortress six days ago. After a whispered discussion, Miri, the Water Maji, and Vuur, the Glimmer Isati, declined. "We will send two Watchers to greet the queen. The rest will remain here to protect Moniah's secrets."

Suru repeated the knocking pattern. Nuala swallowed. She should have made them evacuate. "Do you think they've been found?"

"No. They're here. If Maligon found the waterway's access, someone would have risked life to destroy this entrance."

In the extended silence, they finally heard the clunk of locks turning over and the slide of the heavy wooden beam barring the door's opening. With a groan, the door inched open enough for a face to peer out at them. The Watcher's eyes brightened at the sight of Suru, but she paused and spoke instead of opening the door farther. "Archer's aim."

"Sword and flame," Suru responded.

The heavy door eased open enough for the two of them to pass through. The speed with which the woman closed and began locking the door belied its weight.

The Watcher bowed to them and gestured down the long corridor. "You may join the Maji and Isati at the intersection."

This time, Nuala took more note of the path they traversed. The corridor sloped downward and took a sharp turn to the left. At the next turn, right, they emerged beside one of the famed aqueducts. The sight alone made her mouth water. The water rippled and sparkled in firelight from torches along the walls.

A short way along this stream, a stone jutted out into the water. Suru stepped onto the stone, knelt, and dipped her hand into the water. She drank then bowed her head and said, "Thank you, Creator, for life and sustenance."

When Suru rose and stepped out of the way, Nuala knelt and did the same. The trail of cool water coursed down her throat, the refreshing trickle as if she'd wandered the desert parched for weeks. Suru had told her it always did this when you gave thanks for your first drink.

A swish of leather warned of the presence of someone approaching. Nuala rose and extended her arm to a Watcher with large eyes the green of moss on wet rocks. The Water Maji extended hers, and the two gripped the other's elbow. "Greetings, Miri. We were coming to you."

Miri released her grip on Nuala's arm and shook her head. "Formalities are not important during these days of trouble. We haven't left the waterways since you came through here. Did you bring supplies? Food?"

"Are your stocks low?" Shame over her lack of forethought swept over Nuala in a flash of heat.

The woman shrugged, an odd action from a Watcher, but the maji trained a different path. "Not yet. The storehouse contained food for each squad during their guard. Five squads, plus all the glimmer makers means—" She shrugged again.

A quick calculation told Nuala that instead of food for twenty-five, they fed over a hundred. "I will speak to the queen when I return."

"My thanks to you." The maji led them toward the intersection where Vuur, the Glimmer Isati, waited.

Swathed in a frayed black robe that swept the ground, Vuur nodded to them. His bald pate glistened in the firelight. "You have come to retake the fortress?" His deep voice echoed off the walls.

"No," Suru said. "The queen sends us for information."

Miri gestured for the three of them to follow her into a larger chamber.

Watchers and glimmer makers had begun to emerge, some obviously roused from their beds, and they glided toward them, faces eager for news. Miri, Vuur, Nuala, and Suru entered a rough circle of stone with a small fire pit in the center surrounded by benches, and Miri closed the door on the curious faces. "Please sit."

Vuur sat on one bench, his long legs extended toward the empty fire pit. For a moment, no one spoke.

Then Suru leaned forward. "Queen Adana sends her greetings. I must beg forgiveness from the Maji and Isati for leading a non-trained Watcher into our midst once again."

Vuur frowned at her. "You said the queen sent you. That is all we need know. What do you seek?"

With a glance at Nuala, Suru yielded the question to the older Watcher.

"Information on Maligon's plans. Access to the false queen—"

"So, the rumors are true." Vuur sat forward. "The queen above is not the true queen?"

"No," Nuala said. "A woman with a remarkable resemblance. They used her to protect Queen Adana during the battle. It worked. The enemy grabbed the wrong one."

"She's a spy for our queen?" Miri sat forward, an eager note in her voice.

"Yes. We've been directed to seek her out if possible. Also, to gauge how many loyal Watchers remain in the fortress." Nuala frowned. "If you've not gone into the fortress since the battle, we'll have to go ourselves."

A slight lift of Vuur's shoulder caught Nuala's attention. "Vuur? Have you been above?"

He ran a forefinger down the bridge of his long nose. "Me? No. But we've needed supplies from the giraffes. A few of my makers have ventured up. Only at night."

"What can you tell us?" Suru dropped the Watcher's stoic mask, an expectant look in her eyes.

"Hm. Well." Vuur slid his gaze toward Miri who stared at him, her mouth a firm line. "Not much. The stable access is easy to manage. At certain times."

"What of the other points?"

He shook his head. "We haven't tried. The few who have gone above avoid contact with anyone. All appears normal. We wouldn't know the answers to your questions."

Nuala and Suru nodded to each other. They must use the plan they created on their journey. "Are any of yours above now?"

"No. No one. You can't go up for another hour. Then the stables are clear all the way to the paddocks."

Nuala rose. "Very well. I will use the access to the queen's chambers. Suru will try the stables." She turned to Miri. "Can you spare a Watcher for each of us? One you trust without doubt?"

The maji stiffened at Nuala's last question. "Waterway Watchers remain loyal, I assure you. We know what Maligon will do should he find these passages."

"Good. Bring us your two most loyal and talented Strategists."

No one below Unit Leader rank worked in the passageways. Although all Watchers trained to move unseen through an area, she and Suru agreed that Strategists, with their espionage background, would provide the best guidance during their foray into Adana's View.

4

Something woke Shana. Wide awake, she lay still, listening.

The crescent moon no longer shone through the opening to the courtyard, obscuring most of the room in shadows. Sliding her hand under the pillow for her knife, she closed her eyes and listened. Slow focused breaths fine-tuned her hearing. Just as Honest taught her.

The silence stretched out. Nothing. Then...

There.

A tiny plop. A tiny something thumped on her legs. She stifled a shriek. Brief but gentle points of pressure bounced up the length of her leg. Heart battering her chest, she drew her knife closer.

The small jerboa hopped onto her chest.

She dropped the knife with a clatter, lurching upright in the bed.

Another bounce, aided by the change in angle of Shana's chest, and the jerboa settled in her lap.

With a sigh of relief, she stared at the tiny intruder. "You gave me a fright."

Although Malay's warning of pox rose in her mind, she couldn't help but smile at the tiny animal's presence. It sat on its haunches in her lap, its yellow eyes regarding her.

"Have you decided to return? I have no food."

As if in answer, the mouse leapt to her shoulder, its aim unerring in the dark room. Shana laid back down and let it crawl onto her pillow. "You should disappear before sunrise, little one. I doubt I can protect you from my maid or Malay."

Turning to watch the small animal, Shana stroked its back with her finger, pausing when she picked up voices speaking, quick and quiet. She pulled the animal into her hands and crawled from the bed, turning her head to find the best place to listen. It came from Maligon's rooms she realized as she tiptoed toward the courtyard.

Quiet feet on the stones, she cuddled the jerboa, trying to discern the voices. They spoke in a guttural language she did not understand. Maligon barked something a bit louder, but the words meant nothing to her. After a few more words from the other person, she heard the quiet patter of bare feet leaving his room. The footsteps receded in the night.

She waited through several moments, hoping Maligon might still speak. He did that, sometimes, talking to himself out loud.

When nothing came and the chill of the evening froze her toes, she returned to her chaise, placing the animal on the pillow.

Tensions remained high in the royal wing. Daily, Maligon stormed and shouted at the Watchers to find the aqueducts. Was the voice someone who had found them? No. As far as she knew, she'd never heard anyone in the fortress speak that strange language before.

If only Samantha would shift her loyalties. Then they might find a way to ruin the man from within.

Soon after one of Maligon's special gatherings of Honest, Pultarch, Samantha, and Kalara, she heard Samantha muttering to herself from her guard post outside the queen's chambers.

"First Visions assign guard duty."

"How dare he order me like a trainee?"

"Soon, I'll slit his throat and take control."

Until the last complaint, she'd hoped to turn Samantha back to

Adana's service. Instead, an uncomfortable rushing sound like a hot wind roared in her ears when she heard the last declaration.

Then there was Pultarch. The young lord remained a gentleman, but she knew his affection for Adana weighed heavily on his mind. He'd murmured several comments under his breath in her presence, too. She doubted he would appreciate her pity, but she did pity him and his losses.

A new sound—a *click*—pulled Shana from her reverie. The jerboa jerked upright and, in one great leap, disappeared. A soft hiss, like something sliding open, came from the foot of the chaise. She sat up, her eyes a bit more adjusted to the dark, and stared at the chest that sat beyond her feet.

The quiet whisper of sound came again. From inside the chest. She darted from the bed and scooped up the knife from where she'd dropped it. Her feet quiet on the smooth cool stone, she glided into the shadows.

With a faint *whoosh*, the lid of the chest shifted sideways. Her heart jumping into her throat, she leaned forward in surprise. The top didn't lift. No wonder Samantha couldn't force it open.

Two long-fingered hands grasped the edges of the chest. A person in Watcher's leathers leapt out and landed in a crouch. Chills ran up Shana's arms. The Watcher made no sound with that jump. Without her gift of Listening, she might still sleep in the chaise unaware of this intruder.

"Shana?" the woman whispered.

Back pressed against the far wall, Shana froze.

The woman swiveled on her feet, scanning the room.

Would a Watcher spot her in the darkest part of the room?

Yes. That searching gaze locked onto her spot. "The queen sent me."

Every muscle in her arms and shoulders wanted to relax. Still, she hesitated. Maligon knew her true identity. This could be a trap.

Another faint sound came from the chest. In the dim light, another woman's hand grasped the edges and a second Watcher launched into the room.

The first Watcher straightened and tilted her head toward Shana, alerting her companion to her hiding place in the shadows. "We've both come at the queen's request. She said to tell you the hawk caught a small animal by the pond."

Shana stiffened. Only four other people knew what that meant. Two of them had died in battle. That left Queen Adana and the First Vision, Montee.

Stepping from the shadows, Shana peered at the women. "Adana truly sent you?"

* * *

For the fifth time, Suru's guide parted the ground foliage and scanned the area. She eased back before whispering, "There's no one there, but I think we should wait a bit longer."

Exactly what she'd said the last two times. During the first two, three of Maligon's men stood near the pigeon coop, pissing into the weeds. From the smell, the men used the spot often.

Suru shoved her aside. "When did you become a coward?" She parted the heavy foliage and climbed out of the tunnel. "Are you coming?"

The other Watcher shook her head. "If you're caught, I'll alert the others."

A snort of disgust was all Suru offered her companion. A quick tiptoe run put her at the corner of the stables. No one was visible in the yard. She waited, counting to one hundred. Still no one. Staying in the shadows, she slipped around the corner and hurried toward the barracks.

The expanse of ground between the stables and the Watchers' wing stretched farther than she recalled, but, heart pounding like a stampede of buffalo sensing water, she made it to the building. Now came the difficult part—getting inside undetected.

The long corridor felt like a hollowed-out, abandoned cavern. No movement anywhere; no sounds either. Did so few Watchers remain? She eased along the wall toward her personal quarters. The door curtain half-covered the entry. No light shone from within.

Breath held, she edged the curtain aside, then slid in. Empty. Nothing remained. Her clothes, belongings, keepsakes from home—all gone. A wave of despair rose in her chest, but she took a deep breath and rammed it down. Another breath. Another breath. The Watcher's focused breathing soothed her, but the desired calm felt distant in this familiar but changed terrain.

Moving back into the hall, she eased along the wall, listening for sounds of people. The rooms near hers were vacant, too. No information to be found here.

She headed toward the center of the fortress.

"When will we attack?" A strident voice spoke from the First Vision's quarters near the front entrance to the wing.

Suru halted, then crept toward the room.

"Not soon enough," said another voice, disgust heavy in her voice.

"What's she waiting for?"

"She? Do you really think the queen makes decisions? No. It's him. Maligon. He's stalling."

The voices sounded familiar. Except for their obvious disgust. Watchers cloaked their emotions, hiding thoughts and opinions from others. This skill made them excellent security and warriors for the queen. Either these two knew each other well and trusted each other, or they'd forsaken their training.

The Watcher who escorted her through the tunnels didn't speak like a Watcher either. What had Maligon done to her sisters?

A large sigh escaped one of the women. "I need to go. Sentry on the tower."

"Again?"

Ah. That was Samantha, the one Watcher known for harsh tones even in the company of her sisters.

Before they could catch her, Suru scampered back toward her vacant chamber. The Watcher's voice now came from the hallway as she spoke one more time to Samantha. "You escape it, thanks to your lineage. Unless he can produce more Watchers, we're stuck with this duty twice a day."

Pressed against the wall, Suru moved with stealth toward the vacant chambers, praying to the Creator that the Watcher wouldn't look her way.

"Can't you force his men to take watch?" the woman turned in Suru's direction but continued to look over her shoulder into Samantha's chamber.

Suru dove through the curtain into one of the dark and vacant rooms.

In the quiet that followed, a voice spoke from behind her. "Hello, Suru."

5

Stiffening in surprise, Suru turned toward the voice.

"Hello, Kalara." Of course, the one Watcher known for turning Watchers into traitors would find her.

Kalara stood in the dim light and closed the gap between them. "I don't recall seeing you the last few days. Where have you been?"

What to say? If she said in the aqueducts, she gave away her secret role within the Watchers. One of the main tactics for protecting the water access was to hide the identity of those who worked there. Nuala only knew because she failed the training to work in the aqueducts. It happened. Some Watchers could not handle the tight spaces and closed off sight.

"You won't tell me?" Kalara walked around Suru, blocking the exit. "Okay. How about this? How did you get into the fortress? I know you weren't here after the battle. We searched everywhere. Smoked out those in hiding."

"Smoked?" She stepped back, glaring at Kalara. "You used torture? On your sisters?"

A chuckle escaped the traitor's lips. "Of course. We needed to find those we didn't dispatch earlier."

"What happened to you, Kalara? When did you change?"

"Hah. This is me. It's always been me. I just hid it until..." She leaned against the doorway. "I don't need to smoke you out, but I can force you to talk. Wouldn't you rather just tell me where the aqueducts are?"

She knew. Or guessed. Either way, Suru had taken an oath of death if she revealed the entries to someone without authority or true need. "I wish I knew."

Pain shot through her arm when Kalara grabbed her and dug her long nails into the soft flesh along the underside of her arm. She clenched her teeth and swallowed the scream. Kalara's nails had been filed to a point.

"Tough? Or maybe just stubborn. Fine. We'll see how you feel after a few days in the dungeons."

Dragged into the corridor, Suru cast a longing look toward the exit. A flash of movement caught her eye. Her guide had left her hiding place after all. Kalara, intent on drawing blood as she pulled Suru behind her, didn't see the other intruder.

Maybe the Watcher could get word back. Suru raised her voice. "Why are the barracks empty? Where are Maligon's supporters?"

Kalara yanked hard, making Suru stumble. "We have plenty of men to handle the situation."

"Men? Soldiers?"

A snort gave her the answer she needed. She risked one last glance down the dark corridor. Her gaze met the other Watcher's. She didn't even know her name. The woman gave a quick nod and disappeared in the other direction.

* * *

Nuala waited as Eno, her Watcher guide, slid back through the chest's access to the tunnels. She turned to Shana. "You understand the mechanism, now?"

The decoy queen gave a quick nod.

Sharing this knowledge could bring Maligon's men down on their heads. If Shana chose to betray them. The queen told her to trust her intuition, so she had, showing Shana how to open and close the tunnel access. "You can send information to Eno or the other Watchers below."

Without another word, she dropped into the tunnel and waited until the chest opening clicked shut.

"So few left," Eno said, her voice betraying horror.

"Maybe they escaped or are hiding." Nuala started down the tunnel in the direction Suru should come from. Perhaps she would know more.

"Doubtful they're hiding if they used smoking."

The thought made Nuala cringe. Bad enough she was down in these claustrophobic tunnels again. The thought of the pungent stinging smoke Maligon used against his enemies in the last war made her want to run to the surface, gasping for air.

At the intersection of the tunnels, they waited for Suru, the time stretching interminably. Just as Nuala decided to go in search of her, Suru's guide appeared in the tunnel, face gray with worry.

"Where's Suru?"

The woman shook her head. "Captured."

Eno stepped forward. "How? Why?"

"There were guards."

Shaking her head, Nuala asked, "Suru would never risk being caught by guards."

"Well, no." The Watcher squared her shoulders. "We waited after they left. I wanted to wait longer, but—"

"You didn't go with her." It was a statement not a question.

"No. I stayed behind to alert you if she didn't return. When she didn't come back, I followed her. She was in the Watchers' wing. Kalara had her."

Exasperation, such an unfamiliar emotion, rattled Nuala's body. She started up the tunnel toward the stables access.

Eno raced to block her. "You must leave her. For now. It's not safe if Kalara suspects we're using the aqueducts."

Nuala halted and turned, fighting to hide her feelings. "I know." She turned back to the other Watcher. "Did you gain any information? Anything we can tell our *queen*?"

The woman flinched as Nuala stressed the word queen, but she nodded. "When Suru saw me, she asked Kalara where the Watchers were. The barracks were empty. All of our belongings, everything was gone." The woman paused.

Nuala said nothing, waiting. She fought the unexpected urge to shove this hesitant Watcher against the wall.

"Kalara told her they had enough men. Suru asked if they were soldiers and Kalara only snorted."

"Confirms what we heard from Shana." Nuala shoved past the other Watcher, heading back to the main chamber. "Request a demotion."

Nuala didn't bother to ask her name. As far as she was concerned the woman's name was Okuko, chicken.

6

✥

The dungeons where Kalara led Suru stank of sweat and blood and bodies. Alert for any potential escape routes, Suru focused on their surroundings. Unlike most Watchers, she could see more specific details than most in the dim lighting thanks to time spent in the waterways.

The smells weren't old, but they weren't fresh either. Someone had been imprisoned here recently. A surge of apprehension washed over her for a moment before she turned to her focused breathing, inhaling slowly, then exhaling through her mouth. The stench didn't help, but she knew in a few breaths her focused breathing would negate the smells.

At the intersection of two corridors, Kalara stopped and turned on Suru. "Is this the way?"

She blinked in confusion. "The way?"

"Yes. The way. To the aqueducts."

Shrugging, Suru said, "I have no idea."

She stumbled as Kalara jerked her arm, pulling her closer. "You got into the fortress somehow. It wasn't through any gates we know of. You know where they are." She shoved Suru away from her again, scrutinizing her eyes. "It never occurred to me that you were a Water

Watcher. I guess being underground dulled your senses, though. A true Watcher wouldn't get caught."

The blaze of triumph in Kalara's last words surprised Suru. When had the stalwart Kalara exhibited such emotion? Had this solid supporter of Adana and steadfast believer in the Watcher's role to protect the queen been acting all along? "I'm not a Water Watcher, Kalara. I know as much about the aqueduct's entrances as you do."

"Entrances?" Kalara leapt on the word. "So, there are more than one? How do you know this?"

Forcing relaxation into her shoulders, Suru said, "I don't know. It would make sense, though, wouldn't it? Why would you have only one entrance to such an important aspect of the fortress?"

Kalara paused as her eyes shifted to the right, a sure sign she was forming an image in her mind.

Taking advantage of Kalara's momentary lapse in attention, Suru took a step closer to the woman. "You mean no one has found them, yet? Are none of the Water Watchers still in the fortress?"

Kalara's dark green gaze swiveled back to Suru. "Of course, I haven't found them. Would I be questioning you otherwise?" She shoved Suru against the cold, rough sandstone wall. "Don't try to distract me. I know you weren't here. We searched the whole fortress. You were not one of the Watchers remaining after the Lord took Adana's View."

They still called it Adana's View. Interesting. That must mean Shana was living as Adana.

"How do you know I wasn't here? You yourself said you haven't found the waterways. Maybe you missed me in your counts."

"Then where were you?"

A small bruise covered Suru's forehead. A bang to her head while trying to assist Tonch through one of the smaller chambers during their retreat to safety, it had faded since the day of the battle. She rubbed it and winced in pretense. "I came to later. I don't recall where I was. I woke, my head spinning and wandered around until I managed to get to the barracks. That's where you found me."

Disbelief clouded Kalara's eyes. "Why were you sneaking around?"

"I didn't know who held the fortress. I found my room empty of my belongings. I heard Samantha telling someone about a shortage of Watchers. It didn't make sense, so I hid."

An iron-strong hand clamped around Suru's arm as Kalara pulled her down the hallway again. "I can't tell who speaks the truth these days. You can think about that and how to get into the aqueducts while you rest here."

The woman pulled a heavy wooden door open, the hinges screaming in protest. Then she shoved Suru inside and slammed the door behind her.

Through the solid door, Kalara's last words took on a threatening tone. "If you can't tell me something useful, maybe the Lord will find a way. Sweet dreams, little sister."

Pitch black enveloped Suru, and she held her breath a moment in fright and shock. Watchers feared the absence of light more than anything. Wise of Kalara to choose this place. With groping fingers, Suru felt for the wall and searched the chamber. Cold but dry. Under her feet, the floor felt hard and ungiving. The space couldn't be more than half her height in length or width. No room to lay down. She slid to the floor, eyes closed against the encompassing darkness, and prayed to the Creator to give her wisdom and light.

* * *

Shana woke to sparkling sunlight and the sound of the tiny jerboa hopping away. Malay stood at the entrance to the courtyard breathing in the fresh morning air. Even though she'd slept little, Shana rose to join her, grateful for the cool breeze flowing through the chamber. Across the desert, the sun stood just above the horizon, its reds and oranges fading to the white unyielding light it would become within the hour. Until then, the cool of the night remained.

"Your Majesty." Malay bobbed her chin in deference.

The shorter act of obeisance used in Moniah made it easier for Shana to pretend she was royalty. Not that she'd started that way. The first time someone gave her a slight nod she'd made her first mistake, reprimanding the maid who hadn't even bowed at the waist or attempted a proper curtsy.

Her indignation shriveled to embarrassment when Samantha had turned on her. "We don't bow and curtsy to royalty here, little pretender." Then louder, the Watcher smiled and said to the maid, "It appears our lady has forgotten the ways of Moniah after three years of bowing and curtsying from the fools in Elwar."

Calling Elwarians fools sounded too strong to Shana, but the maid grinned back and nodded. "I've heard they believe we're no better than savages."

That part was true. Shana had heard Quilla tell Pultarch this before their departure.

As if summoned by her thoughts, Malay turned to her. "I'm glad to see you up so early, my lady. Sir Pultarch wishes to dine with you. Will you go to him, or should I send your refusal?"

Not the way she wanted to begin her day after the previous night's surprises, but how could she continue her charade if she didn't accept the invitation from the young son of the Earl of Brom? "Of course. Please tell him I'll be there soon."

As Malay left, Shana wandered back into the courtyard. At the edge of the fountain, she scanned the area looking for the jerboa. The first time it disappeared in the corner farthest from the entrance to her chambers, so she searched the walls and crevices for any clue of its way into her chambers. There were no signs of its means of arrival or departure.

With a disappointed sigh, she returned to her chambers to dress for breakfast. "Perhaps it's just as well. I'd hate for Malay to destroy the little thing."

Slipping out of the loose sleeping robes, Shana donned the everyday uniform of the Monian queen—a Watcher's tunic and leggings. With no multitude of buttons or underskirts, she required no assistance in dressing. At least she didn't have to pretend to that nonsense. Even as a lady's maid years ago, she'd despised the need to assist her mistress in dressing. Clothing that required assistance became a trap for the woman forced to wear it.

As she smoothed the tunic down her front, she considered the meaning of the uniform. Was it a trap for her, too? Most likely, if the game Maligon played no longer required her role.

She recalled Nuala's parting words to her last night. "Remember, the queen doesn't want you killed. If you fear for your life or have urgent information, you must come through the chest. We will protect you."

If only Nuala could sit beside her and tell her what she must say to satisfy the ones she must fool daily. At least she had Brother Honest. At the thought of the Teacher of the Faith, her step grew lighter, and she departed the royal wing to share her breakfast with her betrothed, Pultarch.

* * *

"Ah, there you are, my lady." Pultarch rose from the table and stepped toward her. Ever the Elwarian noble, he took her hand, bowed over it, and placed a small kiss on its back. Despite knowing him for the traitor he'd become, her skin tingled at his touch. What was it one of the tavern maids had told her during her first week working at The Sleeping Dog? *It never hurts to enjoy how they look when they're beautiful. So few are.*

He was gorgeous to look at and could be charming when he chose. A fact that drew her to him that first night he and Lord Sarx graced the doors of the tavern. Though only a few months earlier, the magic of attraction had faded as the true boy revealed himself in his actions. Jealous and pouting, Pultarch wasn't the catch his outward features advertised. And whose were? Not hers, that was sure. Just like him, she had hidden behind the mask of other roles— lady's maid, tavern wench, even dutiful daughter. Now she wore the most frightening mask, queen, aware any revelation about her true self would likely lead to her death.

Several were already gathered at the table when Shana took the seat at the head. She bestowed a smile at them, and they, in turn, bobbed their heads in greeting. No more. No less.

Brother Honest washed down the bite he'd taken as she'd arrived with a draught of wine and turned to face her. "My lady, I met with the Lord for several hours last night."

She nodded. She knew this of course, but besides Honest, no one else knew of her Listening gift.

"We've decided you should return to your archery and sword practice."

What would Adana say to this? At ease with the weapons of her profession, the queen would delight in the suggestion if it were her in this seat. However, Shana thought she might resent Honest's and Maligon's presumption to grant her permission.

"You have?" She arched an eyebrow, picked up a bowl of cut fruit, spooned a large amount on her plate, then set it down. "How thoughtful of you to remind me of my own duties, Honest." Eying a plate of boiled eggs—too large for chickens, but that didn't matter right now—she stabbed one with her knife. "Not that I need your permission, of course."

"Of course." Honest dipped his head in obeisance, but she suspected he hid a smile at her acting.

"But since you've gone to the trouble, when shall this commence?"

"Brother," Pultarch interrupted, a look of shock on his face, "do you really think that's wise? Won't she hu—"

"Hush, my lord." Shana grasped Pultarch's hand where it lay on the table and dug her thumbnail into the soft flesh between his thumb and forefinger. "You know I practiced as I could in Elwar, but not enough. It's time I pick up my bow again. We have a war to fight, my dear."

A flush of red rose from his jawline and over his cheeks. She popped a date into her mouth and chewed thoughtfully. If she waited, would the blush spread to his ears, too? Maybe calling him dear was a bit much, but the boy needed to keep his mouth shut. She half-expected he'd been about to blurt out her lack of experience since he knew her true identity.

After dabbing at her mouth with a napkin, she cast a rakish grin in his direction. "Maybe I'll let you join in my swordplay. Or maybe we should start with knives?" She flipped the knife next to her plate in the air where it somersaulted back toward her. With the ease of many years' practice, she caught the hilt right before it jabbed into the table. Turning it to cut into her egg, she said, "I am a bit rusty."

Now the boy turned pale. *Good.*

7

Two days later, Shana woke to Malay rushing in to wake her, her usual genial manner missing. "Forgive me, Your Majesty, but you must dress and come to the armory."

Confused why her archery practice required her to rise early and bypass breakfast, Shana dressed and followed the frantic Malay.

The tumult of warriors readying for battle buzzed and clanged throughout the armory in the fortress.

She turned to Malay in confusion. "What is happening?"

"The Lord gave the command. We march on the Border Keep."

Gulping down her concern, Shana pretended to stroll along the corridor while her heart tried to catch up to the pace of those around her. Watchers, the women she claimed to command, moved in measured and practiced preparations. Their efficiency of motion and dedication to the kingdom, whether right or wrong, evident in every place she looked.

She dodged out of the way of several Watchers who hesitated as they brushed past her.

"Your Majesty," they said in hushed, hurried tones, a scant acknowledgement of her position within Moniah.

If she couldn't command their respect, couldn't fool them, then how could she help Adana? An urgent need to warn Adana of the coming attack surged in her chest. She turned to rush back toward the royal wing. With everyone in the barracks, no one would notice her slip the chest open and descend into the waterways.

Maybe she wouldn't need to return. Maybe she could stay with those who appreciated her.

A hand grasped her upper arm from behind, and Shana flinched before recognizing Pultarch. She chided herself for failing to listen for someone behind her, letting her concerns prevent her awareness of Pultarch's approach.

"You're not preparing?" Pultarch said, his eyes alight with excitement. "The queen must accompany her Watchers as they journey to fight for her."

Fear taughtened her nerves. She may have practiced a few times over the last two days with Samantha or whichever Watcher she deemed willing to not mention the queen's apparent loss of skill, but that didn't make her battle prepared.

"How, Pultarch? You know what and who I am. I know nothing of warfare." Helpless, she glanced around to be sure no one heard her confession. She felt in her sleeve for the knife she kept hidden there.

Soldiers and Watchers continued in their preparations, unaware of the imposter in their midst. Her heart stuttered at the numbers of them. She'd been told few remained in the fortress, yet gathered in one place, she realized few meant something different to her.

Another squad of Watchers rushed by her, Samantha splitting off from them when she spotted Shana and Pultarch.

"You won't go into battle." Pultarch squeezed her arm again. "You will stand on the hill above the field and observe. They must see you there. Adana would lead the army and beg to fight alongside them. You must be there."

"He's correct," Samantha said. "You must lead us out of the

fortress. When we draw closer to the Border Keep, you must be there to challenge your troops to battle. Come. You will ride with me."

"Challenge?" Shana gulped. "What is that?"

Exasperation crossed Samantha's features, surprising Shana. This Watcher revealed so much emotion compared to the Watchers in Adana's company.

"Can you memorize?"

Blazes! Does she suspect about my Listener's gift? Shana bit her lip, feigning insecurity. "I believe I can."

"Good." Samantha marched on, leaving Pultarch to his own preparations. "It's five days to the keep, four if we're lucky. I'll teach you what to say while we ride. We must hurry, though." Samantha stopped by a wall of weapons, grabbed a sword, and slid it into her belt. She reached up and pulled down another one, handing it to Shana. "Do you remember how to strap this on?"

It was heavy, heavier than the one Shana practiced with, but she'd spent her life carrying trays of full ale mugs at The Sleeping Dog. Strength was not a problem. Strapping it on, she tried to look precise and focused, wishing for once that she might be an Empath, able to copy others' actions. At least as a Listener, she could fake the voice of command and authority, and she would have no problem recalling the words Samantha gave her.

"And don't worry too much about the challenge. No one expects you to sound like Adana anymore. The Watchers expected Elwar to weaken her. Any mistake you make will justify their expectations."

"Oh no!" Shana spoke before thinking, aware her response might give away her true feelings. She scrambled to cover the mistake. "I want respect." She grabbed Samantha's arm. "You must aid me in this."

Doubt crept across Samantha's face.

"I managed to convince Adana and Montee I was a lady. Even Pultarch believed."

Samantha sneered at her mention of Pultarch.

Shana's mind raced through the possible words to align Samantha to her cause and struck on the one desire she knew drove the Watcher. "As my First Vision you know my acceptability bodes well for you. You will command through me. You will have all the power."

The sneer shifted to greed.

Pressing her advantage, Shana leaned closer. "We can control Moniah and forget Maligon."

Those words could make or ruin her, and Shana held her breath waiting for Samantha's reaction.

"My queen," Samantha said, bobbing her head in feigned respect. "With my assistance, we will make you a true queen to those who watch."

With a quick prayer to the Creator that Honest had been right to push Maligon to move, that the attack would not succeed, Shana followed Samantha into the courtyard where a horse and a long journey awaited her.

* * *

Adana paced near the tunnel's exit. Nuala and Suru still hadn't returned. Images of their stumbling into Maligon's hands after escaping his clutches days ago plagued her. Enough that she couldn't sleep. Giving up, she'd dressed and rushed into the depths of the keep.

What time was it? She could open the exit to the outside but hesitated. If they managed to escape the fortress again, they could have soldiers chasing them. Or Watchers. She shuddered at the idea of her own Watchers hunting down their sister Watchers. The same feeling had hit her in the middle of the night. It prompted a strong desire to sneak after them and try to kill the traitor in his sleep. She glanced over her shoulder, noting the ever-present form of one of her Honor Guards, Sinti. Kind and supportive she may be, but she would have stopped Adana before she could have taken three steps out of the keep's tunnel.

The Watcher's gaze caught Adana's, and she stepped forward. "Your Majesty? I'm sure they'll be here soon if possible."

"If possible? Don't even hint at failure."

"No. I meant since it's close to dawn. If they managed to complete their mission in time to leave under cover of dark two days ago, they'll soon be back. If not, they'll stay in the waterways another day."

How did Sinti know dawn approached? Adana shook her head at that useless and distracted thought. "We'll wait a quarter hour more. If they haven't arrived, I'll go up for breakfast. You will, too."

A relieved smile creased Sinti's face. "Thank you. I'm not concerned for me. Just you. We don't know what Nuala learned, but if it's urgent news, you need to rest and eat. To be ready to act."

Deep in worry, Adana nodded, not listening to the Watcher's words. The report could mean a quick action or...Or what? The compulsion to act stung her nerves and throbbed deep in her shoulder.

A shaft of early morning light shone across the flooring in front of her as the tunnel door eased open. Nuala slipped inside and pushed the door closed. The woman turned and started to run but jerked to a halt as she spotted Adana.

"My queen." She bowed.

Adana glanced toward the closed tunnel door, her breath hitching with concern. "Where is Suru?"

"Captured, Your Majesty. We split up and—"

Icy fingers danced down Adana's neck. "How? You're here. How did they catch her and not you?"

"We split up. In hopes of reaching the barracks and the royal wing."

They'd asked too much of them. She'd worried over that yesterday and last night. She, more than anyone, knew the distance from the barracks to the royal wing. And the kitchens weren't close to either of those points. They should have sent them to one place, not suggest three.

"How do you know she was captured? If you split up."

"Miri provided us guides."

A brief lightness fluttered in Adana's chest. "They live? The aqueducts remain hidden?"

"Yes, Your Majesty. Miri and Vuur protect all their people." She paused, then added, "Miri hoped I came with supplies and an army to invade."

The pounding of feet racing down the tunnel corridor distracted the two of them. Kiffen, face flushed with exertion—*had he run the whole way?*—rounded the corner followed by Montee and Simeon.

A quick check along her link confirmed the giraffes had alerted him to Nuala's arrival. Clever beasts. This almost constant awareness between her and Kiffen was hard to get used to.

"It's true?" Kiffen asked, staring at Nuala and the tunnel door behind. "Suru didn't return."

"Yes." Adana gestured toward Nuala. "They split up."

"Where was she captured?" Kiffen asked.

"The barracks."

Those two words revealed a brief frown of worry on Montee's face. "You are safe? Not followed?"

"Yes."

The five of them stood staring at Nuala for a moment, then Montee said, "If you weren't followed, can we assume we're not in danger of imminent attack?"

"Yes. I doubt an attack will come soon. Maligon appears hesitant to engage at this time."

Adana opened her mouth to ask why, but Montee gave a brief cutting motion with her hand. That gesture, learned as a trainee, made Adana bite back her question. Galled at her reaction to a command from her advisor, Adana faced the woman, one eyebrow arched.

"Forgive me, Your Majesty, but I believe we should conduct this discussion elsewhere. The tunnels are no longer a secret to the keep's inhabitants."

True. As far as they knew, all in the keep supported Adana, but there was no need to share every piece of information, adding to the multitude of rumors that spread throughout the keep like an untamed fire.

* * *

By midmorning, the commanders and leaders who gathered in the map room had heard the details of Nuala's and Suru's foray into Adana's View. Quiet settled over the group as they absorbed the news.

Adana studied each one, trying to read the clues available to her. Montee, Kassa, and Sinti provided no outward signs, but she knew each one worried for their sister Watchers. Before Maligon breeched the gates of the fortress, nearly four times as many Watchers as the numbers Shana reported remained there. Were those warriors dead or hiding? Did the remaining ones endure among the traitors, hoping for her return?

The one piece of good news involved Maligon's forces. They numbered few true soldiers or Watchers. Most were civilians forced into service as he rampaged across the kingdoms on his way to Moniah. For this reason, Maligon was hesitant to strike at the keep yet. The others making up his army frightened her, though. Men who sought glory in battle. Mercenaries. Trained but with no loyalty.

She turned to Prince Jerold. He appeared at war with himself; thoughts crossed his face in rapid succession. The signals flashed so fast her eyes blurred trying to discern their meaning. She anticipated his next words, moments before he spoke.

"If Maligon can't attack us yet, we have time to send soldiers to rescue mother."

The thought had occurred to her, although she'd rejected it. They held the upper hand with trained soldiers and Watchers. Halar and Simeon spent hours each day training those who had volunteered to join her army before the last battle, the Battle for Adana's View. She hated that name, but that's how everyone referred to it now.

Halar, now Commander of Moniah's First Soldiers, cleared his throat and spoke, his gaze avoiding Kassa, his wife. "I can lead a small troop of men to accompany Prince Jerold. If we can regain control of Belwyn, we will add to our numbers. For now, you can handle an attack on the keep and won't miss the ones I take."

Adana caught a quiet hiss from Kassa. "Fool."

Amazed, she noticed no one else heard the quiet words. Living in Elwar, although it was uncomfortable and left her feeling claustrophobic, had forced her to rely on other senses besides sight. A benefit and skill she hadn't divulged to anyone. Yet.

Avoiding the former First Vision's hawk-like glare, Adana surveyed the others. Simeon and Montee nodded at Halar's words. Kiffen studied Jerold, his head tilted to the side. An endearing habit of thought she'd noticed him doing in her first weeks in Elwar.

"What of Morana?" Kiffen's brief words cut right to the concern others might have missed. "Do we leave her in Roshar? We have no idea if Ariff made it to Belwyn. We should send you to Roshar, first. Check on Teletia's queen and prince. Recruit those willing to fight for Adana on the way."

The morning wore on, but after long discussions and speculations, they charged Halar and Jerold to go to the village of Roshar and check on the Teletian royals. If King Ariff had succeeded in his attempt to free Empress Gabriella of Belwyn, he would most likely bring her to Roshar. Or at least send word.

Throughout the entire discussion, Kassa remained quiet, not

contributing to their plans. Adana found herself reflecting back on a memory of her mother telling her of Kassa's reluctance to speak when orders involved Halar. She feared her emotional connection might prevent the right decision. Doubting Kassa's ability to have biased emotions at the time, Adana had laughed outright. Kassa never kept opinions to herself. Terse she may be, but not without opinion. Yet, here was the proof.

As if she felt Adana's thoughts on her, Kassa turned to Adana. "We should destroy the aqueducts and bring those in the water-ways here."

"What?" Adana sat forward, convinced she'd misunderstood. "They're our only access to the fortress."

"True," Kassa said. "But what if Maligon finds them? Shana says he's looking for them. In the wrong place, but he's searching. Think Adana. They have Suru. She might tell them."

"She won't." Nuala's voice carried conviction. "She's trained to withstand all torture, even death, to protect the aqueducts."

Kassa shook her head in disagreement. "Trained she may be, but training never prepares you for the reality. We must assume they will force it from her."

Tension in the room was palpable at those words. No one had dared suggest it earlier. Suru did know the aqueducts. Her guide had overheard Kalara question Suru about them. Maligon was known for hideous forms of torture.

Kassa continued, "They provide the only water to the estate. Cut off their water before he finds them, and we cripple them."

"And when I regain my Seat? What then?" Adana's throat turned dry at the thought. She reached for her glass of watered wine and sipped instead of gulping like she wanted to do.

"We rebuild them."

In the silence that followed, Adana set her cup down. She waited for someone to speak. No one did. Everyone had opinions, but now they withheld them? She turned a beseeching look toward Montee. "What do you think?"

For once, Montee did not hide her emotions. She appeared as astonished as Adana. "It's a smart move, strategically. Cut off their water. Protect those below the fortress. But we've an opportunity to invade. The walls of Adana's View are impregnable. The aqueducts will get us inside. We have proof of that." She hesitated before saying what everyone else probably was thinking. "The only reason Maligon succeeded in taking the fortress was due to Samantha's help on the inside."

No one looked at Kassa or Halar at these words. The shock of their daughter's betrayal still hung over the entire group. Adana had never felt comfortable with Samantha, but the Watcher had always been loyal to the kingdom. Until recently.

Montee added as an afterthought, "Leave them open. We can plan an attack and use them to get inside. Do the same thing."

"At night," Kiffen added in a vindictive tone, "to kill Maligon in his sleep."

After much debate, they decided to leave the aqueducts intact. Exhausted, Adana rose and suggested they all get some rest. As the others filed out, Father Tonch stopped her. "If you will, Your Majesty, I have one more matter to discuss with you and Kiffen." He nodded to Montee to stay, too.

As Adana retook her seat, Tonch held his hand out to Nuala who remained in her chair. "You do have it, don't you?"

The Watcher nodded and picked up a sack she'd carried in with her. She set it on the table and withdrew two items, one wrapped in worn leather, the other in a wooden box.

Hands steepled before him, Tonch nodded toward Adana. Nuala rose and placed the two items before Adana.

Heart beating a frantic pattern at the presence of the one box, she felt the blood rush to her face. She ran her hand over the smooth wood, the result of a carpenter's dedicated sanding. Burned into the lid was an etching of a regal giraffe. She stared up at Nuala in surprise. "How did you?"

"It's how we decided who went to your chambers. I knew where these were stored. Suru didn't."

"This was in the queen's chamber?" Adana continued to trace her finger over the etching. Her finger on the wood increased the thrumming tempo throughout her body. She inhaled to regain focus, pulling her finger away. The box beckoned to her, so she folded her hands in her lap, gripping the two together.

"It's kept in a hidden compartment of the queen's chest." Those words came from Montee. The woman's earlier firm countenance had softened as she regarded the box and leather-wrapped item. "Open the leather first."

Adana untied the thick string and folded back the soft material, its colors darkened with age. She inhaled in surprise, and the pull of the box faded. Moniah's crown was nestled in the folds.

Unlike the crowns of Elwar, this one appeared simple and light, yet intricate at the same time. An illusion of the design. Strands of the finest silver and gold intertwined in a delicate braid to form the circlet of the crown. In the front, the braided metals rose to a peak, and the twirls twisted into the form of a giraffe in profile. The spots of the giraffe glinted with stones of citrine, golden topaz, and amber. A tiny stone of dark brown agate made up the giraffe's eye.

Tears clouded her vision. She hadn't realized how much this crown meant to her until she beheld it in front of her. It didn't make her queen. Yet it did. The presence of it on her head would remind those in the keep of her responsibility toward them and Moniah.

"We must crown you, Adana," Father Tonch said. "In front of all of those in the keep. We must remind them you are queen."

"Thank you, Tonch," she whispered as she blinked back the

tears, suddenly embarrassed. If the tears embarrassed her, though, the box...

She turned toward it but held her hands back, aware of what pulled at her from within.

Her shoulder sang with an excitement she wished to embrace after the unending pain. She peered from under her lashes at Kiffen. His gaze was glued to the box. He had no idea what it meant, but it drew him like it drew her.

She reached to open it, then paused, turning to Tonch. "What of Kiffen's crown? Do we have his father's or my father's crown to give him? Or is it lost in the forest?"

"Simeon located King Micah's after the forest attack," Montee said.

Adana reached for Kiffen's hand under the table and gave it a squeeze. Giddy joy flooded her soul at his touch. It centered and thrummed a pleasing warmth in the mark on her shoulder. The puncture spot had pulsed with pain for so long. Now as Tonch presented these items, it bathed her in joy. Did the box cause the sensation or the suggestion that they both could be crowned?

She turned her attention back to the box. Before she opened it, she turned to Tonch once more. "Are you sure we should open this here? Now?"

The pit of her stomach felt empty and wanting as she waited for the man's answer. Almost craving. This box should have remained out of sight for another year. Yet here it was.

Tonch gave the briefest of nods, his expression as stoic as the strongest of Watchers.

She eased the lid open. Kiffen leaned forward, his head tilted in confusion.

The box held a brown glass vial and a conical piece of bone. A curved projection stretched from the wide end of the bone. She had never seen it, although she knew it. Children weren't allowed near it.

The vial resembled the ones Suru saved while escaping Adana's View during the battle. This one, though, was larger and held a more precious liquid, its importance signified by the different color. She picked up the bottle and peered at its contents through the cloudy glass. Giraffe tears washed against the sides, tears from all of Am'brosia's ancestors. Her shoulder vibrated in response. These were the tears infused into the pin Montee used during her recognition ceremony.

While she tilted the bottle to catch the light, Kiffen submitted to the draw of the conical object. His hand hovered above it while his other hand squeezed hers tighter. "Is that bone?"

Adana put down the vial and lifted the bone from the box. She held out the ivory-colored cone to him, sad when he released her hand to take it in both of his.

"We call it the horn," she said. "We use it to collect the residue that becomes glimmer fire and cloth." She turned to Nuala and Tonch. "You prove yourselves loyal beyond expectations."

Kiffen caressed the horn, his expression a mixture of confusion and desire. "Residue? From where?"

Adana leaned close to his ear, inhaling his scent of leather and apples. A new element joined his scent, and she trembled with the urge to bury her nose in his shoulder. He shivered as she breathed quiet words in his ear. "I'll explain later. In private."

The sight of the Great Horn, the official name for the conical object, revitalized her with an energy she had missed. The tiny hairs on her skin and neck stood erect. Touching Kiffen so soon after opening the box had to be a mistake. It heightened the tension. She forced her hands back in her lap away from the box and Kiffen.

Giraffe horns secreted a residue during mating season. Few people knew this. The residue provided the foundational ingredient for many of her kingdom's resources. But the actual presence of the horn carried power, too. A power she and Kiffen could not ignore. Not with it in front of them. The exhilaration from the power made Adana flush with guilt. So many dead, Suru captured, possibly enduring torture this very moment, and her body surged with a need that violated the sorrow with jubilation.

"Are you sure, Father Tonch?" She fought the way her voice sought to rise in pitch.

"Yes," the man replied. He turned to Kiffen, "It means, King Kiffen that it's time for us to celebrate your marriage to Queen Adana. We should not wait the year as planned. Too many seek to destroy your kingdoms. We must make it official."

8

Adana led Kiffen down the Central Tower's stairs and through clusters of gathered people. This proved no easy feat with the Border Keep filling up with refugees. Information traveled fast, and news of the giraffes' arrival, eighty in total by the end of the previous day, as well as rumors of the true queen's presence, drew them.

How had Maligon fared in his attempt to pass Shana off as Adana? She'd seen the notices sent out from Adana's View. If they didn't work, what would the man do? Shana's life might be forfeit if he no longer needed her.

The pang that struck Adana over this concern subsided when the bond vibrated with an urgent magnetic pull. Am'brosia.

Answering the call, she dragged Kiffen around more clusters of people, ignoring the ripple their presence created. The bond swelled with excitement. Adana giggled. An inappropriate sound for a queen, especially one so recently displaced.

Am'brosia shared, through the bond, the quiet and empty fenced-in area housing the two royal giraffes. For once, refugees did not stand gawking at them, most likely drawn to the larger show of giraffes outside the keep. It might be the perfect place to explain the horn to Kiffen. And to try to quell its yearning call. How much of that call was Am'brosia's and how much was her own?

A crowd of refugees clogged the corridor before them. Without warning, Kiffen pulled her down a side corridor. "Did Am'brosia show you?" he asked, glancing over his shoulder as she stumbled behind him, his pace so urgent that he caught her off guard.

"Yes. Bai'dish showed you?" She laughed. "The two must be in tandem with their manipulations."

"Manipulations?" Kiffen stopped short, causing Adana to stumble into him. He wrapped his arms around her and smoothed flyaway strands of hair from her face.

The touch fueled a yearning inside Adana, and she moved closer to him. The explosion of need in the pit of her belly made her lightheaded. Her mother had warned her the horn carried great power. Now she understood the little quirk on her mother's lips as she tried to explain its effect.

She kissed him first. Then answered, "Yes. Manipulations. Where do you think these feelings come from?" She kissed him again and nuzzled his neck. "They know the horn is here, too."

A growl rumbled in Kiffen's chest, not an angry one, but one that drew Adana even closer into his embrace. "I don't need a horn or a giraffe to make me feel like this."

"Oh my." A woman's voice squealed in surprise.

The couple jerked apart. Before them stood a servant, a basket of linens tumbling from her arms. She fumbled to pick up the basket or kneel; Adana wasn't sure which.

"Forgive me," the servant said. "I did not mean to interrupt."

Kiffen rushed over and helped the woman to her feet. He picked up the basket and handed it to her. "It is we who must apologize. We have trespassed into your domain."

Adana looked around, for the first time seeing where Kiffen had led them. The sounds of running water and women singing farther down the corridor suggested the laundry. She forced composure on her face and took a few focused breaths before bestowing a conspirator's look on the servant. "We meant to sneak through and not bother you at your work. The giraffes...called to us. You won't tell anyone we were here, will you?"

The servant gaped and then bowed her head, hiding a conspiratorial smile. Most of the people at the Border Keep found the giraffes exciting and exotic. Few had seen one prior to the arrival of Am'brosia and Bai'dish. When more arrived, talk flourished about the mysterious powers of the giraffe. Hinting to a servant about those powers might help increase the esteem she and Kiffen needed. A queen or king without a throne needed reverence no matter how they got it—or how they behaved at the moment.

Especially with a coronation coming.

"Sometimes," Adana gave the woman a conspiratorial wink, "the giraffes are very demanding."

Kiffen cast a strange look at Adana. "Not that we can't resist their demands, if we choose to."

"You need not fear, Queen Adana. I did not see you."

"Thank you." Adana stood back and gestured the woman forward. The laundress shifted the returned basket in her arms and wobbled down the corridor.

"She's Monian," Adana whispered to Kiffen.

"What makes you say that?" He played with a loose strand of her hair.

"Did she answer you? Or me?"

"Good point." Once the servant was out of sight, Kiffen took Adana's hand and turned to her. His face registered concern. "Is what you said true? Did Bai'dish and Am'brosia do this to us?"

She pulled him after her, anxious to leave the laundry behind before she answered. "I'll explain when we get to the stables."

Once outside in the open sun, she forced her walk to a stroll, dropping Kiffen's hand to prevent him from dragging them through the people going about their duties. No reason to alarm those in the courtyard. She lifted her face to the sun's warmth. The Border Keep, five days north of Adana's View, did not press an unrelenting blanket of heat over its inhabitants. The sun felt glorious on her arms. A tiny taste of the heat that awaited her once she evicted Maligon.

Arms extended, she soaked up the rays of light. It felt incredible, and she relished it for a moment, thankful to be alive in the face of so many deaths.

They walked past several refugees and soldiers. Kiffen watched her, his face inscrutable.

She squinted sideways at him. "You've seen me do this, haven't you?"

"Of course." His gaze swept down her body, lingering on the contours of her legs in her Watcher's uniform.

Her skin grew warmer.

"It looks easier in your uniform rather than those ridiculous dresses my sister wears."

Adana twirled, arms raised. "The dresses keep men from doing exactly what you're doing now." She arched an eyebrow at him. "We better get to the stables." She dropped her arms.

He reached for her, but she stepped away. "Try not to look at me or touch me in front of everyone. It feels improper with so many fleeing to us for protection."

The incredulous look he gave her shot deeper longing into her soul. She reached for her connection with Am'brosia, aware the giraffe heightened the emotions. Am'brosia opened her sight to Adana. In the stables, the giraffes had separate pens, walled off from each other with stone. Bai'dish stretched his long neck across the fence toward Am'brosia.

Their joined sight wobbled as Am'brosia glided toward the wall separating the two.

Adana dropped the connection and turned on Kiffen, her voice sharper than intended. "You need to order Bai'dish to stop. He's torturing us all."

Kiffen looked surprised but stopped and closed his eyes, his chest rising and falling in long, slow breaths. His focused breathing still took a lot of concentration. Kiffen had so little practice, having only been bonded to Bai'dish a short time ago.

Samantha taught him how to do this. That thought curled envy around her heart.

"*Stop,*" she thought toward Am'brosia, aware Am'brosia fueled the sudden spike of jealousy. The emotion diminished but did not disappear. Am'brosia's mood always shifted to fury when Samantha was mentioned.

Kiffen opened his eyes. Exhaustion smudged dark rings under his eyes. A clue to how difficult the connection remained for him. "I'm not sure he'll obey. He's fairly adamant at the moment. Are you sure Bai'dish did all of that to us?"

"Not all of it. But he is an animal. His urges are primal. He responded to what we felt. And we responded to what he felt." She walked a few steps ahead of Kiffen, swaying her hips. "Unless of course, you don't have any of those feelings on your own?"

He grabbed her, and they raced toward privacy.

In the quiet of the stables, Adana stood before Kiffen, holding out the horn. Kiffen studied the bone, running his fingers over its surface, Bai'dish shadowing over him.

Am'brosia grazed from a box of leaves on the far side of the enclosure. A glimpse of Bai'dish as a romping calf and Kiffen as boy of maybe ten flitted along the bond. Adana nodded in understanding. Kiffen still struggled to keep Bai'dish from taking over. The male giraffe played with the freedom.

Distance between the giraffes helped, so Am'brosia attempted to stifle the emotions by keeping away.

"You said the giraffes responded to the bone. Why?"

She ran her finger along the flared edge, suddenly shy. "At certain times, giraffe ossicones—that's the horns—secrete a substance. We run this edge along the horns, and the secretion settles into the bone."

Kiffen thumbed the edge. "What is it for?"

"This." Adana touched the glimmer cloth of her belt. "We add flecks of sandstone to the collected secretion. After it sits several months, we submerge cloth in it. After a week, it's glimmer cloth."

The glimmer cloth wrapped around her waist captured the sun's fragmented light coming through the openings in the ceiling of the oversized stable. An iridescent glow emanated from the cloth. Rare and in high demand, the material accounted for most of Moniah's wealth.

"Very few people know this."

This knowledge placed Kiffen in a small group of people who knew the mysteries of the export. Moniah's glimmer cloth makers protected the secret to its luminosity with a vengeance.

"And glimmer fire?" Kiffen asked.

Adana said. "Glimmer fire comes from the secretion alone. It's very flammable. After we add sandstone flecks and let it sit, the secretion becomes fire retardant, impossible to burn."

Adana thought of the pyres of the dead they had burned on the grounds outside the keep just a few days ago. Sacred glimmer fire lifted each body's remains to the sky. The wind scattered their ashes, giving back to the land that nourished the soul in life. Moniah's wealth depended on the increasing demand for the treasures made from the gifts the giraffes gave freely.

"That doesn't explain the horn. Why it makes me feel—" His cheeks flushed pink as he trailed off.

Unable to resist, Adana kissed him again.

The two of them fell into the embrace, unaware of anything,

even the giraffes. His lips felt soft and searching. The burn in the pit of her stomach forced her to move closer to him.

A snort from Am'brosia interrupted the two, blasting into Adana's mind with agitation.

With a nervous laugh, she pulled back. "Am'brosia doesn't appreciate our ability to—to—um..."

"Do this?" He leaned back in and planted a quick kiss on her lips but pulled back before she could respond. He remained close, the look of need returning to his eyes, "Why did Bai'dish and Am'brosia react this way when the horn arrived?"

Adana turned to Am'brosia and drew in several focused breaths, reaching for the calm of the breathing exercise as well as their joined link. Am'brosia responded with a gentle connection, and Adana gave the animal a memory of her behavior with Kiffen in the laundry corridor.

A bubbling sensation rippled across the link. Laughter? She darted a warning look at Am'brosia, and the bubbling stopped.

The connection deepened, and Adana saw Bai'dish witness the arrival of the horn through Kiffen's eyes. The male giraffe knew the purpose of the horn. He had waited a long time to mate with Am'brosia. Nature would not wait much longer.

Sliding free from the connection, Adana placed her hand on Kiffen's chest and took a step back. "The secretion occurs just after the giraffes mate. The moment we saw and touched it they knew. Bai'dish fights the tension of waiting."

Kiffen swallowed. "You mean the giraffes haven't—"

"No." Adana crossed her arms over her chest, suddenly uncomfortable with the explanation. "The bond forces them to wait. For us to..." She looked at the ground, unable to face Kiffen's gaze. "We must first."

"That's why Father Tonch told Nuala to bring it here? So we can marry?"

"Yes. Now that it's here, we must not delay our wedding. The sooner the better."

She couldn't hide the blush spreading heat over her cheeks. "But we have to convince the others, especially Kassa and Montee."

9

After Kiffen recovered from the shock of the horn's unexpected effect, he could think of nothing else. Was the horn that powerful? An ancient fragment of bone from a long-dead giraffe overwhelming them with irresistible urges sounded like a story his stepmother would shout to the masses. Claim it gave proof of Moniah's savagery. Barbarians given to primal urges. Quilla's thoughts mattered little in this regard, though. He never saw Adana or the Watchers as the savages she claimed them to be.

For now, Father Tonch held the horn in a secure place where it would not affect them or their giraffes. The overwhelming urges soon subsided, but the idea hovered in his mind, even as he studied the map table and waited for all of their advisors to arrive. Final approval, as much as he detested the idea, needed the good will of these people.

Prince Jerold arrived and sat between Father Tonch and Sergeant Markel, the member of Elwar's castle guard who had delivered the warning of Quilla's treachery just a few weeks ago. Sinti, the only surviving Watcher of Adana's original honor guard, along with Montee, Kassa, Halar, Nuala, and Simeon, was already in place.

With a deep breath, Kiffen rose and began the meeting. "This council should be short, but matters have been brought to our attention which need to be addressed today."

Kiffen slid his hand toward Adana, groping for hers, then relaxing when she took it and gave him a gentle squeeze.

"Father Tonch gave Nuala an extra charge when she went into the fortress the other night." He nodded in Tonch's direction. "She managed to bring us Adana's crown."

A wave of relief swept over the group, evident in smiles and relaxed postures.

"We can crown you," Sinti exclaimed, an excited grin lighting her face.

"Yes," Tonch said. "The sooner the better."

"When do you want to do it?" Jerold asked.

"In a few days," Adana said. "We believe the people will rally behind a crowned ruler more than a ruler in name."

"And what of Kiffen?" Simeon said with a nod to his liege, his smile shifting to a frown. "Will you crown him, too?"

"I asked the same question," Adana said. "I want him by my side in everything."

"Which brings us to the other item Tonch asked Nuala to retrieve." Kiffen laid the box on the table.

In a few short seconds, Kiffen knew who understood the contents of the box and who didn't. Halar's eyes widened. Kassa's mouth formed a thin, straight line. Sinti sat forward, fighting a bigger grin. Simeon, Jerold, and Markel frowned in confusion.

"We can't open the box here," Tonch said, "but its presence means, I believe—"

"They are to wait a year," Kassa interrupted. "That is the custom."

"And if we resided at the fortress without a traitorous army challenging their authority, I'd agree." Tonch's voice carried a determination and strength Kiffen had never heard from the man.

"But marry? Now?" Halar's three words sent those unaware of the box's significance into shocked exclamations.

Kassa turned toward Montee. "You didn't share this information with me. Why?"

Before Montee could answer, Adana did. "She is the First Vision, Kassa. She acts in Moniah's best interests, and I asked her not to speak of this before we met."

In the startled silence, Kiffen said, "Father Tonch recommends that we marry. Now. Soon."

Several of them shifted in their seats, but no one spoke.

Kiffen turned to Adana, for a moment lost in the sea of her blue-green eyes. "I'm inclined to agree." He kissed her hand.

Her eyelashes fluttered down, gazing at where his lips had brushed the back of her hand. Then she looked at the people around the table. "I agree, too,"

Father Tonch sat back and steepled his hands, peering over the tips of his fingers, his wooly white eyebrows drawn down in command. "You will marry. But first Adana must be crowned."

"And so must Kiffen." Simeon sat forward, the same intent look on his face.

Montee's gaze pivoted between Adana and Kiffen a few times before she spoke. "In Moniah, the coronation of the queen's husband follows the marriage. In the same ceremony."

Simeon's chair screeched as he shoved back from the table. He didn't rise, though he leaned forward, locking gazes with Montee. "In Elwar, the marriage must wait for a week after the coronation."

The room erupted. Some leaned in, jabbing fingers at the table to make their points. Others half-rose from their seats, shouting. A few sat back in stunned silence, like Adana and Kiffen.

The raised voices clamored in Kiffen's ears. Adana's hand slipped from his. She crossed her arms over her chest and sat back. Kiffen moved to place his arm around her but encountered empty air when she exploded from her chair, slamming both hands down on the table.

"Enough."

Each person turned to her; discussions halted mid-sentence. In the distance, Kiffen heard workers calling to each other below, a horse's whinny, a shout of laughter.

"Unless I've missed something, we are no longer just Moniah or Elwar." Adana searched their faces. "Am I correct?"

No one moved or spoke.

Adana punched an index finger at the table. "So, has no one thought about this? How we will combine our kingdoms and cultures? Maligon moved too quickly for us to work this out, didn't he?"

Kassa shifted in her seat, an aggravated motion, her expression fierce. This woman, a formidable Watcher, served as First Vision to Queen Chiora during her entire reign over Moniah. For the second time in two days, she remained quiet.

Instead, Montee stood and captured each person with her Watcher's gaze, cool, deliberate, and commanding. "Queen Adana is correct. We must make new traditions. Maligon changed things the moment he survived his exile. We've already turned our backs on many customs due to his threat. How can we squabble over the order of things? A marriage still is a marriage at the end of the day. A coronation is still a coronation."

Simeon pursed his lips in thought. When he spoke, all heads swiveled in his direction. "Montee makes sound observations. We must not tear ourselves apart over this."

Here are our clear thinkers, thought Kiffen. These two—the ones we can trust.

"However," Simeon continued, "I propose that the coronation of both of them precede the wedding. And until this war ends, we crown Adana queen of Moniah and Kiffen king of Elwar. We should strategize carefully before moving toward a unified kingdom."

Montee nodded. "That might be wise."

Nuala cleared her throat, a determined look on her face.

So, even the newest member of their council had an opinion.

"I know I'm new to your discussions and plans, but I fear we must not forget one thing. By now, Maligon has most assuredly crowned the imposter. I imagine he will crown Pultarch as the Husband King. Do you plan to make this coronation public? Announce it to the kingdoms as you know he will do?"

Kiffen laughed out loud. Another brilliant mind among them, and still he and Adana were no closer to a final decision. Everyone stared, but he didn't care. The issue was so simple, but politics always made it hard.

Adana reached out to him, but he ignored her and stood, shoving his chair away from the table. He knelt before Adana and took her hands in his, gazing up at her. "Adana, I pledge to you my undying love. I will serve Moniah as I will serve Elwar. What say you?"

Adana's mouth formed a perfect "O" of astonishment, but her gaze never left his. The tension in her face softened, and she nodded. She bowed her head toward his, a gentle peace settling on her features.

"I, too, pledge to you, Kiffen, my undying love. I will serve Elwar as I will serve Moniah. This is what I say."

With his hands gripping the sides of Adana's chair, Kiffen rose from his knees, leaned forward, and kissed his queen. Her lips parted against his in soft yielding, and he tasted the sun on her tongue. She smelled a little of the giraffes. He found the wild smell intoxicating.

When Kiffen stood, he assisted Adana to her feet and together they faced the council. "As far as I'm concerned, that's done. We are committed to a marriage and coronation before the eyes of the Keeper of the Faith and our advisors. We have pledged to protect and serve both kingdoms. Short. Simple. New. If you'll forgive us,

I believe the queen and I have other obligations. We'll leave the planning of a lavish celebration and official ceremony to you."

The two headed for the door, hands clasped.

"Wait." The commanding tone in Father Tonch's voice made Kiffen freeze in mid-step.

The older man rose from his seat and approached the young couple, a look of consternation on his round face. Kiffen's shoulders drooped in resignation, sure Father Tonch would overrule him in this arena.

Adana took a hesitant step toward the Father, her hand sliding out of Kiffen's. "Father Tonch, you know we must marry. What must we do to satisfy everyone?" She gestured around the room.

"You have done well." He beamed at them. "We shall plan the coronation three days hence. The marriage ceremony will conclude the coronation. We won't detain you further, Your Majesties."

With relief, Kiffen rushed through the door and halfway down the tower's stairs. On a landing, he turned and swept Adana into his embrace.

Adana giggled into his mouth as they kissed. "Am'brosia and Bai'dish know. Do you feel them?"

He did. An exultation rushed through the bond enveloping him with overwhelming joy. "Three days."

"Three days," she answered him.

IO

Leera, former princess of Elwar, studied the pack Sariah gave her for the journey. She glanced back up at the Protector of the Faith, unable to hide her dismay. "This is it? All I take must fit in here?

"Yes." The pleasant round face of Mother Sariah smiled down at her. "I don't doubt you're accustomed to more. Probably wagons full of chests, but we travel light. You cannot bring anything but necessities."

"What about an extra horse? One more couldn't slow our progress."

With a shake of her head, Sariah settled on a hay bale and patted the one next to her in invitation. "We don't have the funds to purchase one, my lady. We must make use of what we have."

Dropping down on the proffered bale of hay in the storeroom behind Gerguld's shop, Leera sighed. A stick of hay stabbed her in the rear, and she shifted to shove it down. How had she come so low? Sitting on hay bales. Traveling in servant's clothes? No fine dresses or jewelry. No maid to attend her.

"What do I take, then?" She had no clue what she might need. Except for the ring. Just thinking of it made her aware of its weight on the chain around her neck. It hung between her breasts, the symbol of her father's reign, destined to become her stepbrother Kiffen's. Some mornings when she awoke, it had impressed the face of a lion on her chest.

Had her mother missed the ring? Most likely. Little escaped Queen Quilla.

That thought drew a smile to her lips. How it must gall her mother to know she had escaped from her rooms without a trace. She'd enjoyed the subterfuge. A lot. Let someone call her a spoiled princess now. She'd adapted and transformed into Lily, the young woman who helped out in Gerguld's shop. She swept floors for Ballene's sake.

"We need most of our space for food," Sariah continued. "Bring a change of clothes, a cloak, your knife, and, of course, the few proofs of your identity you carry."

"And my Watcher's uniform," Leera added, ignoring Sariah's reference to the ring. She never told the Protector of the Faith she had it, but the teacher knew.

"Yes. I assumed you'd wear it." Sariah's knowing smile told Leera she enjoyed giving her this freedom. How much Leera longed to don the leggings, tunic, and soft boots given her by Adana. A gift in grayish green meant to hide her in the forests of Elwar, not the sandy browns of a true Watcher's uniform, meant to blend in with the dry, sandy lands of the savanna and desert.

"I will."

"You better." A young boy's voice chirped from the doorway. Catch, the young page who helped her escape confinement in the castle as well as retrieving the uniform, sauntered in. "After all I went through to make sure you have it."

He no longer limped from the vicious kick she'd given him that day.

That had surprised her rescuers—her ability to strike out with strength when situations required it. Helmyra's bruised cheek was only now beginning to fade. Kicking Catch had been necessary. So had punching Helmyra. All part of their plan, not hers. She'd added spite to the punch, though, as well as the flat of her father's ring. One last act of will against the seamstress before accepting her assistance. If Helmyra hadn't expected it, she shouldn't have asked her to do it.

Leera rose and looked down on the twelve-year-old boy. She always did this when he entered a room, Catch being the only person she could look down on. Royals didn't need height to look down their noses, but current circumstances robbed her of the right. A servant didn't act imperious. It might be petty, but she needed to do this to feel better about the situation. "I will wear it, Catch. And thank you for ensuring I have it."

The boy grinned, a big toothy smile she had never seen when encountering him in the palace. It bloomed on his face often in their new environment and company. She liked it.

Sariah rose and ambled toward the rear exit of the storeroom. "We leave tomorrow morning. Before sunrise." She turned a sharp eye on the two of them. "Maybe Catch can help you pack your bag. He knows how."

A flush of anger—no embarrassment—rushed into Leera's face, making her warm all over. Without a fan to hide behind, she turned away from Catch's knowing smirk. He sensed her discomfort over the change in their roles, and she hated to see it revealed on his face. She was no longer a spoiled princess. If they didn't know it yet, they would soon.

* * *

In a fit to prove her unspoiled nature, Leera insisted on helping Gerguld in the store on her last day in Elwar.

The rotund man rubbed his nose and bobbed his head in confusion. "Missy, I know the Mother made you work for me. You done it fine. Tomorrow you go, and you must rest now. I'm fine." The man had glanced around the store empty of shoppers in the early morning. "It's not busy."

Using a smile she'd seen Adana grace on others, she picked up a broom and marched past him. "I will assist you today, Master Gerguld. As you have assisted me." She paused and turned back toward him. "I can never repay you the favor."

"Aye, you can and you have." Gerguld shrugged and picked up a box of goods to stock on his shelves.

In the morning sunlight shining through the store's one small window, Leera whisked the broom across the worn boards of the shop's flooring. She liked sweeping in this spot, watching the dust swirl like specks of gold. Her gaze intent on the drifting motes, she didn't hear the bell ring, announcing a customer.

"Good day, sir," a familiar young man's voice called from the doorway.

Startled, she glanced up then ducked her head, checking the kerchief covering her distinctive curls. She slid into the shadows. *Taren. Here?*

Heart pounding, she continued to sweep, the strokes of her broom counting each beat. She tilted her head toward Gerguld and the visitor. No. Visitors. Several soldiers of her mother's guard stood behind Taren.

"Welcome, sir," Gerguld said as he bowed to Taren. "Do the queen's soldiers have need of my wares again?"

"Need? Again?" Taren shook his head in confusion. "I know not of what you speak. I'm seeking someone."

Her heart gave up pounding and dropped, gluing her heavy work boots to the floor.

Gerguld adjusted the glasses on his nose and peered at Taren. "Who are you looking for? I'll help, but I see very few people these days. My shop being out of the way."

One of the soldiers advanced a step, a menacing frown on his face.

Taren held up his hand forestalling the man.

"Just the reason why I thought to check with you. I don't believe she'll try to hide in obvious places. She's too intelligent for that."

Despite the fear trembling her body, Leera basked in the compliment. She eased a step closer, keeping her body turned sideways to prevent Taren's close perusal of her face if he happened to notice her.

The young lord's long, tapering fingers drummed on the counter where he stood before Gerguld. With a glance around, he leaned in close and whispered, "The queen still seeks her daughter."

Straightening in shock, Gerguld played his part well. "The princess hasn't been found? Still? How frightening for her."

For her or her mother, Leera wondered. Gerguld continued to amaze her each time she witnessed his skills at subterfuge. She knew he meant for Taren and the soldiers to believe he meant her when he was really speaking of her mother.

"Yes. You're quite right." Taren leaned in. "But she's clever, the princess. And lovely. You can't have missed her if she ventured this way. She's a lovely little bird with golden tresses that float around her shoulders."

The look on his face softened Leera's fear for a moment. Did he truly see her that way? Or was he using her as a step toward ruling Elwar? She wished she possessed Helmyra's gift of Seeing the truth. Still, her pounding heart took an extra leap of joy at Taren's description.

Until one of the soldier's snickered. "Come now, lad. You really don't believe miss perfect and pouty would make it this far, do you?" The soldier glanced around, his gaze falling on Leera. "How about you? Have you seen the princess? You wouldn't miss her. Most likely had her nose in the air and complained a lot."

With a quick shake of her head, Leera retreated deeper into the shadows, face down.

"Ernest, must you always speak so rudely of your future queen?"

Taren advanced toward the soldier, his voice calm, but even from afar Leera saw the angry tension in his shoulders, the set of his jaw muscle pulsing in anger.

A loud guffaw bellowed from the soldier. "Future queen? You believe Her Most High and Mighty Majesty will give the chit her throne anytime soon? And sit you beside her?"

As Taren's eyes squinted in warning, the soldier continued. "Yes, yes. We know. We all know the plan for the little rabbit."

With a short clearing of his throat, Gerguld drew Taren's attention back. "Begging your pardon, m'lord. I never seen the princess 'cept from a distance. Even so, I think I'd note a noble lady in these parts. I haven't seen her. May the Creator bless your efforts and upcoming nuptials."

Yes. Gerguld might be rough around the edges, but he knew how to play a person. Yet he'd never played Leera. She wondered why.

11

Adana tossed her sword from hand to hand, swung it in a huge arc, then spun to face...no one. She needed to move, to rid her body of this excess energy.

Sinti, the lone Watcher left to stay by her side this morning, pushed away from the wall of the practice yard. "Shall we spar?"

Relief drained frustration from her shoulders. "Yes."

The Watcher approached with a slight swagger to her stride, pulling her blade from the sheath across her back. "It's been a while, Your Majesty. Should I go easy on you?"

For answer, Adana lunged at her.

Sinti skittered out of the way and to her right.

Adana followed her movements, gauging her weak spots. When last they had sparred, Sinti's weakness had been her left side. Adana feinted for the woman's right but reversed to slam her sword into Sinti's left.

Their blades met with a clang.

A triumphant smile on Sinti's face told Adana she remembered their last bout and had rectified that weakness.

Adana grinned back and shoved Sinti away. They danced around each other. Energy sparked in Adana's arms as she watched for her next move.

Sinti made a right cut from above.

Adana countered with a slashing cut toward Sinti's arms.

Her opponent's blade swung in an arc and made a crosswise cut. An upward thrust stopped the blade.

Thrust. Counter. Dance. Cut.

The two swordswomen fell into the rhythm of the exercise. After a few minutes, the telltale signs of the other's actions became obvious.

Thanks to Quilla's refusal to allow Adana much time to practice her Watcher's skills while living in Elwar, Sinti's expertise outshone her. But only by a bit.

But that bit was all it took and, moments later, Adana's sword flew from her hands and clattered across the stones of the courtyard.

Sinti stepped back as Adana retrieved her sword. "You've conquered your weak spot, Sinti. Do you have one now?"

Readying her stance, Sinti said, "Same as always—the left."

Adana stopped before picking up her sword. "No. You stopped me."

"You revealed too much."

Head tilted in thought, Adana pretended to consider this. She grabbed her sword and rushed at Sinti, swinging for her right shoulder. A quick step to the left put her where Adana wanted her. She upcut toward the left side using the flat of her blade.

Sinti stumbled back.

"Never tell someone your weak spot, Sinti," Adana said.

A disgusted snort from behind sent Adana whirling to face Kassa. The elder Watcher observed the two of them from the entrance to the practice yard. Their gazes upon her, she marched toward Adana, pulling her own sword free.

"I should have made you practice with me more. Kiffen has softened you."

"Yahhh!" Adana ran at her, sword raised.

* * *

At dinner that night, Adana eased into her seat beside Kiffen. Muscles she'd forgotten ached in ways she never knew they could.

"Are you unwell?" Kiffen asked.

She shook her head and reached for her goblet, downing half of it in one swallow.

"Or did you get dishonored by an old woman?"

Boisterous laughter filled the room.

"Everyone knows, do they?" She smiled across the room of Watchers, soldiers, and advisors. She took a daintier sip of wine and set the goblet down. "Might it interest you to know Kassa blamed my dearth of skill on you?"

"Me?" Kiffen spluttered in surprise. "Oh no you don't. We might be wedding tomorrow, but you will not accuse me for your less than superior performance."

A flush ran through her as she realized the import of his words. Tomorrow, she acknowledged him as hers. Another flush spread into her limbs. Am'brosia. A quick command to stop this foolishness didn't change the animal's interest in the next day.

Kiffen gazed at her, a wrinkle between his brows. "Now I am concerned. Are you unwell? You're all flushed like you have a fever."

The Watchers close enough to overhear tittered.

Her husband-to-be glanced around then reddened, himself. "Oh."

"Yes." She set her hand in his. "Oh."

For a short moment, she managed to forget the trials of the last few days and the battles soon to come. For a very short moment.

* * *

Leera thanked the Creator for the sun's declining position in the sky. As she had hoped, a moment later, Mother Sariah called for them to stop.

"We'll make camp over there." She gestured to a small grove of trees by a stream. "Do you need assistance, Lily?"

In answer, Leera tried to swing her right leg over the back of the horse to dismount. Her leg refused to obey her commands to move. Biting her lip as pain shot up her back, she shook her head. "I can't lift my leg."

In a flash, Catch appeared and, between him and Sariah, they eased her off the horse.

"Best walk around a bit," Sariah said. "Get the feeling back in your legs and back."

As she struggled to hobble forward, Catch chuckled. "You're gonna want some of Gerguld's salve tonight."

Ignoring him, she attempted to turn in place to unbridle her horse.

They'd maintained a fast pace throughout the day. At times, Sariah and the others had dismounted and walked, encouraging Leera to join them. She'd wanted to decline. "Ladies don't walk" echoed in her mother's voice. Something in Sariah's face and tone told her to follow the Protector's lead, though. She wasn't a spoiled princess, so she refused to complain. Now she wanted to cry.

One of the men Sariah referred to as soldiers approached her. "No need, Miss Lily. I'll do this for you. You need to walk the pain out."

"Thank you."

He nodded. "No problem. The Mother told me to watch out for you. You managed well for such a long day."

The praise warmed her, and she nodded her thanks and headed for the stream.

Long after their dinner and after the watch was set, Leera struggled to sleep. Every part of her hurt. Her legs felt frozen in place. If she'd wanted to move, she couldn't. Not to mention her seat—a polite word for her bottom that didn't fit this pain. Bruised beyond belief, she lay on her stomach and side, avoiding contact between the earth and the pain. For once, she longed for the volumes of petticoats she often wore. The padding might ease the agony.

Exhaustion overcame her as the watch changed, and she drifted into a dreamless sleep.

The aroma of the strange hot drink the soldiers drank woke her as the sun began to peek over the horizon. She eased herself up, relieved to find she could do that.

"Good. You're awake." Sariah squatted beside her and held out the wooden jar of salve. She nodded toward a cluster of underbrush. "I suggest you take care of your needs over there and rub more of this on your legs and seat. If your back hurts, call me. I'll tend to it."

Unable to express any thoughts, Leera climbed to her hands and knees. The motion didn't send stabs of fire through her legs. Smiling, she rose and found she could walk a bit better. The salve must be a miracle. Another reason to place her in gratitude to Gerguld.

After a quick breakfast, the small crew set off again. The saddle hurt but the salve lent a numbing tingle to the mix, making it survivable. Ahead of Leera, Sariah rode flanked by two of the soldiers. Then in a line came three more soldiers, Catch and herself, and the last two soldiers. Helmyra at the last moment chose to stay in Elwar in case word needed to be sent later. Then the seamstress would come. Or Gerguld. One would stay. One would come.

She kicked her horse up beside Catch. "Have you ever been to the Border Keep?"

"Yes, You'r—um, Lily. I went there once as a boy."

She laughed out loud. "As a boy? Then what pray tell are you now?"

The frown he threw her direction surprised her. "I'm old enough to work for the king," he whispered at her in fast, biting words. "I'm old enough to help you leave."

"You're right. I apologize. How old are you?"

"Thirteen next week."

Three years younger than she. He still looked tiny and young, but he was correct about the responsibilities he'd shouldered. "Then I stand corrected. Thirteen is old enough to join the king's troops."

Sagging shoulders greeted this response. "I know. I planned to join after my birthday. Now..."

The urge to pat his arm overcame her, but she held back. Who was she? Adana?

"You can become one of my soldiers." She glanced ahead at the road extending beyond them. "You already are, to tell you the truth. We just need to make it official."

And with that one statement, Leera gained her first loyal servant.

At midday, they stopped to eat. Leera managed to dismount on her own. Everything still hurt, but she wasn't a spoiled princess anymore. She smiled as the soldiers congratulated her on her recovery.

The hard biscuits and cheese they ate for lunch eased her hunger, but it still gnawed in her belly. Enough that she didn't hear the approach of horses. The rest of her party *did* hear them, jumping to their feet and reaching for weapons. The knife Gerguld gave her the morning they left remained in her saddle bags where she'd placed it. He'd warned her that was not the place to carry it.

Ten men on horseback paused on the road within sight of their group. The kerchief to cover her curls lay on the ground. She grabbed it up and quickly tucked her hair up, hoping the men wouldn't notice the lone person seated on a rock by a tree.

Two of her men walked out to meet the arrivals, both carrying a sword in warning.

She strained to hear their words, but the blood rushing in her ears muffled all noise.

After a moment, her men's shoulders untensed. They sheathed their swords. A few laughs and cheery comments exchanged between them and the others as they waved the rest of the arrivals forward.

A curious expression crossed the first of the men's face as he approached their small resting place. He walked straight toward her, recognition dawning in his eyes. Heart pounding, she rose and backed up until she stumbled over the rock she'd sat on.

With quick grace, the man swooped in and caught her, setting her back on her feet. He bowed low before her.

Bewildered, she glanced at Sariah who shrugged, the same confusion reflected on her face. None of their party seemed alarmed, though. Just perplexed.

When he rose, the man said, "It's with great joy we find you, Your Highness."

That created a shuffle of unease among Sariah's soldiers. Had they known her identity? They'd called her Lily as Sariah had introduced her.

"Forgive me for startling you." He turned to the others, his face reflecting bemusement "Helmyra's message came to us. We thought she told you."

"Helmyra?" Leera held her voice steady, forcing the habitual dislike of the woman down. She'd come to trust her in the last weeks. A foolish move?

"Yes." He frowned with concern. "I see I have alarmed you, Your Highness. I do not mean to. I'm here. We're here to protect you and escort you to your brother."

"Did he send you?" Hope flared in her chest.

"No. We've been hiding in caves since the death of the king. My condolences on your father's death." He bowed his head a moment, and his men followed suit. "Each week, one of our number ventured out to scout the situation in the capital. When we heard of your disappearance, we worried what might have happened to you."

This became odder and odder the longer the man spoke. *They were worried for her?*

"I'm sorry. Do I know you?"

He shook his head. "Not me. But Callan was among the guards in the royal chambers." He waved a young man over.

Tall and lean, the man had deep tan skin and liquid brown eyes. His hair hung long on his neck, and a thick beard covered most of his face. He bowed then rose to smile at her.

She studied him a moment, unsure. "I rarely noticed guards, I'm afraid to say."

"I was there the day after the Princess Adana's Recognition Ceremony. You quarreled with her, I believe."

"I did." She cocked her head to the side. "What else do you recall?"

He chuckled. "You came to her rooms while she was out and bade me fetch you some tea."

Her eyebrows shot up at this statement. She did recall demanding tea. Was he the man? "Suppose I choose to believe you. Why, again, are you here?"

"King Kiffen is raising an army. You are going to him. We will serve and protect you on your journey."

With little effort than a nod at her acceptance, Leera's party grew. Counting the seven with her own party and Catch, Leera's army grew to eighteen soldiers and a Protector of the Faith.

12

The queen's and king's coronation wedding day dawned under gray skies. A warm wind blew from the south, carrying sand and grit from the far-off desert. Some might say the signs were ominous, but Adana didn't care. Today she would wed Kiffen. Today her people would witness her official acceptance of the crown.

Adana gazed from the window of her chambers in the central part of the keep. The view, south toward Moniah, hung heavy with dark clouds. They didn't swirl. No rain fell. The air felt like the pressure before a battle. Tense. Urgent. Ready to burst.

"Never mind the weather, child," Kassa said, pulling her from the window. "No one controls the weather. Some believe a stormy day promises brighter days in the future."

"It's not stormy. I don't see rain. Even in the distance." She sat down on the edge of her bed. "I wish Shana was here."

Both of Kassa's brows shot up at that statement.

"She could tell me if rain was coming. She heard thunder before any of us. Surely, she can hear a storm."

"Maybe. For now, you must finish dressing. Your kingdom's people await you."

"And Kiffen," Montee added as she came in the room. "He's

"

pacing up and down the hallway beside the temple." She grinned, a rare but welcome sight. "Simeon says he's frantic with nerves."

She'd seen him that way one time, on the night of her Recognition Ceremony in Elwar. He'd found her in the hidden balcony spying on her guests and...

She smiled remembering how nervous he'd been but determined to steal one kiss before she became another man's betrothed. Thank the Creator it did not become their last kiss.

A jolt of shock ran through her. Had she really thanked the Creator for this? After three years of mistrust toward the benefactor of her gifts, might she find a way back to the strength of faith she once possessed? Possessed until he took everything.

"Tell me of mother and father's wedding," she asked as Montee and Kassa slipped the flowing royal blue gown of glimmer cloth over her head.

Kassa's firm hands smoothed down the back of the gown, adjusting it at her waist. "You don't want to think on that day today."

"What?" She whirled around, pinning Kassa in place with her stare.

The woman's eyes widened. A twitch in her shoulders revealed the former First Vision's momentary impulse to fight the Watcher's stare Adana held her with. Then she relaxed. "Please child. I'll gladly tell you some other day. Not today."

With a gentle pull, she directed Adana to the looking glass. The glimmer cloth of her dress shimmered in shades of indigo, cobalt, navy, and silver. The skirt swirled around her legs, skimming the floor. Tiny flecks of mica sparkled in the tight bodice, their placement an arrow pointing toward the low neckline. Diaphanous lengths of material flowed from the bodice to braided, off-the-shoulder straps, leaving much of her neck and shoulders bare. The braided material unwound in a cascade down her back, ending in a long train that flowed behind her like a river.

The lengths of Adana's hair, unbound and flowing free, floated around her face in a tawny cascade of curls. One of the keep's maids had spent hours coaxing it into this spiraling mass. For once, Adana did not regret the time spent dressing for an occasion.

Her gaze met Kassa's and Montee's in the mirror. The three women smiled in the way of women, enjoying the beauty of their bodies. Kassa wore a simple but elegant gown of sand-colored glimmer cloth. The long skirt separated to ease access to the short sword and knives she carried strapped to her thighs. Montee wore red glimmer cloth, her dress cut the same as Kassa's, but the color drew out deep undertones of red in her tightly pulled up hair. Tiny droplets of smokey topaz hung from her ears.

Montee turned toward Adana and held out a tiny box of gold. "Kiffen asked me to deliver this to you. His wedding gift to the queen."

Chains of blue sapphires dangled from silver-wired earrings.

Threaded along the edge of her ears, the stones clinked as she walked out of the chamber and left her youth behind.

* * *

The stones of the temple felt cold and rough against Adana's knees. Despite the solemnity of the day and occasion, a thought leapt to her mind of Elwar's subjects. In Elwar, all witnesses to a coronation prostrated themselves before the new king or queen. The position held little appeal, and she gave thanks that kneeling wasn't required often in Moniah.

The air smelled different from this position, too, resonant of wood smoke and freshly scrubbed floors, evidence of people who knelt on these floors with regularity to do their jobs.

Beside her, Kiffen knelt, waiting his turn to receive his crown. Did his heart pound, stop, and pound again like hers?

The blue of his tunic and loose-legged pants held more silver in the material than her gown. Not exactly the same glimmer cloth, but they were well-matched. His gaze as she'd floated toward him in the hallway where he'd paced the last hour in nervous anticipation had revealed a hunger she hadn't anticipated. She felt it, too, but to see it in his eyes? A blessing.

Father Tonch's robes billowed as the man turned toward the podium holding the crown. When he turned back, Adana blinked in the light, awed at the sight of her mother's crown in his hands. Until a few days ago, the last time she'd seen it, the stones ablaze in the light of hundreds of candles, was on Mammetta's head.

Father Tonch held the crown above Adana's head and intoned in a droning melody, "I crown you as the Giver of Sight and Health, the queen of Moniah, the commander of the Watchers, and the blessed of the Creator."

Energy crackled around the crown. Strands of Adana's hair lifted from her scalp as if they reached for the symbol. The hair on her neck stood up too, and she felt her skin pimple with chills. The smell that followed a lightning strike burned her nose.

Father Tonch intoned one more line. "And I crown you as the helper and Queen of Elwar. Both kingdoms soon to be known as the One Kingdom."

The words startled Adana, but she held her tongue, the tension in the air distinct and invigorating. As Father Tonch pressed the crown onto her head, she half-expected the heavy sky of clouds to thunder in response, but she only heard a sigh of relief among the people gathered in the Border Keep's Temple.

White robes swirled again as Father Tonch turned to a second podium and lifted another crown from its depths. This crown represented the Husband King of Moniah, not the king of Elwar. Her heart ached for Kiffen that it was all they had available.

"King Kiffen," Father Tonch said, "we cannot offer a proper Elwarian crown at this time, but we do honor you with the crown of the Husband King of Moniah. It holds great power. Will you accept it as representation of your authority in both kingdoms until we can do better?"

"I will," Kiffen said, his voice betraying no regret over the missing Elwarian crown.

Father Tonch held the crown over Kiffen's head. The chestnut brown hair on his head raised in a similar attraction to the crown, lifting and reaching upward toward the symbol of his new authority.

A jolt of pain and anger almost knocked Adana to the ground.

Ambrosia's connection flooded with warning. Adana grabbed for Kiffen, who stumbled to his feet in alarm, stepping away from Tonch and the crown. He must have felt it, too.

Cries from the outer walls reached them. The bell above the eastern gates began to clang out a warning.

"Attack! Attack!"

Within moments, a circle of Watchers surrounded Adana and Kiffen. She reached for her blade only to remember the wedding dress held none. Monian queens went without a weapon to their coronation and marriage. A tradition. One she'd change if she survived this day.

Through Am'brosia's eyes, she saw troops flow out of the forest and from the plains to the south. The giraffes on the outer shore of the lake bucked and kicked at the encroaching army. The huge hooves caved in the skulls of the first ranks and maimed others. Men fell before the giraffe army.

Pain lanced through her head like the shaft of a migraine as one giraffe fell to a soldier's blade slicing through the tendons of the animal's hind legs. The giraffe went down with a thud and tried to rise. Soldiers swarmed over her like a troop of army ants.

A flash of cold washed Adana from head to toe.

The giraffe had died.

Skirts gathered high, she raced for the walls, Kiffen behind her.

The gates, open for the ceremony, were closing, but not fast enough. Four, seven, nine soldiers rushed in before the gates slammed shut. She watched in fascinated horror as they realized their mistake. Archers on top of the battlements shot them down.

"The walls! The walls!" Shouts from above warned.

Adana yanked up the beautiful skirt and train of her dress and ripped at the cumbersome cloth. It shredded in her hands, and she cast aside the tattered remnants. Unhindered, she mounted the ladder to the battlements. All along the outside wall, as far as she could see, men surged toward the giraffes guarding the keep. In the distance, catapults rolled from out of the trees.

At least the giraffes managed to warn them before the attacking army lined up their machines. And they still held the attackers' numbers back from the walls. She spotted the dead giraffe by the makeshift bridge, its huge body blocking most of the structure. Another giraffe had taken up the spot, but several of the enemy had already shoved past the first giraffe and now ran across the bridge.

Another giraffe fell. The cold rush over her body confirmed its death. She whirled around trying to find the lost one but couldn't. Only a few of the giraffes wore armor. Some refused it. Others waited for more to be made.

A third giraffe fell. Cold plunged over her, and pain lanced her heart.

One look at Kiffen told her he felt the same. Dazed, he turned toward her. Misery swam in his eyes.

"Kiffen." She grabbed his arm and shook it. "Kiffen. We have to shut the giraffes out. Cut the bond." She shook his arm. "Can you hear me?"

He nodded.

Only the day before, she'd taught him how. Not the way she'd been taught. The way she'd figured out three years ago in Elwar, when the pain of separation from Am'brosia became too much to bear.

Along the link, Am'brosia's misery bled into her soul. Cutting her bond felt cruel. To save others and the rest of the giraffe guard she must. Envisioning a knife, she aimed it at a mental image of the tie between them. A quick slice severed the bond.

Sounds rushed over her, and she stumbled at the onslaught of smells and people rushing by. Am'brosia must have softened all of that.

To her left, an archer fell. She rushed to take up the position. Grabbed up the bow and arrow. Stepping into the vacant space along the wall, she nocked the arrow. The man in front of her gaped in shock as she released the arrow into his middle. He fell from the scaling ladder, dragging the next man with him. Others surged up the ladder. She drew another arrow.

"Adana," a voice shouted in her ear. She ignored it, aiming at the men on the ladder. *Where was the pitch for flaming arrows?*

"Adana," the voice shouted again.

"What?" She didn't bother to turn, as she picked off several more men. The ladder fell, unmanned. Her fleeting moment of triumph evaporated when three Watchers rushed the ladder. The warriors— ones who once served her—shoved it back up against the wall.

Adana hesitated, as she sighted along the arrow. She knew one of them. Had trained with her. Shared a tent with her in the desert.

Their gazes met. The Watcher's mouth curled into a vicious snarl.

Adana loosed the arrow, wiping the snarl from the traitorous Watcher's face.

A sudden tug pulled Adana from the wall. "You must fall back, my queen."

Adana blinked. Montee stood beside her, fury clouding her eyes. "You must fall back. Go to the tunnels. With Kiffen."

"Kiffen?" Heart pounding, she searched for him.

"There." Montee nodded toward another point on the wall where Simeon yanked Kiffen back from a rain of arrows.

"You must fall back. Leave this to us."

In seconds that felt like hours, Kiffen and Simeon dodged toward them.

"Get below," Simeon snarled.

Blood smeared Kiffen's face. She reached up and wiped at it. His? He reached up and steadied her crown. "My queen."

With insistent shoves, Montee and Simeon herded the two of them down the ladder. "Go to the tunnels," Simeon said. "Take those inside the keep with you."

Kiffen made a move to follow the man back into the battle. Simeon turned on him and stood firm as a rock wall. "You will not, my king. This is a small battle. A test. Do not give Maligon your heads today."

* * *

From a rise on the plains south of the Border Keep, Shana stared at Maligon's soldiers scrambling for a hold on ladders, fighting giraffes. Giraffes guarded the keep. So many. A huge one kicked out his hind legs, both hooves finding their mark. Many of Maligon's men fell.

She glanced around for Samantha's Watchers. They steered clear of the giraffes. Found holes where the great beasts fell. Ran through those. They knew the animals well. No Watcher drew close enough for a hoof strike.

Some of the giraffes wore armor. She was glad of that. Others didn't. Another stumbled and fell. Screams came from two men pinned under the body.

Along the walls, several soldiers and Watchers scaled ladders. So far, none had made it to the top of the wall. The ladders teetered backward in a cycling display like a child's toy, their climbers shot down. On the wall beside one ladder, a stray sunbeam shot through the heavy layers of clouds. It struck something in a flash of gold. The sparkle short but too small for a sword. No, it was a jewel. A crown? Adana.

Blood surging with worry, she leaned forward on her horse, straining to see the flash again. Oh, to have a Watcher's gift right now; then she would know what she saw.

The sun and jewel didn't reward her with a second glimpse even though she combed the walls seeking it. Had Adana fallen in that flash? "Please, Creator, save her. Save the queen." The whispered prayer melted into the melee of sound. She glanced at the soldiers to her left and right, at Pultarch behind her. Why didn't he fight? Or Maligon? Shouldn't the man who called this battle be here? But Maligon had not joined the troops sent to battle.

Coward.

Sickened by the continued slaughter, she turned to Pultarch. He searched the walls, too. For Adana? Or for Kiffen whom he'd sworn to kill? Another form of cowardice if he hoped the soldiers would take the strike for him.

A screech of pain rushed along the wind. She looked up to find what she'd known would come. Fire. Arrows flamed into the midst of those outside of the walls. Ladders burned as they plunged to the ground, flames whipping into those too slow to jump free. The fires rushed around the dry grass on the edge of the lake, cutting many men off.

A whoosh and roar went up as the two catapults caught fire just before their first launches. Men dove away from them, screaming with pain.

Sickened, she turned away.

At least the battle was lost.

"Call them to retreat," she ordered the Watcher beside her.

The soldier blinked in surprise.

"I said call retreat." Shana kicked her horse into the side of the Watcher's horse. "Do not hesitate under my orders."

Without a word, the Watcher lifted a small bugle from her hip and blew into it. Three sharp blasts.

Shana didn't wait. She turned her horse away from the keep and started the long ride back to the fortress, uncaring what "her" soldiers thought. More than anything, she wanted to see Brother Honest. Not to speak to him. Just see him and his gentle face, kind with concern. Find comfort in the teacher's presence. The only peace she'd known in years.

13

The wounded and innocent lined the corridors in the tunnels. The coolness below ground did little to mask the reek of blood and sweat. The eyes of the refugees haunted Adana as she moved among them, giving comfort where she could.

One woman, wearing the plain gray cotton skirt and shirt of a livestock handler, reached out to her, her face drooping in dismay. "Oh, my lady, your dress. Such a shame."

She followed the woman's gaze to the remnants of her wedding gown. Ripped and shredded by her own hands, the jagged hem hung in a frayed disarray, some lengths to her knees, others to mid-thigh. Flecks of mica dangled from threads on the bodice, and one of the braided straps had slipped down to her elbow.

She patted the woman's hand. "It's only a gown. Lives mean more."

The woman reached out a tentative hand, and Adana fought the urge to jerk back. "At least you still have these."

The sapphires still dangled from the edge of her ears.

"Yes."

"They're lovely. Your husband loves you well."

Husband? Horror coiled in her belly. They weren't married. Kiffen wasn't crowned. The Creator must have been laughing when she thought he might finally be blessing her this morning. What did he want from her? Why couldn't he let her live with some small joy?

"Yes. Well, not yet. A small interruption."

"Oh." The woman's face registered an awareness of the problem. "You're not—"

"A situation I plan to remedy soon, my lady." Kiffen appeared at her side, a wry smile on his face. "My lovely bride deserves her wedding celebration don't you think?"

Celebration? Adana stared at him. After this, he could think of celebrating?

As if on cue, a cheer started from the front of the tunnels. It carried through the numbers of them quickly, smiles returning to grim faces. Simeon and Montee led a stream of soldiers, Watchers, and the occasional workman, wielding a shovel or ax, into the large chamber in the center of the tunnels.

"They retreated," Montee said as a greeting. "We won the day." Her red dress survived better than Adana's thanks to the slits providing space for a sword. Darker shades of red covered areas of the skirt, though. Blood?

The jubilation she should feel over the easy defeat didn't come. Am'brosia had reached out a tentative stroke to her mind moments earlier. She'd taken the bond back, felt the overwhelming grief over the losses among the giraffe army. Fifteen dead. The impact of loss staggered her, but she held her stance firm and sent a gentling croon to the giraffe. A lullaby Mammetta used to sing to her at bedtime. Not enough, but something to reveal her compassion and own pain.

Am'brosia's mourning cry resonated through the link, and Adana turned on her First Vision. Voice sharp, it rang out in the chamber. "At what cost, Montee?"

People hushed and turned her way, joy replaced with anxiety.

Show them your confidence. Her mother's firm words echoed in her ears. Never show them despair or weakness.

She straightened and raised her voice with conviction. "We won the day. We must honor the fallen; we will prevail."

Cheers erupted again. People laughed and slapped each other on the back.

"Well done," Simeon said under his breath.

"Queen Chiora taught her well," Kassa said, joining the small group.

How had she known? Adana tilted her head to the side and regarded the woman.

A thin-lipped smile flashed back at her. "I see the signs, every time you remember her. You shift your stance. Square your shoulders. Your head tilts up a small fraction."

Glancing between them, Montee nodded. "I've noticed, too. I didn't think to attribute it to your mother."

"You weren't present in the first years of Adana's life. The training she received long before she joined the Watchers."

Mammetta had taught her. Each morning after breakfast before meeting with her advisors, she led Adana along the walls or through the barracks or the kitchens, always instructing. Adana had loved those moments her mother devoted just to her and no one else. No matter where they went, no one interrupted them. If something urgent happened, they approached Kassa, who maintained a short distance behind them, not Mammetta.

"My lady?" The woman who'd noticed her dress interrupted her thoughts.

"Yes?"

"I've a good hand with clothing and hair. I could help you straighten up a bit. It won't be perfect but—"

"Don't let Marletta fool you, my lady," a woman behind her said. "My sister can make wondrous magic with cloth. Especially glimmer cloth."

Marletta blushed but didn't deny the claim.

Before she could put off the idea of needing a wardrobe adjustment in the aftermath of a battle, Kiffen answered the women.

"My bride thanks you."

Montee echoed the approval. "The queen accepts your offer."

Then Kassa and the two women pulled her away, the crowds of battle-worn people parting before them. After a few turns, Kassa led them down a dark, unused corridor and through a door at the end of the hallway. The room, a bedchamber, held a large, canopied bed, a dressing table, mirror, and three fabric-covered armchairs facing a cold hearth.

"This is the queen's chambers below ground," Kassa said. She turned back to the door. "I'll get some water. You should find brushes and combs in the dressing table. There should be a small basket of tools below the bed. I believe there's thread there, too."

As fast as she'd herded Adana to this room, Kassa left.

The two women, Marletta and her friend, already bustled about.

"You are called Marletta?" she said to the first woman.

"Yes, my lady."

"And you are?" She turned to the second woman. The darker-skinned woman wore the white of a cook or baker, a kerchief tying back her thick curls of black hair.

"Bellu."

"You said Marletta was your sister, but she doesn't look Monian." Marletta's ecru skin tones contrasted with Bellu's darker tones, defying the claim to relations.

"Yes," Bellu said. "We're neither Monian or Elwarian. We grew up in the keep. Our parents lost their spouses in Maligon's Rebellion. I guess that would be the first war. Now must be the second." Her voice trailed off as she appeared to ponder this idea.

"I was a babe," Marletta picked up the explanation. "Our mother was pregnant with Bellu at the time my father married her. We're sisters."

"And neither Monian nor Elwarian."

A wide grin spread over Bellu's face, her teeth sparkling white against the deep ebony of her skin. "We're whatever yours and King Kiffen's kingdom will be. All of us at the keep are from both."

"And part of neither." Marletta's grin matched her sister's delight, her teeth white against the lighter shades of her skin.

Both women's dark brown eyes sparkled with joy over this announcement. They were proud of their allegiance to both kingdoms.

As the two women began their ministrations, Adana pondered the implications. This fortress, almost forgotten by the nobility of both kingdoms except in moments of danger, offered the proof that a combined kingdom could work. The fortress sat on the original grounds of the former kingdom of Yarada, divided centuries ago when the king gave each twin daughter a portion to rule. If only the rest of the two kingdoms could see how well the people lived together here.

Not as simple as it seemed, but there might be hope yet.

* * *

True to Bellu's words, Marletta's skill wrought miracles with the ruined gown. As Adana walked down the long corridor of onlookers toward the center chamber where Kiffen and Father Tonch waited, the hemline brushed her knees and thighs. She still didn't understand how Marletta managed to adjust the material to a longer length than Adana's frantic ripping left behind. Bellu called it magic, and she believed it. Marletta may not be Monian by birth, but she belonged with the glimmer makers, not tending goats and chickens.

Bellu's deft fingers restored beauty to Adana's hair, piling all of it on top of her head and encircling it with Moniah's crown. This felt more real. More like who Adana wanted to be, with a long knife strapped to her right calf, hidden by the frothy, uneven skirt.

Father Tonch's robes remained pure white despite the earlier battle. They swirled in the silent room as he once again lifted the Husband King's crown over Kiffen's head. Before he could utter a word, the hair on her betrothed's head swirled upward. People gasped as his hair curled around the edges of the crown, as if it lay claim to it before any other disruption might occur.

"Kiffen, son of Elwar, betrothed of Moniah, this crown proclaims you as Husband King." Tonch held the crown just above his head, but it looked as if he struggled to keep the crown from settling too soon on Kiffen's head. Sparks of light danced in the stones.

"This crown today stands for more. I crown you as the Protector of Fairness and Health, the King of Elwar, the commander of her armies, and the blessed of the Creator. And I crown you as the helper and Husband King in Moniah. Both kingdoms soon to be known as the One Kingdom."

The crown slammed down on Kiffen's head, a charge of energy shooting from it to Adana's crown. The energy dragged her closer to him, a pull that neither she nor Kiffen could, nor wanted to, ignore.

Father Tonch looked down the long corridors. People filled three branches joining into the main chamber. "As witnesses to the Creator's chosen, will you support and protect these two rulers in their task of returning Elwar and Moniah to One Kingdom? Will you stand by their sides to protect both ends of this land and its peoples?"

Underground, in the tunnels of a new order, everyone raised their voices in unison.

"I will."

* * *

After the charged energy of the coronation, Kiffen didn't expect much from the simple vows he shared with Adana to join them as one. The two of them rose as the halls resonated with cheers and faced each other as Tonch directed them to do so.

He took Adana's hands in his and stared into the startling blue of her eyes. This one trait she received from her father, once a stranger to these kingdoms like his own father. It set her apart from others and made people whisper about diluted blood. But the gaze she directed at him made his heart soar. Through the link, he felt Bai'dish as he pranced in the paddock above ground, flaunting himself before Am'brosia. He felt Am'brosia, too. Just a flash. Nothing permanent. Was that normal? Or had Bai'dish shown him the female's admiration?

The electric charge from his crown continued to hum, and he felt it draw him even closer to Adana. He wanted to press her to him and never let go, and he struggled to not lose the decorum required for the ceremony.

Adana edged closer, too, and her mouth parted in astonishment as she glanced up at him.

Beside them, Tonch whispered, "I feel the pull between you. Fight it a few moments more. The crowds will quiet, and we can begin."

As promised, Tonch raised his hands above their heads, and the cheers subsided. "More powerful than the bond to a kingdom is the bond between a woman and a man. The marriage of their souls helps them focus on their purpose in this world together. The Creator blesses each couple with this union and forever draws them close to the one they must love."

Kiffen heard the words but only because Tonch stood directly to his left. Adana's hands, slightly moist in his, squeezed his gently, and she smiled into his eyes. She was beautiful. The glow of her skin against the reparation of the gown begged him to reach out and touch her. Only moments separated him from doing that, but he longed to do it now.

A slight murmur of sound rustled across the crowd as Tonch pulled forth the horn from a fold in his robes. Now Kiffen knew why he felt oblivious to all but Adana.

Every tiny motion caught his notice. A dart of her tongue across her lips. A downward sweep of her eyelashes over pink cheeks. The rise and fall of her breasts as she breathed. Slow, deep breaths. Focused breathing. That's what he should be doing to forestall the lure of emotions. With her, he breathed in, feeling the air rush into his chest, then flood his soul. After a pause, they released their breaths together, slowly through slightly parted lips. Once more. Once more. Once more. They breathed in harmony, their union even stronger with the sharing of their breath between them.

"The strength of a union draws each of us in our own ways, but the presence of Moniah's sacred horn creates a stronger power between Adana and Kiffen. The Creator blesses their union. The sacred horn establishes their bond to each other, and thus their bond to our kingdoms. Before the Creator, they must hold the horn between them and speak their vows."

And then the bone lay between them, their fingers touching above and below and sending surges of energy up his fingers. His focused breathing stopped. As did Adana's.

"Adana?" Tonch prompted.

She had a clear and strong voice. Most days. But today, she spoke just above a whisper. "To Kiffen, son of Donel and Roassa, I pledge my home, my health, my hand, and my heart. I stand before you, Kiffen, undone by your presence and wholly willing to join lives with you."

"Kiffen?" Tonch prompted again.

Unlike Adana, Kiffen's joy bubbled over in him, and he fought not to shout the vow at the top of his lungs. As he promised her home, health, hand, and heart, his smile grew wider. The last of his words echoed throughout the chamber, drawing chuckles from those gathered there.

Adana's gaze still held him mesmerized until Tonch leaned forward and removed the horn. "You may seal your union."

Kiffen swept Adana into an embrace, knocking their crowns askew in the process. Each grabbed for the weighty item, as they crushed their mouths and bodies together.

They laughed as they broke free to boisterous shouts of approval and thunderous applause.

They turned and stood before the crowds, facing each corridor one at a time. The rustle of clothing preceded the witnesses bowing low before them.

Tonch laid his hand on Kiffen's shoulder. He didn't have to see the other hand settled on Adana's shoulder. He felt it. Through the bond.

"You should visit the injured while these people prepare your feast," Tonch whispered to them.

They stepped forward, and the crowds parted in a wave. As many people as were gathered in the tunnels, it took them a little time to reach the quarters set aside as the infirmary. As they entered the room, a scattering of weak cheers came from those who reclined or sat awaiting the attention of the healers and apothecaries.

They wandered between those on the cots and pallets, pausing to thank each one. At the end of the room, an old soldier lounged, his arm tied up in a bloody sling. "You best get back to the celebration, Your Majesties." He gave them an impish grin. "We won't be seeing any of that fine food until you're served."

The keep's staff had managed to transfer the feast to the tunnels in a short matter of time. Unlike the formal event they planned, people milled about, nobles, servants, and soldiers intermingling. Food was carried, not served at a table. Except for those who tended to the injured, all joined in the celebration below ground.

Kiffen and Adana found themselves besieged by well-wishers, who crowded in on all sides, sometimes separating them an arm's length but never more. In a small break between embraces and congratulations, Kiffen grasped for Adana's hand and drew her into another kiss.

Adana leaned into him. "Now," she whispered against his lips, an edge to her voice that thrilled him. "The queen's chamber is closest."

"Lead the way," he said.

She took his hand and ducked behind the crowds, following the walls of the huge main chamber. Kiffen ignored the winks and nods as they hurried past.

After several turns, she led him into a dark hallway and gestured toward the door at the end of the hall.

He swept her up in his arms and raced for the door.

I4

The next morning, Adana exited the infirmary and stalked along the corridors without noticing where she went. Kiffen followed her. She could feel his confusion over her mood. Her short-lived joy over their marriage faded as she spoke to the injured and held the hands of the few who might not make it through the day.

Her body recalled the sensations of the giraffes dying in battle, and she shivered.

Around her, people bustled about, setting the castle and the world back to some order they needed—the process of pushing forward with life. She should know. She and Kiffen sought solace in each other's arms the night before. She'd never imagined their first night together filled with a different desire. One that fed the desire she'd anticipated. The desire to remember they lived. For now.

She could ask Am'brosia to help her block the sight of upheaval after a battle, but Am'brosia mourned, too. She deserved her own methods of dealing with the loss.

A strong hand grasped her arm, and she whirled to meet Kiffen, his forehead creased with concern.

"Where are we going?" he said.

"I'm trying to flee my thoughts."

When he tilted his side to the side, she sighed in frustration. "I know. I can't flee something in my mind, can I?"

"You can if you find something else to focus on." He took a step closer, his body warm against hers. "We could go back to our chambers."

There it was. The urge to feel alive surging through her with need. She shook her head. "No. We must be visible to our people today." She leaned in and gave him a quick kiss. "Although it was an excellent suggestion."

He nodded, the acceptance of her refusal telling her he expected it.

"Glume did tell me over breakfast he planned to honor the memories of the giraffes fallen in the battle yesterday. We should find him and find out what his plans are."

"Why didn't you tell me? Or he should have. I must be there." She held her head up with conviction. "They came to serve me. It's my duty."

"Yes, it is. It's *our* duty."

His answer surprised her. His whole demeanor until now radiated a desire to pamper her or please her in some way.

"Did he say where?"

After the crowding in the tunnels, moving through the keep unhindered came as a relief, like a cool drink of water. Glume and several of the refugees had built a pyre for the giraffes in the only area large enough to gather the remains of the animals, south of the lake. When Adana and Kiffen emerged and turned south, her steps faltered as she saw the fifteen animals laid out side by side. Trees cut from the closest edge of the forest surrounded them. At least, in the dry season, trees burned quickly even if recently cut. They would need little glimmer fire to encourage flames.

A crowd had gathered, which seemed impossible, considering how many remained below at work in the tunnels. Glume stepped forward as they approached, standing with his back to the pyre. The crowd parted as she and Kiffen moved to join him.

As he spotted the two of them, Glume gave them a sad smile. He approached Adana as she emerged from the crowd and took her hands in his. "My queen, I was going to say a few words, but I believe you should in my stead."

Adana took a deep breath, inhaling deeper than she thought possible, and then released it slowly through her mouth. With a nod, she said, "I will. But, Glume, I believe you should speak first. You know the giraffes better than I, and your connection reaches all of them. Mine must filter through Am'brosia."

"Of course. She has not touched me today. How are she and Bai'dish?"

"They appreciate what you're doing."

Gasps behind Adana made her turn. From around the lake and the keep, giraffe guards approached. Those on the keep's island remained there but clustered to face the crowd. The ones from the opposite shore of the lake strode forward, and just as the crowd had parted for her, they parted and stepped back, letting these through.

Tog led them. He walked up to the edge of the pyre and lowered his head to the ground. Moments passed, then he moved aside, and another giraffe came forward. Movement on the periphery of her vision drew her gaze back to the ones on the island. They had waited for Am'brosia and Bai'dish. The two royal giraffes led the remaining ones across the low, floating bridge used to cross the lake. The wood dipped and swayed, but it held the full weight of three giraffes at a time. The animals never sent more than three, as if they knew the structure's limitations.

With all the giraffes stepping forward, one at a time, to pay homage to their fallen, the crowd of people stepped back and spread out until they stood in a large circle around the pyre. This provided room for the giraffes to stand close.

After the last giraffe turned and took up her spot in the gathering of mourning animals, Tog raised his nose toward the sky. An eerie bugling rose into the air, its tone loud, grief-stricken, and haunting. Am'brosia and Bai'dish raised their noses and joined him in the song.

Shivers ran down Adana's arms. She'd seen this before. The giraffes had done the same when Ju'latti, her mother's giraffe, died.

Mesmerized, the people around her listened to the dirge. No sounds interrupted them. Bird song ceased. The distant noises of the few people working inside the keep halted. Everyone attended to the mournful melody.

Tears streamed down Adana's face, and, as she swept her gaze over the people, she saw that many cried with her, with the giraffes.

Tears glistened in Am'brosia's eyes, too. Most wouldn't notice, but a Watcher's sight could spot them. For a brief moment, she wondered if Glume held a vial to catch the tears, but shame rocked her out of the thought. These were not tears to enhance the bond. These tears carried private grief.

When she turned back to the pyre, Glume had stepped forward, a torch of glimmer fire in his hand. As the song rose on the air, he set the torch to the logs, then moved farther along the structure and lit more. He continued until he traveled around the entire structure. Glimmer flames licked up the logs and spread with a roar across the bodies of the giraffes. Smoke billowed in the sky. Huge clouds of it.

The crowd of people took involuntary steps back from the overwhelming heat. Nothing burned hotter or brighter than glimmer fire. A blaze this large forced them back against the edge of the lake.

Adana checked the distance to the forest and grasslands, noting with approval the preparations to stop the fire's spread. The ground surrounding the pyre and for several lengths in the direction of the forest and grasslands had been cleared of all growth. Young people stood a body length apart, large tubs of water by their sides. Stacks of buckets sat next to each tub.

Rocks enclosed the space. Inside that area, a ditch encircled the pyre. With surprise, she realized a large plank of wood had been used for her to cross to the giraffes. She hadn't even noticed as she walked over it. That's how deep her sorrow pulled her from the world. Not a smart move for a Watcher or queen. She must be careful.

If Maligon wanted to strike and really hurt them, this would be the perfect time. When their grief and distractions pulled their awareness away.

He wouldn't of course. His losses should be more severe than theirs.

The giraffes' song died out, Tog, Am'brosia, and Bai'dish each bugling one last call on the wind. All faced the fire. It crackled and popped as the fire ate the wood and the bodies of the giraffes.

Without a word, people began to turn and walk away. Adana sensed Am'brosia's approval. The giraffes gave the elegy, not the people. As they should.

The giraffe guard still hadn't moved as the last of the people left Adana, Kiffen, and Glume. Together, without sharing their intentions, the three with the closest bonds to giraffes approached each one and laid a gentle hand of condolence on their foreleg.

When she reached Am'brosia, the giraffe turned toward her and spread her legs, dipping her head low in a bow. Adana dropped into a curtsy to the giraffe.

15

Leera discovered you could cover lots of ground in a day when your traveling party consisted of a small squad of soldiers, everyone carrying the minimum of supplies. After adding the refugee soldiers to their number, they had hurried on, stopping only for small breaks throughout the last two days.

If any of the people in the castle could see her now, they'd faint in shock or split their sides laughing. The spoiled princess of Elwar would never deign to take care of her needs in the bushes like a common peasant. Yet, she did. It was easier than trying to use a chamber pot in a moving carriage, too. A task her mother had forced her to practice ever since she could walk. She chuckled to herself and straightened her tunic and leggings, another reason it was easier and emerged from the bushes.

The smile vanished from her face. The small clearing held double the number of men than before she'd left to tend to her needs. These new soldiers milled around the clearing, grooming horses or sitting on the ground sharing food and water.

Nothing gave warning to this abrupt shift in their numbers. No shouts of alarm. She hadn't noticed the approach of horses. The men looked and sounded Elwarian. Her mother's soldiers?

Talking a step back into the bushes, Leera considered her options.

No one had noticed her yet. She could run. She wasn't quick on her feet, though. She cast a searching glance around the groups of people. Her gaze fell on Callan who rose and approached her, his eyes shining with excitement. Or was that enthusiasm?

She took another step back, searching the area. Where was Sariah?

The Protector of the Faith stood in deep conversation with one of the newer arrivals. An act or had these men fooled her into trusting them, and now, her goose was cooked? She made a face at the phrase, recognizing it as one she'd heard Adana's Watchers use.

Hesitating, Callan bowed. "Your Highness, we've been joined by more men who wish to serve you. Will you accept them into your service?"

The only word she could utter was, "Why?"

"Why what, my lady?"

"Why would more join us? For that matter, how? It's not like we left with huge fanfare."

Another soldier joined Callan, executing a deep bow to her. "Your Highness, I'm Ruslan. We're pleased to locate you."

His words jumbled her thoughts. *Pleased?* "Locate me? You've been looking for me?"

"Yes. We, like Callan, learned of your journey and seek to serve you and the king."

"How?" She glanced at Callan, heart pattering in her chest like the rapid wingbeats of a sunbird. "No one knows I travel with you."

The shrug the man gave her did nothing to quell her anxiety. Did they not know how dangerous her actions were for her? If her mother's soldiers found her before they reached Kiffen, she'd be dragged back, forced to marry Taren and pretend her mother hadn't killed her father.

Shock halted her thoughts over the last realization. She'd known, or at least suspected, her mother's part in his murder, but when had she decided her mother had done it? For she had. No doubts clouded those thoughts. If found, what awaited her might be worse.

With a shake of her head, she didn't hear Ruslan's next words at first.

"—of no concern. We are discreet, as is Gerguld and Helmyra. We've been waiting for word so we could rise from our caves and serve you."

By now, the rest of the camp stood quiet, watching their interaction. She glanced at Sariah and received a half-shrug of apology. She had known.

With a tiny jerk of her chin, she summoned the woman over.

"Yes, Your Highness?"

"What are Gerguld and Helmyra doing? Do they wish me returned to my mother?"

"No, my dear. We've known of these men in hiding. Many we helped flee Elwar. They were loyal soldiers to your father and now your brother. We sent word to them."

"What if others hear of this?"

"It's a chance we take in war. Precautions were made, Lily, but we can't stop all that happens." She turned and surveyed the men, all of whom watched their discussion with unfeigned interest. "They wish to serve you, if you will it."

Leera lifted her chin and straightened her back. The sudden appearances of so many men concerned her, but she couldn't deny the relief at a larger force accompanying her to the Border Keep. "You and your men are welcome to join us. We will not be delayed by your numbers, though. How many men do you contribute?"

She was acting, using the words and tone her father or mother might have used. It worked.

"We number fifteen, Your Highness."

Fifteen! Added to their current party, that gave her a small army of thirty-three men. Three, her lucky number. Not that she believed in luck, but she'd always liked threes of anything.

On Callan's insistence, with no grumbling dissent from the rest, the group swore their allegiance to Leera, and Kiffen by association. Then Leera's small army prepared to mount up and continue on their way. With any luck, they'd make it to the forest before nightfall and camp outside before entering the dark, mysterious place the next morning.

Riding near the front of the column, Leera basked in the sunshine and the cheer of the men around her. They served her. What an odd place to find herself. It felt amazing. If only her mother could see her now. At that thought, the sun ducked behind the clouds, and she shivered with fear. Today, she became not just a fleeing princess, she became an enemy to her mother's claim to the crown.

Before she could fall into a frightening array of methods her mother might use to stop her, one of the newer soldiers rode up next to her. He slowed his horse to match pace with hers. "Your Highness." He bobbed his head. "I am Amar. Gerguld sent the suggestion, and Ruslan agrees, that I teach you to fight. We will begin when we make camp this evening."

With a cluck to his horse, the man nodded and turned to rejoin the ranks behind her.

She hadn't said a word, but a glow grew in her chest. She would learn to fight.

Thirty-three must be the luckiest of lucky numbers.

16

"How dare you call retreat."

Shana raised her eyebrows at Samantha as she stalked back and forth, pausing every few steps to glare at her. The entire journey back to the fortress, Samantha treated her like the queen she was meant to be. She pushed them hard, and they managed the five-day trip in three and a half.

Now, without preamble, the First Vision cornered her in the queen's chamber. Fury rolled off the Watcher, unrestrained now that she lacked an audience. "You aren't the queen, or have you forgotten that? Now I have to explain it to him. Do you know what that's like?"

In the tavern and the great estate where she once worked, people lost their tempers, and in many cases, thought their anger gave them the right to intimidate her, a servant. Amusing, really. She used to laugh with the other lady's maids about the antics of their mistress and her oldest daughter—the one of marriageable age. For all their fine clothes and possessions, they screeched like common fish wives. A lot.

Drunken men challenged her more, but she'd faced down enough at The Sleeping Dog to know what to do. Most wanted a gentle hand to comfort them—something she suspected their wives didn't do—so she listened and nodded and patted them on their arm. A gentle touch, soothing. Nothing strong.

But with this woman...

"My actions made sense," she said into the sudden quiet of Samantha's rage. "Your soldiers were failing."

Nostrils flared, Samantha took an ominous step toward Shana. Unlike drunken men and noble ladies, this was a trained warrior willing to fight a woman. Silence never boded well. Samantha glared. And took another step closer.

Maybe she should tread a bit easier. She fought the urge to step back as Samantha closed the space between them. She must act as Adana even if Samantha knew better. If she dropped that role in anyone's presence, except Honest, she'd never regain the lost ground.

"Enough, Samantha. If you're frightened of Maligon, I'm not." A lie but one she'd never let Samantha know. She pushed past the warrior and headed for the door. "I'll explain how poorly you strategized the attack. Make sure to point out the faults in trying an attack on all sides when a lake separated you from the fortress. How unprepared your men were for an army of giraffes surrounding the lake and the keep."

That last information had surprised all of them.

Where had the giraffes come from?

She knew the giraffes housed in Adana's View remained at the estate only because she'd asked Honest to check. The animals stuck to the outer edges of their territory within the walls, but they remained.

"And they killed giraffes. That offense carries a death sentence."

The snort from Samantha gave the only indication the woman followed her. As she left the room, sweeping the door curtain aside, the heat of the body following close behind her reminded her of the night her father almost threw her in the fire on the hearth. Drunk, he'd turned on her and her eavesdropping. What had she overheard?

Nothing else of that night remained in her memory. Just the heat as he shoved her toward the flames, hands gripping her arms with a strength that kept her from the fire unless he chose to let go.

No. This was not the same. She wasn't a child anymore, and she refused to be intimidated by anyone.

The air around the two women thickened with the heat of the sun. It had shone bright on the kingdom ever since the retreat, as if it wanted to reveal the truths of Maligon's folly to all. At least Samantha chose not to speak, just follow, as they strode down the corridor to the rooms Maligon had commandeered. Larger than the queen's chambers, Shana suspected this room originally served as a receiving chamber instead of sleeping quarters. Maligon desired everything bigger than other rulers and had taken pains to disguise the room as a lord's chamber.

Pultarch hovered outside the entry. A dark purple curtain covered the access. "He's meeting with Kalara and Brother Honest." The young lord glanced between the two women. "I was told to locate you and escort you to him." A sardonic smile crossed his face, followed by the gaze she'd seen him employ when trying to beguile someone. What had Adana called it? Puppy eyes.

"Well?" Samantha's voice carried an annoyed edge but none of the hostility she'd aimed at Shana earlier. "Are you going to step aside, or do I need to move you?"

"She's in a mood," Shana whispered and winked at Pultarch. "Best not stand in her way."

The puppy eyes vanished in wide-eyed alarm as Samantha shoved him aside and slapped the curtain open.

Within the chamber, Maligon reclined on a large chaise, propped up by a multitude of gold and purple pillows. He wore his red robes today, the glimmer cloth sparkling in the sunlight streaming in from the courtyard. A fire blazed in the hearth despite the day's oppressive heat. Honest stood propped against a writing table, head bowed except to glance up at them as they entered. Kalara paced much like Samantha had done moments ago. Yet her actions revealed a measure of stoicism more common for her.

"Welcome ladies." Maligon graced them with a weak grimace.

The control it took Samantha not to snarl at the word "ladies" reminded Shana of a cat, desperate to snatch a mouse but forced to wait until the perfect moment to seize its prey.

While the five other people in the room studied each other, Shana tried to gauge Honest's thoughts. He appeared in deep thought, not looking at anyone. As if he felt her stare, he raised his eyes, not his head, toward her then slanted them toward Maligon. There was a message there. If she were a Watcher, she might understand.

Instead, she relied on her ears. She took a focused breath and tried to drop her awareness deep within her chest as the air filled her lungs. She exhaled, slow and quiet, and repeated the exercise. After several inhalations, she concentrated on sound, shutting out everything else.

People didn't realize the tiny noises they made. Pultarch sniffed. Not a cold, more like an indignant gesture. What had he noticed? She hid the urge to snort. Maligon hadn't addressed the young lord, unless he included Pultarch in the "ladies" comment.

Kalara still paced, her footfalls even. A knife slapped against her leggings as she walked.

Heavy breathing came from Samantha. An effort to seek focused breathing and calm herself? That would be the smart thing to do.

As for Maligon, she caught hints of wheezing in his chest. Louder than before. The sound never ceased, and the traitor's skin looked paler than normal, a bit green beneath the surface.

She turned back to Honest and blinked twice. *Yes. He still wheezes.*

In the short moments it took Shana to tune in on those in the room, Maligon had also studied each of them, his gaze greedy like the orphaned pickpockets she used to pass on the streets in her village.

"Kalara informs me the Border Keep is protected by giraffes." Maligon's voice carried no true volume. They could be having tea in a fine parlor, not a care in the world.

"Yes," Shana said. "A circle of them around the lake, and another circle of them around the keep."

He nodded and turned to Samantha. "Your scouts didn't share this information with you?"

Eyes wider than Shana thought possible, Samantha shook her head. "No. Not a word."

"Kill them."

Samantha and Shana jerked their heads up in surprise. "Kill who?"

"The scouts of course." Maligon waved his hand in dismissal of the topic. "And the giraffes. The ones here. They remain, don't they?"

"No." Shana seethed with fury. "It's forbidden. They're sacred."

Black eyes under thick graying eyebrows pinned her to the spot. "I'm aware they're sacred, Shana." He placed strong emphasis on her name. "That's why we must kill them. They aid Adana. We'll send a message by doing so."

A message? She shot a questioning look toward Honest who rose and nodded. "With Adana and Kiffen bound to their giraffes, they'll feel it. It will devastate them and their bonded beasts. A wise move, Lord."

Revulsion churned in her belly while the rest of her body flushed cold with horror. Honest played his part, and he appeared indifferent to the implications. Memories of Adana enveloped by her giraffe, a peaceful smile on her face, came to her. "You can't do this. It's cruel, even for you."

With precise and careful movements, Maligon eased himself upward from the chaise and shifted toward the edge of the cushions. Pultarch rushed to his side to aid him, but Maligon slapped him away. In slow increments, the man rose and approached Shana. "My dear child, what would you do? We must send a message. This one will shatter the young queen. Drop her to her knees. Wouldn't you like that?" He glanced over his shoulder at Honest before continuing. "Honest tells me she did nothing to endear herself to you. Surely, it would bring you satisfaction to see her dropped so low."

She kept getting colder the more the man talked. Was there no end to his cruelty? Squaring her shoulders, she fought off the emotional tug of compassion. "Yes. That would give me joy." She bared her teeth and stepped toward Maligon, aware that few dared do that. "How will you do it?"

A dismissive hand wave answered her. "I would use lions." He turned and captured Samantha in his gaze. Now she was the mouse and he the cat. "But I'll leave it to the First Vision to carry out. There will be an outcry, I suppose, from the Watchers. You will deal with it."

"Yes, Lord." Samantha's voice didn't betray any emotions, but Shana saw her throat bob in a large swallow. She hoped the Watcher tasted bile the rest of her life.

17

Nestled in Kiffen's arms, Adana woke with a start. The bed-chamber in the tunnels remained dark save for a small candle nearly guttered out on the table. The dark hours of night, still.

With care, she slid from the warmth of his body and sat on the edge of the bed. Cold pimpled her skin as she evaded his still-sleeping form as he rolled toward her.

What had woken her?

Unease trickled down her spine. Pain, hot and lancing, stabbed her shoulder.

"What?" Kiffen jerked awake as she moaned, reaching for her. "What's wrong?" Sleepy-eyed, he rubbed at his face and raised himself to sit beside her.

"Do you feel it?"

"What?"

"I don't know. I feel..."

"This?" Soft lips caressed her bare shoulder. "Or this?" He kissed her neck.

The draw of his closeness shuttered the worry for a moment.

Arms encircling her waist, he pulled her back on the bed.

The emotions his hands and lips prompted swathed her in momentary bliss.

Sharp, stabbing heat throbbed in her shoulder. She yelped, jumping from the bed. Her hand groped for the spot, and a whimper escaped her lips.

"Adana?" Leaping from the bed, Kiffen reached for her.

She dodged, avoiding contact. "Something's wrong." Her right arm dragged as if the weight of every soul in the kingdom hung from her hand.

They dressed quickly. Kiffen ran a stream of questions at Adana, but the pain prevented her answering. He assisted her with the laces of her boots when her fingers refused to grasp them.

Within moments, the two rushed from the room. The pain eased enough for speech when the door closed behind them.

"Do you feel anything, Kiffen?" Adana raced down the hall, her feet pounding the stones. "From Bai'dish?"

In the moments of dressing, she'd sought the link to Am'brosia and found it tattered and weak, unresponsive.

He paused, making her sigh in frustration at his inability to work with the bond while in motion. Horror dawned across his face. "Monsters."

With a nod, she grabbed for his hand. "Come."

They raced through the still forms of those who slept along the corridors, some who woke in surprise as they rushed past. The halls near the tunnel's access to the keep above lay deserted. Their footsteps kept time with the pounding of their hearts.

At the top of the circular hidden stairs, they activated the lever to open the exit. Light and musty air washed over them as they circled from behind the great statues of Yarada, Moniah, and Elwar that hid the tunnel's entrance.

The echoes of their footfalls continued to surround them in the deserted keep. Under Montee's orders, all had come below to the tunnels. Except the giraffes.

Adana reached for the bond again. A surge of desperation hit her, but she cried out in relief over the connection, stronger now. "Try Bai'dish now."

A grunt accompanied Kiffen's efforts as it appeared his link solidified with the animal. Once again, she felt that strange sensation from their marriage ceremony where she glimpsed Bai'dish's sight for a moment before Am'brosia took over. The bull's desperation ate at his nerves. She felt the sway of the animal pacing.

The night sky glistened with stars as they stumbled into the open courtyard and headed toward the paddock. In the shadows, Adana slid to a stop as she spotted Glume. His slumped form pushed away from the wall where he had been leaning.

"Mistress. Sir." He gazed up at them, eyes red-rimmed and puffy. "Thank the Creator you've come."

Glume's presence reminded Adana of his absence after the battle when most everyone in the keep celebrated their victory, followed by their coronation and wedding. Everyone had pushed so hard for them to complete the ceremony. Overcome with the pressure from so many, she never missed the man.

"What is wrong?" The question sounded stupid to her, but she needed to hear it from Glume. Hear she had forgotten Am'brosia's continued mourning for the lost giraffes. That she'd ignored the connection and given into her own pleasure and desire.

"No, no, Missy. Don't blame yourself."

Once again, he knew her thoughts thanks to his incredible bond with Am'brosia and all the giraffes. She felt the spiral of his pain over all that happened feed back to her in the bond.

"They rejoiced in your marriage. The giraffes know we must prepare for battle and not forget the important roles you play."

"Then what is it?" Kiffen asked. "Why are they upset? What have they done to Adana?"

Until then, Adana didn't know if Glume knew about the

puncture on her shoulder. Concern in his eyes, he focused on her shoulder. "How bad?"

"She woke screaming."

She had?

"She couldn't dress herself. She couldn't use her arm." Kiffen's voice rose in frustration. "I had to dress her."

A gentle nod toward Kiffen's outburst provided the only acknowledgement of those words. "Am'brosia mourns, but she senses something else. Something neither I nor Bai'dish yet feel. She closed the bond to us."

Behind the giraffe keeper, the two giraffes loomed in the paddock. Bai'dish paced like a frantic lion. Am'brosia stood rigid, her face turned south toward Moniah and Adana's View.

With gentle steps, Adana approached Am'brosia, crooning the lullaby she'd sung earlier through the bond. She slipped through the slats of the fencing and reached out to touch the animal's flank. A shiver ran through the animal at her touch. Am'brosia's long neck dropped toward Adana with agonizing slowness. Caressing the side of her beloved giraffe's face, Adana stared into the liquid brown eyes. Tears brimmed there. Precious tears, the source of their bond.

Then the bond blazed with anger and pain. A giraffe calf in Adana's View, separated from the others, being herded from its mother by women dressed in Watchers' uniforms. They led the giraffe into the large arena reserved for great gatherings of battle sport. The audience stands stood empty, but several soldiers stood in a circle holding lit torches against the night.

The calf shied away, but the soldiers closed it in.

One Watcher stepped forward and faced the giraffe. Samantha. She raised her hand, the blade of a long knife catching the firelight.

And stabbed the giraffe in the heart.

Adana fell to the ground screaming.

18

Kiffen couldn't hear the stampede of people racing toward him. Not with Adana screaming. His link with Bai'dish still radiated confusion and a frantic need to do something. How much was his emotion and how much the giraffe's?

Montee got to them first. She skidded to a halt beside Adana, still rolling on the ground screaming. When Adana didn't respond to her efforts to stay her, she turned on Kiffen, fury darkening her eyes.

"What have you done?"

Beside his own worry, the realization that he still stood as an outsider and potential threat struck him harder than any blow.

By now, several Watchers surrounded Adana. They managed to lift her to a seated position, whimpering but still not speaking.

Montee left her charge and stalked toward him. "What happened? What did you do?"

"Nothing."

The ground drummed with more people racing out of the keep into the paddock. They surged around him, gasping in shock. Many turned furious glares in his direction.

"Kiffen." Montee's voice rose in warning.

He took a step back, arms raised to ward her off, and backed into Glume.

The man stepped in between them. "He tells the truth, First Vision. Kiffen knows no more than you do."

Defeat sagged her shoulders as she stepped back. One step. "What's happened?"

"Am'brosia shared something with the queen," Glume said. "Not with Bai'dish or Kiffen. Not with me."

The Watchers encircling Adana managed to get her to her feet and lead her away from Am'brosia who still stared to the south, body rigid. Bai'dish pounded back and forth in his side of the paddock. Kiffen recognized the urge to release pent up nerves and wished he could join the giraffe.

"What happened?" Montee spoke but didn't look to them anymore, her gaze fixed on Adana.

A steady hand settled on Kiffen's shoulder. He looked up with relief into Simeon's reassuring presence. "I apologize, sire, for not being here sooner. Someone needed to prevent the people from trampling each other."

The paddock was overrun with people. All the ones from below save the wounded must have poured up the stairs. Still, they came.

"Of course, Simeon. I'm sure your quick actions saved many from harm."

With an absent nod, Simeon turned to Montee with an eyebrow raised. "Would it be best to remove the queen from here? Out of sight of the people?"

Unspoken were the words, "where others won't see her devastation."

"Already taken care of." Kassa's sharp tones came from Kiffen's other side. She glanced up at him and nodded. Unseen by the others, she patted his arm twice.

Sinti and Nuala guided Adana from the area. People began to follow them, so Kiffen, Simeon, and Kassa blocked them.

"You go." Simeon nodded to Kiffen.

"She needs you." Kassa nudged him behind her. "We will deal with the crowd, for now."

Thankful for the reprieve, Kiffen followed Adana. He wanted to go. Worry tensed his muscles and drove him to want to protect her from this. Whatever this was. But part of him didn't want to go. Screaming women reminded him of Quilla's histrionics. Adana's lack of emotional outbursts drew him to her at first, before he knew the strong warrior underneath. Yet here he was, not married five days, and she exhibited behavior he never expected from her. Some soldier during their wedding reception warned him, clapping a heavy hand on his shoulder, "Now, you'll find out who she truly is."

At Kiffen's confused response, the man bellowed in laughter, took another gulp from his goblet, and stumbled away. Drunk. Kiffen ignored him.

But now...

Sinti grabbed his arm. "Come in. Now. We can't shut the door."

He blinked. The room they'd taken her to looked like an armory. Was that wise, bringing a hysterical woman into close reach of so many weapons?

He inched inside enough for Sinti to close the door behind him. She and Nuala turned to him, expectant looks on their faces.

He took another step, then another, toward Adana who was slumped into a stiff chair in the corner of the room. She looked drained. Her left hand was clamped over her right shoulder in a reflection of a soldier staunching an injury.

"Adana?" He knelt before her, peering up into her face. Her eyes were shut tight. "Adana, my love? What happened."

She didn't respond.

He touched her face, just a slight graze of his thumb over the high cheekbone.

She gasped. Grabbed his hand and cradled her face in it. A huge tear rolled down her cheek and over his fingers.

"They killed her." The words came out in a hoarse whisper. "The poor baby. They killed her."

"Killed who?" Maybe Am'brosia had shown her a prophetic vision. The thought stole the breath from his body. A baby. Killed. Theirs?

Fingers dug into his hand. She tugged him closer and collapsed on his shoulder, throwing her arms around him.

"Adana? Please tell me."

She nodded. "I know. I told her not to show you."

He waited.

She lifted her face to look into his eyes. The pain in hers stabbed his heart. He would fix whatever this was. "Samantha and the Watchers..." She paused and ground out the next words. "No, they're no longer Watchers. They took a giraffe, a calf. Surrounded it. Killed it."

The gasps behind him reminded Kiffen of the other Watchers' presence.

"She drove a knife into its heart while men with torches kept her from escaping."

He wanted to retch.

Sinti did, rushing to a bucket before losing control.

Comfort. He wanted to comfort her, tell her it was a nightmare, but he'd wondered how long it would be before Maligon tried something like this. The surprise attack had alerted him to the presence of their giraffe army. His abhorrent response made appalling sense.

"Now or soon? Do you know, Adana? Did you see it as a prophecy?"

She shook her head. "No."

Whatever control Am'brosia held over their bonds disintegrated at this point. The images rushed through the bond to Bai'dish, to him. The ruthless act bowled into Kiffen's sight. He teetered with the impact but held fast to Adana. He would not let her fall.

One swallow of bile. Two. "Bring Montee and Simeon. Now."

Nuala raced from the room.

In moments, the two, followed by Kassa, rushed into the room. The looks on their faces told Kiffen Nuala had told them rather than make Adana or Kiffen repeat it.

"We must act." He stood, holding Adana close in his arms. Fury over the pain caused by Samantha—the irony of who did it clear to him—set his jaw firm. No one would hurt Adana this way again.

"What do you suggest?" Simeon asked, his voice quiet, speculative.

Kiffen opened his mouth to speak, but Nuala spoke ahead of him. "Send me back. I'll release the giraffes before they kill more."

Kiffen shook his head. "Too dangerous. We must destroy the aqueducts. Drive them mad with thirst."

Montee and Kassa exchanged glances. Something passed between them because both gave the other a grim nod.

"I will take a small squad into Adana's View," Kassa said. "We will release the giraffes and destroy the aqueducts as we leave."

"No." For the first time, Adana showed awareness of their discussion. Voice still hoarse but firm, she said, "I won't lose you to his schemes."

"My queen." Kassa bowed her head in a formal gesture, it's rarity more striking than her words. "I'm expendable. I'm past the years of fighting. You have a First Vision, Watchers, soldiers. You don't need me."

"But I do."

It struck Kiffen, then, why Kassa volunteered. Her daughter. Her own daughter killed the giraffe. He studied her face, impassive and stoic as always, seeking a clue to what she planned. For plan something, he knew she did.

19

They moved quickly. Before most of the keep's inhabitants knew what upset their queen's perfect balance. Before anyone could question their motives or plan.

Kassa took two Watchers, two of the oldest warriors at the keep, with her. At the fork in the tunnels where one led back to the keep and the other led above ground, she turned to Montee.

"You're positive about this?" Montee asked.

"Yes. More than most of the decisions I've made over the last thirty years."

Had it been thirty years since she first stood at Chiora's side, a Watcher achieving the rank of Tactical Command, the highest except for the First Vision? And twenty-five years since Chiora's mother chose her to serve Chiora as First Vision?

"Tell Halar—" Kassa hesitated. He and Jerold had left the day before the wedding, headed for the village of Roshar, and then Belwyn or Teletia. He had his role to play serving Adana, as did she.

"Tell Halar, I love him."

Without another word, she led the women down the quiet tunnel.

* * *

They emerged from the tunnels into the pre-dawn light. Kassa had wanted to reach Adana's View before sunrise in two days, but it couldn't be helped. May the Creator give them time to reach the giraffes before Maligon—she refused to think her daughter's name—killed the rest.

"We must hurry," Kassa whispered to her companions, women she'd known since her first days as a trainee.

Umgani, a sinewy, battle-scarred Watcher with dark skin tough as leather, nodded once. Behind her, Dosata's russet brown eyes met Kassa's in acknowledgement. The three women darted across the landscape, keeping to the brush and undergrowth.

At daybreak two days later, they reached the entrance to the aqueducts below the southern wall.

The Watcher, Eno, met them at the final gate, the door swinging open before the echo of their knock disappeared. At their surprised looks, she said, "We anticipated you. Too much goes on above for us to miss it." She bowed her head in acknowledgement of Kassa's former rank. "Former First, Miri and Vuur await you in the master chamber."

After performing the ritual of sharing the water of the aqueducts, the three women followed Eno. Kassa glanced around, her gaze absorbing the wonder of the waterways. A shiver ran down her spine, chillier than normal due to the unfamiliar moisture in the air. How Miri managed to live down here, never coming above except in ceremony, Kassa never understood. But then, the two of them never did see things the same way. The Water Maji would object to destroying the aqueducts. Her old competitor loved this dark, dank space. If she hadn't, Miri might have become First Vision to Chiora instead of herself. For that, Kassa thanked the Creator.

Miri rose to greet them, her face composed and serene. In the torchlight, her moss-green eyes glowed. "Kassa, my sister, your presence confirms the depth of our concerns. What do you know of above?"

Kassa filled Miri in, glancing at Vuur occasionally. His ebony eyes gave nothing away, and he sat with the torches behind him, which, combined with the darkness of his skin, obscured her ability to read his face. The clever man used this ploy often in the presence of Watchers. She admired his caution while fighting annoyance over it, too.

Miri's concern for the giraffes' safety shifted to outrage when Kassa ordered them to prepare to evacuate. "Ballene's fire, no." Miri jumped to her feet and took a menacing step in Kassa's direction before composing her face and halting her forward motion. "These aqueducts will take years to rebuild once we win."

"We must destroy them." Kassa stared her down, not surprised by the maji's refusal. "It's the fastest way to weaken Maligon's army."

"What of your Watchers still above?"

Her Watchers. An interesting choice of words. Kassa wanted to explore that, but time remained a larger issue. "Very few remain. They appear to support Maligon."

"And your daughter, I assume." A cat-like smile spread over Miri's face as she settled back into her seat.

Why was the maji goading her?

Vuur leaned forward and cut her response off. "How do you plan to destroy the waterways?"

Releasing a long breath, one she hadn't realized she held, Kassa said, "I hoped you and Miri would know how." She forced her body to loosen the tension from Miri's stab at Samantha. "You're most familiar. Surely you know areas of weakness where we can do the most damage."

"Not only do you want me to leave my home, but you expect me to help you destroy it?" Miri seethed, her eyebrows raised in sarcasm. "It never occurred to you we might know how to stop the water's flow without destroying the tunnels, did it?"

"Do you?" Kassa leaned forward. She'd considered it. Discussed it with Montee prior to leaving, but Miri's words confirmed the small hope she'd held in her heart.

The woman sat back and crossed one leg over the other, looking off to the side instead of at Kassa. "I don't know if it will work. We've never attempted to stop the flow."

The undercurrents in what the maji said and did concerned Kassa, but she needed to focus. She turned back to Vuur. "What can you do?"

The man straightened and glanced at Miri before shaking his head and turning to face Kassa. His deep voice resonated throughout the stone walls of the chamber. "My predecessor began creating traps after Maligon's Rebellion. At crucial locations. They might work, but we'll have little time to leave the tunnels once we activate them. The tunnels will flood."

"How much time will it take you to get the glimmer guild and their supplies out?"

Miri sniffed.

Kassa frowned but turned to her. "And your Waterway Watchers? How long to get them and whatever essential supplies you need out?"

Silence ticked by while the two leaders of the waterways regarded each other. Meanwhile, above, Kassa feared giraffes might be dying or already dead. She opened her mouth to speak, but Miri spoke first.

"We can have our supplies and Watchers out by nightfall."

Vuur nodded. "The guild can be done sooner and will help them. You will not want to attempt firing the traps before then, anyway. Night provides the best cover. We have many to evacuate."

Kassa sat back and sighed with resignation. When she left the

Border Keep tunnels, she'd known how soon they'd arrive and how much longer she must wait. It annoyed her, but she no longer held the rank to move things faster. And they were right. Tonight, there would be little to no moon.

"Dosata will stay below and aid you. Umgani and I have to attend to a different matter."

Miri stiffened. "You're going above. In daylight. Are you sun-maddened?"

"Possibly, Miri. You always said I was."

That drew a wry smile from the maji, a sign her sister hadn't changed as much as it appeared.

"I need to determine where the giraffes are held and see if I can locate Suru. If she still lives. I'd ask for one of your Watchers to aid us, but it makes sense to leave as many below as possible to aid in your evacuation."

She didn't share all the plan. Umgani didn't know either, but she doubted the woman hadn't guessed her motives. The chance to locate Maligon and kill him presented itself, finally. Something she'd sworn to do after Chiora sentenced him to the oxen head years ago. It was time she fulfilled that promise and correct what Chiora failed to do. It wouldn't end the war. Her daughter had plans and the ability to step into the traitor's role. But removing Maligon took them a step closer.

And if she saw Samantha? She'd chosen Umgani for a reason.

20

By the time Kassa and Umgani headed for the above-ground access, Dosata stood shoulder to shoulder with Miri, directing the evacuation process. Despite Miri's estimations on time, with Dosata overseeing the move, they would be ready well before nightfall.

Kassa led Umgani to the waterways access behind the stables. By now, the sun had begun its climb into the sky, halfway to its zenith. The heat as she lifted the door to check their surroundings washed over her in a blast. After being below in the cold, stony underground, she embraced it.

No one in sight, the two Watchers exited and skirted the edge of the stables. They peered around the corner, checking the wide yard between them and the barracks wing. Voices and the occasional clank of equipment or armor told them people went about their daily tasks, but the yard stretched before them unoccupied.

"Odd to see it empty," Umgani whispered, stating the same thought coursing through Kassa's mind.

At any hour of the day, Watchers used this space for training and practice. When not training, many congregated here to relax and watch others spar. It seemed impossible no one would appear, so the two waited through six focused breaths while they surveyed the area.

"Shana said their numbers are low," Kassa whispered. "Which means, if Suru still lives, she's probably locked in a cell below the barracks."

"That's what I'd do." The muscles in Umgani's body tensed as she prepared to leave their hiding place. "Ready?"

They trotted across the broad yard and ducked into the shadows of the Watchers' quarters. Sweat trickled down Kassa's back in the short amount of time they'd been above ground. The stream made her want to fidget. It had been a while since Monian sweat bathed her in response to her work. She'd missed it but needed to retrain herself how to ignore it.

The overwhelming heat and unrelenting days of dryness kept enemies from laying siege to this fortress. Few had the fortitude to linger outside the impenetrable walls. Impenetrable, at least, if you didn't know how to reach the aqueducts.

Kassa led the way into the barracks.

Just as reported, most of the quarters were empty, as deserted as the yard outside. The two women crept along the walls, their footsteps silent in the huge corridors. A shiver ran down Kassa's spine as she peered into vacated room after vacated room.

At the cross-section of corridors, they turned left. The door to the dungeons stood at the end of this short hall. Unused since Maligon's Rebellion over twenty years ago, it had become storage for excess supplies. Just before they reached the door, Umgani flattened herself to the wall. "Someone's coming,"

Voices drifted from the main part of the wing. The footsteps of at least three people echoed in the empty space.

Kassa eased the dungeon's door open, waiting for the hinges to squeal their presence. No noise—a good sign Kalara was using the cells below. She eased through the opening followed by Umgani.

Spiral stairs wound to the floors below. It should have been dark, but dim torchlight flickered on the walls, moving upward and closer. Someone approached.

"Ballene's fire," Kassa pulled her knife. "Here or outside?"

Umgani drew her blade. "Here."

The two warriors backed into the shadows opposite the door. Heavy footsteps trudged closer. One person, better odds. Gaze focused on the top of the stairs, Kassa jerked in surprise as the door they just came through swung open. A Watcher slipped inside and closed the door behind her. She turned and gaped at them.

Before the woman could shout, Umgani grabbed her. She slapped one hand over the woman's mouth and shoved her against the wall, pinning her arms to her side by the force of her muscular body. "Not a word."

The warrior stilled as she met Umgani's gaze. Wide green eyes darted back and forth between them.

Kassa spun to meet the oncoming threat from below.

"What's this?" A man in the gray shirt and tan pants of a stable hand emerged into the light.

Kassa drove a kick into his gut.

He tumbled down the steps, dropping the torch. Feet grappling for purchase, he slammed into the wall, pushed off, and lunged upward.

His gaze locked on the Watcher held by Umgani.

Kassa, face half-hidden in the shadows, grabbed his dropped torch and shoved it in his face. "Who are you?"

Holding empty hands out, he shook his head. "No one."

Umgani struggled against the Watcher who chose this moment to fight back. "Stay still, you fool."

"Please don't harm her." The man started to step forward, but Kassa blocked him.

"You know her?" Kassa kept the surprise from her voice. Watchers did not associate with stable hands as a rule. Not by command, though. They had nothing in common to draw them together.

"Yes." He dropped his hands by his sides, shoulders slumping.

Kassa took another step forward. The man really was no more than a boy, not even Adana's age yet.

"Please don't whip her." He straightened, jutting his chin out in defiance. "Punish me instead."

Shocked, Kassa eyed Umgani's captive. They'd interrupted a lovers' tryst. An odd place to meet. Tilting her head toward Umgani, she said, "Let her speak."

"If you scream, I'll slit your throat." Umgani waited a moment for the warrior to nod understanding.

Kassa switched places with Umgani. "Why does he think I'll whip you?" She focused a binding gaze on their captive, preventing her from lying.

The woman swallowed so loud, all of them heard it. The man took a quick step toward her. Umgani snarled at him, knife drawn in warning. He stopped.

"That's what they do to traitors," the Watcher stammered. "Or send them to—"

"Charissa." The man's voice carried enough warning to stop her.

"It's quiet here," Charissa whispered. "I hid here when Maligon came. We found each other, and..." She swallowed again.

Kassa could see the moment Charissa remembered her training. She squared her shoulders, raised her head, and met Kassa's gaze straight on. "You're Kassa, aren't you? The former First Vision?"

Umgani and Kassa exchanged glances. The man swore under his breath.

"What makes you say that?" Umgani barked the question, an order not to be ignored.

"No one forgets." She swallowed again. "That look."

Umgani snorted. "I know I don't."

Standing taller, Charissa whispered, "Creator save us, are you?"

For a long moment, no one spoke. The Watcher dropped any pretense of hiding her emotions. Her face told a story Kassa dreaded to hear. It had not gone well for these two since the Battle at Adana's View.

"I am," Kassa said. "How long did you hide here?" She glanced back at the man, including him in her question.

"Not long," Charissa lifted a shoulder. "Soldiers searched the cells for anyone hiding. They didn't find us."

"How?"

The man cleared his throat. "There's a ledge. Above one of the doors. It's well-hidden."

"Why did you leave?" Umgani prodded.

"We feared we'd get caught and sent away, so we returned to our posts." Charissa took a step away from the wall, her gaze wary on Umgani and Kassa.

"Sent where?" Umgani glanced at Kassa in concern.

"We don't know." Charissa shook her head. "People come in the night and take those like us. Those who don't…"

Kassa studied the two. They'd caught this Watcher off her guard, but she'd recovered quickly. Then she chose what she showed them. The man's body, on the other hand, revealed much—fear, anger, guilt. She leveled the binding gaze on the woman again. "You convinced them you support Maligon."

"No. I mean yes, we are seen as loyal."

"If you're here, you have no choice but to stand with him." The man spat on the steps. "If you're who she says, will you help us?"

"We aren't to that point yet." Kassa refused to look to Umgani for guidance. This was her mission. Her decision. "How do I know you speak the truth?"

"You used the binding on me, First Vision. I can't lie under it."

Kassa paused to consider her words. A well-trained Watcher

could overcome the binding, but she didn't sense any attempt from this one to do so. Their story fit what she'd heard about the days following the battle.

"Is anyone below? Locked in the cells?" Umgani gestured down the stairs.

"Not anymore. There was one. Suru." The woman stepped forward. "We brought her food when we met here. We tried to free her but couldn't open the door. They took her away a few days ago."

"Like the others?" Umgani asked. "The ones who disappear in the night."

Kassa's stomach churned. If she'd come earlier...

"I don't—" Charissa said.

"Moved to the paddock," the man said at the same time. He nodded up at his love interest. "I saw her that night. They..." His tongue darted over his lips.

"Go on," Kassa said.

"They made her choose a giraffe from the herd."

Umgani moved fast when angered. The man quailed as she loomed up over him, muscles bunching. Her voice came out soft and low. "They forced her to choose the giraffe they killed?"

"Yes, Watcher." He bowed his head. "She cried. I've never seen a Watcher cry."

Sickened, Kassa sought action. She tilted her head toward the door. "Check the door. We waste time here."

"It's safe, for now" the man said. "No one comes through here during late morning."

She nodded at him. "Let's go."

"'Let's'? You mean we're going with you?"

Taking a step toward Kassa, Umgani lowered her voice. "Wouldn't it be wiser to lock them in here until we're done? We don't know if we can trust them."

Umgani's caution and concern had a lot to do with Kassa's

choosing her for this mission. One of the oldest active Watchers, she possessed the wisdom that came with those years. And the physique of a much younger Watcher. She trusted no one else at her back more than Umgani. Still, today, wandering around without knowledge of the fortress' schedule could prove dangerous.

"They know the estate—"

"So do we."

"Yes, but they know it *now*. The patterns. The timing. If they help us and still wish to leave, I will help them while we still can."

The two of them turned to look at the couple who now stood in an embrace. The warrior pushed at the man's encircling arms and straightened her back as she noticed their attention. Kassa fought down a smile at that. This warrior cared how Kassa saw her. A true Watcher would. A traitor wouldn't.

Umgani must have seen it, too, because she gave a brief nod. "You are right, Kassa. As always." She turned to the man. "What is your name?"

"Ramil."

With their new guides, Kassa and Umgani followed them to the paddocks unseen. The stall where Ramil last saw Suru was empty.

Fighting down frustration, Kassa turned to him. "Have they moved the giraffes? Or are they still in the High Field?"

The High Field ran along the southwestern edge of the estate's lands. The giraffes chosen to serve at the estate changed ranks only when a queen died, so the ones living within the walls had arrived three years earlier through the north gate or had been born inside. Somehow, she needed to encourage the current tower to move northward. Open the gates at the right time. Umgani hadn't asked how she planned to do that. She would not appreciate the answer.

In a stealthy, round-about path, Ramil led them to the High Field. Thirty giraffes gathered under the trees. Was that all? Reports sent to Elwar didn't include the giraffe population. It wasn't part of the reports after the attack on Adana's caravan, either.

"Creator bless me. If there are more, let me see them."

From their hiding place within some thorny bushes, she scanned the field. Unused by the people in the fortress, this field posed little danger of discovery, but she refused to draw closer. No more giraffes came into sight. "Have they killed any more?"

"No." Charissa stiffened. "The first one caused great distress on the Watchers. They turned from listening to Samantha."

Satisfied, Kassa motioned for them to head back to the estate. Her daughter deserved whatever they did to her after that act of betrayal.

Outside the household wing, Kassa stopped. "We must go without you here. When the bells ring after sundown, head for the gate." She turned to Ramil. "Prepare two horses for you. There will be confusion. Take advantage of it. It may be your last chance."

"But what do you plan to do?" A wrinkle ran down the center of Charissa's brow.

Kassa wanted to say, "Don't do that, the sun will wrinkle you soon enough."

"The less you know the safer you will be," Kassa said, instead. "Head for the Border Keep if you succeed. Don't be caught with your eyes closed."

When the two departed, Umgani turned to her. "What is your plan? I've joined you, but I still do not understand."

"You will." She turned and headed back for the stables. "We must check the progress below."

21

Kassa nodded with satisfaction as she heard Dosata's report about evacuating the aqueducts. Hand-picked for her ability to organize and persuade people to action, Dosata, with Vuur's assistance, overcame Miri's reluctance to relinquish the waterways to destruction. They would be ready for a nightfall departure.

Leaving Umgani to add her incredible strength and determination to the task, Kassa took the moment of that distraction to return to the tunnels. One more thing must be completed above, and she needed to go alone.

A few steps away from the bustle of people packing, Kassa saw a shift in the light from behind her. Someone followed her. She turned and came face to face with Vuur.

He didn't bother to apologize or ask her intentions. "I wanted to speak to you a moment, away from everyone else."

Agitated by the delay, Kassa raised her eyebrows in question. By now, the sun was halfway down its descent. To succeed, she needed to slip into the royal chambers unnoticed. Soon, before the queen's attendants arrived to prepare the chambers for evening. Assuming they still followed protocol.

Her own lack of emotional control caught her off guard. She relaxed her brows, presenting a stoic face. Between Adana's hysteria and interacting with Miri, her abilities had waned. She must steer clear of Miri. All the Water Watchers for that matter. None of them seemed to maintain the true Watcher composure anymore. The Watchers at the Border Keep would remind them of their proper training soon.

Unfazed by Kassa's countenance, Vuur gestured for her to continue along the tunnel. "You have little time, Kassa, so I will accompany you and await your return at the entrance."

They walked in silence. As they drew closer to the opening in the royal chambers, Kassa paused. "Thank you for escorting me, Vuur. But I sense you have a purpose beyond awaiting my return."

He nodded. "Forgive me if I overstep, Kassa, but how do you plan to release the giraffes? The gate is too far."

Of course, he would strike at the stray arrow in her plan. Vuur might be the Glimmer Isati, but he would have served well as a commander of the First Soldiers. "I will get them to the gates." She paused and looked at him in the dim light of the tunnel. The whites of his eyes gleamed back at her. "By a stampede and a second diversion at the same time."

Vuur nodded. "If I may, I can offer a diversion. One that will distract and create an easier escape for the giraffes."

What had this man devised? Halar always told her Vuur possessed great intellect and curiosity. "What kind of diversion?"

His deep voice carried pride and conviction. "I would need to show you, but we don't have time. Trust me. It will work."

For some reason, she did. Unaccustomed to leaving crucial plans to someone else, she stiffened at even considering it, but now was not the time for control. Her focused breathing, a quick exercise for her, brought the calm and peace necessary. The calm also confirmed her instinct to rely on Vuur.

"I accept your offer. In case I don't come back from my scouting above before you destroy the aqueduct, plan to activate your plan two hours after sunset."

"Of course."

The man didn't object to her expectation that she might not return. She appreciated that about him. Another sign he would have done well as a commander instead of a glimmer maker.

A short while later, Kassa crouched in the pathway that led upward into the queen's chest within the royal chambers. Still and silent, she strained to hear any sounds. After five focused breaths, she deemed it safe and slid the lid aside.

A rush of memories bombarded her as she climbed out of the chest. The chamber, bathed in the late afternoon sun, looked just as it had the last day she stood here as First Vision. On that day Chiora succumbed to her illness and sent Adana to Elwar for three years. Montee walked out of the room that day as First Vision, not her.

So much had happened since then.

Fighting to suppress the sudden and sharp pang of loss, she inhaled, her breaths too shallow to help at first. "Ballene's fire," she muttered to herself. "This is no time for mourning."

Using slow, cautious motions, she closed the chest. In the courtyard, the fountain still bubbled. That would halt soon. Deserted, the room and courtyard continued to wrap her in familiarity.

Shoving those thoughts aside, she took a few quick steps to the curtained-off doorway leading into the corridor. All was quiet beyond, but she waited. Guards, silent but ready to act, often took positions along the halls near the royal rooms. With a careful hand, she parted the farthest edge of the curtain just enough to observe the length of the corridor before it turned to the right toward the meeting chambers. Empty.

Shana had reported Maligon claimed the meeting rooms as his official chambers. With quick steps, she moved down the hallway and paused with her back against the wall at the corner. A stillness had settled over the royal wing so absolute as if no one breathed the air in these rooms. She slid around the corner toward the chamber, confirming the eerie silence—no one, not even a servant going about their duties. This reinforced Shana's news that Maligon's numbers were stretched to their limits.

Just before the entrance to the royal meeting chambers, a small room, no more than a walled-off alcove, opened to her left. It provided a space for the staff in attendance when the queen held counsel here. She ducked inside, noting with displeasure the dust collecting on the shelves and counters. The room remained unused.

A heavy curtain of black and gold glimmer cloth separated this room from the chamber beyond. Focused breathing helped calm her heart. It pounded as it had on her first day of Watcher training. This could be her last. An ironic end if it was.

She parted the curtain and checked the room. A low cabinet blocked this entrance, explaining the lack of cleanliness in the alcove.

Silence pervaded the room, but not the same one she felt in the corridors. This stillness sat heavy with tension as if everything waited for an explosive outburst from the room's owner. Maligon always poisoned every place he went. She'd told this to Chiora after the then-princess had invited him into their close circle of friends. Chiora had laughed and assured Kassa he was merely amusing.

A tiny sliver of space between the cabinet and the wall gave enough room for Kassa to edge into the empty chamber. She swept through it in quick, silent, efficient steps, searching for any information about Maligon's plans. A sedan chair stood near the window. The sharp iron odor of blood permeated the hangings and cushions as she drew closer. Something else putrid entwined with the stench.

Unable to discern the source, she moved on but jerked up in surprise when she heard a voice. Darting back to the alcove, she vaulted over the cabinet, pulling the curtain closed behind her.

Dropping to her knees, she grasped the bottom of the curtain to stop its swaying.

Someone stalked into the room and flung their body into one of the few chairs, the legs of the priceless furniture screeching on the stone floor with the force. A few moments later, two more entered, one light of step and one heavy. Without looking, Kassa knew the light steps came from a Watcher.

No one spoke. Liquid flowed into a goblet.

"Well?" The voice she'd never forgotten even after twenty years spoke. "Why does she wait? The disposal of the first one posed no problems."

"It's not an easy request, Father."

Kalara? It must be. Only two Watchers served in his circle, and the voice wasn't Samantha's. A rush of relief washed over her at her daughter's absence. She dreaded an encounter.

"She's had time to plan."

"If I may." Another voice, male, spoke. "You do ask them to do something against their beliefs, Lord. Giraffes are sacred."

"Even you, Pultarch?" The voice dripped with sarcasm. "Why am I not surprised. You still harbor love for the true Adana. The girl Shana suffices for now. And without this constant concern over giraffes."

Cold anger gripped Kassa. She forced her body still. He spoke so casually of killing the revered animals. Such an act threatened the alliance Queen Moniah struck with the giraffes centuries ago.

"No. I'm merely pointing out that we must assign this task to those less threatened by the act. Let me handle it. I can choose men to carry it out without qualm."

A snort came from the other side of the curtain. Kalara stood nearby.

The chair screeched as Pultarch stood and approached her, his voice growing closer. "I weary of your opinions of me."

"And?" Kalara's tone reflected nonchalance and amusement.

"I am the son of an Earl."

"So you've told me. Many times."

"And the Lord believes in me. I'm by his side, day and night."

"Because he needs to keep a close eye on you, little earl."

"Enough." Rather than the sharp voice of command she'd come to know from Maligon, his voice croaked with exhaustion. "The way you two bicker. It does nothing for morale. People look to the two of you to lead them in my stead. You represent me and all we've striven for to honor Chiora's memory."

Kassa had risen to go, but this last statement stopped her. *Honor Chiora's memory?* Conquering her kingdom, putting a false queen on the throne, killing giraffes. The desert must have baked the last vestiges of sanity out of him. He had to die. She reached for her knife, a desire to do it now flooding through her. Then she dropped her hand to her side. She needed him alone. Pultarch presented little problem. She'd kill him if she must, but Kalara was known for her fighting prowess. The Watcher's youth and skills would best be avoided.

"Leave me, Pultarch," Maligon said, his voice weaker than before. "Send Samantha and Brother Honest to me. Maybe the good teacher can help her see the wisdom of our actions."

Once Pultarch stomped away, Kassa waited to see what Maligon and Kalara might say in Pultarch's absence. The two remained silent, so she slipped from the room and down the hallway to the queen's chambers.

Sapped of strength, Maligon might be easy to kill if no Watchers attended him. Umgani could handle any surprises they encountered. From the sounds of it, she must hurry. Maligon planned to kill the rest of the giraffes soon.

The exhaustion in his voice betrayed something else. He sounded ill. She felt sure he planned to command from his chambers. His illness might kill him first if she didn't act soon. She hated to be cheated of the honor. Even if it was the Creator who stole her chance.

22

The glimmer makers and Water Watchers were working in steady rhythms of purpose when Kassa and Vuur returned to the main chambers. Miri sat in her seat, gaze distant, but she jerked back to awareness as the two of them entered the room.

"Did you find what you seek, Kassa?" she asked, an edge of sarcasm in her voice. "And you Vuur? Did you?"

If she survived this night, Kassa would need to find out what plagued Miri so. True, they'd never been close, but the veiled animosity from the Water Maji concerned her.

In his deep, melodious voice Vuur spoke for the both of them. "Yes, Miri. All is well. Are you ready now to confide in Kassa? Share your plan with her?"

Plans. The maji had plans. At this late hour.

"Miri, we don't have time for altered strategies. Whatever you have in mind, forget it."

Miri opened her mouth to speak, but Vuur interrupted her. "Kassa, you want to hear these plans. They align with my diversion."

Kassa turned to Miri and waited. "I'm listening."

"I do not wish to go above ground—"

"We've been over th—" Kassa jumped in.

Miri held up her hand to stall Kassa. "Let me finish. I don't plan to stop you from evacuating my Watchers. I hand them over to you with gratitude. But be aware, they are unaccustomed to the ways of the land Watchers. The waterways do that to you."

"I've noticed."

"I'm sure you have." Miri sat upright and grimaced at Kassa. "I will be the one to trigger the traps. There's one that leaves little time for escape. I'll trigger it last."

"A wise decision."

"I'm not finished. Upon the Creator's words, Kassa, have you led so long that you can't stop adding your thoughts to everything?"

That stung. Especially after spending three years at Quilla's mercy while she accompanied Adana in Elwar.

Miri nodded and continued. "I will remain below. There is one more thing I can do." At this, her gaze darted to Vuur's. He nodded in encouragement. "The diversion Vuur told you of. It will destroy a section of the wall close to where the giraffes graze. I will ignite it."

"Not Vuur?" Kassa turned to the man in surprise.

"He must live." Miri turned away. "I don't wish to. Not above."

Kassa roused at her words as if she'd been dunked in the cold of the waterways. Miri's behavior made sense now. She planned to die. To go down with the fort in one last effort to save what she'd protected her entire life. Not spineless. Bold. Strong. Courageous. The Miri she remembered.

"Miri, I—"

"Don't." The maji held up her hand to forestall what Kassa might say.

"I will convey your bravery to our queen when I next see her."

At this Miri turned her full green-eyed gaze on Kassa. "If you survive what you plan. Don't think I don't know what you seek to do up there. We've known each other far too long for any doubts."

"Agreed."

Soon afterward, Kassa stood at the exit beyond the fortress from the waterways as the sun dropped below the horizon. The last of the guild and Watchers left through the entrance she'd led Dosata and Umgani through that morning. Dosata and Vuur came last.

Before Dosata ducked through the door, Kassa pulled her into a fierce hug. "I've been honored to serve with you sister. Carry the tidings of sacrifices to our queen should we not return."

Hugging her back with as strong an embrace as she received, Dosata nodded against Kassa's shoulder. The two stepped back and regarded each other, then Dosata turned and left.

Another reason Kassa chose Dosata and Umgani—neither one objected to the suggestion she might not survive. They'd been through so much over the years. With a deep breath, Kassa turned away and left Umgani and Dosata to their own goodbyes.

"Kassa," Vuur's voice called to her. "Stay clear of the wall to the west of the gates until after Miri triggers the diversion. She will do that first, before triggering the traps. You will know when."

"As you warned me. Go safe, Vuur."

Without another word, she and Umgani turned and strode back through the tunnels. This time, they risked the entrance to the Great Hall. With the Creator's good favor, they would not be seen.

Miri followed them to an intersection of tunnels. They grasped forearm to forearm. No more needed saying.

* * *

Shana pretended to drowse in the first cool moments of the evening. Under a small cave formed by her pillows, the jerboa perched, waiting for Malay to quit stalking around the chamber. The Watcher's head shot up when Pultarch's and Samantha's voices rang in the hallway as they left Maligon's chambers.

Shana hadn't needed her Listener skills to overhear most of the discussion. It was doubtful anyone in the fortress missed what the three of them shouted about. She hoped she would find a chance to slip through the chest and alert Eno of the danger to the giraffes.

Malay darted from the room to confront the two in the corridor, not even bothering to take her leave of the queen.

The jerboa hopped out of his hiding place onto Shana's shoulder. As he landed, Malay's worried questions reached her ears. "You're not going to do it, are you?"

The bite in Samantha's voice made even Shana recoil. "I don't have much choice, do I?"

"You always have a choice, First Vision. Exercise your authority. The queen won't stop you."

At those words, Shana sprang from her chaise and rushed toward them, pausing before the curtain a brief moment for the jerboa to leap off her shoulder and out of sight. She burst through the curtain. "She's correct. I won't stop you from disobeying him." She straightened, surprised she hadn't thought of this before. "I command you to disobey Maligon."

People talked about Kassa's hawk gaze pinning them in place like quivering prey. For the first time since she'd met her, Shana saw it in Samantha, but the Watcher's next words would never have come from the former First Vision's mouth.

"You command me, oh great queen?" Samantha took a menacing step in her direction.

Pultarch grabbed Samantha's arm. She halted, a sneer turning her face ugly. Another sign Kassa's daughter didn't carry her mother's power.

"Don't listen to her," he urged Samantha. "She's of no consequence."

Jerking her arm free, Samantha glared at Pultarch. "Never touch me, you fool. She's no consequence now because he hasn't forced you to wed her yet."

The young earl paled at that.

Malay looked between the three of them in confusion. "Why do you speak to Queen Adana this way? You're supposed to stand with her."

The harsh gaze swiveled to Malay. "Are you that blind?" Samantha took another step toward Shana, but Pultarch once again stopped her. This time blocking her path.

"Don't." His voice carried a warning.

The venom in the glare Samantha shot her way made Shana gasp, her heart faltering for a moment, only picking up its pounding pace when the Watcher whirled around and headed the other direction, Pultarch on her heels.

Malay watched them for a moment. "My lady, I do not understand the First Vision."

"Unfortunately, I do, Malay."

Again, Malay looked after the two. When they disappeared from sight, she returned her attention on Shana. "Do you require anything?"

The word "no" almost escaped her lips, but Shana paused, contemplating. "Yes, I do." Taking a few steps into the corridor she motioned Malay closer. "Do others agree with you about the giraffes?"

"Of course, my queen. We're Watchers. We're sworn to protect them."

"Good. Gather as many as you can to stop Samantha." Then a brilliant thought crossed her mind. "I know Kalara imprisoned the Watcher Suru. She can help you. Do you know where she is?"

"Yes, but I can't get to her. She's guarded by Maligon's men. The ones he brought from the desert."

That complicated things. "Where?"

Would they deny the queen access? Maybe, if they knew she wasn't Adana. Somehow, she doubted Maligon wanted that information spread among his soldiers.

"The stables." At Shana's confused look, Malay nodded. "Kalara has her in a pit dug on the other side of the stables. She said to prevent her screams from disturbing you, my queen, on your orders."

"My orders?" Shana channeled Adana's indignation, something she knew only too well. "Kalara takes liberties, too, I see. Go. I will see to Suru."

Bright relief shone in Malay's eyes. "Yes, Your Majesty. At once." And she dashed down the hall.

Shana rushed back into her chambers and discarded the robe she'd worn to cover her leathers. With a click of her tongue, she summoned the jerboa who hopped across the floor and bounded to her shoulder. "I think I'll call you Bauns, little bouncer." The animal scurried down into the confines of her tunic, tucked tight in her cleavage. "Let's see if I can fool some idiot guards."

* * *

The door under the base of the queen's throne in the Great Hall opened with a soft *whoosh*. Kassa moved to heave herself upward, but Umgani stayed her.

"Let me, my friend. I will clear the way for you." The sinewy muscles in Umgani's arms bunched as she drew herself up enough to see the floor of the hall.

With no moon, they knew she might miss something, but the lack of moon worked for them in this wide-open space. With a quick push, Umgani vaulted out of the tunnel and crouched behind the throne.

With the time of her revenge near, a soothing calm focused Kassa's thoughts. Umgani would follow her to the royal wing where they would separate. Umgani to provoke the giraffes into stampeding and Kassa to kill Maligon. She counted on his death going unmarked until long after they fled the fortress.

A low whistle from Umgani signaled the courtyard safe, and Kassa pulled herself up into the night air.

The women ducked as a guard crossed the hall, heading from the servants' areas to the barracks. He whistled a tuneless song, unaware of his audience. After he disappeared, the two loped along the edge of the hall, only to drop to the ground when the figure of Adana slipped out of the royal wing.

"The queen?" Umgani turned to Kassa, bewilderment in her eyes.

"No. Shana."

They watched the woman pull up short and turn their way. Kassa laid a finger to her lips. The girl's keen hearing could give them away, but she did not possess a Watcher's sight. After a long pause, much longer than Kassa anticipated, Shana turned away and scurried to the temple wing. Once the door closed behind her, Kassa touched a hand to Umgani's shoulder.

"She has the Listening Gift. I'm sure she heard your whisper, but she doesn't share our sight."

"Then I'm pleased she went into the temple. I may know stealth, but I doubt I could evade a Listener."

"Probably not. She is quite strong. Go quick and return to me." Kassa nodded toward a small bag Umgani carried across her back. "You are comfortable with the device?"

"Yes."

Vuur had bestowed a glimmer fire starter on them, a new creation of his. He'd directed Umgani to go to the trees in the middle of the High Field and set them on fire once the giraffes had moved below that point. The timing needed to coincide with Miri's diversion on the western wall. If all went well, the giraffes would not balk at her efforts.

"Be quick," Vuur had said. "The trees will burn much faster with this. Don't stay to watch the flames."

True words for a glimmer fire maker. The blazes they created mesmerized them. Not so with Watchers.

Kassa watched Umgani disappear into the Watcher barracks then turned to her own task.

At last.

23

The glow of the polished wood in the temple wing always impressed Shana. It revealed a warmth she never knew wood could possess except for when burned. Each time she entered the sanctuary, she couldn't help but run her hands along the smooth railing, polished to a deep veneer. Candles along the walls and hanging from ceiling fixtures added to the welcoming atmosphere.

Before meeting Honest, she never felt welcome in a temple. Now she embraced it, reveling in the quiet and peace.

At the altar near the front, the teacher knelt with his head bowed, green robes pooling around him. She could stand here forever, content to meditate in the tranquility, if it wasn't for the urgent need to save the giraffes.

Stepping forward with a purposeful tread to alert Honest of her presence, Shana broke the spell of quiet.

He was up and facing her before she took a second step. He glanced behind her, checking for others, then smiled. "Shana. What brings you here?"

"The giraffes."

The smile slipped into a frown. "I thought Samantha refused."

"She did. Maligon is forcing her hand. I'm surprised you didn't hear the two of them and Pultarch bickering."

His green robes swished as he approached her. "The temple shuts out the world in more ways than you know. What do you wish?"

"I sent Malay to gather more Watchers to stop Samantha. She still believes I'm queen."

"I told you most did. You worry too much. You have a plan?"

She bit her lip, a habit from childhood she'd never managed to stop. "I took advantage of Malay's apprehension over the giraffes and suggested she free Suru to help her."

"And?"

"She told me she couldn't because of where they're keeping her. I need your help. She's in a pit beyond the stables. Guarded by Maligon's true soldiers."

He strode toward the altar and picked up the long wooden staff from the floor. "What is your plan?"

"I will attempt to use Kalara's voice. If I fail—"

"Clobber the guard with my staff. Agreed." He started toward the exit. "Do you know how many guard the pit?"

"Sorry. No."

"No matter. We will soon."

The fortress lay quiet as the two hurried toward the stables. To avoid notice, they took the longer route, going around the barracks wing. Shana matched Honest step for step, something he'd commented on once before, about how nice it was to walk next to a woman of height again. His mother had been a Watcher. She had died in Maligon's Rebellion. Somehow, when he said this, it made Shana feel special. Appreciated.

As they rushed along the unused path, voices came to Shana from inside the barracks. When she paused, Honest sensed it and paused with her. She tilted her head toward a dark window where the voices came from.

Clipped voices overlapped each other. Urgent. Hurried. Indignant.

"She can't do this."

"It's an abomination."

"You must be mistaken."

"She promised me she wouldn't."

"She can, and she will if we don't stop her." The last words came from Malay, silencing the rest.

After that, the rustle of running feet sounded inside. Then they were gone. In the direction of the High Field.

Straightening, Shana signaled to Honest.

"What did you hear?"

"Malay and the other Watchers. They've gone to stop Samantha."

"Good."

The two turned in the opposite direction and headed for the stables.

At the end of the barracks, Honest checked the courtyard. He straightened and turned to her; eyebrows raised in question.

She shook her head. No sounds.

Sticking to the shadows, they hurried through the yard, arriving at the stables without mishap. Through the walls, she could hear stable hands joking and laughing, dice clacking together, and the slapping of a hand on another's back.

They ventured behind the stable, searching in the dim light for the pit. A person with a torch rounded the corner from the other side of the stable, and they jumped back. They couldn't see who it was, but Kalara's voice rang out in command.

"Bring her up. The Lord asks to see her."

Shana fought back the urge to cry out in frustration.

Honest peered around the corner, then gestured for her to step up beside him. Three burly soldiers lowered a ladder into a dark hole. "Ya coming up? Or should I send Forn to get you?"

After a few moments, the ladder shook as someone climbed it. Then a person emerged. In the torchlight, they could see bloody scabbing streaking her legs and arms. Bruises encircled her neck and wrists. As she turned to limp after her captors, Shana gasped. Suru's braid had been cut off.

Kalara paused, raising the torch higher, peering into the darkness. "What was that?"

Honest and Shana jumped backwards.

"What was what?" one of the brutes asked.

"I heard something."

"Probably Ralf. He ate onions again." The three men exploded into laughter.

Kalara stared into the dark. "Go check." She nodded to one of the men.

"Fine with me," the man said. "Them onions messed me up. I'll stay here. Maybe shat in her pit. A nice gift for the Watcher."

"You will not," Kalara said.

The man ambled toward the corner of the stables, moving slow and uncaring.

"Never mind." Kalara's tone rang with frustration. "By now, whatever it was probably fled."

With Kalara in the lead, Suru limped behind her, and the three men's broad backs blocked the captive from view.

* * *

"We must hurry if we're to stop them." Shana stepped around the corner of the stables ready to follow, but Honest pulled her back.

"Wait. We must think. You wanted Suru to help stop Samantha, and, I assume, to help her escape somehow."

"Yes." She had hoped to lead her out through the aqueducts once they'd stopped the killings. Honest would want to know how she planned to save Suru, since she hadn't shared her knowledge of the aqueduct access with him. Or that Nuala had visited her. He'd been monopolized by Maligon over the last few days, so they hadn't spoken in private.

While these thoughts ran through her mind, the teacher watched her. He waited for her to continue, she realized. "You want to know how."

He nodded. "And what else you've learned my little mouse."

"Mouse?" She squeaked out the word, suddenly aware of Bauns' weight inside her tunic.

"Yes, Shana. You're quiet as a mouse and as alert as one, too." He tilted his head, regarding her. "More so, tonight. Your hearing seems improved. Stronger. I wonder why."

She shrugged. "I haven't noticed a difference."

"No matter. What plans of escape have you concocted?"

"A few nights ago, I learned of access from the queen's chamber to the"—she paused and glanced around, then lowered her voice to an even softer whisper than before—"to the aqueducts. I can send her below."

Mirth danced in Honest's eyes.

How could he find humor at a time like this? "What?" Her voice reminded her of her youngest brother every time their mother suspected him of mischief.

"You leave much out of that story, my queen."

He'd taken to calling her that in private. She liked it even though it felt odd for the man who set her on this path to false identity.

A shout in the distance drew her attention back to the matter at hand.

24

Umgani trotted along the exterior of the temple wing, headed for the giraffe paddocks and the High Field. Nothing stirred in the area, but she heard people in the distance, quarreling. The atmosphere in the fortress felt foreign to her. With the true queen in residence, the place hummed with action. Purposeful activity. Everyone focused on their responsibilities of protecting the queen and the kingdom.

The place under Maligon's hand reminded her of an abandoned fortress with several opposing groups sneaking around to avoid each other, each one believing they were in control. No discernible rhythm and flow.

In the darkness, the paddock appeared empty as she approached it. Good. If all the giraffes were in the High Field, that would save time. She circled past the paddocks and headed into the south-eastern part of the grounds. She continued to trek across the empty field, no giraffes in sight. Fear gripped her stomach. "If Samantha killed them all, I swear I'll kill her."

These words shifted her focus for a brief moment. She recalled a little toddler, already fascinated with Watchers, tumbling along behind Kassa. She shook her head. Samantha was no longer a sweet child.

A rush of movement near the lower part of the fields caught her attention. She slowed her progress, and moved with stealth, a Watcher's focus taking in as much detail as possible in the dark night.

The sight, when it became clear, drew her to an abrupt halt.

Several giraffes clustered together in an agitated group. They shuffled and milled around each other, none willing to go farther. Below this restless gathering, people shouted, waving torches.

If she followed Vuur's direction and started the fire in the trees, what would it accomplish? Trapped between two threats, her fire above and the torches below, the giraffes would trample anything or anyone in their way. If the torchbearers planned to kill the giraffes, her fire might help them succeed while dying in the process.

She eased downhill, straining to see and hear beyond the giraffes.

"It's the queen's wish," a woman's adamant voice rang clear over the shouting and cursing.

Voices roared their approval.

"My orders come from a higher order."

"Whose?" Sarcasm dripped in the voice of the first speaker. "Maligon's?"

"Yes."

A rumble of male voices shouted their approval while many female voices shouted, "No!"

"Take care your words, Watchers." A new voice, a man's, spoke above the rising din. "The Lord doesn't abide malcontents."

More shouting, individual voices no longer distinguishable.

Blazes, they were trying to do it now.

Should she set the fires? Or move closer to the crowds to see who stood on which side?

A concussive blast threw Umgani backward, flung to the ground on her back. Ringing in her ears drowned out sound. She rolled to her side, directionless. It took forever to rise up on one arm. She faced uphill. She rolled the other way.

Fire blazed along the walls. Where were the screams of people? The roar of the blaze? She stumbled to her feet. Stared at the confusion below. A large hole gaped in the southwestern wall. "Miri."

The ground rumbled as the giraffes fled from the blast. Toward Umgani.

"No."

She yanked out the glimmer fire starter and slid open the tip of the stick. Inside, a tiny flame flickered. How had it not burned through?

The giraffes pounded closer. Umgani grabbed a tree branch and flicked the stick toward the leaves. The flame jumped from the stick. Its iridescent glow ate up the leaves and raced over the branch, hopping and dancing.

The giraffes veered. Umgani followed, trying to outrun them. She grabbed another tree branch. Flicked the starter. The flame jumped.

The giraffes continued to run. They drew her in the wrong direction—toward the wall. This was taking too long. Kassa needed her in the royal wing.

Keeping pace with the giraffes, sound began to return to her ears. The thunder of hooves to her right. Screams from below. Umgani searched for a way to turn the giraffes toward the hole.

Ahead, the largest acacia on the grounds loomed into sight. Rumors said it was hundreds of years old. The branches stretched over the others. Tears streaming at the need, she flicked the starter. The ancient tree embraced the flames with a *whoosh*.

The flames danced in reds, oranges, and blues. Other colors, unnatural shades of green and light blue and pink, joined it.

"What have you made, Vuur?"

With a start she turned to check the giraffes. They had swung downhill, away from the blaze.

"Go with the Creator," Umgani breathed, bent over. Behind her a wall of fire blazed across the field as the trees continued to burn.

As the first giraffe galloped through the gap in the wall, Umgani turned and ran back to help Kassa.

* * *

Kassa thanked the Creator for large blessings. Maligon sat in his chambers, alone, asleep in a chair positioned to look out into the courtyard. His breaths came uneven and labored.

Knife drawn, she inhaled and focused her own breathing. Two breaths. Three. Four. Her vision blocked out all but the man she hated. The man who took what he wanted with no regard to anyone. The kingdoms, lives, giraffes, and Adana's destiny, all torn away by him.

She inched toward him. It couldn't be this easy.

A thunderous blast rocked the night. She stumbled and fell, her knife skittering away.

Maligon jolted upright. "What?"

He rose, staring into the courtyard. He didn't see her. She fumbled for and grabbed her knife. Quickstepping toward him, she raised the knife to drive it into his back.

Something jerked her backward. She flew through the air and slammed to the ground.

"Father!" Kalara's urgent voice rang out.

A hoarse voice called, "Kassa!"

Kassa shoved herself up from the floor, grabbing for the hilt of her knife. She spun to face the voices.

Kalara, Suru, and three soldiers blocked her exit. She raised the knife shouting, "Aaaay!" and ran at Kalara.

The traitorous Watcher stumbled but stayed on her feet. She grabbed Kassa's wrist, twisting, wrenching.

Kassa drove her knee upward, catching Kalara in the groin. The strike drew a grunt. She dropped Kassa's hand, swaying on her feet.

Bent over in pain, Kalara bared her teeth. "That's all, Kassa? You're weak, old, useless."

Words burned to be thrown at her. Kassa refused. First year training: don't get drawn in by taunts. She circled Kalara. The shadows of the three soldiers hovered beyond them. A fourth person, Suru, darted forward.

Bruised and battered, the Watcher rammed into Kalara.

Kalara rebounded with a leap. Suru stumbled backward. Kalara spun, snarling at the soldiers. "Bind her."

The three soldiers lifted Suru off the ground. She fought, legs kicking in the air.

In horror, Kassa saw the extent of Kalara's cruelty—Suru's body was covered in bruises and blood.

Taking advantage of her shock, Kalara pounced.

Kassa dodged.

The two circled each other. Kassa focused on Kalara but kept the burly soldiers and Suru in her sight.

The men stood, grins of enjoyment on their faces.

Filthy scum.

* * *

Shana strained to hear voices from the southwestern part of the fortress grounds.

Honest followed her gaze. "Do you hear something?"

"Arguing."

Honest took her by the hand and led her around to the deserted front of the stable. "I will follow Suru. You go stop Samantha."

Before she could respond, two horses clattered out of the stables. The first horse reared up, and Honest slammed his body into Shana's, shoving her away from the dangerous hooves. The second horse shied and tried to bolt, but its rider reined him in.

"Watch where you walk," the rider's sharp voice rang out.

Stepping into the meager light, Honest confronted the man. "I could say the same to you. What business do you have with the queen's horses?"

The rider snorted. "The queen's horses. I await her ladyship's command every day. It never—"

A loud explosion shook the ground. Fire shot into the sky over the western wall.

The ground rose up and slammed into Shana. Stunned, she tried to rise. Persistent ringing drove into her skull. She slapped her hands over her ears. It didn't work. The unbearable clanging drowned everything out.

She rolled to her back. Gorge rose up in her throat.

A man hovered over her. His mouth moved. Who was he?

Not Honest.

Ballene's fire, her head hurt.

The man grasped her by the arm. Jerked. He fell away.

Nothing made sense. She rolled to her side, spitting out bile.

The ringing must stop. She whimpered.

A shadow fell over her. Honest hovered there.

His lips moved. Eyes crazed with worry, he hauled her upright. Cushioned against his green robes, the muffled bass of his voice resonated in his chest, words indistinguishable. The ringing hurt so much. She burrowed into his robes. Then screamed as something skittered across her shoulder. Bauns bounded out of her tunic. The jerboa landed on Honest's shoulder. He jerked in surprise. With two large hops, the jerboa disappeared beyond the stables.

Smart mouse.

"Ramil." A woman's high-pitched voice penetrated the cotton in her ears.

Above them, a woman sat astride a horse. That's right. Riders. Horse. The blast of pain and noise.

Honest rose, placing himself in front of Shana.

The woman's gaze darted around as she edged her horse out of his reach. Her companion, now on foot, moved to follow her.

Honest blocked him. He spoke, words faint under the ringing. "What have you done?"

"Brother." The man reared back. "Forgive me." He swung a blow at Honest's head. The teacher spun out of the way and swept his attacker's feet out from under him with his walking staff.

The woman kicked her horse into a trot toward Honest.

Honest spun sideways.

The woman grabbed her companion, dragging him up behind her. She cantered out of reach and called, her voice faint, "Forgive me, my queen. I pray you survive."

Shana blinked after them. Her hearing opened up with a *pop*.

"What in blazes?"

Honest struggled with the man's bucking horse. After he calmed the horse, he studied the large saddlebags. "They prepared for a journey."

In the distance, Shana heard screams of terror, anger, pain. The sky in the distance glowed golden. Fire.

"Honest! Fire!" She jumped to her feet then swayed. Her vision swam. Eyes closed, she held her arms out for balance. When she reopened them, the world stood still. "The giraffes. We must save them."

"No," Honest said. "We save you."

"But..."

He swept her off the ground and dropped her onto the horse. Jumping up behind her, he turned the horse away from the blaze.

The pounding of hooves shattered her brain. Pain, awful pain, knifed into her skull.

People scattered before the horse. Most ran toward the fire. The clatter of hooves on hard stone came soon, more painful than before.

She squeezed her eyes shut. "Where?"

"The barracks."

"With a horse?"

"Yes. I'm sending you into the aqueducts before they kill you."

She fought through the pain and grabbed the reins. The horse stopped in the middle of a corridor. "No. Adana sent me."

Honest kicked the horse in motion. "It's no longer safe."

She reached for the reins, again, but he dodged her grasp. "Honest. Stop. It's never been safe."

"I take full blame."

"No. You—" What could she say. He wouldn't stop, and it hurt to listen. She'd failed Adana.

25

For a moment, Kassa had a clear strike, but a soldier grabbed her from behind, and his arms squeezed the breath out of her. The burly man lifted her off the floor. Her knife dropped from her grasp.

With a loud cry, Suru broke free and tackled Kalara to the floor. They rolled, screaming, fighting for Kalara's knife. Pinned by the soldier, Kassa could only watch.

Suru broke away. She dragged herself to her feet. A vicious and angry growl spewed from her mouth.

Kalara still wielded her knife. She advanced on Suru, crowding her toward the courtyard.

With an agonizing howl, Suru dove for Kalara's mid-section.

Kalara side-stepped.

With a calculated smirk, Kalara moved toward the courtyard.

Suru tackled her again.

The two plunged into the courtyard.

The numerous candles inside blinded Kassa from seeing them in the dark.

The scuffle continued with grunts and screams. Kassa sagged in her captor's arms, her sight going dark as he continued to squeeze her.

Then there was silence.

Kassa kicked at her attacker. He tightened his hold.

A long howl of fury thrust through the darkness. It faded. Then sudden silence.

Kassa stared at the doorway, praying for Suru to return.

Kalara sauntered back in. Except for scratch marks on her arms, she looked unharmed.

Kassa's heart froze.

She struggled and squirmed against the soldier. Sparks flashed in her eyes. She couldn't breathe.

Forcing her body to sag, she feigned unconsciousness.

Shouts and screams still rang from below in the distance. But no sounds came from Suru.

Maligon rose from his chair. When had he sat back down? Didn't he care what happened outside?

"Well done, daughter." His voice drew closer. "Lift her head."

The soldier yanked her braid.

She glared into the one face she hated more than anything. It wore a look of pleasant surprise.

"Kassa? It is you, isn't it? You've aged so much. Almost didn't recognize you."

She spat. Missed. She *was* getting old.

"Why do high-ranking women spit on me? First Gabriella. Now you. So unladylike." He stepped away from the glob and wandered toward the courtyard, almost as if taking a leisurely evening stroll. With a crook of his withered right hand, he motioned the man who held her to follow.

Maligon ambled toward the wall framing in the open space. The man dragged her along. Kalara followed, two soldiers clomping behind her. Suru's body was nowhere to be seen.

They took her straight to the wall. Was she next? Not with Maligon still alive.

"See?" Maligon flung his hand beyond the wall. "Look at what's become of your savior."

Suru's broken form lay still on the rocks below. The sight of her body goose-fleshed Kassa's skin.

Then Kassa tensed. She smelled smoke. The air crackled with the deadliest enemy, fire. In the distance, an inferno engulfed the High Field. Not since the infamous Ballene's fire had a Watcher willingly set anything but a controlled blaze.

Umgani had succeeded. The blast must have been Miri's diversion.

Creator's Hope Umgani escaped, and Miri's sacrifice went fast and painless.

Shadows raced in front of the huge crater blown into the western wall. Cries echoed in the night, almost drowned out by the roar of destructive flames.

She blinked at the size of the opening and the iridescence of the flames eating up the grass nearby. Glimmer fire. How? What new weapon had Vuur created? Her warrior's brain fought to absorb the power of such a weapon.

"I assume I have you to thank for this disruption of my evening?" Maligon's dark voice invaded her thoughts. "I must admit, I'm impressed. How did you manage it?"

Lips clamped shut, she glared at him.

"No answer. Too bad. Quite an interesting weapon. So much damage. To your home. Adana's View."

Don't speak. Don't speak. She breathed in deep. Choked on the smokey air.

Kalara interrupted his careful address to her. "We must do something. The fire will destroy everything."

He waved his hand in dismissal. "Replaceable, my child, replaceable."

Anger coiled in Kassa's guts at his willingness to destroy. This fortress had stood for over three hundred years. It had withstood everything nature and enemies threw at it.

His gaze still on Kassa, Maligon said, "We should, I imagine, do something to stem this tide." He turned to the three soldiers. "Go. Help."

"Lord?" The deep voice of the man holding Kassa rumbled. "What of her?"

"She won't go anywhere. Will you, dear Kassa? I have Kalara here to protect me."

The man dropped his hold, and Kassa teetered on her feet a moment. She sucked in air. Coughing, she bent over.

Maligon turned back to gaze over the wall. "I do love a good fire. Don't you, Kassa?"

She fought spasms from breathing the heavy smoke .

His nonchalance didn't fool her. He perfected this act in their youth. He'd practiced among their friends, most of them roaring with laughter over his unruffled brilliance.

"No? Oh well. We have a hot one, don't we? I sure hope the giraffes are safe. And my people, of course. You see, I sent quite a few down to deal with the giraffes this evening. Under the command of—" He paused, a wicked gleam coming to his eyes. "Oh, yes. Under the command of the queen's First Vision, Samantha. Your daughter. I ordered her to kill all your beloved giraffes. Your little fire seems to have handled that problem for me."

He scanned the area. "But where are your Watchers? Surely, you brought an army to back you up?"

Kassa ignored the jab. She scanned the High Field looking for evidence of the giraffes. She found none. Unbidden, the boast snapped out of her mouth. "I believe our little fire foiled your plans, Maligon. I see no giraffe corpses."

"You believe they escaped?" He peered over the wall in curiosity. "What about them?"

She curled her fingers. Two giraffe bodies blocked the hole in the wall.

"Only two. No matter." He shrugged. "I have soldiers combing the land with orders to exterminate any giraffes they find. And recruit more soldiers to my cause. Quite a few Monians willingly gather under the banner of their true queen in Adana's View. Not to mention the disgruntled Watchers heading this way, relieved to know the true First Vision claims her rightful place. You should be proud of your daughter."

A ruse or was he really mustering a larger army? He needed one. Quite a few people rushed about below, more than she expected, trying to put out the fires, but not enough to wage a successful battle. How many wished to leave as did Ramil and Charissa?

"Are you done yet, Father?" Kalara's voice rang of anger and disgust.

"With what?" His jaw tensed.

Good. Kalara may be his child, but even she didn't escape his temper.

"What do you plan? For her?" She nodded at Kassa.

"What would you like?"

Shoulders hunched, she took a menacing step forward. "To kill her."

"By all means. Just clean up the blood afterward." He turned his gaze back to the scene below.

Kassa sprang sideways as Kalara lunged for her. She still went down, her body wracked with pain from the earlier fight.

"Make it fair. Give me a weapon." Kassa dodged away from the wall and the obvious fall intended for her.

"No. I don't think so."

"You have no honor." Gaze fastened on Kalara, she circled, easing closer to the chamber. If she timed it right.

Fast as a cobra, Kalara leapt at her, the knife driving deep into the inside of Kassa's upper right arm. The blade dragged a jagged gash almost to the elbow.

She fell hard. Agony shot through her as she collided with the stone floor. Fiery pain streamed down her arm. Blood shot across the room.

She shoved the pain into a corner of her mind. A warrior fights. She clamped her left hand down hard on her arm. It took every bit of focus to roll left and shove herself to her feet. She stumbled toward the room.

Kalara tracked her like prey.

Kassa didn't see Umgani as she passed from darkness to the bright lights in the room. The woman leapt from behind the curtain. Pinning Kalara to the ground, she shouted, "Go, Kassa."

Kassa slumped against the nearest chair. She yanked a cloth napkin from a tea tray. Fighting to stay alert, she tried to tie her arm off, using her good, but weaker, hand and her teeth. Accomplished as best she could manage, she fell into the chair, unable to move or leave her friend.

The two Watchers wrestled on the ground. Both wielded wicked knife blades. Either they both died, or they both lived. No other option.

Spots sparkled in Kassa's vision as she slumped lower. This time the sounds of the skirmish faded to black.

* * *

Unbearable pain lanced up Kassa's right arm. She jerked upright. The room swam. A vise squeezed her tight. She blinked. Umgani in front of her, braced to leap.

Kassa swallowed back a cry of pain and froze.

A knife pressed against her throat.

"Drop your knife, Umgani." Kalara bit out the words, her voice close to Kassa's ear.

Umgani's gaze flicked from Kalara's hand to Kassa's eyes.

Kassa blinked once. *No. Don't do it. Let me die.* She fought the urge to blink again. Not because she wanted to say yes. Because her head felt cumbersome. Her vision blurred.

She'd brought Umgani for this reason, to do what must be done. Kassa closed her eyes and waited for death.

From the hallway came the clatter of hooves and the improbable neigh of a horse.

Kassa's eyes refused to open at first. She forced the lids up.

Umgani's eyes had widened. Still, she focused on Kalara's hold on Kassa. She didn't turn to check the horse's approach.

A huge black stallion burst into the room, a rider ducking under the frame of the doorway. Honest.

Kassa fought the urge to laugh. Hysteria? Not her. She ground her teeth together.

The horse reared, its hooves scraping at the air. Kalara dropped Kassa and darted out of the way. The horse's hooves struck the stone floor with a clang where she'd stood moments before. Kalara backed farther from Kassa as the horse pushed between them.

Umgani raced in and grabbed Kassa, lifting her good arm to her shoulder. "Move."

She dragged Kassa into the corridor and rushed toward the royal chambers. Kassa's feet wheeled under her, useless.

They burst into the queen's chambers. Shana spun from the chest, hand flying to cover her mouth.

The chest lay open.

"Good," Umgani said. "We must leave."

Shana shook her head. "Something's wrong."

The rush of water sounded from below. Miri had sprung the traps. They were too late. And Maligon still lived.

"Kassa?" Umgani shook her; her worried gaze searched Kassa's face.

Her head wobbled. In a fog, Kassa remembered. Umgani followed her directions.

Vision swimming on the edge of consciousness, Kassa said, "How deep?"

The responding silence from Umgani calmed her. Was she staring at her or measuring the water's depth? Kassa didn't care.

The next moment, a huge splash provided the answer. Umgani pulled her into the water. Icy waves washed over her. They drove needles into the long gash in her arm.

"Stay awake, Kassa. It's not over our heads, yet."

* * *

Shana watched the woman, dark skin crisscrossed in old scars, haul the bloody body of Kassa into the water.

The woman looked up. "Can you swim?"

"Yes."

"Come."

The shouts of voices sounded in the corridor. Honest and Kalara headed this way.

She shook her head. "I must close it. They don't know it's here."

The look she shared with the Watcher said everything. This was her last chance of escape. She could go, and maybe they wouldn't follow. Or she could save them and continue her farce.

Had Honest fooled Kalara into thinking he came to protect Maligon? She hoped so.

She closed the chest and dropped to a cowering squat, arms over her head, moments before Kalara dashed into the room. Honest followed on her heels.

26

The cold water drove Kassa back into consciousness. Her arm throbbed from its cold embrace, and she struggled against whatever held her.

"Hush, my friend." Umgani's melodious voice soothed the frenetic pounding of her heart. "We are almost there."

"Where?" Kassa croaked. Water washed into her mouth, and she sputtered and coughed.

Like a small baby, she felt Umgani lift her above the surface. It felt wrong, letting the warrior carry her. Why was there so much water? And where were the lights?

"The aqueducts." Umgani's deep voice echoed off the walls. "Miri flooded them."

Memory surged into her mind. "We were late. Too late."

"We're almost there."

She faded into unconsciousness again, her mind floating on the edge of awareness for a moment longer before she succumbed.

*　*　*

Adana paced the walls of the Border Keep. Sinti and Montee stood nearby. Both objected to her coming into the open. No one knew what Kassa's mission might cause. Would Maligon retaliate or had Kassa succeeded before he knew she was there?

She cursed the woman for leaving her behind. Too frail? Too overcome with despair. Kiffen and Montee threw those concerns at her when she discovered Kassa's absence. She was the queen, not a withering flower on the vine. How dare they move without her approval. And now, days later, she still burned with the heat of exclusion.

Steps pounded up the ladder and Kiffen walked toward her. She didn't need to turn to know it was him. Since their wedding, she'd known his whereabouts at all times. A comfort, but at the same time a complication. She couldn't rush into anything without his knowing. Did he sense her agitation?

For the hundredth time, she reached out to Am'brosia. What was happening with Kassa?

There had been a flurry of frantic energy from the giraffe a short while ago. It hadn't lasted. No hysteria afterward. That meant they'd succeeded in freeing the giraffes. Right?

She whirled to face Kiffen as he hovered to her left. "Does Bai'dish know anything? Am'brosia—"

"Seems fine," he finished with a gentle touch to her cheek. "I believe the giraffes are safe." He looked into the darkness facing south. "I felt something, though."

When he hesitated, she said, "A surge."

"Yes. Powerful."

Their words drew Montee closer. "What kind of surge? Adana couldn't describe it. It doesn't make sense."

"I think we must wait for Kassa's return."

"Hopefully, they bring the Water Watchers and glimmer makers with them." Sinti joined them at the edge of the wall.

"I hope not." Adana peered into the darkness.

Shock laced Sinti's response. "My queen?"

One of these days, she'd learn to hold her tongue. "I hope they come, yes. But Kassa can travel faster. Or one of those with her. We need news. I don't want her delayed by an entire caravan of refugees."

"Of course, Your Majesty." Sinti backed away, but Adana caught the side glance she gave Montee.

It felt strange, standing on the wall staring into the peace and quiet of the night when she should be sound asleep. Something massive had happened. Her body thrummed with apprehension. She turned back to the wall.

Her shoulder hurt, too. Not the agonizing pang from the giraffe's death. But a deep, ache in the bones. She rotated her shoulder trying to relieve it.

Kiffen's warm hands covered both her shoulders. He began to knead, applying more pressure on the right shoulder. As if he knew where she ached.

She moaned with relief as his fingers dug in.

A sudden rush of hope and warmth spread over her. From Am'brosia?

She reached behind her and touched Kiffen's leg, letting her fingers rest there. Did Bai'dish convey the same feelings to him? There was so much about the bond between queen and king that her parents never told her. Her mother knew time was running out and made plans for her training. Her father shared so little with her. He must have expected to live a long life. To bounce her children on his knee.

Where had that thought come from? She ducked her head, a warmth spreading over her cheeks. Thank goodness the darkness hid her blush. As if drawn by her thoughts, Kiffen leaned his body closer, his arms slid down around her waist and pulled her to him. She relaxed, head resting over his heartbeat. His scent of apples and horses drifted over her. She traced her fingers along his forearms while they stared into the distance.

Montee and Sinti stepped away from them. Not leaving, but giving them distance.

"Should we retire, my queen?" Kiffen whispered in her ear, his breath sending a tendril of longing down the length of her body.

"But we must watch for—"

He twisted her to face him and cut off her words with a gentle brush of his lips on hers. "I can think of a better way to wait. Montee and Sinti will continue to watch for news of Kassa's return." He chuckled. "Simeon, too."

Surprised at the mention of Elwar's advisor, she glanced to the side. The man, as quiet and unobtrusive as any Watcher, leaned against a post near the top of the ladder. He appeared to be carefully not looking at them.

"They will know what we're doing." Again, heat washed over her. She longed to say yes, but she never imagined the first weeks of her marriage to Kiffen would be spent in crowded quarters with little privacy. Adana's View, her home, her fortress, spread out vast and open. Soldiers and Watchers guarded the royal wing, but she never noticed their presence. Not like here with people everywhere, especially now that they'd moved everyone into the tunnels for safety. She couldn't move without stepping over someone or something.

He nibbled her ear sending shivers along her spine.

"We don't have to go into the tunnels. There are many rooms to choose from in the keep. All vacant."

Worry gave in to a wanton feeling of abandon. She grasped his hand and started toward the ladder, forcing her steps to a sedate pace. "Montee," she called out, voice thin and wavering, "I am going to try to sleep. Rouse me when we have news."

"If she can find us." Kiffen chuckled under his breath.

She giggled and fought the urge to run. What was happening to her? She managed to exhibit some decorum while they remained in sight of the others.

* * *

Adana woke with a start. Kiffen's body curled around hers, his arm draped over her hip. In the darkness, she listened, heart thudding so hard in her chest she wondered it didn't wake him.

She slipped from the covers and found her clothes, sliding them on in the darkness. A vision, something fragmented, had come to her in her dreams. It edged from her grasp every time she tried to focus on it. Something about water. Had the plans for the aqueducts invaded her dreams or was it more?

It felt like more.

She brushed a kiss on Kiffen's brow, grabbed her weapons, and slipped from the room, throwing the bow and quiver over her shoulder and sheathing her knife on her thigh.

The corridors of the keep echoed with quiet as she rushed toward the tunnels. As if compelled by some outside force, she knew she must go in search of Kassa and the Watchers who accompanied her.

Before she reached the statues guarding the entrance to the tunnels, Nuala emerged from the shadows and fell in step with her. "My queen."

"Nuala. Why are you up? Sunrise is still hours away."

"The First Vision asked me to watch for you."

They arrived at the statues and Adana took a moment to activate the hidden door before responding. "Why?"

The warrior bowed her head and gestured for Adana to proceed her through the doorway. "She suspected you would not rest for long. Where are we going?"

They descended the winding stairs in silence. At the bottom, they entered the main tunnel. Down here, the sounds of people reverberated, mostly snores as the keep's inhabitants slept. Only a few moved about, slowly, as if wading through water.

Many of the soldiers and Watchers gave the rooms to others, sleeping in the halls where they could respond quickly to danger. Winding her way past them, Adana tried to determine how much to trust Nuala. She might agree to go with her over concern for Suru. Or she might try to stop her.

People always wanted to stop her.

She fought the urge to kick at the ground over that thought.

They rounded a corner and headed for the above-ground exit. She was queen after all. What could Nuala do? She outranked the woman several times over.

As they skirted around yet another sleeping form, a person in the distance raised up, gaze fastened on the two of them. The person leapt lightly to her feet. A Watcher. Wonderful, more barriers to her plan.

With a quick, "My lady," the warrior fell into step with Nuala. "Where are we going?"

Adana shook her head at the enthusiasm these two held for staying with her. Well, if they genuinely wanted to know, she'd tell them. Then send them to Ballene's fire and back if they tried to stop her.

"I am going to search for Kassa's returning party. By now, she must be on her return. If not, I must know what's happened."

Both women nodded.

"How many do you require to go with you?" the second Watcher asked. "My unit is resting down this side hall."

Adana paused and studied the woman's tunic. She wore the patch of a Unit Leader, a small tower of giraffes. That meant five Watchers. A good number if she wanted to move fast and quietly. "Yes. Thank you—" She hesitated, not knowing the Watcher's name.

"Greti."

"Greti, yes, but quietly. We don't want to rouse others or worry them."

In mere moments, the Watcher returned with five others.

Adana surveyed the seven women in front of her. "I plan to move quickly. We don't know where they are or in what condition. Keep your silence. Sounds carry in the dark."

Nuala, to her surprise, nodded in agreement. "We are with you, my queen."

They followed her out into the night air.

* * *

Kiffen awoke to a cold bed. His hand snaked out, looking for the warmth of Adana's body, and found empty space.

His sleep-addled brain sent a searching tendril out to Bai'dish, seeking Adana's whereabouts.

The answer, a clear image of her trekking south across the land, propelled him out of the bed and through the door, yanking clothes on as he went. Fully awake, he probed the image further, trying to grasp Am'brosia's emotions through Bai'dish. Their response made him grunt displeasure down the connection. She was in no danger, according to the giraffes.

They should have alerted him to Adana's departure, he shot back.

Amusement rolled over him. Bai'dish telling him a Watcher goes into danger every day. "Not without telling me, she doesn't," he spoke out loud, his voice echoing off the walls of the keep.

When he entered the tunnels, he barreled through the rest of the keep's inhabitants as they began their early morning preparations. The aromas of eggs and other breakfast delicacies mingled with the amalgamation of body odor and mustiness. The musty smells were beginning to give way to the overwhelming presence of bodies packed into a closed space.

Simeon leaned against a far wall, spooning a brown substance out of a bowl. When he spotted Kiffen, he smiled, followed by an immediate frown. Straightening, the man handed his bowl off to a maid as she pushed by him. Lucky for him, she was alert, or the bowl might have crashed to the ground.

"What's wrong?"

"Adana left."

"Where? When?"

Kiffen shook his head, but the same maid who caught the bowl said, "The middle of the night. She took one of her guard and a unit of Watchers with her."

"Where?" Simeon asked again.

"I overheard her say she wanted to find Kassa."

His advisor stopped, but Kiffen pushed forward unaware of the man's absence.

"Kiffen."

He pulled up short and rotated his neck far enough to spot Simeon standing a few steps behind him, amusement twitching his lips as if he watched children at play.

"Are you coming?" Kiffen fought not to shout.

Simeon shook his head. "No. And neither are you."

In answer, Kiffen narrowed his gaze at Simeon then turned away. "Suit yourself."

The man caught up to him. "She left hours ago. It's doubtful you'll catch up to her until she's headed back. How do you think she'll react to you charging after her?"

His feet slowed as if he waded through thick mud. "She won't be pleased. But I'm not pleased with her at the moment."

"You have to learn to trust her. She's the queen, a trained warrior. She's prepared for this all her life."

Kiffen glanced around, noticing how normal everything looked. People went about their tasks as in any other day. Did they know the queen left, pursuing the Creator only knew what?

"What do you feel from Bai'dish?" Simeon said.

A kind voice from behind Kiffen said, "He feels fine." Glume peered up at Kiffen. "Well-rested and hungry, but fine. He said you might be here, ready to wrap your neck around someone."

Wrap my neck? Kiffen blinked at the man. "You knew she left." It wasn't a question.

"Yes. Many hours ago."

"Why did she go? Why didn't she tell me?"

The round man spread his hands out. "I understand giraffes, not women. Am'brosia sent her. She did not send you." He leaned in close and whispered, "And neither did Bai'dish."

The truth of this hit Kiffen like a broadsword to the head. No one but he worried about Adana this morning. Ever since her arrival in Elwar at fifteen, he'd been tasked with watching her and making sure she remained safe. It was how he fell in love with her. Did she not need him to protect her anymore?

Glume, obviously tuned into the giraffes, shook his head. "Not protect her. Stand with her."

"How do I do that when she doesn't take me with her?"

Glume shook his head. "I do not know, but she needed to go without you. That is all I can say. The giraffes know it, too. Come. Let's find some breakfast. Then we'll go see the giraffes. I think it's time I started teaching you more about the bond. It appears you've progressed faster than expected, and we need to help you take the next step."

Kiffen followed the giraffe keeper, mind racing with worry for Adana, frustration over Simeon's and Glume's lack of worry, and a bit of curiosity over what Glume meant by "the next step."

27

A runner caught up to Jerold and Halar seven days after they departed the Border Keep. Her face looked composed, but she refused to look Halar in the eyes as he took the missive and read it. His face paled with the news.

"What has happened?" Jerold asked, heart plunging to his feet.

Without a word, the man handed the note to Jerold.

Border Keep attacked during coronation. Border Keep safe. We prevailed. Giraffes killed. Here and at Adana's View. 1V

"Blazes," Jerold said. He studied the note again. "1V is...?"

"First Vision," Halar said. He took the note back and reread it, wrinkling his brow. "She doesn't say how they know about the giraffes at Adana's View."

Memories of Adana's reaction to the villagers of Roshar surrounding and herding Am'brosia gave Jerold a clue. "I've seen Adana react to her giraffe's emotions. Do you think Am'brosia felt the loss of the giraffes?"

The Watcher who brought the news confirmed his thoughts. "The queen sensed it." She looked away, shoulders stiffening.

"Is the queen well?" Worry thickened his throat. If Maligon managed to eliminate one more ruler...

"Yes, Sir Jerold. The First Vision acted quickly to help her. And the king, of course."

What did that mean? Had Adana been beyond control as he'd seen her that day?

Before he could ask, Halar spoke up. "The coronation? Did they finish?"

She nodded. "The attack interrupted it, but they held the ceremony in the tunnels later. And the wedding. After the battle."

"Good," Halar said. His color came back, and he looked more like the soldier Jerold had come to know. "How are they responding to the attacks?"

"They're sending someone to try and free the giraffes at the fortress."

"And the aqueducts?" Halar asked.

"They plan to destroy them."

With a nod, Halar pocketed the note. "Do you need to carry word back to the keep?"

"I will join you and carry back any news once we reach Roshar."

The three struck out again. Jerold kept an eye on the Watcher from his horse. She didn't ride but didn't appear to need to either. She not only kept their pace, she quickened it.

* * *

Shana woke with the sun halfway between its zenith and the horizon, going down. Body aching, she wrinkled her nose. Thick air permeated with the odor of smokey residue hung over the fortress like a fog.

After a convincing act of innocence concerning knowledge of the intruders in the fortress, Shana had insisted on helping fight the fires the night before. Kalara believed she was no more than a weak puppet, so, with little question, she accepted her claims of knowing nothing. As for Honest's part in the attack, he ranted and raved for quite some time over Maligon's and Kalara's safety and the obvious attempt on their lives.

Putting out the blazes took most of the night, and she'd fallen into her sleeping chaise without bothering to wash the smudges of soot and ash from her body.

As she trudged to bed in the early hours of the morning, Honest caught up to her. According to him, Maligon never revealed any emotion, positive or negative, about the intrusion, explosion, and escape of the giraffes and rescuers. He'd sipped his tea and listened to the reports as they came to him.

The most devastating report was the news of Suru's death, shared in an offhand manner by Kalara as she recounted the events in Maligon's chambers the night before. The other, equally devastating news reported the deaths of two of the oldest giraffes in the fortress. These two had foiled Samantha's attempt to lead a unit through the destroyed wall and pursue the escaped giraffes. Standing in the opening, their huge bodies and lethal hooves blocked any exit through the wall. Samantha ordered the Watchers to fire on them, and they eventually succumbed to the arrows and fire. Even then, they continued to block the opening with the weight of their massive bodies. Somehow, Shana suspected the giraffes knew what they did and why.

She'd shed tears for all the giraffes as she joined a bucket line to put out the fires, all the time knowing they used the last of their precious water supply to quench the blaze. No one else knew the waterways were destroyed during the night. No one but her and Honest.

As she blinked and tried to open her gummy eyes this afternoon, she wondered who discovered it first, and how Maligon reacted.

A tiny skittering sound caused her to pop her eyes open. She grinned at the sudden appearance of Bauns. The tiny rodent hopped up her leg and landed on the pillow. "You're alive." She ran a light finger over the jerboa. "I worried about you."

He stared at her, whiskers twitching, then bounced away. Moments later, Malay entered her chamber.

"Your Majesty, you're up." The woman hurried to the chaise and knelt before her, eyes downcast. "Forgive me. I failed you."

"How so?" Shana tried to imagine what Malay blamed herself for. Caught up in events beyond any of their imaginings, how could this one Watcher find fault in herself?

"I was unable to stop Samantha or save Suru. If it hadn't been for the explosion—"

Shana bolted upright on the chaise, checking Malay for signs of injury. "Were you there? Near the wall?"

Malay nodded. "We were. Arguing with Samantha and Sir Pultarch. So many stood with her, my queen. The ones who followed me now fear for their safety. Samantha is not known—" She bit her lip and did not continue.

"Yes? Samantha is not known for what?"

"It is not my place to question the queen's selection of First Vision."

It was. That's what Shana wanted to say. To shake the warrior and tell her the true First Vision earned the position through honor and loyalty to the queen, the true queen. Instead, she said, "No Malay, it is not your place. She made a mistake last night, but Samantha is tough. Moniah needs a tough Watcher to lead and guide us during these trying times. If we're to survive."

"Of course, the queen is right." Malay rose. "I saved water for your bath." She paused. "I'm afraid our water source is gone. Nothing flows into the fortress, now."

Nodding with understanding, Shana said, "I suspected the explosion might cause more damage. What plans are being made to ration water?"

"I do not know." The look in Malay's face said different, but Shana did not pursue it.

"I will clean up, then I must go to Brother Honest and discuss proper rationing to feed those under our protection. Has anyone checked on the condition of our people?"

She suspected the answer even though it saddened her when Malay confirmed her feelings. Maligon worried about himself. He didn't care for others unless, or until, he needed them.

"However," Malay hesitated for a moment, but then blurted out the rest, "Kalara was injured while helping with the fire last night. A beam fell on her head. She has not woken yet. Maligon is terribly upset."

"I'll bet he is," Shana said under her breath.

Malay raised an eyebrow but said nothing.

"Bring me the water for my bath. It appears I have even more to deal with today than I thought."

"Yes, Your Majesty."

Once the Watcher left, Bauns ricocheted back into her lap. "Where did you hide, little one?"

While she stroked the jerboa, her ears picked up Maligon's voice drifting from his chambers. "Get me Pultarch. And Samantha. And Brother Honest."

She waited. He did not add her name to the list. The patter of running feet told her his attendant had left. If Pultarch wasn't with him, who was?

She grabbed her knife, slipping it into her sleeve, and stalked toward his chambers. Could she do it? Finish what Kassa came to do? Creator help her, she thought she could if the man truly was alone.

Maligon looked up in surprise when she entered. He sat at his table, reading some papers. A cup of tea, steam visible even in the sultry heat of the day, sat by his left hand.

"You're up." He sipped the tea and sat back in his chair; hooded eyes focused on her. "You gave quite the show last night. I'm glad to see you've embraced your role as a caring queen. The people will follow you with love, now. Good move."

She frowned, gauging the distance to his chair, and trying to devise how to surprise him. She could throw the knife. Her aim remained true, but she'd prefer to strike closer. To know without a doubt she'd succeed.

Misreading her frown, Maligon continued. "You didn't think about the effect it would have on the people to see you help put out the fires? I thought you were smarter than that." He took another sip of tea then searched the papers on his table, sliding one sheet out from the others. "At least that's what my friend Sarx says. You remember him? The one who lifted you to this great height."

"I do." Need to see the missive from Sarx fed energy to her legs. "What else does he say?" She took a few steps closer. A few more.

Maligon raised an eyebrow at her and tucked the note away. "No concern of yours, Shana." He emphasized her name heavily.

"If it's of interest to the kingdom, it's of interest to me."

A bark of laughter erupted from his mouth; it dissolved into a coughing fit.

She rushed to his side, grabbed the teacup, and urged him to drink. The rattle in his breathing came louder as the coughing subsided.

He pushed the cup away. "No. It doesn't help."

"Lord." She tried to hide the cringe she felt at using his preferred name. "Are you ill? Your cough sounds bad. Worse than before."

That got her a glare.

She hadn't meant to anger him. Most men responded with relief and a bit of self pity over a woman expressing concern over their health. Not this man. He tried to hide all signs of weakness. Not an easy task with his right hand deformed beyond use and left shoulder scarred enough to limit any decent range of motion with the left arm.

Gaze fixed on his, she eased the knife down her sleeve and palmed it. She stood over him. A downward strike to the heart would do it. He'd collapsed into more coughing. Wouldn't see her move. The hilt felt heavy in her palm. She prepared to lunge.

Footsteps sounded in the hallway, headed for Maligon's chamber. Shana stayed her hand. If she struck, she needed to escape unseen. No possibility of that now.

Samantha, Pultarch, and Honest entered the room. Honest's brows shot up as his gaze registered her proximity to Maligon, her hand at an unusual angle. With a shrug to her mentor, she tucked the knife back up her sleeve and eased away from her target.

"Ah, First Vision, Brother Honest, we have much to discuss." Maligon, recovered from his coughing fit, leaned back, steepling his hands, and his gaze fell on Shana by his side. "Run along and clean up, Shana. We have no need of you now."

She opened her mouth to protest, but Honest beat her to it.

"Do you believe that's wise, Lord? She's won the loyalty of the people, but rumors abound. Most know you don't include her in your meetings. If you continue along this path, you will undermine what she's managed to do in spite of your unfair treatment of her."

Leaning forward, Maligon drew in several short breaths, his face reddening. After two coughing fits, Shana marveled that this sure sign of impending rage didn't choke him. The rattle reverberated in his chest, though, like the popping of grease in a cookfire.

Shana waited for the onslaught, disappointed in her inability to act fast enough to rid them of this menace to Moniah. Courage and time failed her. Even the great Kassa failed to kill him. Why did the Creator let such evil abide in their presence?

The rattle in his chest proclaimed the body's effort to end his life, though. Maybe the Creator could accelerate that process.

Maligon managed to breathe enough to unleash his anger. "You dare speak of my mistreatment? This young wench should crawl to me on hands and knees, thanking me every minute of every day. If not for me, she would still work in that filthy establishment, serving the basest patrons of Elwar."

Maligon rose to his feet, his face transforming into benevolent kindness in the matter of one heartbeat. He looked upon her. "I'm sure she realizes how blessed she is."

Her position at The Sleeping Dog in Elwar gave her far more liberty and respect than he did. Not that someone like Maligon understood honor. Still, she played a role and must abide by the rules of this two-sided game. Without a pause, she dropped to her knees and grabbed his right hand, planting a fervent kiss upon his cold, dry knuckles.

He lifted his hand and draped it over her head. It remained there, a weight of reminder. "See? Shana understands her position. The two of you could learn something from her." He sat back down, hand still pressing down on her head. "But in truth, Honest, you do make sense. I will abide her presence." He pressed harder. "Shana you will be quiet as a mouse, though. Not a peep out of you. Your opinion is of little value."

He released her, but she kept her head bowed. "Yes, Lord."

In a fortress full of bustling people, the only sound she heard as she rose came from Maligon's chest. She walked on shaky legs toward Honest. She would stand behind the others and listen. If Maligon knew her gifts, he might realize his error, but he didn't. Not that it mattered. She eavesdropped from her rooms, anyway.

A profound wish for Bauns' presence ran through her thoughts as she took up her position. Two realizations hit her. First, nobles never understood their servants' submissive postures, choosing to see the people as conquered, instead of appreciating the quick minds hidden behind the downcast eyes. The second drew her focus from the room for a moment. She needed the jerboa. The animal's touch amplified her Listener's gift, picking up distant notes of sound and the tiniest noises that surrounded her every day. For today, it didn't matter, but in the future, she must find a way to hide him on her person.

"Thank you, Lord," Honest's voice brought her back to the moment. "As you know our water has been cut off. The aqueducts destroyed. We must start rationing. The rainy season—"

"Samantha." Maligon angled his dark eyes, shrewd and accusing, toward the Watcher. "What did you know of your mother's plans?"

The quick intake of air and stiffening of the Watcher's already rigid posture told Shana the alarm this question caused. Then the perpetual stiffness of anger Samantha carried as a weight on her shoulders overcame the shock. She drew in a breath, then another. "Nothing, Lord. I knew nothing."

"Hm?" He rose and paced toward the courtyard, hands steepled before his mouth. "Nothing?" He pivoted on his heel and nailed his gaze to hers.

"Yes. Nothing."

With slow, deliberate steps, he returned to his desk. "You knew nothing of her ability to enter the fortress?"

"I told you—"

"Ah. Ah. No interruptions. You told me she might use the water-ways. I recall this. Yet you never found them despite my orders. Or did you?"

"No." Tension warred in Samantha's voice as she fought to maintain her control. "We still can't locate access to them. No one saw her come into the fortress. No one knows how she left."

At those words, Maligon's gaze swiveled to Shana. "And you never saw her? You wish to stay with that statement?"

So much for not saying anything. "Yes, Lord. I did not see her."

Leaning over his table, hands supporting his weight, Maligon said, "Then someone tell me how in the blazes she managed to infiltrate the fortress, free the giraffes, blow up the wall, and cut off our water? How could no one see her?"

For a moment, Shana thought Bauns lay inside her tunic, kicking her chest, her heart pounded so hard. From what she could see of Samantha's profile, lips white and thinned in suppressed anger, she suspected her heart might jump across the room any moment, too. Could she hear Samantha's heart? For a moment, she strained but heard nothing extra. Maybe with Bauns.

Honest cleared his throat as he stepped forward, placing himself between Maligon and Samantha. "If I may, we must remember Kassa's history. She's an accomplished strategist. We know she anticipates possibilities well. She's a Watcher, Lord, gifted with the ability to see danger and avoid it."

"Yes, I'm amazed she managed to escape unnoticed. But she made a mistake. Otherwise, we would never know who to blame. A mistake like that tells me she got emotional and lost self-control. Her famous self-control. Just for a moment. She left here injured. Lost a lot of blood. Mayhap, she's dead." Maligon smiled at this last part while Samantha's shoulder twitched. Enjoying his own words, Maligon missed the Watcher's reaction. Shana didn't.

Maligon reseated himself, then turned to glower at Samantha. "Until Kalara improves, you will lead the Watchers. An opportunity for you to prove to me you are capable as First Vision. I expect you to discover how Kassa got in and out of this fortress. Also, add a rotating detail of Watchers to help rebuild the wall."

Samantha nodded but said nothing.

"It takes courage to sneak into your own fortress and destroy it from inside," Maligon continued. "A shrewd woman. At one time, I thought Kassa and I...Alas, she's too devoted to Chiora, but she can't stop us if she's dead. The Creator hopes, we'll find what we dreamed of many years ago." He smiled, most of his teeth showing. "Let's hope she's dead."

Compassion for Samantha filled Shana's heart. The Watcher remained impassive, but her breathing hitched in a tiny gasp at those last words.

The more worrisome words were about Chiora. He spoke of her as if she still lived and longed to join him.

28

Adana and her small band of warriors made great time and caught the first glimpse of people early on the second day as the night sky began to lighten with the coming dawn. Adana, trying to decipher the tumble of Kiffen's emotions across the bond, missed the first sighting.

Greti took that honor and sent two of her unit to intercept the first of what now appeared to be a long line of evacuees. Three Watchers broke into a trot to greet them. Adana longed to run forward and hear the news firsthand. It took every piece of Watcher control, including ignoring the giraffes' confusion over Kiffen's frantic worry, to hold her urge in check.

After a brief exchange, the five Watchers trotted toward her. They stopped and bowed their heads.

Dosata, one of the two who had gone with Kassa, spoke for the group.

"Your Majesty, my sight is pleased to find you. I have brought those who lived in the waterways as well as Vuur and his glimmer guild."

She waited for her to add the Water Maji's name.

She didn't.

"What of Miri?"

Dosata turned to one of the other two accompanying her. The Water Watchers tucked their chins, shuffled their feet, and would not look at Adana. A Watcher might choose to reveal emotion in their face, but one never revealed so much through their body. What had happened to these Watchers? Adana's skin crawled at the idea of calling them warriors. If they'd used their face to convey discomfort, she would have thought they chose to honor her with the visible emotions. To use the body—messages others can see from a distance—reminded her of Leera and her childish behaviors.

When the women continued not to speak, she arched an eyebrow at Dosata. "Explain."

Steeling herself, Adana waited for Dosata's answer, her fears mounting.

After casting a glance of compassion toward the women, Dosata said, "The Water Maji volunteered to remain and trigger the last trap to stop the water."

"And?" Must she pull the information from Dosata, too?

Before she could answer, Vuur stepped forward. He'd been at the front of the line of people who had reached them. "Your Majesty, I'm pleased to answer your questions."

"Thank you, Vuur."

"We set traps many years ago. Traps to stop the water but keep most of the tunnels from damage. The last trap...it must be triggered last because it's the one that does the most damage. You cannot escape it. Miri volunteered."

The relief Adana felt at the dark man's offer to explain evaporated.

"She's dead?" Adana forced a solid note to her voice, aware she must not reveal too much emotion, even though the Water Watchers did.

"Yes, my queen. She chose to sacrifice herself to your cause. She did not wish to live above ground after so many years below."

Adana nodded, numbness threading along her shoulders and arms. It vibrated in her shoulder. Was this the cause of the deep ache in her shoulder the other night?

"She asked me to give you a message, Your Majesty." Vuur's eyebrows drooped over sad eyes.

"Of course." Adana straightened and focused on the Glimmer Isati.

"She said to tell you, 'When you reach beyond yourself, you're closest to spreading your wings to fly.'"

"When you—" She was a child again, her mother taking her by the hand to greet a Watcher with the greenest eyes she'd ever seen.

"This," her mother said, "is Miri. She has chosen to go to the waterways to serve us."

The notion of someone choosing to live below ground confused her young mind. How old had she been? Six? Seven? Young enough to ask an impertinent question. "Why would you choose to leave the sunshine?"

Miri had smiled and said those very words to her.

It took years of her mother repeating them to her at difficult times to grasp the meaning. As a child, it made no sense. One did not fly, and definitely not below ground. Now she knew. Choosing the difficult path led to the best outcome.

"We shall honor her sacrifice and flight."

Vuur's brow wrinkled a bit, and she waited for whatever else he felt compelled to say. Was it Kassa? Had she assisted Miri? All the sounds of nature greeting the morning faded from notice as she waited.

"I left Miri with one more task, Your Majesty. If it worked—I believe it did—we destroyed part of the southeastern wall. Below the High Fields. If Umgani managed to do her part above ground, I feel assured the giraffes escaped."

"Destroyed part of the wall." Adana stiffened with horror. "Why would you do that?"

"Ah. I thought you might not be pleased over that news. We had little time. The main gates would not do to get the giraffes out. It's a new use of glimmer fire, my queen. The blast was..." He studied her.

Waiting for some response? "Yes? The blast was what?"

One of the Water Watchers said, "Amazing." She straightened as if refilled with energy. "I've never seen such power. The fire raged. We could see its light most of the night as we traveled to you."

"The fortress is on fire?" Her voice sounded high and shrill. So much for controlling her emotions. She inhaled, trying to conceal the deep intake of breath, then exhaled slowly. She did it twice. Vuur must have seen because he waited until after her third exhalation to speak again.

"It's possible it still burns." Vuur's deep voice rumbled without an apology. "We chose the only method we thought would work. My queen, this weapon gives us the advantage."

"Weapon?" She struggled to keep up. Miri dead. The waterways flooded. Destroyed? Maybe not. And a hole in the solid protective walls of the fortress. Her home on fire. Glimmer fire used as a weapon.

"Yes. I needed to test it. Once Kassa and Umgani return, we shall know."

She seized on that bit of information and turned to Dosata. "Where *are* Kassa and Umgani?"

Dosata spoke up. "They went above to release the giraffes. They were to come out of the waterways soon after. We waited some distance way, but they did not return at the specified time. We dared not wait any longer."

Dread iced Adana's veins. "You left them? Inside the fortress?"

"On Kassa's orders, yes, we did." Dosata stood straight, looking into Adana's eyes. She didn't flinch or back down from the confession.

That sounded like Kassa, giving an order to leave no matter what. It's what she would have done. Why had Am'brosia sent her to meet Kassa, then? The elder Watcher must have made it out. Otherwise, the giraffe would not have sent her.

"Very well," Adana said, pushing steel into her voice. "We will continue in search of Kassa and Umgani."

"I am to go with you," Dosata said.

Adana rolled the Watcher's words over in her mind. "You know something?"

With a nod, Dosata said, "Miri gave me supplies." She pointed to a large pack; one she'd set down by her feet. "She said I would need them for Kassa."

Need them for Kassa. Miri knew something. "Did she give a reason?"

"Only that I needed to finish the mission with those I started with."

Yes, Miri knew something, but either not enough to explain, or she chose not to share it. Either was possible with a Watcher of her advanced experience.

"Of course," Adana said.

She turned to Greti. "Choose two of your unit to escort this group back to the keep."

After the two took up positions, Adana directed Nuala to continue on their path. Before she left Vuur and the others, Adana fastened on a point she'd failed to note over the devastating news. She turned back to Vuur. "Do you have more of this weapon?"

He shook his head. "No. I had one batch. I must make more."

"You have the ingredients?"

"Yes."

"Speak to King Kiffen when you arrive. Tell him what you told me."

"Of course." Vuur bowed his head as she turned away.

That would give Kiffen something else to worry about besides her exploits. His words, she thought, based on how it floated down the bond with the giraffes.

A release of tension flowed over her as Am'brosia embraced the strategy. It seemed the giraffes felt her husband needed something to occupy his mind, too. *Good.*

Somehow Adana suspected Kiffen would know of the weapon before Vuur arrived.

<h1 style="text-align:center">29</h1>

Umgani carried Kassa through the day and night, but as the sun rose, her energy waned. They'd made it to the edge of a small copse of trees. Not much concealment, but it would have to do. She lumbered under her friend's weight, seeking a spot out of direct sunlight and with decent grass to lay her down. The rainy season would be on them soon, so most of last season's grass was long gone, eaten by some traveling herd months ago.

With a sigh, she eased Kassa's unconscious body off her shoulder. Her arms almost gave out as she lowered her to the ground. "My friend, life in Elwar put weight on your old bones. You've grown soft."

Umgani wished for Dosata, the healer within their ranks, as she examined Kassa's injury. Her skin had turned ashen gray. Most of the blood had washed away in the flood of the waterways. Still, blood stained the tourniquet and more seeped through the weave of cloth.

Nearby, the trickle of a stream sang to Umgani, another reason she chose this site. Removing her canteen from her pack, she hurried toward the sound, filled the canteen, and returned.

Kassa's deep brown eyes darted toward her as she approached. Her friend relaxed and closed them again when she saw Umgani.

"I'm not dead yet?" Her voice croaked.

"No. You're too stubborn to die." Umgani knelt and slid an arm under Kassa's shoulders to lift her a bit. "Here. Drink."

The muscles in Kassa's throat flexed rapidly as she gulped at the water. She groaned a protest when Umgani pulled the canteen away.

"You've lost a lot of blood. We need the water to stay down. I'll give you more in a moment."

Kassa's eyes fluttered closed in response, and Umgani settled her back to the ground. "I'm going to examine your arm."

A brief twitch around the mouth told her Kassa heard.

"Try not to hit me."

That produced a weak snort.

Umgani lifted Kassa's arm to her lap and studied the tourniquet. The cloth had been tied to Kassa's arm before Umgani managed to pull her to safety She could only assume Kassa somehow managed the first tourniquet. Clumsy, but effective, it saved her from bleeding out while she fought the devil's daughter.

Outside the fortress, Umgani had improved on the bandage, using a stick tied to the cloth to increase the pressure. If she loosened it, would Kassa lose too much blood? "Kassa, why didn't you keep Dosata with you?"

She'd whispered the complaint, but a low murmur came from her friend. She turned from studying the bandaged arm and laid a hand to Kassa's cheek, drawing back in concern. Fever wracked Kassa's body, something she'd been unable to tell while traveling in the heat.

Battlefield medical training came back to her—something about checking for a pulse in the injured arm. Pressing two fingers over the inside of the wrist she searched. No pulse. Nothing. She shifted her fingers and shifted them and shifted them again. Still, no pulse. She grabbed the other hand, nearly sagging with relief as she found a thready pulse there.

The injured arm had died. It needed amputation. That required fire. She pulled the fire starter from the bag on her belt. Would it work after a swim in the tunnels? She flicked open the top and gazed down on the tiny flickering flame. The momentary relief faded as exhaustion overcame her. Feet giving way, she dropped to the ground.

"I may have fire, but I don't have the energy, skills, or tools, Kassa. We will rest a moment, then continue. I need assistance."

Umgani must have slept, because she woke with a jerk, her eyes flying open, searching the area. Next to her, Kassa moaned. From the angle of the sun, they had not been there long.

Kassa's body still raged with fever. After offering her a trickle of water, Umgani trotted to the stream and refilled the canteen. Setting it aside, she plunged her head into the shallow stream. The cool water bathed her with relief. For a moment, she considered carrying Kassa to the stream and laying her in the bed, but the rocky bottom would complicate the situation.

Canteen filled, she ran back and spilled the contents over Kassa's body, sluicing the water along her arms and legs, avoiding her injured left arm. Not a flinch of a reaction from Kassa. Blinking back hot tears of frustration, she ran to the stream and refilled the canteen.

Resolved to see her friend make it to the keep alive, Umgani gathered the few tree branches scattered on the ground and crafted a makeshift stretcher. Awake, Kassa would complain, but that didn't appear to be a concern for now.

By midmorning, she'd set off again, muttering pleas to the Creator to help her make the journey and keep Kassa alive.

* * *

Kiffen met the caravan of waterway refugees a short way outside the entrance to the tunnels. He and Montee, with a small force of Watchers and soldiers, stood sentry over the last stretch of their journey. He'd wanted to strike out on horseback to meet them, but Bai'dish overwhelmed him with a sense of foreboding about that choice. Would he really encounter harm? The giraffe refused to reveal his full opinion on that.

When he'd received word of the refugees' approach, Glume had been helping him develop the skills of the bond. The keeper gave an excited crow of glee when Kiffen explained what he'd felt from Bai'dish.

Chuckling, the man said, "Foreboding? You felt foreboding? You're sure of this?"

"Yes. I don't see the humor in such a warning." Kiffen had fought down his annoyance over being laughed at. Or maybe it was laughed about. Whichever it was, he didn't like it.

"No, Kiffen, I'm sure you wouldn't." Still Glume grinned ear to ear.

"Well?"

The man had settled against the railing of the paddock and eyed Kiffen. "Giraffes use emotions to guide us to do something. They don't know many. If they find one that succeeds in a person, or giraffe, doing what they want, they stick with it. One Bai'dish likes to use is foreboding. You're strengthening your bond if you could interpret that."

"But I don't understand. What does he mean by it?"

"Any number of things." The keeper cast a sidelong glance at Kiffen and straightened his back with purpose. Gone was the jovial man, and now the teacher of giraffe-speak addressed him. "He's telling you no. I'm not sure why. It could be dangerous, but I doubt it. We'd feel something from Am'brosia, too, if it was."

"So, foreboding means no? How did you come to learn this, Glume?"

The man shrugged. "I've had years. I was there when Bai'dish dropped from his mother. I've watched every event in his short life."

"Why no? What happened to him?" The idea that Bai'dish first learned no through something ominous twisted Kiffen's gut.

Suddenly, the dirt ground held Glume's interest. The man shuffled his feet a bit, discomfort evident in the tensing of his shoulders.

Kiffen waited. The one thing he'd learned from his stepmother—through experience, not a lesson—was to wait someone out. If they appeared to be fighting within their mind, silence usually prodded them to voice their concern.

"He found his emotion to say no later in life than some do. Unusual, but Bai'dish experienced little trouble as a young giraffe. I felt his 'no' the day Serrin chose him. I remember what a shock the feeling gave me. Everything from Bai'dish until that moment oozed joy and contentment."

A pang of memory sliced at Kiffen's soul. He'd managed to get past the idea that Serrin had chosen Bai'dish and bonded with the giraffe. At his brother's death, the animal remained alive because it chose another, himself, as the true bond. Bai'dish had bonded with Serrin, but a part of that bond attached to Kiffen instead. Not that he could explain how the giraffe managed a dual bond, but he had.

"The foreboding was his awareness of Serrin's fate?"

"I believe so." Glume tilted his head upward to look at the towering beast. "He sensed he was meant for you and not Serrin. He felt something that told him it was terribly wrong, but he couldn't know what at the time."

"And you knew? All this time?"

"No. At first, I thought he didn't want to be chosen. Then he tried to show me the two of you, but Serrin looked weak. You didn't. I suspected something might go wrong but did not expect your brother's death."

Kiffen's shoulders drooped with relief and a bit of despair. "I suppose not. If you had known, you would have warned us."

Glume surprised him by shaking his head. "No. I wouldn't have.

My gift was a secret. I couldn't risk it. To this day I wonder what might have happened if I revealed it to the queen. But Montee's vision took care of that need. Not that I knew it at the time."

As he had trailed off, Bai'dish filled Kiffen's mind with the sight of a line of people, weighted down with packs, a few pushing single-wheeled barrows, all piled down with their possessions. At the front marched a man, skin as dark as night, his gaze strong and purposeful. Bai'dish focused their joined sight on this man, and something rippled along the bond that gave Kiffen hope. The man carried something important.

Now he stood near the tunnels, ready to intercept the evacuees' path.

It wasn't until they came into view that he realized Adana was not with them. A spark of worry hit him, and Bai'dish responded with foreboding. No? Or something bad? Or both? He should have asked Glume to join him as he waited, but the man preferred time with the giraffes at the keep. He had his duties.

At the front of the caravan marched the man Kiffen had seen through Bai'dish's connection. He turned to Montee. "That man, at the front, who is he?"

Montee squinted at Kiffen. "Is he the one you saw?"

"Yes."

She smiled. "That is Vuur. The Glimmer Isati. He leads the glimmer makers."

They strode forward to meet him.

Vuur folded his right arm in front of him and bowed at the waist. The man's voice washed over Kiffen like a deep, refreshing pool of water after a long, exhausting hike. "King Kiffen? You must be he. And First Vision. The Creator knows my thanks for finding sight of the two of you."

"Master Vuur, you are welcome." Kiffen made a show of studying the people gathering behind Vuur. "I had hoped to find the queen with you."

"She sent me to you and has continued in search of Kassa and Umgani."

At that, Montee interrupted. "What of Dosata?"

"She accompanied us until we met with the queen's party. She joined them. Miri alerted her to this path, I believe."

"And did Miri go with them, too?" Even Montee could not hide the disbelief in her voice over this question.

Kiffen wondered about this evident display of emotion, but his thread of thought evaporated with Vuur's next words.

"No. Miri went to the Creator two days ago." He glanced around, then stepped closer, his voice dropping to a quiet hush, remarkable for the depth of his tone. "We should not discuss this here. I bring much news, but I would see us safely within the keep, first."

"Of course." Kiffen nodded, then waved for the soldiers with him to assist their exhausted arrivals. As they continued the trek toward the tunnels, he couldn't help but ask, "I received word that you bring something I will appreciate." He paused a moment, thinking over the sensation from Bai'dish. "At least, I believe that's what was meant by the message."

Vuur's lips curled in a pleased, but slight, smile. "Yes. Queen Adana directed me to speak to you of it." He lifted his gaze to Kiffen's. "I believe you will be most pleased, sire. Most pleased."

Heart pounding, Kiffen fought the urge to command the man to speak now. Short of leaving the people Vuur led on their own, he could do nothing but wait.

* * *

The wait proved its worth.

Vuur, along with Montee, Sinti, and Simeon, sat in a small receiving room in the Central Tower. The man assured them he did not need to climb the stairs to the tower room with the map quite yet. His news did not require a map.

Kiffen, anxious to hear what he carried with him, paused with frustration when Simeon stopped him from barging into the chamber where Vuur waited. "Sire, Vuur is Monian. It might be best, at first, to allow Montee to conduct the inquiries."

The man knew Montee. The two kingdoms might be reuniting, but no one knew what different factions thought of this yet. The Isata's respectful address to Kiffen indicated acceptance of him as king, but the advice was good.

After Vuur finished the goblet of wine they'd offered him, Montee sat forward. "What, Vuur, have you discovered?"

Discovered? Kiffen turned to the man, curiosity begging to ask questions, but he held his tongue.

Vuur set the empty goblet down. "A weapon, I believe." He raised his hands in precaution as Kiffen leaned toward him. "I hope. Umgani and Kassa would be the best to tell us if it worked. They were in the fortress when Miri triggered it."

To Kiffen's surprise, Simeon overrode his own warnings. "What kind of weapon?" The usually silent man sat forward on his seat.

"An explosive. Using glimmer fire."

Glimmer fire. It burned hot, yes, but it didn't explode. Kiffen, heartened by the silent amazement on the others' faces, couldn't hold back his question. "I thought it was too stable to explode."

"So did I, Your Majesty." Vuur looked around, spotted the wine decanter, and rose to get it. He came back and poured more in his goblet, then topped off the untouched ones before the three of them. "I found it quite by accident."

"So you say." Simeon grabbed his goblet and took a big swallow. He set the cup down, chuckling. "Just like you found how to make glimmer cloth fireproof by accident."

Confusion sparked along Kiffen's nerves. Simeon was laughing, even joking, with the glimmer maker. He turned a questioning eye toward Montee.

She blinked at him for a moment, then recognition of his confusion crossed her face. "Vuur is known for *accidentally* discovering all sorts of uses for glimmer. Most minor. But the fireproof discovery was invaluable in the last war. Now he's found us a new weapon."

"*Think* I've found one, Montee. Don't get ahead of this idea. We must have confirmation."

"No disrespect to you, Vuur, but if you suspect it worked, even if you suspect only a slight bit, I will stake my position on the fact that we have a new weapon."

"How does it work?" Kiffen jumped in, growing tired of the banter.

Vuur took another swallow and smacked his lips together in appreciation. "I don't know why or how it works. I only know what I did to make it."

"How did you test it?" Simeon asked.

"Ah. And now I must share the other news. To aid Kassa and Umgani in the rescue of the giraffes, it became obvious the main gate would not be a feasible option. We used this explosive to open a spot in the southeastern wall."

Montee leapt to her feet. "You took out part of Adana's View's defenses?" She paced across the room. "Did it work?"

"That, I do not know. The explosion was magnificent in the night sky, though."

Spinning to face him again, Montee said, "Why do you question its viability if you saw it?"

"I did not truly see the explosion. We were well away from the walls when Miri set the trigger."

"But you saw something?" Montee leaned toward the man.

"Yes. It lit the night up. We saw it burning even as we traveled farther from the fortress."

"Brilliant." Montee grinned. "You managed something many a Monian enemy has attempted—infiltrating our walls. And from within. With the wall down, we can do it again. How much of this explosive do you have?"

"None. We used the one batch I made. I must make more." He turned an apologetic look to Kiffen. "The queen bade me find you and ask you to help me find space to work."

"We have an entire keep," Kiffen said. "But I assume we should not test this within the walls."

"Quite right, sire. Quite right." The inventor raised his goblet to the three of them, drained it, and slammed it down on the table with a loud clang. "Can we begin tomorrow? After this old man can rest his bones?"

As the sun traveled its arc across the sky, Adana and her small crew continued searching for Kassa and Umgani. She felt a nudge from Am'brosia, pressure to veer to the right. Curious, Adana stopped and scanned the area. It was grassland, just like ahead of them, with the occasional tree breaking the landscape. Still, the bond leapt with energy each time she turned that way.

"Am'brosia wants us to change direction," Adana announced and started along the new path.

When nothing of interest appeared within the hour, she began to question Am'brosia through the bond. She'd asked questions of the animal before, while Am'brosia responded with images or feelings. Only once had she ever managed to sound a word in Adana's mind, and that had been "No."

She'd tried to explain the understanding of the giraffe's communications to Kiffen, but he couldn't grasp the idea. He would have to learn that on his own.

For now, her doubt annoyed Am'brosia, the bond stinging with energy, almost painful in its forcefulness.

They continued in that direction, then.

The moment she agreed to maintain their heading, the stinging stopped. Its absence enhanced her awareness of the ache in her shoulder. The intensity of pain, while not pleasant, lessened a bit. Could they be close?

"There's a stream ahead," Nuala said, interrupting Adana's musings. "We should refill our canteens."

Adana paused and recognized the light babble of water flowing ahead and to their right. She altered her path, heading for the stream. The lightness of relief washed down the link. She picked up her pace. "I think they're near the stream. Am'brosia wants us to go this way."

The seven of them hurried after her, and Greti sent two of her unit ahead to scout the way. Before long, shouts of greeting came to their ears. Ignoring the need to stick within the middle of her Watchers for protection, Adana raced ahead.

Before she saw them, she heard the shift in their tones. At first their voices sounded joyful, but now they sounded worried. She ran faster.

"Your Majesty," Dosata called as she attempted to stay with her, but the heavy pack slowed her down. "Wait. We don't' know—"

She ignored the warrior's urgent tone. At the top of a small rise, she spotted them below. Blood rushed to her head at the scene unfolding in front of her. Kassa lay still and gray on a frame of vine-wrapped tree limbs. A cloth tied around her left arm was brown with old blood. Beside her, Umgani stood, sweat streaking rivulets through a fine layer of dirt on her skin. The woman spotted Adana and moved to stand at attention, but Adana waved her hand in dismissal. "Tell me."

While Umgani explained what had happened, Dosata got to work, ordering two of the Watchers to build a fire while she took items from her pack. She blinked and looked up at Adana, whose eyes were wide in surprise as she withdrew a short saw and a bottle of some sweet-smelling potion.

Adana stared in shock at those and the other items in the pack

—dressings and straps for making a carry-bed. Her time in Elwar dragged her away from the amazing phenomena of a Watcher's prophecy. She'd forgotten their power, absorbed in only one vision over those years.

"Bless the Creator for giving Miri the sight," Dosata said, her voice a quiet hush of awe.

Yes, Miri had known. And the vision came from the Creator. Had Miri known that Kassa walked into danger and let her go?

Heat rose in Adana's cheeks at the thought of Kassa's choice. She wanted to rant and rave at her mentor for pursuing a fool's path into danger. News of Maligon's death would have heartened her; thrilled her, actually. But not at the cost of Kassa's arm or life.

A gasping voice, slight but unmistakably Kassa's, brought her back to the moment. She knelt by the woman's side, staring down into the face she'd come to think of with the fondness of a child for their mother. That thought drew her short. She'd never put words to it, never admitted to the significant shift their relationship took in Elwar.

Still in training, Kassa had treated her as a Watcher, but the closeness Kassa held with Adana's mother softened the woman's bite. Or maybe it had been the harsh treatment Adana received from Queen Quilla. For whatever reason, Kassa had become more to her than a senior Watcher.

The faded green eyes sought Adana's face and locked on her. "Failed you." Her words came out in a hoarse whisper. "Failed you."

"No." She stroked the loose strands of Kassa's braid back from her face. She wanted to yell at her. Tell her she should never have done this alone. She should have sought permission for such a risky act.

She said none of that; she breathed in deeply, letting her anger slip between her lips with each breath.

Did Kassa somehow feel responsible for her daughter's actions, seeking redemption by removing the man who drew Samantha away? No. Kassa's hatred of Maligon went deeper. Adana had seen it many times reflected in the woman's eyes, the one window to her mentor's thoughts that she sometimes failed to control.

Kassa winced and attempted to shift, winced again.

"Breathe with me," Adana urged her. "You must find your center and hide there until this is done."

Beads of perspiration slid down the woman's forehead as she shook it. "No. Broken. No good to you."

"Nonsense." The urge to comfort and the urge to chastise fought within Adana's soul. All she could do was shake her head and smooth Kassa's brow. "Now breathe with me."

"She's correct, my sister." Umgani's deep voice pulled Adana from her conflicting thoughts. The Watcher knelt on the other side of Kassa. "You are not broken. No. You are not beautiful for the shape of your body, but for the shape of the soul it holds. You, my friend, hold a strong and formidable soul full of courage and wisdom."

The words resonated with Adana, and she reconsidered them, knowing she'd heard them before.

"Let us breathe, Kassa, you, I, and our queen."

Kassa locked her gaze on Umgani and began to breathe slowly, in and out, in and out. With time, she faded into unconsciousness again.

Finally, the sounds of Dosata and the others' preparations ceased. As silence surrounded her, Adana lifted her head to meet Dosata's gaze.

"We are ready," the warrior said. "She may fight us if her body wakes her to the injustice we must do to it." She held out a cloth to Adana. "She will rest easier if you can hold this over her mouth and nose."

Adana hesitated. "What is it?"

"It will help her sleep. As long as you keep her mouth and nose covered. If you let it slip for long, she will awaken to agony."

For a moment, Adana's throat worked but would not emit sound. Finally, she swallowed hard and nodded her understanding. The cloth felt damp and a sweet smell wafted from it.

"Don't inhale it yourself, Your Majesty," Dosata ordered, softening the command with Adana's royal title. "We need you awake."

Adana returned to kneel beside Kassa, keeping the cloth at arm's length. She clamped it over Kassa's face. "She can still breathe?"

"Yes, as long as you don't press down too hard."

The others took up their positions. The drug on the cloth might keep Kassa asleep, but they prepared for a fight, anyway. A warrior of forty years didn't forget how to defend herself because she was unconscious.

Umgani knelt at Kassa's head, her hands braced to hold down Kassa's shoulders. With one Watcher each at her right arm and two legs, Dosata approached. She handed Umgani a thick wooden spoon. Without direction, Umgani placed it in Kassa's mouth. "Bite on this when it's too much," she whispered to the unconscious body.

Adana swallowed. Umgani and Dosata had done this before. Their motions, their actions, revealed a muscle memory ingrained into them. Another gift of Maligon from the first war, Maligon's Rebellion.

While they held Kassa down, Dosata returned to the saw. It hung from a rope, cooling after its scorching in the fire. Dosata picked up another bottle and poured it liberally over the saw blade. Then she approached Kassa and poured more over Kassa's arm.

She set the bottle down beside Adana, the thick pungency of liquor spilling from the bottle. "If the cloth doesn't work, pour some of this down her throat."

Adana nodded.

They began.

* * *

Kiffen's vision flooded with a scene that made his stomach churn. Kassa lay still as death, skin ashy, while several Watchers held her down. Adana held something over the woman's face. Was Kassa dead? No. They wouldn't need to hold her.

As if Adana heard his question, the scene focused on the woman's left arm. Then he saw Dosata approach with a sawtooth blade. Realization hit him with a sickening grip.

Just before the vision faded, it shifted to Adana's face. Her sorrow-filled eyes peered at him in a wordless plea. For what? Comfort? He had no clue how to do that across the bond even though he'd managed to do so during her father's funeral. He'd stood before King Micah's pyre, then. It had been easy to share their misery. He'd had no way to stem the wave of emotions overwhelming him as the flames engulfed King Micah's body.

"Kiffen? Sire? Your Majesty?" Simeon shook his arm, deep grooves of worry wrinkling his forehead.

He blinked and straightened. Shoving the man's hands off, he took in the curiosity in Montee's and Vuur's faces. Unlike Simeon, they knew when a giraffe bond overtook a person.

"Apologies." He cleared his throat and straightened. "Adana. Am'brosia." The impact of the message stilled his tongue. A mentor to Montee, Kassa's condition might come as a shock.

"She sent news of Kassa and Umgani?" Montee's mouth pressed in a thin line.

She knew, as any great Watcher would, that he had received bad news. "I'm sorry, Montee, the news is disturbing." He suppressed a sudden urge to reach out and put a comforting hand on her arm. "Dosata is about to remove the former First's arm."

Vuur fell back in his chair, one hand scrubbing at his face.

Simeon swore under his breath. Sinti gasped.

Montee remained still, immobile, no response. Had she heard him?

The four eyed her as she sat motionless, gaze focused on something internal, the occasional eye blink the only indication she lived.

Simeon, not deterred by her strength like Kiffen had been, walked over and lightly touched her hand where it lay flat on the table. "Montee?"

She blinked twice, rapidly, then looked up at him. "Kassa's alive. For now. We must prepare for her." She turned to Kiffen. "Does Adana need anything?"

Comfort from him, but he didn't say that. "I don't know."

Rising to her feet with purpose, Montee faced south as if she could see them through the thick stone walls. "Do you know where they are?"

The surroundings were not part of the vision, or the stark reality of what he saw forced his attention elsewhere. "I'm sorry. I saw nothing but Kassa surrounded by other Watchers."

Montee took a step toward him. "Ask Bai'dish."

Kiffen frowned. He had no idea how to ask a question, then recalled his lesson with Glume. *Think what you need if you can't picture it. Sometimes the giraffe understands.*

Thanks to his recent contact with Bai'dish, Kiffen didn't need to go through the focus exercise first. He drew in one deep breath, released it, and tried to picture Adana as he'd seen her a moment ago. *Where are they?*

A wavy picture began to surface in his mind. Adana and the other Watchers surrounding Kassa. The edges of the image blurred into nothing.

Can you step back and look around?

Nothing happened. Focusing harder, Kiffen pictured himself standing a few lengths behind Adana, then he took an actual step backward within the keep.

Again, time passed, agonizing in the slow response, but this time, Bai'dish showed him a stream rippling over rocks, the ground flat with a few trees. On the bank of the stream, a tiny cluster of stones rose in a small pillar.

More.

Bai'dish raised their sight to survey the surroundings. A low hill rose behind Adana and her party. A narrow path of trampled grass, recent or long used by animals he could not tell, led up the hill.

When he described the scene to Montee, she smiled. "I believe I know the place. The rocks. Do they tilt toward the water a bit?"

He nodded.

She turned to Simeon. "We must send soldiers to carry Kassa back. A wagon, horses, not only for the wagon but for the Watchers."

At Simeon's raised eyebrow, she said, "Even Watchers require rest occasionally."

He nodded. "I will see to it. Do you plan to send more Watchers?"

She shook her head. "No. I shall go. And you, Kiffen. I believe you should come with me."

"Agreed." For once, he didn't mind someone else directing him. "I'll let Adana know we're coming." He started to reach out and felt a slap along the link. Of course, the giraffe knew not to interrupt Adana while they operated on Kassa. "Once they finish the surgery."

"A wise move." Montee smiled, but sadness remained in her eyes. "Was Kassa awake? When you saw her?"

He shook his head. He first thought her dead but didn't share that.

* * *

Adana still knelt by Kassa, fighting tears of exhaustion and frustration. Everyone else moved about setting up camp. Dosata had proclaimed the operation a success, stating recovery was up to the Creator and Kassa, now.

For the first time in years, Adana turned her thoughts toward begging the Creator to help. Turning to the Creator, a huge comfort in her youth, no longer came to her naturally. Did she trust the Creator? No. But the need for his healing drove her to a desire to trust.

Thankfully, Dosata had wrapped Kassa's severed arm in a cloth and taken it away. What would she do with it? It must be disposed of. Would they bury it only to invite a hyena or lion to find it? Predators drove Monians to the practice of fire burial hundreds of years ago. To bring the arm with them felt morbid, though, not to mention the stink of dead flesh and the cloud of flies that would swarm and track them.

As she shifted from her knees to a seated position, Dosata and Umgani approached the edge of the stream. The two pulled several large stones from the rocky bed and set them in a circular hearth. The two worked in tandem without words, selecting stones with care, throwing back some with a plop in the water. When they'd created a large stone bowl, they gathered and laid sticks, grass, and twigs in it as if they meant to start a fire. Adana suppressed her surprise. Wet stones would douse the fire.

Umgani withdrew a long stick-like tube from a fold in her tunic and flicked her arm toward the small pile. A tiny blue flame spun out of the tube and landed on the sticks. Within a few breaths, a colorful blaze ate up the kindling.

Adana had never seen glimmer fire in those colors before. The orange, red, and blue danced with green, pink, and a lighter blue. Umgani fed it more sticks, the unusual colors jumping to eat the kindling, while Dosata picked up a long, wrapped item from the ground. Kassa's arm.

The two faced each of the compass directions as they would in a funeral, ending with the arm pointed south toward Adana's View. When they laid the arm on the fire, it popped and crackled its pleasure. The arm disappeared in flames.

One of the blessed things about glimmer fire, because this

colorful fire could be nothing else, was it burned so hot and fast that the smell of burning flesh rarely hit the senses.

With a quick check to ensure Kassa still rested, Adana rose and walked toward the two elder Watchers. The flames whooshed as the last of the arm caught fire. It no longer looked like an arm by the time she reached them.

It felt right that Watchers from Kassa's first years in training undertook this sacrament. She joined them, and the three stood together, silent within their own thoughts. At some point, Adana felt a prickle on her neck as the weight of their gazes shifted toward her.

"We have much to tell you, Your Majesty," Umgani said, her voice thick with emotion. "I apologize for not sharing everything when you arrived."

"No. Kassa's life depended on your actions." Adana held back her many questions. She still felt awe over the depth of experience and wisdom in the Watchers before her. The fact that Kassa chose them to accompany her over any of the Watchers in their prime of life hinted at something more about them. Strengths Kassa had desired.

Instead of mentioning this, she asked the question foremost in her mind. "Why did you give her arm a funeral? Is that normal?"

The two women eyed each other for a moment, something unspoken passing between them. Dosata answered her.

"It is not always done, but it has been in the past. Under special circumstances. Kassa is the last person who touched Miri. We cannot give Miri the rites she deserves. We had worried over this, but when we realized Kassa's hand had touched hers in formal farewell, we thought it appropriate."

As Dosata tapered off, Umgani added to their answer. "In the wilderness, an arm will draw undue attention from animals and flies. Unlike a battlefield that attracts birds and flies more interested in the dead than the living, we are a thriving company. Kassa's arm would draw predators we wish to avoid. Her hands served Moniah in many ways. More than any of us, she's struggled to prevail under the blows dealt by Maligon. We hope the Creator will give her peace where the arm once was and not plague her with its ghost."

Its ghost. Stories told around the hearth talked about missing limbs and the ghost of an arm or leg plaguing its owner. Adana nodded at their wisdom. "You have done well by both your sisters. I am sorry for the loss of Miri. I recall her as powerful and encouraging. Thank you for the honor you do her as well as Kassa."

The three of them, as one, turned to watch the unconscious form of Kassa on her makeshift pallet.

Adana returned her inquisitive stare on the two women. "Miri honored all of us more than we can imagine, especially Kassa. I have many questions, but you both must need to cleanse yourselves as the others have already done. Then we will hear what you have to share."

As the two turned toward the stream, Adana felt the surge of Am'brosia's presence. Relaxing into the strength of the link, she opened her mind. She'd closed the bond as much as possible during the surgery, but now she hoped to find Kiffen's presence on the other end. It was. In a way. Through Am'brosia's eyes she saw Kiffen and Montee followed by a wagon, several riderless horses, and a mixed unit of soldiers—Elwarian and Monian. They could remain here and let Kassa rest until they arrived.

Her heart lifted in relief. Maybe the Creator did care after all.

* * *

Charissa crept along a narrow gully, a remnant from the rampage of last year's rains. She led the horse in slow, careful steps. Ramil followed. The late evening sun didn't penetrate the shallow ravine and the sparse shrubbery where they hid from the uniformed soldiers a short distance away. Safe as long as the horse didn't snort and the soldiers didn't come too close.

The men in the distance wore the blue of Elwar. Beyond them, many ordered lines of soldiers marched. Nothing mercenary about these men; their uniforms looked clean and formal.

One of the guards raised his head and looked around. She ducked, gesturing a warning to Ramil. Not much she could do for the horse, though. The army would seize their mount if they discovered them. Not much she could do about that, either, unless she wanted to be captured by the enemy.

Ramil crawled up beside her and whispered in a low voice. "Are you sure they're Maligon's?"

She nodded. "I saw Queen Quilla riding near the front, behind the standard bearer."

In the distance, she could still spot the Elwarian standard of blue with the golden eagle stretched out in flight. A woman, the only woman from what she could see, rode behind the bearer. Queen Quilla. She'd seen her once sixteen years ago, a month before she came to Moniah for her training. She never forgot this tiny woman and how she frowned down her nose at the people gathered along the route through Elwar City. The people had sung and reveled and cheered the health of the new queen and the small baby princess cradled in her arms.

Today, the queen radiated the same disapproval of her surroundings as she looked around, disdain set in her thin mouth.

The dark-haired man beside the queen did not look familiar, but he regarded the area with contempt identical to the queen's. Most in Adana's View did not know Quilla had seized the throne with the help of a man known as Lord Sarx. Maligon and his close circle managed to keep this truth hidden, a fact she and Ramil overheard while in hiding. Later, Suru confirmed it. The man must be Sarx.

Charissa and Ramil remained crouched under the slight cover as they waited for the large caravan to pass, wagons with food and supplies rumbling near the end. Among these, she spotted a woman here or there, but few.

Once the signs of the troops' passing became a heavy dust cloud in the distance, she turned to Ramil and motioned for him to follow her along the gully. It took careful precision to navigate the uneven terrain, but she didn't dare climb out until confident any stragglers had passed.

With the sun kissing the horizon, they finally emerged from cover. The vast plains stretched out before them.

"How many soldiers did she have?" Ramil asked. "I tried to count, but—" he shrugged, "—you're the Watcher."

"They marched ten across. Forty rows in each troop. I counted twenty troops, but I missed counting at the beginning."

Ramil's eyes bugged out. "Over eight thousand trained soldiers? Headed for Moniah?"

With a nod, she squinted at the dust in the distance. "We must warn the Border Keep."

"I don't think so," a gruff voice came from behind them.

They whipped around. Four soldiers leapt across the narrow stretch, swords drawn.

Charissa grabbed for her own sword, but one of the men rushed her, grabbed her arm, and twisted her around. "Not a good idea, Watcher."

The sound of their horse galloping away drew the man's attention. He gawked at the sight of Ramil whipping the horse with a frenzy. She jabbed her free elbow in her captor's gut, stomping on his instep at the same time.

Howling, the man released her, and she ran after Ramil. The other three pursued her. Ahead, she saw Ramil look over his shoulder, rein in, and kick the horse back in her direction. "You fool," she muttered but felt glad he hadn't deserted her.

She outran the men, thanks to her Watcher training and gifts.

Long legs ate up the distance between her and the horse. No person could outrun a Watcher except another Watcher. She happened to be one of the fastest.

Ramil halted the horse and waited for her. She vaulted behind him.

He kicked the horse away from the soldiers.

"No. Go back." She turned to check the progress of the men. They had stopped running. "We can't let them go."

"There's four of them," Ramil said.

"Get me within range." She withdrew her bow and pulled an arrow from her quiver. "I don't need to be close to stop them."

31

Several days had passed since Amar began teaching Leera sword skills. Over that time, her little army grew to three hundred. Each day brought a few more men out of hiding. At first, Leera could only stare in astonishment at the hum of soldiers working around her. Each arrival marked a new swearing of allegiance, a formality she enjoyed maybe a bit too much.

The soldiers worked around her in constant motion but bobbed their heads in acknowledgement if they caught her looking their way. Only when she and Amar sparred did many of them stop to watch.

As they were doing now.

Hair pulled into a tight braid wound into a bun, Leera bounced on her toes, her body light and quick. She lacked strength, Amar had warned her, but her size and speed could overcome that weakness.

The sword felt comfortable in her hand, although she regretted the callouses wearing across her palm. At least the burning blisters had healed thanks to the miracle salve Sariah gave her.

"Today," Amar said, "we must work on your parries."

A thrill somersaulted up her spine at Amar's familiar address. She'd insisted on this after the first day of Amar spewing her title every time he spoke. It wasted time. They didn't have time. She needed to defend herself, especially if they encountered her mother's loyal soldiers.

She swung the blade in a slicing motion. "Like this?"

Amar took an easy step away from the strike and shook his head. "No. You parry with the flat of the blade." He lifted her sword arm and ran his finger along the blade's flat side. "If you try to parry with the edge, like you just did, you'll break it. Maybe even shatter it. That would not bode well for you." His dark eyes bored into hers, but she noted a hint of amusement flirting in their depths.

She swallowed and nodded. "Duly noted. Let's get started."

With a shake of his head, Amar directed her to stand aside. "First, I will demonstrate." He waved one of the willing audience members forward, and the two men began to circle each other.

"Now when I swing my blade in from above, notice his response."

A loud clang rang across the clearing as his opponent swung the flat of his blade up, blocking Amar's blade crossways.

After a few more demonstrations, first at combat speed and second done with slow deliberation as Amar explained the steps, he invited her to try. "I want you to focus on doing this parry until it's comfortable. Then we'll try a new one."

They sparred for some time as evening fell around the camp. Settling on the outer edge of the forest, they had taken several extra days to traverse the heavy wood. Maligon's gathering troops prowled the forest, too, looking for deserters and men to force into service.

Each time the scouts spotted signs of soldiers, they shifted their route, sometimes doubling-back on their journey. But this after-noon, they had emerged from the dark and somber trees. The sky finally visible above her, Leera had breathed in the clean scents of grass and wildflowers and exclaimed over the huge expanse of roll-ing hills stretching to the horizon.

Now, as they practiced, the clang of their swords was joined by others in their party inspired by her efforts. The first time her men did this, many of the soldiers pulled their sweaty shirts off and battled in a display of muscles, lean and toned.

The distraction proved problematic for Leera, unaccustomed to any proximity to a man's bare chest, especially a whole army of them. She kept missing her marks, her gaze wandering to the lure of muscular, bare arms, shoulders, and stomachs.

Callan had called a stop to the practice, ordering them to don their shirts and never practice without them in her presence again. Disappointed, but aware of the necessity, Leera smiled at the men with the charm her mother had taught her and thanked them for their modesty. Inside, she tried to quell the butterflies of interest that sprang to life at such an enticing sight.

Now, as she practiced the parry, Leera's arms protested with each impact. She refused to complain or give in. She was not a spoiled princess. None of her men saw her that way, and she wasn't about to let them hear her whine or pout.

Despite the pain, the swing of her blade thrilled her, and the freedom of motion from her gray-green Watcher's uniform made her feel more alive than she'd ever been.

With this many men rising up to support her, Sariah had even quit calling her Lily. Leera had an army now, and they should think of her as their princess. Not that any of them didn't know her true identity to begin with.

Focused on this joy of exercise and freedom, Leera missed the sudden hush of sound and motion until Amar pushed her behind him.

She stumbled at the hard shove and swung to strike at him, stopping mid-stroke. A small group of her men encircled her. They held their blades raised in protection. The rest fought unknown soldiers in earnest.

Training forgotten, Leera huddled behind Amar and the others, trying to make herself invisible. She searched through the mass of men to see which of her mother's hated soldiers had found her.

Fear rippled down her arms, making it hard to hold her sword, when the Protector of the Faith, wearing her white robes of office, strode into the middle of the chaos. "Hold. We will not fight." Sariah's voice resounded louder than Leera thought possible.

Was the Protector going to hand her over without a fight? Leera's stomach dove to her feet.

Sariah's obvious voice of authority froze the soldiers, though. Even Leera felt the power behind the command, unable to run from her position.

"We have no fight with Halar of the First Soldiers," Sariah said as she walked between the soldiers. "Nor the first knight of Belwyn, Sir Jerold."

"Jerold?" Leera blurted the man's name, shock in her voice. She pushed through the men who hesitated to give way at first. They still held their swords at ready.

A tall man with thick brown hair stood before Sariah, a smile of greeting on his face.

Leera broke free of the front line of men and stared up at the tired, grizzled face. "Is it truly you?"

The knight she remembered standing beside Empress Gabriella at all times during the Kingdoms Council almost three years ago stood before her. Leaner and less formal in dress, but it was him.

"Princess Leera?" he asked, eyes wide in astonishment. "Forgive me, my lady, but I saw a Watcher—you—fighting these men and thought to help you." He studied her clothing with curiosity. "When did you become a Watcher? I had no idea you possessed the gift of sight."

She blushed as his gaze traveled up her body. Did he enjoy what he saw?

"I am not a Watcher. The uniform was a gift from Princess

Adana." Around her army, the scandalous leggings and tunic never caused any concern or embarrassment, but now, before Empress Gabriella's knight, she longed for a cloak to cover herself.

"And the sword? Is that a gift from Queen Adana, too?"

Queen. She'd forgotten that Adana was now a queen. And her brother a king. So much shifting in their lives.

"No. My men are teaching me to fight."

Eyebrow raised, Jerold looked around the clearing. "Your men? Whatever do you plan to do with them?"

Was he laughing at her? "Take them to my brother, of course." Leera straightened her back and stared down her nose at Jerold. He may be taller, but her mother taught her height had nothing to do with looking down your nose at someone.

At that point, Halar stepped forward, his face amused and pleased. He bowed at the waist. "You won't recall me, Your Highness, but I am Halar. I serve Queen Adana as the Commander of the First Soldiers."

"Commander Halar?" She turned to the tall and lean, white-haired man, a long mustache curling beside his mouth. "What of Commander Linus? Adana spoke of him often."

Profound sadness drooped his whiskers, revealing a frown. "Killed, my lady, by traitors within Adana's View."

Leera looked around for Sariah, unsure how to respond. Spend a few days traveling with roughened soldiers, and she'd lost all of her training for polite company. As always, the Protector hovered nearby. Almost as bad as a Memory Keeper, Sariah eavesdropped everywhere she went. Not that they held this conversation in private.

"Commander Halar, I am sorrowed to hear this," Sariah said. "But we thank the Creator we find you on our journey to the Border Keep." Then she turned toward Jerold and took the man's hands within her own. She spoke with deep respect. "I'm pleased to find you well, my lord. Do you rally an army for...the empress?"

Why had she paused? Leera caught the hesitation but found no basis for it. Something passed between Sariah and Jerold, though, for he nodded in reply. "Soon."

"Come." Sariah beckoned to him, Halar, and Leera. She led them to the small tent her men insisted on erecting for her and Sariah every night. It provided room for two to sleep or a few more to sit and talk in private.

There were two seats inside the tent, and Leera took one. To her surprise, Jerold displayed little respect for Sariah by taking the other. She stared at him until she felt Sariah's birdlike gaze focused on her. The woman's eyes sparkled with amusement. Instead of addressing Leera, though, she turned to Jerold. "Shall I or do you prefer?"

The knight turned to face Leera, his face intent. It made her flush with embarrassment. No man, save her brothers or Taren, had ever looked at her with such unbroken focus.

"I think she must know. She'll learn soon enough. At the keep."

"Whatever are you two on about?" Leera burst out then clamped her mouth shut. She was not a spoiled princess who thought everything centered around her. But right now, it felt like it did. Heat built up in her body as she watched Jerold cock his head and study her. She fought the urge to cross her legs, an unseemly position for a woman. How could this knight regard her so casually?

He rose from his purloined seat. "I believe I shall tell her." His gaze never left hers as he knelt before Leera. "Princess Leera, I travel to Belwyn, gathering an army as I go. Much like you do. You bring an army to your brother the king. I bring an army to my mother in hopes to find her safe and well. Then I'll return to the keep to stand with Queen Adana and King Kiffen."

It took a few moments for Leera's mind to catch up with Jerold's words, her attention first focused on the fact Jerold mentioned Adana before her brother. The last time she saw this knight, she'd suspected he held a deeper relationship with Gabriella. She even pointed it out to Adana and joked about it. The two had appeared attached. In love. Maybe in lust, her impressionable young mind decided at the time.

The heat in her body surged to her face as she processed his words—my mother—and realized the mistake she and Adana made that night. "Gabriella is your mother? You are a prince?"

"I am."

For some reason she could not explain, Leera's heart soared. She dipped her head in acknowledgement of an equal. "Well met, Prince Jerold of Belwyn. I am pleased to make your acquaintance."

Later that evening, she sat by the fire, enjoying the soldiers' storytelling and banter. To her right, Jerold sat on the ground, one leg stretched toward the fire, the other leg drawn up, his hands draped over his knee. No matter how hard she tried, she could not ignore the warmth of his presence.

Eventually, Callan cut off his men's tall tales and turned to Jerold. "You saw Maligon take Adana's View?"

"Yes." Jerold sat upright. "I did."

"Will you tell us of the battle? Of King Kiffen?"

"I rode with Queen Adana, not King Kiffen, but I am glad to share the news."

The fire popped and crackled as Jerold spoke, his voice as gifted as a Memory Keeper's in holding their attention. The men stilled, their antics and side conversations tapered off to silence as he spoke.

Leera's heart rose and dipped like an eagle on cross currents as the tale unfolded. When Jerold reached the point of Samantha's treachery, she exclaimed in shock.

Jerold turned his gaze on her, nodding. "Yes, it came as a huge blow to all of us. Especially to Kassa, Halar, and Montee."

"Montee?" Leera leaned toward him, urging him to explain.

Like an accomplished storyteller, Jerold glanced around the gathering, leaned forward, and whispered, "Because she loved Linus."

The men rewarded him with exclamations and gasps of shock. A thrill of intrigue stroked Leera's mind. The stoic Montee led a secret and forbidden love affair with the only man in Moniah equal to her rank. She wanted to melt like butter on a hot roll over the idea.

That night, she tossed and turned, her mind playing over the chaos her brother and Adana's betrothal wrought. According to Halar, they had married a few days earlier. She'd missed it.

Her disappointment faded, though, with the last bit of the story. Jerold had saved it for hers and Sariah's ears only, aware it might dampen her army's fire for a fight.

In quiet conversation, he told them of the giraffes' deaths. The Watcher accompanying his troop confirmed this news. The idea that someone could strike down and kill giraffes in battle fueled Leera's wrath. The idea that someone would kill giraffes within Adana's View made her fury boil to an intensity she didn't know she possessed.

Aware the next day's ride came soon, she couldn't stop her mind from wandering to some less disturbing, albeit interesting, news— Jerold's identity. His face floated in her memory, brown eyes hardened as he related tough details then softened with compassion as he spoke of the devastation Samantha's actions caused her family and Montee. He'd held Leera's gaze several times during the story, each time her heart spiraling into her throat as if it had wings. She drifted asleep wondering what it would be like to kiss Prince Jerold.

The next morning, the two armies parted company. Jerold and Halar, delayed on their own mission by avoiding several of Maligon's troops, too, continued on their way westward.

Leera hoped, for Jerold's sake, that King Ariff had returned victorious from his self-appointed mission to save the empress. The lack of news concerned her as it did Jerold and Halar.

Astride her horse, Leera gave her farewells to the prince, drowning in his brown eyes. They reminded her of the gentle liquid brown of the giraffe's eyes. He had little wrinkles in the corners of his, casting a distinguished air to his once-boyish features. His horse, drawn up beside hers, whinnied as Halar called for departure.

Jerold took her hand in his and planted a kiss on the back. "I hope to see you soon, Princess Leera, our fighting princess from Elwar." He grinned, then turned his horse to follow his troops, whistling a jaunty tune.

For a long time, she watched him ride away. When she turned to order her army forward, she found them watching her, mouths twitching. An urge to order them to behave came over her, but she was no longer that princess. She relaxed her face into a silly grin and shook her head. "Callan? Let's move."

The last of Maligon's new recruits arrived several days after the explosions. Shana and Brother Honest, practicing in the archery grounds, stopped to watch the mercenaries and conscripted soldiers tromp in. The men from Maligon's private army surrounded the motley group of disgruntled men, forcing them into tight lines and barking orders at them.

The cacophony of their arrival threw off Shana's focus, ruining her last shot. The arrow vibrated in the outer circle of the target. "Blazes. If soldiers distract my aim, how will I ever manage in battle?"

"You will," Honest assured her, turning to study the men. "They don't look like much, do they?"

Pulling her gaze from her miserable results, Shana studied the men. Then, as she'd always done, she closed her eyes and listened.

Heavy breathing, some coughing, and a few muttered words ran an angry undercurrent to the mercenaries' shouted orders to "Keep moving" and "Stay in line, you scum."

She shook her head. "How do they expect to transform this group into a combat force willing to stand or fall for Maligon?"

Aware she repeated this question every time a new group arrived, she turned back to her bow.

Archery, it turned out, soothed her mind even if she failed to perfect her aim—a problem they tried to hide since Adana's prowess surpassed many in this area.

She nocked an arrow and studied the target, inhaling slowly to reset her focus. The dryness in her mouth distracted her. Why couldn't she find her center when aiming? She swallowed, trying to create moisture, cursing Maligon's refusal to deal with the water shortage.

The fortress limped along with little to no water. For some, it was no hardship. Drought came to Moniah often enough, so the people knew and accepted its limited supply. Shana, raised near a river, never went without it. Her family had very few possessions or wealth, but they always had water.

Approaching footsteps distracted her again, this time from her thirst. Unable to stop the involuntary response to sound, she slid her gaze to the side and confirmed what her ears already told her. Pultarch approached, the hint of his swagger reflected in his steps. The young lord stopped just inside the fence, leaned his back against the railings, and crossed his arms over his chest, a smirk on his face. He said nothing.

Ignoring him, she lifted the bow and sighted down the field at the target. As Honest had taught her, she attempted to focus again, drawing in a slow breath and releasing it through her lips. She did this again, then again, then again. Just as she began to release the arrow, a quiet scuffle of sound came from where Pultarch stood. She whipped around, the arrow pointed just over the young man's ear.

Pultarch jumped in alarm, hands thrown up. As if his hands could stop an arrow. Beyond him, a hyena slinked. Ever since the fire, animals continued to creep into the fortress. No manner of temporary construction over the large hole in the outer wall stopped them.

She dropped the bow and grabbed her hatchet from her belt.

She flung it. Somersaulting past Pultarch's hip, it plunged into the hyena's head with a pleasing thunk.

Pultarch jumped as it skimmed past him, yelping in alarm. The hyena fell on the spot.

"Nice control." Honest beamed in approval.

One didn't work in a tavern, armed with all manner of knives and tools, without picking up the ability to use them. She glanced at Honest, noting his efforts to not laugh out loud.

Pultarch's reaction came too late. *If* she'd been aiming for him. She stifled a desire to chuckle and approached her quarry.

The hyena lay in a pool of blood, the last spasms of death jerking its limbs.

Pultarch pushed up from the ground, dusting off his pants as she approached. He eyed the hyena, his shoulders tensed. Speculation ghosted in his eyes. "Did you mean to threaten me with that move? Or did you seek to protect me?"

She smiled, said nothing, studied the hyena, shoved it with her foot, and, convinced it was dead, yanked the hatchet free.

"Whatever do you mean, my lord?" Her voice dripped like sweet, golden honey while she wiped the blade off on a patch of dried grass. "Would you rather I jump on the fence and scream? Maybe, I should call to you, 'Watch out, my love'?"

She sauntered back to her bow.

One foot shoving the animal to double-check her effectiveness at killing it, Pultarch grimaced then followed her. "You're in a fine mood this morning, my queen. What can I do to serve you and improve your day? Shall I stand against the wall with an apple on my head?" He studied the target with its array of arrows, none near the center. "Maybe not. You really are not good at this, are you?"

When had they resorted to sarcasm? She couldn't recall. It just came out one day and never stopped. Pultarch embraced it as much as she. So much that Maligon had berated them the other day for acting childish. At least, it hadn't gotten her thrown out of his planning sessions. In fact, just the opposite. Most of the time, Maligon appeared entertained at their constant barbs. Honest, too, but she expected for a different reason than Maligon's.

"Did you come to torment me, my lord, or do you have a purpose for this lovely visit? Maybe you wish the services of a teacher? You could learn a thing or two about decorum toward a lady from Brother Honest, I'm sure."

In an obvious effort to appear unaffected by his near-miss with a hatchet, Pultarch put on his practiced smile and sauntered closer to her. "No. I'm well-graced with a fine education befitting a nobleman, just like our queen...should be."

A taunt unworthy of her attention, Shana turned toward the target again. An education outside of formal arrangements gave her far more understanding of this world than his. "So, you're here to pester me. Wonderful. Honest, would you like to keep score?"

"Tempting, but no," Pultarch said. "Maligon asked me to locate Brother Honest. You may come, too, of course, as his ever-present shadow."

That jibe hit the mark. Shana paused and thumbed the hatchet blade's edge. Sharp, smooth, easy to plunge into his gourd of a head.

"Please tell the Lord that Shana and I will attend him soon." Honest's face revealed nothing regarding the request.

His ability to hide his feelings about Maligon and the offal scum surrounding him amazed Shana. Instead, she took her frustrations out on Pultarch. Who could blame her? The boy presented so many opportunities.

After Pultarch strolled away, Honest turned to her, lips twitching. "I worried when you two started fighting each other with words. Today, you turned up the heat, little queen. An act to defer any concerns over your strengths—and you possess many—or is the young noble destroying your incredible sense of control?"

"Both." She didn't hesitate to answer the question, one she'd worried over several times. "What if Maligon forces us to marry? He hasn't brought up the betrothal since the attack on the keep. I'm afraid he'll spring it on me one day, and by the end of that day, I'll be owned by that pompous bag of camel dung."

Rather than chuckle at her word choice, Honest stared at the ground, his gaze unfocused. She waited, aware he would speak when ready. It didn't take long.

"I should have found a way for you to escape that night. Maligon doesn't even mention you as the true queen anymore. All pretense disappeared like ashes on the wind after the fire."

She'd noticed. "Do you think he's changed his plans? Or is it due to Kalara's injuries? He's worried about her."

The pounding of many feet in perfect cadence kept her from saying more. A more organized line of soldiers marched past them. Most of these soldiers looked intent on their duty. To her or to Maligon?

The man bordered on crazy, but most in the fortress never saw the truth behind his benevolent façade. She'd seen people driven to madness enough times in her other lives to recognize the signs. Most crazy people posed no threat due to their inability to focus, but others destroyed everything in their path. Maligon was the second kind of crazy.

"How does he expect to provide food and drink for this many, anyway?" Shana watched the troops disappear around the corner. Still no plans for rationing existed. Maligon refused to acknowledge the blow Kassa's attack delivered him.

Honest shook his head, no answer available today as in every day since the attack. They gathered her wayward arrows, asked a soldier to dispose of the hyena, and headed for the royal wing and the crazy traitor controlling their lives.

Before they reached Maligon's chambers, Shana laid a hand on

Honest's arm. She tilted her head toward the room, a silent hint she wanted to eavesdrop. Within the special pocket she'd sewn into her tunic, the jerboa rested, warm and helpful.

"You're too weakened to fight." Maligon's voice sounded tired as if he repeated this not for the first time.

"I'm not." Kalara's voice struck with the iron of conviction. "You want to rely on her? She couldn't do the simplest tasks you've asked."

Who? Shana lifted the jerboa from his sleeping position and cradled him in her hands. Honest didn't even blink when she withdrew the rodent. She'd told him how contact with Bauns helped her hear better. It worked best, she discovered, when holding him in her hands.

Maligon heaved a deep, rattling sigh. "I need you well, fully recovered. The rains come soon, and we must strike before then. Sarx will be here before long with Elwar's troops."

Sarx. His name sent ants skittering along Shana's nerves. She shivered at the possibility of facing his sleazy gaze again. And now the arrogant man brought Elwar's troops. She'd seen the size of Elwar's army. Watched them march on holidays, line after unending line of well-trained soldiers. If Sarx commanded the same army, Adana wouldn't stand a chance.

"You don't need her. You need me. I possess more experience leading armies. She's a trained scavenger. I'm the leader." Samantha's boast echoed with agitation.

Kalara went on as if Samantha hadn't spoken. "Are you sure you trust him? Or Quilla? I was not impressed by her. Moving troops just before the rains is not wise, either."

"That's why I need you returned to health and Elwar's troops backing us up," Maligon said.

"Will you listen to me?" Samantha said. "You don't need Quilla, or Sarx, or Elwar, or your daughter. We have enough men and

Watchers. We can't wait any longer. My sources tell me the numbers at the keep dwindle. People escaping before the rains."

The rains presented a problem. According to Malay and the others in the fortress, torrential rains would soon drown the land, forming massive violent rivers, dangerous with power.

"Jealousy doesn't become you, Samantha," Kalara said, a sneer in her voice.

"No. Not jealous." Unlike before, Samantha's voice revealed a return of her Watcher's control. She sounded like the high-ranking soldier she was. "I'm stating facts. When have you ever led a raid? I'm not counting those ridiculous attacks on the villages of Moniah as you escorted your father across the kingdom. You didn't fight trained soldiers then. I have."

"You've commanded more, but I've led Watchers into places no one else could go. I know how to plan. I know how to disappear from sight then strike."

"You plan to sneak into the keep and strike? What of their army?"

"You claim it's smaller," Kalara said. "With Sarx's arrival, we'll have the numbers."

"My informants say it's smaller. Any soldier knows to doubt their sources. I prefer a large-scale attack, leaving nothing to chance."

"On the walls? We failed in that attempt already." Kalara's voice drew closer as if she approached the doorway. "They hold the fortified ground. Not us. But we'll have the numbers."

Honest tapped Shana's shoulder and tilted his head back toward the hallway. She followed him and, out of sight, whispered what she'd heard.

"Sarx?" Honest searched her face, asking a question she wanted to avoid for now. He, more than anyone, knew the turmoil the man's presence left in her stomach. "When?"

"I don't know. Soon."

Maligon's army numbered several thousand already. Adding El-war's army would triple their numbers, or more.

How large an army did Adana have? Questionable sources claimed Jerold and Halar left the keep gathering troops. Had they succeeded or run into Maligon's scouts?

"They'll notice our delay if we don't go in now." Honest started down the hall. "We must find a way to send warning to Adana."

Shana scurried behind him, stowing Bauns inside her tunic where the jerboa nestled in a warm heap and went to sleep.

33

The tunnels grew overly warm with the gathered refugees, soldiers, and Watchers, but Adana forced herself to embrace the heat after her brisk walk in the cooling air on the ramparts. Rain would soon come to Moniah. It arrived early this year; she could feel it.

Here on the border, the keep's inhabitants predicted an early snowfall, too. The chill air outside agreed with them.

The numbers of people in the tunnel, although not enough to carry out a successful attack on Maligon, still filled her with pride like when her mother used to talk with her after a long day of training. She would build her up to face the trials of her eventual reign, never doubting her ability to achieve all they set before her.

These people believed in her and Kiffen. They embraced the plan to reunite the kingdoms and rid Moniah and Elwar of Maligon once and for all. She would succeed where her mother had failed. Complete Kassa's mission and eliminate the traitor forever. For this, she'd been born.

A year ago, the thought of eliminating someone, snuffing out their life, would have horrified her. War changed people. Montee told her this often.

Many called out to her as they went about their work. Except for the closed-in surroundings, the industrious activity reminded her of her youth when she wandered the wings and grounds of the fortress.

A jolt slammed into her shoulder, and she stumbled to a halt, gasping from the intensity. Her vision danced with lights and went black. She leaned against the wall, eyes closed, breathing deeply.

Her shoulder hurt most days, a dull throbbing she'd learned to ignore. Ever since she'd found Kassa and Umgani, it had remained steady, neither increasing nor decreasing. Until now.

What had happened? She blinked until her sight cleared, then rushed forward. Kassa would know what to do. No, not Kassa, Montee. She must find them both.

A young page flailed his arms and danced out of her way as she rounded the corner, almost bowling him over.

He bobbed his head, cheeks flushed with high spots of red. "Forgive me, Queen Adana."

With a distracted nod she pushed by him. "No matter. We did not collide. Please remember, stay on the left side to avoid collisions." It took only a few days of life in the tunnels for Montee to create that plan.

When the page turned to follow her, she tilted her head in question. Annoyance at the delay tightened her chest, but she fought it down and stopped to face the page, eyebrows raised.

"Forgive me, but the First Vision sent me to locate you," he said. "She's with the former First."

That solved one thing—where to find both Watchers—but the boy's words increased her shoulder's throbbing. Her pulse became a tangible percussion beneath her skin. "Is something wrong?"

After returning to the keep, Kassa stayed alert long enough to share the news of Suru's death. The rest of her report came from Umgani and Dosata. For five days, the former First Vision had refused to rise from her bed and slept most of the time. Two days ago, she refused food or water.

The page jogged to keep up with Adana as she hurried toward the room where Kassa recuperated. "She didn't appear worried."

Aware of the boy's frantic effort to keep pace with her, Adana slowed. Whether urgent or not, she should not leave the boy panting in her wake. Rumors started that way. A lesson Montee taught her only a few weeks ago.

"Did she send someone for the king?"

The boy nodded.

"Good."

The word didn't match her feelings though. If Montee sent for both of them, either Kassa decided to return to the living and demanded to talk with them or...

Adana refused to consider the other option.

She spotted Kiffen passing through the crowds from the opposite end of the hallway. They would reach the hospital corridor together. Gazes fastened on each other, she sensed his concern through the tightness of his jaw and the link. He tilted his head, gaze darting to her shoulder. A question.

After her brief nod, imperceptible to anyone not looking for it, he frowned and picked up his pace. A young boy trotted along in his wake just as her own page shadowed her. Sharing the sight of Kiffen strolling without concern to Am'brosia, she waited for him to slow as she had done. It took mere seconds. He raised his head in sudden awareness and slowed his feet.

She sent an apologetic smile in his direction.

Then they were together, turning down the corridor. This part of the tunnels, the infirmary, was not overrun with crowds, so they reached the door to Kassa's room all too soon. She longed to push it open yet hesitated to do so. Kiffen turned to face the two boys following them.

"Remain here in case we have need of you," he said. "Thank you for finding us quickly."

The boys beamed at each other, unaware of the serious nature of their tasks. All the children raised in the keep thrilled at the hustle around them. Childish ideas of valor and strength and, of course, winning battles probably populated their waking hours, and dreams, too.

Kiffen reached for her hand, twining their fingers together. They pushed open the door and entered the room together.

Kassa lay on the bed. Her wiry body appeared bent into sharp angles in the candlelight, as if the skin sticking to her bones might slide off at any moment. Father Tonch sat on one side and Montee on the other. The First Vision rose and faced them, not diminishing the concern in her eyes. "I don't think she'll last much longer."

Blinking back a sudden surge of tears, Adana stared at the bed. Somehow, she managed to approach it and perch on the edge. She lifted Kassa's hand and brushed a kiss across it. This hand commanded obedience with a simple twitch, held a bow and shot with impeccable aim, brushed her hair and helped arrange it to Quilla's satisfaction in Elwar. Now, it felt like dry bones in her hands. "Kassa?"

The woman did not move or open her eyes. Hearing was supposed to be the last sense to go, so Adana bent close to her head on the pillow. "I love you, Kassa. Please stay and teach me." The words clogged in her throat as she whispered them, but she managed to choke them out.

She flashed back to that dreadful morning when she sat by her mother's side as she died, then ran, unable to face the end. She would not do that today.

Kiffen's hand came to rest on her shoulder. She soaked in his comfort, aware he knew the bond she'd formed with Kassa, the only constant guide during her nine seasons in Elwar.

Kiffen spoke, his voice soft in the room. "Have you summoned Umgani and Dosata?"

"Yes. And Vuur. We'll take her above once they arrive."

The instant flex in Kiffen's body hinted that he stiffened at this plan. He hadn't grasped this part of being a Watcher, yet. How could he, having never lived in the fortress surrounded by their ways and customs? Watchers yearned for sky and land and sight to the horizons. One did not deny them one last look. Kassa provided it for her mother, and she meant to offer her the same blessing.

At least he didn't voice his objection. A flicker of her thoughts washed through the bond with Am'brosia and on to Bai'dish. This odd way of communicating between them, still new and uncomfortable, offered help in the strangest ways.

When the others who had been called had gathered in the corridor outside the tiny room, Vuur came in and bowed low to Adana, Kiffen, and Father Tonch. Then he lifted Kassa in his bulging arms and Montee tucked a blanket around her, the gesture so maternal it drew Adana from the reality of the moment.

Kassa murmured something, but her eyes did not open.

"Yes, First, we do," Vuur responded, his deep voice soft and gentle.

When they entered the main hallway, the cessation of all activity struck Adana like a gong ringing in her head. People lined the corridor, four or five deep, heads bowed in respect. She and Kassa's closest companions walked in a solemn line toward the hidden stairs leading into the keep.

Simeon and Glume waited at the stairwell's entrance. Their procession wound up the stairs, Vuur in the lead, followed by Adana and Kiffen. All the Watchers within the keep followed, Montee taking up the rear position.

Adana swallowed hard to keep the tears from streaming down her face, but as Vuur turned a corner, she saw streaks of wetness on his cheek. If a man of such strength and power could cry, maybe she could, too.

She'd never believed Kassa would die, just like she never believed her mother would die. Even when she found Kassa injured by the stream, she expected her to push through. A force to be reckoned with, this frail body in Vuur's arms could not be the Watcher all trainees feared and longed to please.

As she followed Vuur onto the wall, streams of Watchers and the keep's inhabitants emerged from other points and stretched in a line along the ramparts. The absence of Halar and Samantha gnawed at her soul. Kassa should not die without her family to say goodbye.

A breeze had picked up in the short time since she'd left the walls. It dispersed the banks of clouds hiding the sun, uncovering the azure blue of the sky. As sunlight spilled over them, Kassa stirred and blinked up at Vuur. A thankful smile spread over her face. She lifted her hand and patted his cheek, once, twice. He took her to the midpoint of the southern wall and stopped there, smiling down at her. She stared up at him, her face relaxed and grateful.

The Watchers along the walls undid their braids, their hair catching in the breeze. Adana reached up to follow their actions, the ritual dredging up more memories of her mother's death. She'd refused to do it then, to offer the Watcher's promise she would not battle her in death. Weak and close to releasing her soul, her mother had found strength one last time to order her to do it.

The chill of the wind whipped around her, running through her hair like Kassa's hands once did.

A quiet murmur started to her right and spread down the line of Watchers. Each watched something over the wall. Adana inched forward in time to see the giraffe guard in a silent rhythm of movement turn sideways, one at a time. The ripple of motion created a wave like wind blowing over the grasslands. Each one kept an eye on the territory beyond the keep while focusing the other on the gathering along the wall.

Adana sent a swell of appreciation to Am'brosia, and she returned it with an embrace of peace and love.

When she returned her gaze to Vuur and Kassa, the Isati motioned for her to step forward and speak to her mentor. With a gentle hand, she stroked Kassa's forehead. "The sun chased the clouds away for you, my teacher. And the giraffes stand with you." She blinked, unable to conquer the surge of tears anymore. Eyes welling, she did not turn from the green-eyed gaze of her stand-in mother. Kassa's eyes glowed with a depth of light Adana never saw there before.

She moved her lips a bit, gaze transfixed on Adana.

Adana leaned in.

"Trust Creator." Her voice came out dry and crackling like wheat dried in the fields.

Cold not caused by the wind chased down her arms. The hawk-eyed glare flashed in Kassa's eyes, momentary but evident.

"I'll try." She couldn't offer more.

The lips moved again, and the words croaked out slow but determined. "Kill. Him. For. Me."

No question who Kassa meant. Conviction filled her chest, and she straightened into the stance of a Watcher before her commander. "I will," she said, voice firm. She grasped Kassa's bony hand until the woman dropped her own from the comforting grip. Then Adana stepped back, allowing Umgani, Dosata, and Montee to approach.

The breeze blew toward her, so she heard the words Kassa gave to them. "Samantha...has...part. Must...do...it."

The three Watchers, Adana, and Kiffen stiffened at these words. Had Kassa received a last vision? It often happened at the end of immensely powerful Watchers' lives. Miri had done so. Now Kassa.

The witnesses to this honorable warrior's life remained on the walls looking to the horizon as the sun climbed to its peak and shone over the gathering, lending warmth to fight the cooler winds of despair. Kassa said nothing else, turning her head to stare toward the south, the one place where the trees did not block her sight. As the sun began to inch toward its descent, she breathed out a sigh.

Breath caught in Adana's lungs as she waited for Kassa's chest to rise again.

It did not.

Overhead, a screeching cry tore through the air. A hawk winged above them, circling the keep, then soared southward on the wind.

The giraffes lifted their heads to the hawk. An eerie bugling rose from Tog first, then the others, their tone grief-stricken and haunting. Adana shivered. She'd heard this lament twice—when they mourned the loss of giraffes lost in battle and on the day her mother and her mother's giraffe died. So many reminders of her mother's death surged into her thoughts today.

A sudden bustle of movement behind her interrupted Adana's thoughts. People began to step aside, one after another, making room for someone who pushed toward her. Glume, unchecked tears running down his cheeks, emerged from the press of people.

When he reached her side, he took a moment to look upon Kassa's still face, peaceful in repose, an expression of acceptance sweeping his features. The giraffes continued their lament as he spoke, his voice full of wonder. "The giraffes honor Kassa's long service to them and Moniah. She's not a royal and did not bond with a giraffe, but they choose to mourn her as one and help send her soul to the Creator, anyway."

On the wind, the scents of dried grass and the promise of coming rains combined with the giraffes' song. It echoed across the lake and followed the flight of the hawk.

Adana's gaze found the fading shape of the bird in its flight south toward home. Without conscious thought, she laid her hand on Kassa's shoulder. In a flash, she soared with the hawk over the ground. Below, a huge undulating snake slithered out of the forest. Tilting her head forward to see better, the bird responded and dove toward the snake. They skimmed above the constant motion. The snake shifted into thousands of snakes coiled over and under each other. Lifted higher on the breeze, she and the hawk rose above the massive serpent and glided to the front of the slithering mass. An icy fist gripped her insides when she saw the front of the snake. It had two heads with the faces of Quilla and Sarx. They slid across the land.

In the distance, the walls of Adana's View loomed.

34

A chilly wind swept over Leera's troops as they trudged toward the keep. Today, as every day, more and more soldiers found them, emerging like wraiths from their hiding places. Some wore simple clothes, others the uniform of Elwar. All warned of Sarx and Quilla leading an army toward Moniah to help Maligon.

Leera's army, if Callan's count was accurate, numbered over three thousand. Enough to cause them to break into smaller camps, each focused on their own food and needs.

According to today's arrivals, many fled her mother's army at night, one after another slipping away in the dark of the forest. All claimed allegiance to her and, through her, to Kiffen.

The earlier confidence Leera found among her men extinguished like a doused campfire at the news of her mother's proximity. Elwar's army numbered tens of thousands of soldiers. These deserters to her mother's cause brought hope, but the majority still rode with Sarx. Quilla would not take their desertion well. Scouts would seek them.

Catch, caught up in the excitement of traveling with soldiers, had stopped riding by her side days ago, so she blinked at him in surprise when he guided his horse next to hers. He searched her face with a worried frown.

"What?" she asked, the old crossness returning to her voice.

"You look worried. I wanted to check on you."

A wry smile crossed her face. "You've stayed away for many days now. Why check on me now?"

"You didn't look like you needed me before." He shrugged. "Today, you remind me of this spoiled girl I knew whose mother locked her in her chambers."

That straightened Leera's back. Her action straightened Catch's too. He leaned toward her and whispered, "I know who you are if you don't."

"What is that supposed to mean?" she said.

"You are the princess who defied Queen Quilla's plans. The one who kicked me in the shins and made me limp for a week. You are the king's sister. And you lead an army to aid him."

"You see all of that?"

He gave a big nod. "I do. And more. Your men do, too. They brag about you around their campfires."

That made her want to squirm with pleasure, but she forced herself to sit still. "That's ridiculous. What do they brag about?"

"How you embrace responsibility and stand up for those who can't defend themselves. They hope your brother and the queen are as special as you."

His words pressed the weight of her father's ring against her chest. Hanging from the chain around her neck, she'd become accustomed to its presence. A memory flashed in her mind of sitting in her father's council chambers as he used the ring to press his seal into orders. When he set it down, she'd reached for it, tiny fingers itching for the shiny object. Her father had covered it with his hand and turned a serious face toward her. "This ring, my little one, carries much power. It's not a toy for you to play with."

When she pouted, he sat back and patted his leg, an invitation to crawl into her favorite spot, his lap. He held the ring over her cupped hands and let it drop into them. She gasped at the weight.

His plump fingers rotated it in her palms, revealing the lion head engraving. "This seal is as good as me standing in front of someone giving a command." Pulling the parchment he'd been reading toward him, he spilled a bit of wax on it. With a light touch, he lifted her hands and the ring and together they pressed it into the wax. "Now this can go anywhere with my seal, and it's as if I delivered it myself."

"Oh Papa," she'd said, "when can I have a ring like this?"

His face turned somber then. "The Creator willing, you never need one."

She'd pouted again, and he'd laughed at her and told her to run along. The next year on her birth celebration, he gave her a tiny wooden ring with a swan engraved in it and a stick of wax. She wondered whatever happened to it.

As if it branded her, the ring warmed against her skin. Soon, Kiffen would wear the ring and protect the people. Not her. She was the swan.

She thought about Catch's words. "They see me as a protector?" The idea sounded ludicrous. Did she really seek to help those who couldn't? Maybe. She'd been one of the downtrodden most of her life. That thought made her want to snort. No one who knew the spoiled Princess Leera would ever describe her as downtrodden, would they? But then Catch had done so a moment ago, comparing her to the girl locked in her chambers in Elwar.

"They will be pleased in what they find in my brother and Adana," she said. "Tell them for me."

Together, the three of them would stop Maligon. With Jerold's help, of course.

As she pondered these thoughts, a hawk flew overhead, screaming. It swooped low over the group and circled them, its wings outstretched. One of the men raised his bow to shoot it, and Leera kicked her horse toward him, frantic to reach him before he shot. "Stop! Do not shoot it down."

The men around her stopped and stared at her. She'd sounded like the spoiled princess just then, but their faces revealed confusion and curiosity, not the disrespect or dislike she'd known in the past.

The soldier lowered his bow. "If you say so, Your Highness. But it would have fed a few of us."

"Maybe. But not that hawk."

That hawk was not meant for dinner. She knew it, somehow.

* * *

Jerold and Halar rode into the village of Roshar late in the afternoon. Unlike the last time Jerold visited the small village, it bustled with energy. Several of the villagers crowded around them or scurried to the outskirts of town where they'd left the recruits they'd gathered along the way.

Adana built her first army in Roshar, finding refuge here after Maligon's attack on her caravan when traveling from Elwar to Moniah. When she left Roshar, brimming with confidence in their plan to stop Maligon, the village's population should have dropped to less than forty people. Except more houses lined the road, now. Several new shops filled in the gaps on the main road. It appeared many of the refugees remained here, making Roshar their home.

Where else would they go? Maligon still held most of Moniah thanks to Samantha's treachery. She delivered the death blow to the battle outside Adana's View when she struck down Linus, the Commander of Adana's army, and then opened the gates to Maligon. That knowledge still made Jerold's body tense with a need to strike out at her.

He glanced sideways at Halar. A true soldier, the man never revealed his thoughts toward his daughter's choices. Jerold doubted anyone plucked up the daring to ask either, at least not Kassa, anyway. Her tongue remained strong and dangerous when she spoke of her loyalty to Adana. He'd seen new lines on her face since Nuala brought her the news, though.

Halar might want to talk about it. Just not here in the open.

"Shall we go to the temple or the inn?" Jerold said.

"I think the inn," Halar answered. He glanced over at Biaji, the Watcher who traveled with them. "Do you have a preference?"

Astride a horse—because the men insisted until she gave in—she studied the people going about their business. "We'll learn more at the inn, but Queen Morana resided in the temple when we were here before."

"Would you prefer to go to the temple while we go to the inn?" Jerold asked.

"No." The word came out clipped and blunt, her eyebrows turned a slight angle downward, the closest a Watcher came to showing displeasure.

"I meant no disrespect to a warrior of Moniah," Jerold said, once more aware of the Watcher's concern that their recruiting efforts so far only produced men.

No women came forward in the villages. Even the few who showed signs of Watcher gifts hung back or, most likely, were forced back by their parents. A drawback of the two cultures of Moniah and Elwar merging. Women served with pride in Moniah. In Elwar, where part of their journey took them, women looked askance at Biaji's uniform and scoffed at the idea of fighting a battle.

Her face relaxed. "I accept your apology, Sir Jerold."

He hadn't shared his identity with her. A few people in Roshar knew him as the Belwyn prince, but hopefully they continued to protect his secret.

Before they reached the inn, the plump innkeeper, Talia, hurried down the street toward him, her billowing green pants and white shirt rustling. She stopped before him, a wary look on her face.

"Greetings, Sir Jerold, First Soldier, Watcher. How may our village serve you?"

Jerold leapt down from his horse and beamed at the woman. "Talia, it is good to see you well. We've come in search of news."

She glanced between the three of them, then took a moment to stare in the distance where their ramshackle army went about making camp. "Another army to share our meals?" Her tone hinted at dismay. "We've barely recovered from the last army's time here."

For the first time, Halar stepped forward. Intent on Talia's reluctance, Jerold had missed the man's dismount and tried not to jerk in surprise when the commander's deep voice spoke to his immediate left.

"InnkeeperTalia, well met. I am Halar, Commander of the First Soldiers of Moniah. I wish to thank you personally for the hospitality and aid you provided our queen during her sojourn here. Without your help, we might no longer command an army."

"Pretty words for a soldier." Talia squinted up at him. "Well, Commander Halar, we were honored to share our village with the queen, but we have little left to share. Yours isn't the first, second, or third army to travel through here since."

Jerold stiffened at these words, even though he knew other armies patrolled across Moniah and the border. "Whose armies?"

Talia shook her head. "Not here."

People around them pretended to continue their daily tasks, but Jerold noted many worked without the laughter and conversation of a few moments ago. They leaned in closer to overhear.

"We bring our own provisions," Halar said, dipping his head in respect. "The goods we ask from you are words not food."

"For your men, that is good. I do have food, not much and not fancy, but I can spare a bit for the three of you." She turned and headed toward the inn.

The inn had been small and simple when he'd last been here.

Built from earthen walls on the first floor with a wooden porch and second floor above, it provided a few rooms for lodging and a tiny tavern for food and drink. That building was gone. In the same spot sat a large, three-story inn constructed of the finest wood. A sign over the door read Talia's Tavern.

Jerold whistled through his teeth, a habit his mother detested. "Your establishment appears to have flourished from the inconvenience of travelers."

A deep chuckle sounded from the woman. "I didn't say *all* had gone poorly, mind you. We gained a certain level of fame once two queens stayed here." She strode up the stone steps to the porch. "I couldn't ask Queen Morana to stay in my humble hovel, now could I?"

"She's here then?" Jerold hurried to catch up to the innkeeper's stride. "The queen?" Hope pounded his heart against his ribs. If Morana lived at the inn, then she must fear less for her safety. "And the empress? King Ariff?"

"You best come in," she said.

Talia's reticence plummeted his heartbeat. Jerold fought the urge to pepper Talia with questions but followed her inside. The woman was right. They should not discuss royalty in the streets like common peasants.

Inside, wooden floors gleamed with a high polish. Huge candelabras cast a bright glow around the main tavern. The first inn held four maybe five tables. The new one had three times as many and a hearth large enough to stand in. At this hour of the day, the aroma of a stew wafted from the rear of the building and several patrons relaxed at the tables, eating and drinking.

"Back here." Talia led them through the room and into a side hall. "These doors lead to private dining rooms."

He counted five. "You have done well, Talia."

"I have." She pulled a key from her pocket and unlocked the last door on the left. "This is the room the queen uses to receive visitors. It provides access to her rooms on the third floor." Talia locked the door behind them and crossed to another door in the rear of the room. "I think it might be best if she receives you in her rooms. She's not been well."

"Wait a moment." Jerold stopped in the middle of the room and waited for Talia to turn around. "Has she received bad news? Of King Ariff. Have you heard from him? Or the empress?"

Talia's shoulders sagged, her hands falling to her sides. Even the billowing innkeeper's pants lost the ability to flap around her as she moved.

This reaction rocked Jerold's calm demeanor on its side.

Until then, he'd maintained hope. No one needed to remind him of the prolonged period without word. Someone would write or send a message if anything had happened, he'd told himself over and over. A tiny reminder whispered to him that absence of information rarely meant good news. No one held back good news as a surprise. Not this long.

"How bad?" Halar asked, keeping a cautious eye on Jerold.

Talia gestured for them to sit. When they did, she lowered herself into the chair closest to her. "Some of the Watchers who accompanied King Ariff to Belwyn returned three days ago. With them, they brought three Watchers rescued from the dungeons."

Jerold jumped to his feet. "And the empress?"

Patting her palm in the air, Talia gestured for him to sit again. "They rescued her. She remains in Belwyn, but she's weak and ill. Once Maligon left Belwyn, the soldiers he left in charge mistreated all the prisoners."

Sweat beaded on Jerold's forehead. He flushed hot, then cold, then hot again. What torture had his mother endured? Fists balled at his sides, he paced the room.

Before he or Talia could speak, Biaji spoke in a low, urgent voice. "Ten Watchers went with King Ariff. Did all ten return?"

Talia shook her head. "It's best if—"

"It's best if I tell it, Talia." A firm voice came from the doorway. Queen Morana, dark shadows under her eyes, stood at the foot of the stairs beyond the door. "Will you bring up some wine, Talia? But only you, please, no one else. I would prefer no rumors getting out at the moment."

Dread squeezed Jerold's heart as he rose and greeted Morana, placing a kiss on both of her cheeks. She gripped his arms as he held hers, noting her frailness, her bones like a small bird. Her hazel eyes faded almost to yellow as if most of the color had leached out of them with her tears. She didn't cry at the moment, but her red eyes left no doubt.

"Talia didn't mention Ariff."

She shook her head. "He's gone." Before Jerold could react, she turned and started up the stairwell. "Come. We must discuss what to do."

35

⚜

The stairwell led to a large room filled with comfortable chairs and couches upholstered in deep burgundy fabric. A desk sat in front of a large window, a sheaf of papers jumbled on its surface, writing quill tossed to the side.

Following Jerold's gaze, Morana grimaced. "I've tried to write you many times."

He nodded and took her by the elbow, leading her to the chair he suspected she used. Beside it sat a basket with needles and thread. She settled in the seat with a nod of thanks then turned to stare out the window. The fields of Roshar's farms stretched into the distance. The window faced north, toward Belwyn. How many days had she sat there watching for her husband's safe return?

When all were seated and settled, Jerold swallowed hard. He wanted to know everything, but questions felt wrong under the circumstances. Should he ask Morana to re-open the wounds of loss so soon after they were inflicted on her?

Morana decided for him, turning to face them. "For a time, Ariff hid in the foothills of your kingdom, gathering news. Remnants of the force King Donel sent from Elwar several months ago stumbled upon his camp late one day. They never made it to Belwyn after being attacked in the middle of the night, just like Queen Adana. The survivors loyal to Elwar fled and hid. They knew nothing of what's happened since. Still, Ariff managed to piece together information about the army left behind in Belwyn."

A door on the far side of the room opened, and Talia entered carrying a tray with two carafes, five goblets, and a plate of bread and cheese. "Supper is almost ready. I'll bring it when you're ready. Meanwhile, I thought you'd like something to tide you over. The bread is fresh out of the ovens." After placing the tray on a table near Morana, she began to serve. Halar rose to take over, but she waved his efforts away.

Halar blinked at her in shock.

Jerold echoed his reaction, realizing the woman meant to stay for their meeting.

"If you're concerned about privacy, Commander, Talia knows everything," Morana said. "She and I run a network of spies from here."

An unexpected, but welcome, piece of news. Jerold turned to Talia with new interest. "You never cease to find ways, do you?"

Talia gave each of them a filled goblet. "We, the queen and I, decided we needed to stay aware of any happenings in the area. Especially once the messenger birds quit arriving. We learned about Adana's View, first. I'm sorry for the pain that must have caused the queen and Kassa and you, Commander Halar."

The man waved her condolences away with a shake of his head, an expression of gratitude washing over his face for a moment. Jerold watched this; he should have spoken to the man about his losses sooner.

"So many people remained here, stuck with no plans or place to go while Maligon held their lands. We decided to give them a purpose." Talia sat back down.

"Did you learn of Ariff's movements through your spies?" Jerold said.

"Spying on Watchers and a king is a difficult task for a trained spy, much less one without experience," Morana said. "We learned nothing of use until a week ago. Ariff suspected the bulk of Maligon's army rode out of Belwyn to aid in the siege of Adana's View. We're not sure when they left, but they left very few in place."

"Quite a few left before I came to you," Jerold said. "That's why Ariff decided to attempt to rescue my mother."

Biaji gave a slight jerk. She turned to look at him, speculation on her face. "Your mother?"

"Yes, I'm sorry to not tell you." Jerold bowed in her direction, chastising himself for the slip. "It's been a secret for so long."

Morana waited until Biaji settled back in her seat, stoic face returned.

"Ariff led a force into the castle with little trouble," Morana said. "Found your mother and the Watchers in the dungeons. Three of them still lived. All had been blinded."

A sharp gasp escaped Biaji's controlled demeanor, but she said nothing when the others turned to look at her. Even a Watcher could only handle so many surprises.

"Yes, Biaji," Morana said. "The injuries to them troubled all of us. They are here. You will want to see them soon."

Morana's gaze wandered back to the window. Every time she did this, her recitation tapered off as she watched for a man who would never return.

"Your mother was ill and malnourished. They all were. Ariff ran into little resistance until they tried to leave the dungeon. Soldiers waited for them and cut down many as they exited the stairs." The tiny queen shuddered and took a sip of her wine. "Ariff, the Watchers with him, and ten of Elwar's men fought them off while the others escaped. Only eight of his soldiers survived—two Watchers and six from Elwar. And your mother and the injured Watchers."

It felt like someone shoved Jerold in the back, a blow that sent you sprawling, unable to draw air. One you didn't know was coming but should have anticipated. Jerold stared at Morana, amazed at her calm, flat narration. Shock. He sank back into his chair.

No one spoke or moved until a rap on the door made all but Morana jump. Talia rose and opened it a small crack, whispered something, and closed it, again.

"Dinner is ready," she said then returned to her seat. "I told them we will call for it in a moment."

Unable to stay quiet any longer, Jerold leaned forward, directing his question toward Talia. "Eleven people returned? Six soldiers, two Watchers, three injured Watchers."

"No." Talia sat back. "Belwyn soldiers escorted them. Several of the military remain loyal to your mother. They pretended to support Maligon's cause to survive. I believe you have a few hundred soldiers guarding the castle against attack and thirty here, waiting for you."

"And my mother?"

"Too weak to travel," Talia said. "It was cold and damp in the dungeon. She went days without food or adequate clothing."

Another punch, this one squeezing the breath from his chest. Rising to his feet, Jerold said, "I must be with her."

Talia nodded. "We sent one of the brothers from our temple to heal her but have not heard from him. It's good you arrived today."

Morana reached out and touched his hand. "You must know everything first."

Running his hands through his hair, Jerold began to pace the room, again. "What else is there to know?"

At the same time, Biaji sat forward. "Are there any remnants of Maligon's men still in Belwyn?"

"No," Morana whispered but everyone heard her. "The kingdom is Gabriella's again. Those who remained to protect the empress started cleaning out the riffraff while the others brought word here. They are making it suitable for you."

The ramification of her words struck him. Jerold spun on his heel. "For me? How would they know it's for me?"

The deep-set, hazel eyes of Teletia's widowed queen regarded him. "Your mother's first action after retaking the castle was to announce your true birth. She told them you are now emperor."

"No. She lives." Jerold marched toward the door. "I need to see my mother."

"And you shall," Morana said. "You can be there by morning if you hurry, but I will ask a favor of the two of you."

Jerold whirled around, frustration burning a fever in his body, but paused at the sight of the small queen. Her husband, in an effort to save his own mother, had lost his life. He owed her everything. "Forgive me Morana. Your loss." He bowed his head. "I regret the sacrifice King Ariff made to rescue Empress Gabriella. Whatever you seek, if I have the ability, I will aid you."

"As will I," Halar said.

"I have sent a Watcher to Teletia, Halar. I know I had no authority, but I needed to know what the situation is like there. Ostreia stayed in Roshar at Adana's behest. She and the other Watchers remaining here helped train our spies. Once we learned of Belwyn's limited guard, she insisted I send her and four others to Teletia. She left three days ago."

At her words, Jerold swallowed his fury. He'd planned to add the Watchers in Roshar to his gathering army. Losing the gifts of five Watchers crippled him more than losing five soldiers.

While he fought an internal battle of frustration, Halar spoke. "You were wise to employ Ostreia's talents. If she asked to go to Teletia, I support the decision. But, Queen Morana, what do you wish of us?"

"Will you lend me an army, some of the one you brought with you? When she returns, I would lead whatever army Ostreia gathered to aid Adana. She told me to give her six days, no more. If she's not returned, we must head for the keep. She had a vision. I don't understand the interpretation of it, but she said I should not wait more than six days. I'd like to have an army at my back when we leave, no matter how small."

The army following him and Halar consisted of Elwarians and a scattering of refugees from all four kingdoms. Would they follow a widowed queen and her young son on the journey to the keep? Maligon's men scoured the area for deserters and to force men into fighting. He raised an eyebrow toward Halar. The man shrugged and tilted his head toward Jerold, indicating he must decide.

In the past, he would have ordered it. He owed that much to Morana, but the events of the last few months revealed how easily soldiers shifted their loyalties when orders did not suit them. "If they're willing. I will not trust your safety to men disgruntled by their change in purpose."

"They'll be willing," a young boy's voice piped up from across the room. Prince Navon, the six-year-old son of Morana and Ariff, stood in the doorway, the set of his shoulders echoing his belief. From the look of him, Jerold thought he might be correct.

As twilight fell, Jerold, Halar, and Morana divided the army. Many of the men volunteered to follow Morana and Navon. Jerold, aware an army awaited him in Belwyn, urged her to take all who offered, but she refused to take more than half. The other half would follow him to Belwyn.

Thirty Belwyn soldiers waited for Jerold and Halar in the street in front of Talia's Tavern. Their horses stomped and snorted, reacting to the soldiers' anxious energy as they waited to escort their prince to their ailing empress.

Morana gave him a quick embrace for luck. "I will send word if you haven't returned before we depart. The carrier birds finally returned today. I already sent one to Belwyn, so they know to expect your arrival."

"May Ostreia find your home unguarded except by fools and return with the full force of Teletia's military," Jerold said then mounted his horse.

The small band of soldiers rode east into the night. The larger army followed but would not try to keep up. He'd made this trip before, in the opposite direction in the dead of night. If this small band of men kept quiet, drawing no attention, and rode hard, he could be by his mother's side by midmorning.

If the men delayed him, he'd leave them behind.

36

Charissa growled at the trussed-up soldier stumbling behind her horse. His eyes grew large, and he froze in his taunts as she snapped her teeth at him. To her amusement, this simple tactic worked. During her Watcher training, they learned other kingdoms feared Watchers. Believed by farmers and peasants to live like savages, the rumors suggested a Watcher would slit your throat given the slightest reason. Some claimed Watchers ate their captives. Although the nobility knew better, most foot soldiers came from outlying areas, so many feared them.

None of it true, she wondered how the rumors started. It served her well if this soldier's response indicated anything. He had courage if he believed the stories, otherwise, he wouldn't have followed them for three days to steal her horse.

She stopped when she came across a small clearing with a large jumble of rocks on one side.

Ramil slid from the horse's back and stumbled toward one of the rocks. He dropped down on it and bent over, head grasped in his hands.

He looked pale. She handed him a cask while she considered their options. The Elwarian soldier might find more truth in the myth soon if she didn't find a way to help Ramil. His injury slowed

275

her down. So did the prisoner. She could kill the soldier but arriving at the border keep with a prisoner as a special thanks to Kassa for helping them escape Maligon appealed to her.

A heavy sigh drew her attention back to Ramil. For all his muscles, he had little stamina for long journeys. Before the soldier attacked Ramil, they rode together, or she trotted beside the horse while he rode. She would give her Watcher's braid to have the second horse they left behind when escaping the fortress. Not that she or Ramil anticipated the need to wander the plains for days, changing routes to avoid groups of armed soldiers. She'd killed three and captured one. She could do nothing else until freed of her burdens.

Her heart twinged a little over that thought. Ramil, her comfort as they hid from Maligon's followers, now became a burden. She loved him, but he was no trained soldier.

"How is your side?" She bent to check his bandage while keeping an eye on the prisoner. The rose on his bandage no longer bloomed with fresh blood.

"It's sore but nothing bad." His voice came out hoarse and strained.

"That's what you said yesterday, last night, and this morning." She handed him her reins, hoping he'd do nothing to startle the mount. The prisoner would get a bumpy ride dragged across uneven territory if he did. She doubted he'd survive. That would solve one problem.

She shook her head to clear her thoughts. "Let me look at it."

The cloth, torn from their captive's shirt, peeled away, sticking in spots as she unwrapped it. No blood seepage. Good. No swelling or puffiness. Good again. She laid a hand on Ramil's forehead and the tension in her shoulders spilled away. He wasn't warm. The willow bark she'd found the night before appeared to have done its job. As well as the medicinal she thought to pack at the last minute before escaping Adana's View.

"You need a new bandage, but we'll have to wait until we reach the keep." She rewrapped it.

Unless someone in Quilla's army doubled back and found the bodies of her prisoner's comrades, no one knew to search for her and Ramil. Unwilling to tempt that fate, she'd taken a winding path, often in the hard gullies that would fill with rain soon. The men she'd killed probably deserted the army, but that didn't mean Quilla wouldn't look for them.

This morning she realized her mistake in trying to confuse their tracks. To the southeast, she saw the telltale dust in the air. It stretched out a long way, indicating the perfect lines of soldiers had stretched out, leaving huge gaps. If only she had a squad of Watchers with her, she could strike.

She gave Ramil his water flask and took a pull from hers. The weather had turned cooler in the last day. A good thing. Less sweat meant the water went further. She walked back to the prisoner, who had dropped to the ground when they stopped, and handed him her flask. He didn't look like much, but he did catch Ramil unaware yesterday morning.

She'd woken to scuffling and had leapt to her feet, knife in hand. Ramil howled in pain before she could make sense of the two bodies wrestling on the ground. When Ramil fell back from the man's grasp, she'd snarled and tackled the intruder, her knife pressed close to his throat.

She'd meant to kill him, too, until she realized he might have information.

"Let's get moving," she said as she took her flask back. After she helped Ramil into the saddle, she gave the prisoner's rope a yank and moved forward. They were too far east, thanks to avoiding other troops and hiding their tracks. Ramil needed rest, and she needed to warn Kassa about Quilla's army.

A cool air blew across the low hills as they trudged onward. The farther north they traveled, the more the seasons shifted. Moniah awaited the rainy season, while the mountains expected snow. She didn't care which came as long as she made it to the keep first. Hopefully, Quilla's army would get caught on the plains.

37

A cheer went up from the walls of Belwyn's castle as Jerold and his men rode into view. Along the high stone walls of the castle, soldiers shouted greetings and banged swords on their shields. The worry constricting his chest throughout the long night eased some at this welcome.

Moments later, he rode his horse into the familiar courtyard. The *clop-clop* of hooves on the cobblestones resounded in his heart. The fresh scent of scattered hay tickled his nostrils. Home.

Leaving Halar to deal with the men and their mounts, he jumped down and tossed the reins of his horse to the first stable hand he saw.

"The empress?" he said to a guard.

"Welcome home, sir. The empress resides in her chambers." Dropping his voice to a level only Jerold could hear, he added, "You should hurry."

Ignoring all other greetings, Jerold raced into the castle and bounded down the main hall, up the great staircase, along the wing of his ancestors, their portraits watching him as he ran to the empress' chambers.

Her mother's favorite attendant, Salora, with her head covered in puffy gray hair, jumped to her feet when he burst through the door. A sad smile came to her round face. "Thank the Creator, you're home, little prince."

The affectionate name drew him back to his childhood when Salora watched him as his mother worked. Although she never had called him that in front of others.

"Salora. Mother? Is she—" The rest of his question died in his throat.

She gestured toward the entrance to the royal sleeping chamber. "She's waiting for you, Your Highness."

As soon as Salora spoke, he started for the far door, but her beloved voice, giving him the royal title she never dared to speak before, slowed his feet.

His mother told everyone. The Creator save her, she still fought against her bastard cousin through this last act of defiance. When would Maligon learn that Belwyn still had an heir to the throne? A legitimate heir.

When he stopped, Salora came to his side, the thick carpet muffling her footsteps. "Would you like me to come with you?"

Her deep brown eyes looked at him with the same care and concern she'd given each of his fears and childhood injuries.

"No. Thank you." He took the last decisive steps toward the door. On the other side, his mother waited. Eyes closed in a brief prayer to find her healthy and whole, laughter in her eyes, and wisdom by his side, he grasped the doorknob. It felt cold and impersonal as he turned it and eased the door open.

The chamber lay in dark gloom, its curtains drawn over the windows. A wheezing came from the bed, a sound he'd heard before and detested for its promise of impending death. An overwhelming scent of spicy herbs flavored the air, indication of a teacher's presence and the final preparation for his mother's end of life.

As expected, the Teacher of the Faith sat in a corner but rose when Jerold entered. With a brief nod, he glided toward him, laid a comforting hand on Jerold's arm, then left him alone with his mother.

The canopied bed stood in the center of the huge room. He inched toward it, feeling like a small boy seeking his mother's comfort after a nightmare. Yet, the bed held the nightmare this time.

He stood at the foot, staring at her lying there. The lustrous dark hair everyone associated with his mother was gone. Hacked off by something blunt. Who had done that? Uneven and lank sweat-soaked strands stuck to her face.

Wheezing, slow and punctuated by a gurgle, sounded deep in her chest. No rhythm counted the breaths, just agonizing moments between each one. The luminous bronze of her skin had faded to yellow, and veins pushed against the skin in the one hand he could see tucked into the edge of the covers.

As he tried to reconcile this shell with the vibrant mother who raised him, she opened her eyes, the motion so slow he didn't notice at first.

She rolled her head on the pillow and focused on him. "Jerold?" She croaked his name then licked her lips.

A small cup sat on a table by the bed. He picked it up and sniffed the contents. Watered wine. "Here, Mother, drink." He slid his arm under her shoulders, prepared to lift her.

She tried to wave a limp hand at him. "No. Can't." A racking cough shook her body.

He rolled her to her side and rubbed her back.

Through her nightdress, he felt the hum of wheezing and the *click-clack* of the rattle as she coughed. When the spasms subsided, he eased her body back, taking her hand in his. Her eyes fluttered closed.

"Mother? What can I do? What do you need?"

For a moment, he thought she'd slipped into unconsciousness, but when he rose to adjust the covers, her hand gripped his with an intensity he found remarkable. Dark eyes searched his face, the fiery spirit he associated with his mother revealed in their depths. She dragged him close with a strength impossible for someone so ill.

He leaned in, letting her pull him close to her face.

Moments ticked by while she sought something in his eyes. "What mother? What do you need?"

"Kill him," she whispered, voice strained and angry. "Kill him for me."

The lovely face, now shattered with illness, blazed with a ferocious intensity. When he didn't respond, she squeezed his arm and gave it a shake. "Do it." An explosion of coughing pulled her into a protective ball, but she glared at him between each spasm.

He knew that glare. It dared him to defy her. The consequences of ignoring this side of his mother meant horrible punishment. He never had and would not now.

Somewhere in his rational mind, he wanted to cry at the concern she'd punish him for going against her will. His mother would never chastise or rebuke him again. She would never walk her lands or greet her people. She would never see her grandchildren. With a start, he realized he'd hoped to tell her about the young warrior princess he'd met on his journey. Surprise her with the girl's name, the same as the spoiled child they'd chuckled over three years earlier. She'd grown and changed, and his mother would never know.

Rather than say any of those things, he stroked his fingers through her shorn hair. "I will, Mama. I promise."

He sat with her throughout the day, stroking her hair, easing her to her side when the coughing attacks wracked her body. Just past sundown, one hand clasped in his, her soul escaped the ravaged body. Jerold lifted her body in his arms and held her tight against his chest. He cried until Halar came for him.

38

A fine mist fell in the morning hours as Leera's army prepared to mount up. Astride her horse, Leera looked around for Sariah, Callan, and Amar. The air warned of snow, and she preferred a warm hearth when it started.

She spotted them at the edge of the group talking to a Watcher. So far, they'd only encountered men as they traveled. When had she arrived? Dismounting, Leera strode across the ground with purpose. They had received contact with Adana, at last, and no one thought to summon her?

Sariah turned as Leera approached and motioned for her to join them. As if she wouldn't. Her annoyance fled as she saw dismay and sadness in the Protector's face.

"What is it?" A chill, not from the cold drizzle, seized her.

"Your Highness, this is Charissa, a Watcher escaped from Adana's View. She says we're within a few hours of your mother's army."

The chill turned to ice in her lungs. "Which direction?"

"Southeast," the Watcher said.

"All the more reason to be on our way." Leera itched to return to her horse.

"Think about it, Your Highness." Callan's voice urged her to wait.

She shot him an incredulous look. "You don't want to go after them, do you?"

Callan cleared his throat. "Yes. We do."

She stared at him. He swallowed.

"We could stay out of sight and attack them at dawn tomorrow."

"In the dark? In this weather?" She shivered.

"Exactly," Callan said. "My lady, we can't stop them, but we can hurt them. If we cut their numbers before they reach Adana's View, we improve your brother's cause."

"The rear of their caravan is mostly food and livestock," Charissa added. "They've fallen behind the army. It wouldn't be hard to strike at them."

Leera stared at the woman then turned to Callan. "Last night, you said no one will attempt to fight once the weather closes in. You stressed the need to get to the keep now. This rain is a hint. Snow will be here within a day or two. Shouldn't we get to safety and wait to fight in the spring?"

"Normally, yes," Sariah answered instead. "But the Creator gives us this opportunity. It's your decision, of course."

If only she could stamp her foot and demand to head west for the keep. A spoiled princess would do that.

She let go of her snide tone. "What's your plan? Or have I heard all of it?"

No one had ever taught her warfare or strategy or anything related to politics. She knew a different kind of warfare, the kind women in Elwar undertook in society. She'd been raised to decorate the arm of someone who fought battles outside. On the ground. With bloodshed.

The odd thing was she no longer desired to be a decoration. Wasn't that why this army followed her? To help her brother and Adana regain their titles?

"Do we send our entire army?" With that one question, she fought down nausea.

She'd committed herself to their plan.

* * *

While Sariah tended to the wounds of the Watcher's companion, Leera followed Callan and Amar to the part of their camp where her most trusted soldiers surrounded the Watcher's prisoner. The man sat on the ground, shoveling food into his mouth. Greasy strands of long hair draped his face. Callan started to push through the guard to question him, but Leera grabbed his arm. "Wait."

The shock on Callan's face must have registered on her own. Except while sparring, she never touched the men. She dropped her hand and tilted her head away from the guards and led him far enough that no one could listen. "This man came from my mother's army."

Callan wrinkled his brow and nodded.

"How many of our army deserted hers as she traveled south?"

"I don't have an exact number, but most of the last ones to join us." He shifted his stance, feet spread apart, gaze steady on hers. "Do you suspect our soldiers or seek help from them?"

That was the problem. Until now, she'd trusted those who joined them, but what if traitors infiltrated their ranks? "I want Charissa to observe the man. Assign guards from the ones who deserted Elwar's army last while we discuss our plan."

Callan nodded. "A wise move. I'm unaccustomed to using the skills of a Watcher."

If someone told her three years ago that having a strange half-princess, half-warrior as a friend might teach her some useful things, Leera would have tittered and skipped away. Who knew she'd been paying attention? Adana would relish this moment if she were here.

A wave of loneliness for her friend rocked her for a moment, but Leera turned from it. "I'll go speak to Charissa. Meanwhile, gather a few of the deserters. Keep some of our loyal men in the group, too. We don't want anyone to attempt a coup when we're this close to the keep and my mother."

Leera found Charissa watching as Sariah cleaned Ramil's wound. She pulled her aside and explained.

The Watcher nodded in understanding. "I did not know your army included deserters, or I would have suggested this." The look she gave Leera reminded her of Kassa's looks of approval when Adana performed well. Warmth of pride tingled all over her despite the cold rain.

She and Charissa moved along the edge of the camp, heading in the direction of the prisoner, but approaching from behind. As the guards changed watch, Charissa settled into an unobtrusive spot where she could observe all the men.

It took only a short time for Charissa to return from her post. "There's one who's familiar with him. I could not determine if they share a desire to defeat Quilla or not. I would keep him out of the attack in the morning. I'll watch him throughout the day to see what he does. When Callan questions the prisoner, make sure he asks if he recognizes any of your men."

"We can do this." Worry for the outcome and pride over her forethought tangled in Leera's chest.

Charissa said, "If he says he doesn't know anyone, we know he lies. I will remain and observe the interrogation if you wish."

With a nod, Leera dismissed Charissa.

A short time later, they knew the answer. The soldier lied. Maybe he feared to admit knowing anyone, but they couldn't ignore the fact he might spy on them and disappear to share any intelligence with Quilla.

Afterward, Callan ordered his own men, the most loyal of her army, to listen throughout the day for any indication of support for Quilla.

The rain continued, and winds swept over them as they traveled. Leera huddled under her cloak, disheartened but determined to not show it to her men.

39

A cool rain began to fall on Morana around mid-afternoon of the second day of their journey. She regretted leaving Roshar two days early, but Ostreia's return gave her no reason to remain. Jerold, if he headed for Roshar would know soon enough. Talia would share the news about Teletia with him.

Teletia, her home, stood in ruins. The few survivors still in the city reported the rage Maligon unleashed on the kingdom when she, Ariff, and Navon escaped his clutches. He destroyed the capital city and killed all their servants. As if that wasn't enough, he burned villages to the ground in his search for them. Most of the surviving men he conscripted into the army. Nothing remained for her son to inherit.

Navon accepted the news with a strength of will surprising even her. "I'll rebuild, Mama, and make it better than before."

"Yes, you will. I will make sure of that."

Even Ostreia, the Watcher representative assigned to Teletia, promised help.

As if summoned by her thoughts, Ostreia trotted up beside her horse.

"Your Majesty, our scouts found signs of a large group traveling through the area ahead. Maybe a day ago. A very large force."

"An army, then?"

"We believe so."

"How many?"

The Watcher shook her head. "Thousands."

Morana stared into the distance. They'd left the mountains behind and traveled below the foothills of the forest. The plains of Moniah stretched out before them. "Headed where?"

"South."

She nodded. "Whose?"

"Most likely Elwar's. I sent scouts to check."

Quilla's Elwar or Kiffen's? Their heading suggested Quilla's, not that Morana believed Quilla wished to travel to Moniah. "Very well. Increase the patrols and perimeter guards. We don't want to be caught unaware."

Ostreia nodded and trotted ahead.

"Mother?" Navon's voice still sent a pang of regret through her. His youthful innocence had vanished since his father's death. "Shouldn't we pursue? If it's Elwar and they reach Maligon, he'll be..."

A tiny part of his six-year-old's childish voice returned with his last words.

Her heart broke that he understood enough to know the ramifications if these reinforcements made it to Maligon. He may be aware, but he was still just a child who needed his mother's assurance.

"This rain will slow them down." The realization hit her as she said it. "We'll travel through rain or snow between here and the keep. Any army headed for Moniah will run a race between the weather and themselves to reach those walls. If the rain wins, the land will flood." Should she say more? He was only six.

He nodded, his face drawn into serious contemplation. "They'll get stuck. Or drown."

"Yes, that could happen."

As he considered this further, an idea rose in her mind. Surely, she wasn't the only one who saw the opportunity laid before them. She kicked her horse forward to catch up with Ostreia. *Could they afford to pursue and harass the army?*

* * *

Jerold paced his mother's rooms—his quarters now—going over the options. He needed to reach the keep before the valley through the mountains became impassible. What remained of Belwyn's advisors to the throne waited in his receiving chamber to report on the kingdom's conditions and advise him. Belwyn's army, half the size it was before Maligon overthrew his mother, awaited his command.

He must decide who went and who stayed. Maligon failed to leave enough of his supporters behind to keep Belwyn from falling back into Jerold's hands. What if he took too many soldiers with him and left the kingdom the same way? Or didn't take enough and failed to defeat Maligon?

The air smelled of snow. He doubted they'd make it to Kiffen and Adana before it fell. By now, Morana had left Roshar, he hoped. He didn't have time to backtrack there, first. Unfortunate, but it would save time as long as he beat the snows through the pass.

"I'm not a Watcher gifted with prophecy," he muttered, wishing for Biaji's or Ostreia's presence. Biaji remained in Roshar with the blinded Watchers, awaiting Ostreia's return from Teletia.

He paced the room two, three more times, running his hands through his hair. The result left it standing on end, but he left it that way as he went to meet the advisors. Odds are, he'd mess it up again before the day was through.

What he would give to have his mother here to guide him now.

Three men and one woman remained of his mother's advisors. They their own territories in Belwyn and bowed to the empress' throne. His now. Where were the other five? Dead or in hiding?

After Jerold's return, his soldiers conducted a thorough search of the city. Maligon had taken his anger out on his people, exacting vengeance over something no one could change—an unacceptable claim to the throne due to his illegitimate birth.

Many homes stood empty and deserted, or, worse yet, they found entire families killed in their sleep. He still had four out of nine council advisors, at least, and Halar, for now. Those who remained began to rebuild the moment Jerold arrived.

The council stood as he entered the cavernous room. A long table sat in the middle of the floor. Portraits hung on the walls of his mother, grandparents, and other ancestors, witnessing the decisions made here. The four remaining advisors sat scattered down the table, taking their usual seats. They bowed as he approached. Halar followed him in.

Jerold stopped to study them before approaching the table. "Please, I would prefer you move to my end of the table. No need to stand on ceremony at the moment."

They complied, although the two older members frowned over it. Of course, they already held some of the higher-ranking chairs.

"This is Halar, the Commander of the Soldiers of the First Sight in Moniah. He has accompanied me for several weeks. I would like him to join in our deliberations."

Four faces turned to stare at Halar, each reflecting displeasure over offering him an advisor's seat.

"Thank you, Your Majesty, but I will stand by the door in case you have need of anything." Halar took up this position without any sign that the advisors' reactions bothered him.

Jerold took his seat and the council followed suit. "I've gone over our options. Every one carries concerns. I would like to know your thoughts before I decide on a course of action. But keep in mind, I must move soon, or the storms will trap us here, unable to contribute our aid to this war."

The two elder men, gray-haired and wrinkled, had been old

before his mother became empress. He'd called them grandfather because he had never met his own grandparents; they died at Maligon's hand. Everyone in the royal line, save he and his mother, died in Maligon's Rebellion. These two grandfathers turned to the younger—although not by many years—two of the council. The four appeared to share a silent battle of wills for several long moments. Jerold fought the urge to drum his fingers on the table as he waited. At last, the only woman, Dara, rose.

"Your Highness, first let me express the council's remorse over the empress' death. We wish we could have saved her and seek your forgiveness that we did not."

"Thank you." Jerold nodded and waited.

His mother always told him the council worked up to their advice through flattery and praise. This wasn't flattery or praise, for what could they flatter or praise right now, but he recognized the tactic.

"The council is unclear on the action we wish to take." Dara sat again and stared at her folded hands on the table.

What? He expected rambling and speculation before they provided clarity, not ineptitude.

He leaned forward and pinned each one with his gaze before speaking. "I accept your condolences and do not blame any of you for the empress' death. But we must take action, now. I doubt you don't have opinions and thoughts. What actions have you considered? What are the merits of each?"

The four stared at him, unblinking.

Jerold fought the urge to run his hands through his hair again. "We've lost precious time as I put my mother to rest. I don't regret that time, although it created unrest when I chose not to wait the prescribed three days. I moved forward quickly because I must act. Today."

One of the elder men, Tomas, cleared his throat. "The kingdom reels from its time spent in oppression, sire. Your mother's, our lovely empress', death shattered what serenity we regained when King Ariff freed her from the dungeons." He frowned and his voice grew louder. "Her own dungeons. He treated her like a dog. We're in shock and mourning. Belwyn needs time. It needs an emperor to restore our faith in ourselves. We need you here."

Dara slammed her hand down on the table and rose before Tomas uttered his last words. "You old fool. We need to stop this blight upon our kingdom's soul. In case you forgot, Belwyn gave the world Maligon. Belwyn outcast him and sent him as a squire to Moniah as a youth. It's our fault, and we should act."

The other two joined in, all of them yelling. Tomas wanted him to remain, plan his coronation, and send no soldiers. Another wanted him to take the entire army to the gates of Adana's View and destroy Maligon. Dara wanted him to send all of their forces to the Border Keep. And the last wanted him to send half his forces to the keep while he remained in Belwyn with the other half.

Jerold rubbed his head. The council proved another thing his mother told him not long ago. This council needed new, fresh minds. The current advisors, both present and absent, guided the council through the dark years when Maligon destroyed the royal family. They lent their support to the last war. Embarrassment over not recognizing the threat his cousin posed until too late weighed on them. Their struggle threatened to keep them from acting at all. Gabriella saw it and warned him. Now the truth of it argued in front of him.

"Enough." With that one word, Jerold released all the anger he'd felt since he first tried to stop Maligon in his mother's throne room months ago. Angry heat burned up the back of his neck. He glared at the four of them who sat frozen in place, their mouths gaping open like the stone fish in the fountains of the city. "Halar and I will decide. But I can tell you this. I will not stay here for a coronation. Not while our army is needed. We can deal with that after we deal with my family's contribution to this evil. You are dismissed."

The advisors sat for a moment looking back and forth between them. None met his gaze. One by one, they rose and left the room, the older two casting disappointed glances at Jerold. He'd probably pay for that later, but for now, he needed to make a decision.

"What a disaster," Jerold said and flopped back into one of the chairs.

Halar cleared his throat and stepped closer. "If I may, Jerold, I would share my thoughts. I do have some familiarity with the kinds of troubles your kingdom suffers under."

Curious, Jerold raised his head.

"Belwyn struggles with a history no one saw coming. Who knew a vagrant might sneak into the gardens and attack the heir to the throne? Or that your aunt would become pregnant from that one attack? When she died soon after his birth, her baby's opportunities died with her, but the child still lives. Maligon still lives. If she'd survived, she might have given him the love he craved. Maybe."

"And?"

"It can't have escaped your notice that my family now deals with a similar problem—a child who craved more than she received and now strikes at the entire kingdom with her anger."

"Samantha." Jerold sat up straight, aware he'd failed to think beyond his own problems. "Halar. I'm sorry. Of course, you understand."

A wry smile flashed on Halar's face and disappeared. "Why do you think my wife is so hard on people? She believes she failed our daughter, and in so doing, the kingdom. But she didn't. She gave Samantha a life full of adventure and training and...love. Samantha had love, but she wanted more. I remember Maligon as a boy. He had joy and your grandmother loved him like her own. She wasn't enough. He wanted more, too."

"My grandmother?" Jerold shook his head. "He killed her first."

"Yes. Who knows why. Maybe because her love didn't solve his problems."

"You are a wise man, Halar. I would ask you to serve on my council if you weren't Monian. But for now, I need you as my temporary advisor. What do I do?"

"What do you want to do?"

Jerold opened his mouth to object.

"No," Halar said. "Don't think about the impact. Don't weigh the options. Just tell me what you want to do."

With a sigh, Jerold sagged, his voice weary with fatigue. "Take as many of my men south as possible. Except I don't have supplies for that many men."

"You don't, but your soldiers catalogued what you do have in storage. While you mourned your mother and put her to rest, I made some inquiries. You have enough supplies for half of your army."

Had his advisors not known? He should have asked them, but no, their positions required them to know and share essential information. He wouldn't berate himself over their inaction. How much could one person handle on his own? That was the purpose of a council.

"Then I'll take half my men." His body felt lighter as he spoke. "We will leave at dawn. That gives the council all afternoon to hold my coronation and for me to consider who might best serve on my new council."

"We better get started, then." As Halar followed him out of the chamber, Jerold felt the weight of indecision over the last few months dissolve.

40

By early afternoon, Leera's scouts returned with confirmation on Quilla's location. They planned to ride until nightfall, then set up a simple camp. In the middle of the night, Callan would lead the troops and attack the stragglers at dawn. She and Amar would lead the rest of the army to the Border Keep. To her surprise, Sariah planned to accompany Callan.

"What did you think a Protector of the Faith does, child?" she asked, regarding her with kind, motherly eyes. "A protector defends. That sometimes means fight."

Until then, it never occurred to her that Sariah or Tonch did anything but encourage the faithful and guide the Teachers of the Faith. "Be careful, Sariah," she said. "If I find Father Tonch at the keep, I don't want to bring him ill news."

"It's not the first time I've ridden into battle." She patted her hand. "These bones might not look capable, especially with all the layers of meat I carry on them, but Tonch knows I will return to him if the Creator wishes it."

The scouts also reported Quilla's army traveled under heavier rains. Welcome information for their plans.

The dry earth of Moniah repelled the deluge, as it did every rainy season, and rivulets grew into creeks that grew into raging rivers, tearing up the ground and anything in its way. Forced to navigate these changes, Quilla's army moved at a snail's pace. The line spread out, large gaps forming between them as they encountered more and more obstacles.

The notion of her mother, who detested wet weather, slowed down by nature filled Leera with glee. The closest she'd come to such a feeling had been when she punched Helymra.

"Why are you laughing?" Catch asked her.

The boy's face held a permanent frown today due to Callan's refusal to add him to the troops for this mission.

Unaware she'd been giggling, Leera attempted to suppress the bubbles of humor riding up her throat. Attempted but didn't succeed. "My mother detests wet weather. I would give anything to see her try to control this."

Catch snorted. "No one can control the weather."

"Try telling my mother that."

No doubt her mother pushed the army to move faster. Even Leera knew the hazards of a decision like that. Those who couldn't keep up would fall prey to whatever came for them. Even her daughter's army.

Lost in her mirth, she'd forgotten Catch until he spoke again. "No soldier will do that."

Had she spoken her thoughts out loud? She blinked water from her eyes, trying to pull her awareness back to the path before them. "My mother can be quite persuasive."

"I've seen that, but Lord Sarx knows better. Even his nephew, Taren, knows better, no matter how poor a swordsman he may be."

The name of her former suitor dammed the humor in her throat. *Taren. No, please no. Not Taren.*

She tried to swallow but struggled to do so. Or even breathe. Chills flashed across her neck and down her arms. She gasped. Her heart pounded like a racehorse pushing for the finish line. Fingers gripped for the reins. She could not feel the leather straps through suddenly numb hands.

"Your Highness?" Catch's voice rose in alarm.

She looked up at him, fright overtaking her senses.

Catch called for help as she tumbled from the saddle.

* * *

The tiny flame of a small campfire called to Leera, drawing her from the place she'd fled to in her mind. Blinking, Leera tried to take in her surroundings. A steady drum beat just above her head. The rich smell of churned up dirt and vegetation filled her nostrils. As her eyes focused, the drumming turned into steady rain hitting the canvas stretched above her. She tried to sit up, but a hand pressed her down.

"Slowly. You took quite a fall." Sariah's face loomed over her, recognizable by her voice more than her face hidden in the shadows.

"What happened?"

"I was hoping you could tell me." Sariah slid an arm under Leera's shoulders. helping her to an upright position. "Catch couldn't explain."

At the mention of his name, the boy's trembling voice piped up from outside the makeshift cover. "Are you well, Princess?"

Was she? Bit by bit, she began to notice her surroundings: a horse's whinny, the clank of pots, the quiet, deep voices of her men. "We've stopped?"

"Yes." Sariah settled down next to her and clasped one of Leera's hands between hers. They felt so warm. "We were about to when you fell."

"I fell?" The sensation of losing control returned. She fought it into submission. Worry streaked through her mind, shoving away the confusion of moments ago. "But my mother's army. We must catch them."

"We're close enough. You needed attention, and luckily for us, you fell in a good area to camp." In the dim lighting, Leera squinted at Sariah. Flickers of the small fire nearby revealed and hid the woman's face in a continual dance.

"Now"—Sariah patted her arm—"tell me what happened to make you pass out."

"I didn't pass out." Leera snapped the words.

She hadn't, had she? No. She never lost consciousness unless planned. Staged, her father had called it once he understood what his wife chose to teach their daughter. His face loomed in her mind, smiling, joking, always loving toward his daughter.

"You did, too." Catch squatted down beside her. He wore an oiled cloak, the hood pulled forward hiding most of his face.

A brief gasp of laughter escaped her at his tone. It sounded like the way she and Serrin used to argue. "Why would I pass out?"

"I don't know, miss," Catch continued, his words tumbling over each other. "You were laughing about your mother trying to push her army faster. Then I said—"

She remembered. "You said Sarx or Taren wouldn't let that happen."

A vigorous nod confirmed her statement and splattered her with water.

Chills threatened to return, but Leera inhaled deeply. "Do you think Taren came with mother?"

A flicker of understanding passed over Sariah's face as the firelight revealed her face again. "I see. You hadn't considered he might."

"No." Leera shook her head.

Why would her mother drag Taren, a foreigner, across the kingdoms to Maligon? He wasn't a swordsman. What good would he do Elwar's army? Unless, of course, her mother planned to force their marriage the first time she held her daughter's life in her grasp, again.

Another shiver rippled over Leera.

"Catch, go get the princess some soup." Something in Sariah's tone told Leera the Protector sought to get rid of the boy.

He scurried off, thankful, like any boy, to be given something to do. Why did men prefer action to words? Before Leera could ponder this, Sariah shifted to face her.

"Before you fell, do you remember anything?"

"No." She shook her head. "Except I felt like I was laughing, then..." She stared into the surrounding dark, trying to remember. Jumbled sensations emerged. Cold hands. Chills. Numbness.

"I think I got a chill. My hands went numb. I couldn't..."

"You lost your hold on the reins, didn't you?"

Yes. That was it. She nodded. "The cold of the rain must have gotten to me."

"No. I don't think so. I believe you panicked when Catch mentioned Taren."

The rain drummed harder over her head as if confirming Sariah's guess. "I never expected to see him again. Then Catch, he said Sarx and Taren wouldn't let my mother lead the army astray."

Thudding footsteps approached and Catch returned with a small gourd filled with hot soup.

The warmth of the bowl seeped life back into her fingers as she grasped it. She huddled over it and took a cautious sip. The heat of the savory broth coursed through her body. "Thank you."

"Catch," Sariah looked up at the boy. "Will you please alert Callan and Amar that the princess is awake and eating?"

"But I—" Catch stopped as Sariah's body stiffened. "Yes, Mistress."

"No matter what happens, I will not let your mother take you," Sariah said after Catch left. "You have three thousand men, more than that, I believe, who will fight to keep you from your mother's clutches."

When Leera thought of her mother, she saw a powerful woman,

larger than life. All her life that power had supported Leera. It felt odd, and thrilling, to have a different power support her. Especially against her mother.

"Let's hope it doesn't come to that." She sipped more soup, looking down in surprise when she realized the bowl was empty.

"I'll get you more." Sariah took the gourd. "You rest. You have a long ride ahead of you, and since you won't be headed for your mother's army, you will be safe. Amar will see to that." The Protector of the Faith rose from the ground as agile as a newly promoted Watcher.

They had made a simplified camp, each person rolling up in whatever cloak or blanket was available to them. Except for the small fire near Leera and the one used to heat the hearty soup, they lit no more fires. The clearing where they camped echoed with the sounds of rain drumming down on the ground, the leaves, and each of them. No one talked. They waited, tense with anticipation.

Leera spent the night fitful and cold. Visions of Sariah and Callan back-to-back fighting off droves of her mother's soldiers plagued her dreams. The only respite from that dream was another. In this one, her mother yanked her up by the throat of the Watcher's tunic she wore and tossed her onto a heap of dead bodies. Taren stood atop it, dressed as a king. He took her hand and lifted her from the bodies of the very men who marched with her. A voice, deep and sonorous spoke. "Taren, you have come forward to serve and wed this princess."

For the first time in her life, she rose before the sun with gratitude to be up at an early hour. The sooner they moved, the sooner her army could return to her in victory.

41

Snow began to fall on Morana's troops as they plodded southwest, following the well-worn trail of the other army. The farther south her band traveled, the warmer it became. Snow turned into a steady rain. The cold settled over her, but she refused to let it distract her. Mid-afternoon, they paused to rest the horses and eat a small portion of bread and cheese. As she watched over Navon, studiously nibbling at his food, Biaji approached.

"Here, take mine. I'm not hungry." Thrusting her portion into his small hands, she followed the Watcher.

Biaji waited a short distance from the prince. "We've spotted them. Elwarian. As expected, the weather impedes travel. The rear of the caravan carries food, supplies, livestock. They've fallen far behind the main force. Few soldiers guard them."

"Good. How much of this army can we cut off?"

The Watcher hesitated. "Ostreia wants to go after the supplies, not risk an attack at this time."

Exactly what Morana expected to hear. "Let's go talk with her."

They found Ostreia under a tree, the branches providing some protection from the weather. She held a crude map. "We're here. The end of their troops is here." The points she indicated looked close to each other although Morana knew the distance represented a couple of hours of marching in this rain.

"How far ahead is the front of the army?"

Ostreia shook her head. "Too far. And too many. We hurt them best by stealing supplies."

"But if we can stop them now, we keep Maligon from receiving a large army."

In the gray light of day, Ostreia's teeth shone in a conspiratorial smile. "The weather fights for us, Queen Morana. We need not waste our troops on pursuit."

"You're sure of this?"

"Nothing is sure. But water is a formidable weapon. We don't want to fall prey to it, too."

As they spoke, the members of her small army started to move about and prepare to depart. No one wanted to linger in this rain for long. The sooner they carried out their plan and headed for the keep, the better.

"Very well," Morana said. "How many do we send?"

"Two small parties will succeed better than larger ones. I would like to take twenty with me and send twenty with Biaji. She'll cut them off at the divide, and I'll block their rear. We surround them." As she spoke, Ostreia had slashed her hand across the map indicating where they hoped to cut the lines.

"And if Quilla has more guards than you think?"

"A risk we take. Our scouts saw only a few, but that can change. That's why I would like to leave at once."

Those words—"leave at once"—echoed in a memory from Morana's youth. She'd played on the floor of the king's council chambers as her father, primary advisor to the king of Teletia, outlined plans to join forces with Chiora and Roassa to put an end to Maligon's Rebellion. Those were the last words she ever heard her father say except that he loved her. Orphaned by that battle, she came to live under the care of Ariff's father.

That would not happen this time. Ostreia and Biaji knew the territory and the season better than Quilla's army or most of her own. If anyone could succeed here, it was a Watcher.

"So be it," she said to Ostreia. "I do make one request. Send one Watcher to alert the keep of our plan and that we soon join them."

"Done." Ostreia left to carry out the orders, her straight back and squared shoulders a formidable sight.

Thank goodness she fought on their side.

42

In the days following Kassa's death, Montee paced the ramparts even when not on duty. The chill winds, according to the keep's inhabitants, meant snow soon. Maybe tonight. She shivered but embraced the cold.

A First Vision must not show doubt or fear. She didn't fear, but she doubted. Not their cause, but her ability to lead them to victory without Kassa's presence. Somehow knowing she could ask for advice, though she only had twice, heightened her self-confidence. Kassa would snort at the idea, but it was the truth.

The clomp of boots walking along the wall alerted her to Simeon's approach.

"Aren't you cold, Montee?" He came to stand beside her and stare into the trees beyond. "Most Elwarians huddle by fires or dress in many layers to ward off this cold. Yet you stand out here in your uniform and cloak. Not much protection against the elements."

"I welcome the cold for now. It keeps my mind clear."

The man turned toward her, his breath clouding in the air. It smelled of the barley soup from the midday meal. "What does your mind tell you?"

Had he read her mind? No one ever knew her thoughts, not

unless she chose to show them. Even Linus struggled to see beyond her façade once their roles diverged their paths.

"We must wait out the storms for now," she said. "That gives Maligon time, though. Somewhere out there, I feel the presence of an army moving. Our scouts have seen the signs. Given his history, Maligon will use this weather to his advantage. Try to catch us unprepared. Unless we strike first."

"What are the chances for an army traveling across Moniah now?"

Montee considered the coming rains that would flood the savanna. She loved to watch the flooding. It brought much needed water and the abundance of plant life. As a child, she found its ability to reshape the landscape thrilling. Her home stood above one of the known flood areas. Every night, the rush of roaring waters lulled her to sleep and woke her the next day.

"It depends on a lot of factors."

Simeon raised his eyebrows at her.

"A small army can manage. A large one will have to split up. The land is unpredictable. I've seen water choose a path no one expected. They will lose some of their numbers. If the army is close to the walls of Adana's View, most will probably make it. If they're in the middle of the plains..." She glanced southward wondering if an army did traverse the plains. "They must keep moving in order to survive. If they stop in a dry area, it won't stay dry for long."

"Would it make sense to send out a party to scout for this army?"

It was her turn to raise an eyebrow. "I send them every day. Three units of Watchers."

"Did I hear you discussing the scouting reports?" Adana's clear voice rang from the ladder as she jumped over the last rung and walked toward them, her steps brisk. Kiffen followed close behind.

Montee and Simeon turned to greet them. "Your Majesties."

Montee added, "No, I was telling Simeon how often I send them out."

Eyes bright with unconcealed excitement, Adana looked from one to the other. "Have we received news?"

Kiffen, standing behind her, radiated a similar energy.

What had them so excited?

"No more than we knew two days ago. I sent the last groups farther. There's lots of territory to cover."

As if she hadn't heard, Adana's face split in an ear-to-ear grin. "You must come with us. We have something incredible to show you."

Exchanging perplexed glances, Montee and Simeon followed the two into the keep.

Instead of heading into the tunnels, Kiffen and Adana followed the outer circle of the keep toward the western side and the deserted armory. All the weapons and armor had been transferred to the tunnels to provide room for Vuur to work on his weapon in the large space.

Montee tamped down a rising hope. Even fighting down the surge, she couldn't help but feel her own steps grow quick and light. "Has Vuur done it? Made more of his weapon?"

"Yes." Kiffen pushed through the door to the armory.

The large room now resembled a huge kitchen. Large pots bubbled over small pots, the smaller pots holding the flickering light of glimmer fire. The heat after the cold outside hit Montee in a welcome wave, although she doubted she wanted to stay there for long.

Around the room, bowls and bottles were piled on different tables. Several glimmer makers scurried around, focused on tasks unclear to Montee.

Distinctions between groups became obvious as she studied the bustling workers. Some makers stayed on the far side of the space, decanting fluid into stone bottles. To her left, others wore heavy aprons and leather gloves, and paid careful attention to the pots they tended—a good sign they worked with glimmer fire.

Far from the rest, Vuur bent over a small set of bottles, his attention riveted on the task of pouring gleaming liquid into a flask. Marletta, the stable hand and seamstress, worked alongside him. She measured several small vials of liquid into a larger vial. Intent on his task, Vuur did not look up. Marletta did, then leaned in to whisper something to the Isati.

Vuur nodded, finished pouring the contents into his flask, and turned to greet them. "Your Majesties, are we ready to show your commanders our results?"

Kiffen spoke with the zeal she'd witnessed earlier. "Do you have a small one, or should we test a larger one?"

White teeth gleamed against Vuur's dark skin. "King Kiffen, I applaud your enthusiasm, but let's begin with something small."

Marletta handed Vuur a vial no bigger than her thumb. The care they both took in handling it made Montee sweat with concern.

"Follow me." Vuur led them to the far side of the room and through a single door.

This room, stripped bare of its contents, also bore scorch marks on the stone floor. Simeon tilted his head in question and walked over to drag his boot over the marks. No track appeared from the swipe. "Did you cause these?"

"Yes," Marletta breathed the word, her eyes dancing. "Wait until you see."

The excitement radiating from the four made Montee uneasy. *What kind of weapon is this?*

"If you will, Simeon." Vuur gestured for the man to return to them. "It's best if you stay near the door. This one is small, just a hint of what we can do."

Marletta handed each of them leather aprons she pulled off hooks along the wall. "There is no way to shield your eyes, so I suggest you cover your eyes. Look through your fingers. Like this."

She placed her hands across her eyes and spread her fingers enough to leave tiny slits between them.

Horrified at the idea of damage to her greatest weapon, her eyes, Montee complied without question. She stood waiting; breath held.

"Brace yourselves." Vuur leaned against the wall beside them. "Three, two, one."

She felt the motion of his arm throwing. A sound like thunder rattled Montee's teeth as a blast of fire shot upward. Heat washed over them. Tiny shards of debris pinged on the stones. Her ears rang with an alarming gong that didn't fade.

"It is safe now." Vuur dropped his hands, the pride of creation clear in his face.

Montee dropped her hands. Where were the flames she'd felt? No shrapnel from the vial either. A new scorch mark stained the floor and the far wall.

"What was that?" Simeon asked, crossing to study the new marks.

"A tiny sample of what glimmer explosives can do." Vuur reached into the pocket of his apron and withdrew a flask three times the size of the one he'd just thrown. "That one was a sample, nothing more than a blast toy. This—" he held up the larger vial, "—this is the size of the one Miri used to destroy the wall in Adana's View."

"And what does it do?" Montee asked, stepping closer to examine the flask.

"Destroy," Adana and Kiffen said. "It will destroy anything within a large area."

"How large?" Montee pulled her hand away from the flask and focusing her Watcher's gaze on Vuur.

"A well-placed throw will take out an area the size of the giraffe paddocks in the keep."

"What happened to the vial?" she asked. "I heard pieces of it hit the floor."

"Melted. Gone."

Horror swept over Montee like a swarm of bees on attack. "How do we ensure it doesn't melt us? Or the keep?"

"We've kept everyone below in the tunnels as a precaution," Adana said. "We don't think it would blast through the floor, but this part of the keep is farthest from the occupied parts."

"How is it made?" Simeon stared at the flask in Vuur's hands, his arms folded close to his body as if he fought the temptation to reach for a snake.

Montee understood his concern.

Vuur and Marletta turned to Adana and Kiffen who looked at each other. Adana took a visible breath, her shoulders rising and falling, a good sign Montee would not appreciate the answer. "For now, we prefer to keep the recipe protected. Vuur, Marletta, and two other glimmer makers know the secret to the explosive. No one else."

Incredulous, Montee opened her mouth to object.

"We don't want to risk anyone associated with Maligon to learn of this." Kiffen stepped closer to Adana, the two of them presenting a solid front to their advisors.

"How much?" Simeon asked.

At the same time, Montee asked, "How do you carry it?"

The two young rulers sighed in relief.

Clearing his throat, Vuur shot a bemused sidelong glance at Adana and Kiffen. "I have enough to take out a large army. And I do have a plan for transporting it. We must train the warriors who will carry it, though. Or we can use glimmer makers. Only two know how we make it, but several of those who work with glimmer fire helped me devise a carrying and launching device."

"And how far can you launch it?" Simeon's question held a note of disbelief and unease.

Vuur met his gaze unswerving and in a quiet, confident tone said, "I could stand behind four full troops of Soldiers of the First

Sight lined up in formation below the southern cliff of Adana's View, and land it inside the walls."

Montee wanted to stagger back at the implication. The walls of Adana's View were impregnable due to their height. No catapult existed that could breach those walls. If Vuur had this, who else might discover it? Her stomach cramped. Now, instead of doubt, she felt fear.

43

Adana walked with the decorum of a queen but wanted to run through the halls shouting a Watcher's war cry.

They had a weapon. One never seen by anyone in the four kingdoms. Its power shifted the entire balance of this war.

Reports of a large army crossing east of them, headed south, had plagued her over the last two days. Enough that she had haunted Vuur's workroom, begging him to finish. And he had.

Now they had a means to stop Maligon and his traitorous supporters. And stop them she would.

The restraint of her outward emotions echoed across the link and rebounded back from Kiffen. The two of them shimmered with joy and relief. Unlike Montee and Simeon. Those two did not react as she'd hoped. Their solemn response surprised her. She slid her gaze toward Kiffen, catching his brief grin. Yet, their advisors didn't laugh or express much of any emotion. She'd just hoped for something less pessimistic.

As Montee and Simeon rounded the corner ahead of them, Kiffen grabbed her hand and pulled her to him. He wrapped his arms around her. Eyes shining with the same joy she felt, he leaned in to kiss her. How much of this joy was hers and how much his? It didn't matter.

Her skin burned at his touch. They kissed once more, long and breathtaking.

With a sigh, Kiffen pressed his forehead against hers. "We will win."

She grinned back. "Yes. We will."

Despite the solemn moods of their advisors, the joy zinged between them as they followed Montee and Simeon. The two stood at the end of the corridor solemnly waiting, faces still devoid of any response to the weapon.

They descended into the tunnels and made their way to the map room. Once behind closed doors, Adana spun toward them. "We will win. You see that, don't you? Maligon can't have anything like this."

"He's seen it, though." Simeon stabbed at the map, running his finger along the location of the destroyed section of the wall. "Are we sure he can't reach the glimmer maker's chambers in the aqueducts? If he finds a way, he might discover our secret."

Adana shook her head. "Umgani assured us the entire area flooded. She almost drowned trying to bring Kassa out. Vuur left nothing behind. He didn't dare let glimmer fall into Maligon's hands."

The evacuation and destruction of the waterways, as well as part of the wall, still stung. Necessary, she knew, but heartwrenching if she allowed herself time to think about it.

Montee stood by the map, her chin in her hand as she studied the markers. They knew nothing of Halar and Jerold. The runner, Biaji, had yet to return. Another reason the glimmer explosive thrilled Adana. She needed to put an end to their losses before Maligon annihilated Moniah's warriors as he'd done Belwyn's royal family.

Only she stood between him and the end of Chiora's line. Once before, a Monian queen died without a child. Many centuries ago. Queen Enuli died in childbirth, losing the heir to her throne at the same time. Her cousin, Nnochi, who happened to serve as First Vision, became queen. In the absence of a cousin—the rest of Adana's family died in Maligon's Rebellion—the First Vision would take the Seat of Authority. And if Montee died, too? The cold outside couldn't match the tremors that thought created.

As she tamped down these concerns, her sight vanished, replaced by a blur of gray and blue. It swirled and undulated until she saw the snake from the vision Kassa gave her.

But now the serpent became an army snaking across Moniah's flooding land. Several thousand stretched to the horizon. Gaps in the lines formed as the rains ravaged the ground. As if she flew with the hawk again, she rose above the army and soared to the front. Quilla, unfazed by the weather, head held erect and unyielding against the rain, still led this legion. In the distance, the walls of Adana's View loomed.

Her stomach lurched as her sight wheeled around and faced the lines. A torrent of water surged over the land and washed a section of the army away. Still, the rest of the army plodded forward, not reacting to this loss.

She winged over the rear ranks. Lions raced from the hills, chasing down the livestock and wagons. Some lions fell to swords, but others tore into the wagons and guards. The rear ranks halted and turned to fight off the lions. As a gap opened between the army moving forward and the army returning to protect the supplies, water surged in and cut them off. Then a mass of horses and lions launched into the divide.

Around the fringes of the battle marched a few giraffes, flanking the wedge and protecting the horses and a second group of lions in case the main army managed to navigate the waters. They did not.

The vision turned toward the front again, where Quilla pushed the rest of the army hard toward the walls of Adana's View. Adana stretched toward the walls, longing to see her home, but her vision blurred into blues and grays.

She blinked and looked around the room. She sat in a chair against the far wall while Kiffen and several others gathered around the map. The candles had burned halfway down.

"How—" she croaked.

Kiffen spun around. "You've returned." He rushed to her side, grasping her hands in his. His felt so warm. Her teeth chattered.

A gentle warmth settled over her as Kiffen wrapped a cloak around her. "What did you see?"

"How? How do you know?"

"Bai'dish. He couldn't show me, though."

"Of course." Her throat felt dryer than the dust of Moniah in the season of sun.

"Here." Umgani stood by her with a goblet of sweet wine.

The wine raced down her throat like the torrents of water she saw in her vision. She drank it all and handed the goblet back to Umgani. "Thank you."

"Of course." She refilled the goblet from a flask on the table beside her chair. "I tended your mother many times during a vision. She always came back to us parched like the desert. I thought you might react the same way."

"Thank you." Adana drank again, then shifted and tried to stand. Her legs refused to cooperate.

"Not yet." Umgani placed a warning hand on her arm. "Stretch them out in front of you and rotate your feet. The blood needs to flow again."

Where had this woman been during all of her other visions? The tingle of blood returning to her limbs made her wince, but at last Adana could stand. She wobbled toward the map, determined to share the vision while it remained fresh.

The long, thin stick they'd used to mark the snake coming out of the forest felt cold and smooth, just like a snake. "I saw the snake with Quilla in the lead. She has a big army. Today, I saw the soldiers instead of other snakes. They wore Elwar's blue." She forced herself to look up at Kiffen as she said this. He only nodded.

"Present or soon?" Umgani asked.

The question made Adana pause. "Is it day or night now?"

"Night," Kiffen said. "You were gone for a few hours."

For so long. It felt like minutes. "Then, I think soon. Sometime tomorrow morning."

"We'll never reach them in time to stop them. Not with the rains." Montee's even tone revealed a hint of frustration.

Eyes wide in surprise, Adana stared at the First Vision.

Montee shrugged. "I believe my frustration worth sharing. In here. With this small group."

"Flooding separated the troops. Quilla left them behind. Some drowned. The tail of the snake has supply wagons and livestock." She paused unsure how to explain the next part. "Lions and horses ran down from the hills and cut this group off from the rest. Quilla left them to die."

Kiffen frowned.

The markers on the map showed Elwar's army still in Elwar. Adana picked up the blue lions and placed them beside the snaking line. Then she took several more lions and placed them behind the snake. "I believe some of Elwar supports you. Either that or these are deserters stealing supplies. For whatever reason, they attacked."

Then she took Teletia's red war horses and more of Elwar's blue lions and placed them to the northeast ahead of the same section of the snake. "It appears Teletia and Elwar also will attack from here. At least, that's what I assume the lions and horses represent." Picking up a few giraffe markers, she added them to the Teletian army. "Watchers accompany them. They guarded the others from a rear attack."

She frowned at the map. Something felt wrong. Eyes closed, she tried to recall the details, saw the swarm of the different attacks.

There had been another force. She'd missed it in the heat of the vision, but her Watcher's sight had not. She transferred half of the lions from the northeast to the rear of the ones coming from the northwest. "I think there were two forces of lions here. It felt like they didn't work together."

"Could they be those Quilla left behind?" Kiffen studied the configurations of markers.

"I don't think so. I think they have the same purpose as the first group, but I'm not sure they planned together."

Someone rapped on the door, and Nuala stepped away to answer it. Voices murmured, then she pushed the door closed and turned to Adana. "A Watcher has arrived with news from Queen Morana. Shall I allow her admittance?"

"No." Montee strode toward the door. "We should meet with her in your receiving room, Queen Adana. This map and your vision remain a secret for now."

A Watcher spy or ally? Adana followed Montee. She hoped to find Biaji waiting to confirm her vision and tell them of Gabriella's rescue, but Nuala didn't say it was Biaji. She would have. She hadn't said anything, but everyone must have noticed her vision did not include Belwyn's eagles.

* * *

The Watcher turned out to be one Adana recognized but did not know.

When she shared the news of Ariff's death, the destruction of Teletia, and that Gabriella was dying, if not already dead, Adana grasped for Kiffen's hand. He squeezed hers hard, the shock of the news reeling through their bond.

Prince Jerold's face as he danced with his mother three years earlier floated into Adana's memory. The two glowed with health and happiness. They even looked carefree. She knew they weren't at the time, but Maligon's threat felt distant then.

After Montee questioned the Watcher, she gathered the rest of them far enough from the messenger to avoid being overheard. "This matches the vision." A vicious grin flitted across her face and disappeared. "They are within our reach if you wish to send aid."

Rather than answer Montee, Kiffen turned to the Watcher. "How long ago did you leave your troops?"

"Midday today. They were a few hours behind the enemy." The Watcher flinched momentarily as she said enemy, her eyes darting away from Kiffen's focus on her.

Aware of the Watcher's discomfort in calling Elwar's military the enemy, Adana took up the questions. "When do they plan to strike?" It could already be over if they were that close.

"In the morning, just before dawn, Your Majesty."

"Did you see other forces?" Montee asked. "Signs of another army behind this one?"

"No." The Watcher's skin paled a moment. "Are they riding into a trap?"

Everyone turned to Adana. She shook her head. "I don't know."

"A vision? You had a vision, my lady?" A look of awe crossed the Watcher's face. "What does the Creator wish?"

The reference to the Creator disturbed Adana, but not as much as it would have before Kassa's last words to her. "I saw an army attack. It looked like they succeeded. But there was another army."

"It could be us," Simeon said. "If we choose to send help, we would come from that direction."

Montee turned and dismissed the Watcher. "You should go get some rest and food. We may need your guidance soon. Locate Greti. She'll help you."

Once the door closed behind her, Kiffen said, "We should send reinforcements. And use Vuur's weapon."

Montee studied him. "Reveal its power now? We have one chance to surprise them with it."

"They already know," Adana said. "The wall."

Montee shook her head and paced across the room. "I wager they have no idea what caused the explosion. Once is an odd fluke. Twice confirms we have a weapon."

"I don't see why it matters," Kiffen said. "They don't know how it's made. Even if they did, they can't make it. They don't have the supplies."

Simeon shook his head. "This may be the last battle before weather shuts us off from each other. That gives him time to find a way to retaliate against it."

Montee nodded. "He'll have at least sixty days when none of us can act. Sixty days before the rains drain off the land."

"Or longer, isn't it?" Adana turned to Kiffen. "Won't the snow last longer than that?"

"In Elwar City, yes. It's farther north. Here, the snow could be gone in forty days."

The weather complicated everything. Adana rubbed her head, feeling the beginning of a headache. Visions sometimes did that to her. Without speaking, Umgani appeared at her side with a goblet of water. She drank it, the cool crispness biting at the pounding in her head.

"It's snowmelt," Umgani said as she refilled the goblet.

"It's snowing?" Kiffen exchanged a worried glance with Simeon. "We're running out of time. We must send reinforcements and the weapon now. Or it will be too late."

* * *

Within the hour, they had formed a force of two hundred Watchers and soldiers to aid Morana in her battle.

"My queen may choose to journey with us, but we wade into dangerous grounds," Montee said as they discussed who would lead this strike. "If you fall in this battle, we have little more to protect. The keep needs commanders to remain here. This is where you should stand."

"You are correct today, Montee." Adana held back the desire to say Montee could ascend to her position. She doubted the First Vision would appreciate that point. "I will remain here, but do not try to prevent me from battle later. I will not be a figurehead."

"Of course, my queen." Montee nodded her head in obeisance. It still felt odd to see her succumb to her authority, and Adana doubted she would ever feel differently about it.

Montee and Simeon would lead this strike while she and Kiffen remained at the keep.

Two of Vuur's glimmer makers accompanied the troops, transporting two flasks wrapped in heavy animal skins and placed in crates packed with multiple layers of furs to pad the weapon against jarring. Montee had eyed the crates, a frown creasing her forehead. She and Simeon consented to bring the weapon but did not confirm any plan to use it.

Vuur's eyes glowed with excitement as they rode away. "I would go with them."

Adana opened her mouth to protest, but he waved a dismissive hand.

"I know my place and your needs, Your Majesty. I remain here to protect the secret and concoct more."

"How much more can you make?" She'd wanted to ask earlier but feared to do so in front of Montee's and Simeon's less than enthusiastic response to its power.

Vuur squinted as if he read a tally of supplies. "That depends." He eyed her. "How much do you want me to hold aside for glimmer fire, fire starters, and glimmer cloth?"

"What are our options?"

"We've enough to make twenty flasks if we make nothing else.

That would make over a hundred pots of glimmer fire, or fifty fire starters, or hundreds of yards of glimmer cloth."

"Make five more." The number felt small and inconsequential, but what else could she do? Glimmer fire and cloth fed Moniah's treasury. Their rarity allowed them to charge a dear price for any of the items made from the secrets of glimmer. She did not plan to sell the weapon, though.

Then Adana tried to calculate whether five was enough while she stood on the ramparts with Kiffen. Snow blanketed the land and decorated the trees with sparkling jewels of white, except for the path left by her army trudging through it. It fell in a heavy blanket and would cover those tracks soon enough.

The crisp air stung her nostrils as she gazed down on the giraffe guard outside the keep. A rush of warm gratitude filled her. Nothing in the histories hinted at giraffes doing this for any queen before.

All the giraffes wore armor, now. After the loss of fifteen of their own and Maligon's determination to kill others, none balked at the weight of the heavy material. It probably helped with the cold, too.

Accustomed to hot weather, the giraffes gathered near fires spaced around the keep. The giraffe keeper placed them at intervals where the giraffes could stand and not leave large gaps in their guard.

As Adana leaned over the edge of the rampart, Glume hustled to one of the fires. The giraffes encircled him. When Glume pulled something from his pocket, each one dipped its head toward him. A treat of some kind. How he found enough food to offer treats beyond their normal feed, Adana could not imagine.

Whatever he gave them or said, each giraffe straightened and looked more alert following his visit. Then Glume hustled to the next fire.

Breath fogging in the air, Adana sidled up next to Kiffen. They huddled together under the weight of both of their blankets, bodies pressed close to ward off the cold. "What do you think will happen when Montee and Simeon reach the others?"

The blankets shifted as Kiffen shrugged. "I'm wondering if Simeon will even use it."

He didn't have to say what "it" was. "Or Montee. I expected excitement when we showed them. Not worry and mistrust."

Kiffen sighed, the air thick with his breath. She breathed in the smell of him and the sharp wine they'd drunk at dinner. Overlaying the intoxicating aroma, the crisp, clean smell of snow, layered with drifting woodsmoke, filled her lungs. The tang of cold, something Adana never knew before living in Elwar, always awoke her mind to possibilities. Maybe that's why she didn't understand their advisor's reluctance about Vuur's weapon. When the weather wiped away all other smells, except for the sweet aroma of the fires below, she felt like nature told them anything was possible. "Why do they object?"

"The weapon is unknown." His arm tightened around her. "And powerful. They're right, I suppose. I just want to use it and put an end to this war."

"Even if they do use it, Maligon still holds Adana's View."

"And Quilla still commands my army."

"Kiffen?" Adana's voice lifted as she realized something. "From the report, it sounds like Quilla left Elwar with over half of your army, right?"

He nodded.

"Jerold regained Belwyn because Maligon left a small force there. What if she left Elwar open to recapture?"

"Quilla would leave someone to lead those she left behind. I know her. She leaves little to chance."

"But who?"

His brown eyes regarded her with iron surety. "Leera."

44

Leera had risen with her men a few hours past midnight. Astride her horse, flanked by Catch on one side and Amar on the other, she bade the men farewell. Never gifted with encouragement, she found herself unable to form the call to victory Amar said she must give. She floundered until he began to murmur words to her. She, in turn, shouted them to her men. Now, she recalled none of it except the soldiers cheering and departing with enthusiasm and confidence.

"Shall we go find a warm hearth, Princess?" Amar had steered his horse toward the west.

"Yes." She followed suit, but her mind stayed with those who traveled south. A whispered prayer to the Creator did not improve her concerns.

Soon after they began their trek, snow began to fall. First, it came in large wet flakes, then the flakes turned smaller and more plentiful. The ground embraced it, and they chose to not stop for a break. All around her the world turned quiet and muffled.

"What do you think King Kiffen will say when you arrive at the keep, Your Highness?" Catch's voice pulled her from her reverie.

She snorted. "Something spiteful. Did you enjoy the scenery on your ride?"

The boy chuckled. "You're his sister. Surely, he'll welcome you to safety with relief. I would if it were my sister."

"You have a sister?" Leera turned toward him in surprise. "You've never mentioned her."

The boy wrinkled his forehead. "She's ten by now."

"Are you worried for her safety?" She'd seen that look on Kiffen's face when Serrin fell ill. He never used it when he thought of her, though.

"We're at war. What if Maligon took her or my parents? He's destroyed many villages. Maybe mine."

"But you're from Elwar?"

Catch nodded.

"I don't believe Maligon attacked Elwar. She should be safe and warm at home." At least she hoped the girl was. Who knew what her mother or Sarx had done in the last few months.

At that moment, one of their advance scouts rode out of the trees and joined Amar. He had a wide grin on his face as he turned toward Leera.

With a swift kick, she advanced her horse forward and reined in beside Amar. "What is it?"

"The keep. Just a short way ahead, through the trees." Amar gestured toward the sky and its continued gift of snow. "We'll be out of this and warm, soon."

Relief streamed down her back and shoulders like melting snow. "At last, we've made it. It will be wonderful to see my brother's face when I deliver my gift of an army to him."

The expression she imagined, pleasure and pride, did not match the reality of what stared down at her an hour later.

A great horde of giraffes blocked her way from crossing the lake, and atop the walls of the keep, her brother frowned down at her, Adana by his side. All along the wall, Watchers readied arrows to fire at her party.

"This is ridiculous." Leera ignored Catch's yelp of alarm and pushed her horse to the front of her men.

Amar looked up as she approached, a frown of displeasure crossing his face. "Princess Leera, you should remain with Catch, where your men can protect you."

"Nonsense." She glared up at her brother. The lake, a perfect barrier to their admission, separated them beyond the act of gentle speech. "What have you said to him so far?"

"Nothing." Amar gestured toward a soldier who rode forward holding up a white banner. "They must think we serve your mother. I'm hoping they will honor our request to speak with them unarmed."

"Unarmed?" Leera's voice rang with the indignation she felt. "And will they be unarmed?"

"If your brother has honor and accepts, they should be."

Leera didn't like the way he stressed the word should. "And do you suspect my brother of treachery?"

"I'm not the one creating this stand-off."

Well, he wasn't. That much she could see, but why was Kiffen acting this way? She scanned the lines of Watchers and soldiers amassed along the wall, but her gaze kept returning to Adana. She looked different, older, maybe. Even from here, Leera saw the stern look on her face and wanted to shout at her to quit frowning before she developed wrinkles before her time.

At the thought, Leera spurred her horse forward, riding straight up to the giraffes, their lines and the lake beyond uncrossable.

"Mother forgive me for yelling in an unladylike way," she whispered to herself, then looked upward. "It's cold out here. Please let me in."

The two, her brother and closest friend, turned to each other, then looked back at her. Did they understand? She crossed her arms over her chest and tried a different tactic. "Adana. That frown will mark you old before your time."

Adana leaned closer to Kiffen and said something that made her brother stiffen. He shook his head. Adana did not break eye contact with him, and it looked like neither one of them spoke again. It was getting harder to discern their actions in the dark.

As Leera drew in breath to shout again, Adana stepped away from the walls. Coming to greet her or something else?

The young soldier with the white cloth caught up to Leera. He continued to wave it like a fool.

"I am sure they saw it by now. Please stop."

Above, Adana had not reappeared, and the remaining Watchers prepared to rain arrows down on them. Was she within range? The thought had not occurred to her, but it was too late now. Either her brother accepted her aid or made the worst mistake of his short reign.

Kiffen shouted something, but the wind had picked up. Blinking up at him, she saw him, blinked again, and he disappeared. A flurry of motion swept along the line of Watchers on the wall, but no one turned away from their targets.

"I didn't suspect this," she said to Amar. "My brother and Adana have cowered below, leaving their army to protect them."

"I don't think so," Amar said as his horse sidled closer to hers. "I believe they come to speak with you. See?" He nodded toward a door beside the huge gate. In the dim light, she saw it open, torchlight flickering from within, then Adana marched out.

"What happens now?" Leera asked, keeping her gaze on the two.

Adana raised her hand, and a quick flurry of sound echoed the action across the wall.

Amar grabbed Leera's bridle. "Either they shoot at us, or she's beckoning you. I don't think either side knows."

"She wouldn't shoot me." Leera dismounted and strode between the giraffes. The massive animals didn't stop her, although one dropped his head to her height, his brown eyes tracking her movement.

By the time she navigated the long legs of the animals, Adana was skimming a small rowboat across the water.

"You have to admit," she whispered to herself, "this lake is perfect for warding off an attack." All she wanted to do was find herself on the other side of the lake, behind those walls, the damp boots and outer clothing she wore shed while she baked the cold out of her by a hearth fire. "In a few more days, we could have walked across."

When the boat drew close to the shore, Adana leapt out and stopped, staring at Leera. "Why have you come?"

The harsh words stung. No hugs or welcoming smiles. Not that anything they'd done so far indicated she should expect that.

"I escaped." Leera took a short step toward Adana, keeping an eye on the soldiers on the walls. "I brought you an army loyal to King Kiffen."

Adana stiffened at those words. Wasn't he king? Or had they decided only she would be queen? That was the problem with uniting the two kingdoms.

Leera pinched herself to force her thoughts back on track. Adana studied her, head tilted to the side, those startling blue eyes reading her like they'd done every day she lived in Elwar.

"How?"

"How?" Leera took another tiny step forward. A rustle of movement along the walls followed her action. Maybe it wasn't a good idea to come any closer.

"How did you escape? How did you bring an army? Your mother's army marches—"

"Across Moniah. I know." Leera glanced up at the wall again. Her brother had not returned. "I've been avoiding her and Maligon's troops for a long time."

The door in the wall opened again, Leera alerted by flickering torchlight before someone stepped out. She recognized her brother's walk approaching the shore. An idea struck her.

"I wish I could have been here for your wedding." She did, too. When Jerold shared the news of their marriage, Leera fought to not cry over missing it.

"You have heard?" Adana took a half-step in Leera's direction, followed by a shout of warning from Kiffen.

Heart shattering over her brother's mistrust, Leera forced herself to look only at Adana. The sounds of oars stroking through the water told her Kiffen had decided to join this reunion. "Yes. Several days ago, we encountered Halar and Pr—Jerold. Jerold told us."

Did Adana catch her slip? She had blinked an extra time when Leera stopped herself from saying prince. That blink provided the only evidence Leera knew to her thoughts. The blink meant shock or surprise.

"He told you?" Another half-step from Adana followed by Kiffen leaping out of the boat and rushing to her side, his hand landing in protection on Adana's arm. She glanced down at his hand and a look of peace pushed the worry from Adana's face.

"Yes." Leera waited then added. "Everything. He told me everything."

"What?" Kiffen glanced between the two of them, confusion clouding his face.

"He told you who he is?" Adana started to reach for Leera.

Kiffen held her back. "Wait. How do we know Quilla hasn't set her up for this? Maybe Quilla told her."

"Quilla doesn't know. Didn't Simeon tell you who had access?" Exasperated, Adana glanced between brother and sister. "Leera, do you offer any proof for the king?"

If Sariah were here, they wouldn't doubt her, but the Protector wasn't. Instead, she fought to protect the rights of these two fools to rule.

The intensity of Kiffen's mistrust bubbled uncertainty in her chest, reminding her of the weight that hung on a chain around her neck.

"Kiffen." She lifted the chain over her head, surprised at the odd feeling of loss once it no longer rested on her breastbone. "I brought you Father's ring."

Her brother narrowed his gaze at the ring. "Why do you have it?"

She stomped her foot in frustration. "If you must know, Mother gave it to me. She wanted me to be queen. The ring is not mine. It's yours." Her voice rang across the lake, the peevish tone she'd managed to hold back while among her men resurfacing.

After a silence that felt like it stretched forever, a loud cheer started from behind her. A flush of pleasure washed over her. They'd heard her words and added their support to her, and if he was smart, her brother.

"Kiffen, these men fled from Quilla after—" She couldn't go on. She couldn't say their father was dead. Not now. She hadn't said it to anyone who mattered.

Arms engulfed her, first Adana's, then Kiffen's. She collapsed into their embrace and wept.

45

For the fourth day in a row, Maligon summoned Shana to his chambers. He smiled at her as she entered and gestured for her to sit on the chair specially reserved for her. This sudden shift toward including Shana concerned her. She and Honest had tried to piece together the clues of why he summoned her, but so far, nothing explained this move.

Rain drummed on the roof of the fortress and lay in puddles on the balcony as she entered. At least it no longer ran into their rooms. The destroyed, but never found, aqueducts prevented flooding inside through a special drain system. Even following it kept them from finding access to the aqueducts. Meanwhile, a replacement drainage process became necessary.

One of the newer soldiers went through the entire fortress followed by a herd of house staff, building structures that captured the rain and pooled it into casks. It worked well, and no one went without water, now.

"Good day to you, Lady Adana," Maligon said, using the new name he'd adopted when speaking to her. Unusual and not appropriate for the queen but better than being called Shana, wench, or tavern maid.

Today, Pultarch sat in the chair across from hers. He rose and sketched a short bow to her as she entered. "My lady." He smirked. "You managed to arrive much sooner than I anticipated."

"I could not wait to join in your company, I'm sure, Lord Pultarch. It is so pleasing and humorous."

She turned to Maligon, hoping today he might explain his purpose behind these summonses. He didn't look up or even stop in his writing. She settled into her chair to wait.

As in the previous three days, someone remained in the room with them. Never just her. Today Pultarch, the two days before, Samantha, and on the first day, Kalara.

At first, she worried Maligon knew about her plan to kill him. Honest thought not, reminding her Maligon suspected anyone except his three shadows.

Patience kept her going, though. Someday, Maligon would need to send one of them away without a ready replacement. Then she would strike and accept the consequences. Fear of exposure stopped her once. Never again. She'd die if necessary.

She stared out at the rain, disappearing into her thoughts to drown out the irritating scratch of Maligon's pen. For exercise one day, she'd attempted to discern what he wrote just by listening to it being written. Without an example to work with, she failed or at least expected she failed.

After writing and sealing four or five different parchments, Maligon signed the last one with a flourish and pushed it across the table. "We're waiting on Brother Honest and Kalara."

Pulled from her reverie, Shana realized he addressed her and Pultarch.

Maligon looked gleeful. "Exciting news today."

A quick intake of breath told her Pultarch was surprised by this announcement. Good. She hated his superior attitude and feared one day she'd be expected to bow down to it.

"Lady Adana, would you serve me some tea?" Maligon nodded toward the tea kettle settled near the hearth for warmth.

One of his favorite commands for her, she accepted it far better than she imagined the true Adana would. She rose and performed the service, cocking an eyebrow toward Pultarch.

"No," Maligon said. "He needs nothing. Nor do you. Youth gives you the strength you need."

Over the rain, the rattle in his chest became harder to hear, but she caught remnants of it when she drew close enough to give him his tea. The damp appeared to ease the problem, for reasons she could not imagine since she felt like she breathed through a soaking wet cloth every day.

While Maligon sipped his tea, he hummed. The tune, one he hummed when in a good mood, was unfamiliar to Shana. At last, Honest entered, with Kalara soon after. Maligon straightened and beamed at each of them. He opened his mouth to speak, but Samantha hustled into the room, interrupting him.

"I apologize for my tardiness, Lord. No one alerted me to this meeting."

Curious to see Kalara's response, Shana tried to watch Maligon and his adopted daughter. Kalara half-rose from her seat.

Maligon waved her down and peered over his steepled hands at Samantha. "Of course, Samantha. We can't proceed without our First Vision."

A tiny snort, so minuscule only Shana heard it, erupted from Kalara.

Once Samantha settled in the only remaining chair, one set behind the others, Maligon leaned forward, the same look of anticipation on his face. "My scouts tell me reinforcements will arrive today. By this evening at the latest."

Samantha sat forward. "Why wasn't I notified?"

At the same time, Kalara said, "What reinforcements?"

Neither woman looked nor sounded pleased by the news.

"Please, don't trouble yourselves." Maligon made shooing motions with his hands. He rolled his eyes at Honest and Pultarch, a move that couldn't gain him much favor with Kalara. Did he care?

"I commanded my scouts to keep me informed. Not you."

Both Watchers' stiffened. She couldn't blame them. He treated them as nothing but decorations. Something she knew a lot about.

"Queen Quilla and Lord Sarx are bringing the bulk of Elwar's army to us."

The words dripped like ice in Shana's veins, slowing her heart-beat to a deathly pace.

"Where will you put all of them?" Samantha edged forward to see between Pultarch and Honest. "We have no room."

"Since you ask and insisted on joining us this morning, I'll leave that arrangement to you. Some of your Watcher quarters remain vacant. Let them berth there. Stack them four and five to a room if you must."

Aghast, Samantha sat back. He'd reduced her to garrison com-mander in one stroke.

"Do you truly trust Quilla and Sarx?" Kalara asked.

Shana wanted to lean forward and add her concern to Kalara's but kept still. Her skin crawled with the knowledge of the man's impending arrival. He dressed like a noble but acted no better than the worst scum who frequented The Sleeping Dog.

She'd met Queen Quilla and found her obstinate and grasping but sensed no real danger from her. Of course, that was before the death of King Donel. She'd overheard Adana speculate on Quilla's involvement in Donel's murder, a truth that would place her on the same level as Sarx.

Maligon ignored Kalara and focused his heavy black gaze on Shana. "As for you, Lady Adana. You will officially greet our visitors as Queen Adana. It is time you retake the role Sarx planned for you."

A knot formed in her belly and continued to grow as Maligon continued, swiveling toward Pultarch next.

"And you will stand by her side as faithful betrothed. No more of this battle of words between the two of you." He leaned toward Pultarch, which gave Shana some pleasure, although she knew the message was meant for her, too. "We must present the queen and future king to these officers and soldiers as besotted with each other. You must convince them of your love for each other and for Moniah."

Shana struggled to swallow, her mouth dry in spite of the damp day.

"Brother Honest," Maligon continued, "you will begin to prepare these two for their happy nuptials."

Bile rose in Shana's mouth. Pultarch shifted in his seat. Neither spoke.

Maligon continued, oblivious to their reaction or uncaring, anyway. "They must appear as a blissful, happy couple. I want them so enraptured that they can't stand to be apart. Understood?"

Honest nodded, avoiding Shana's gaze.

"What of me, Father? What do you wish of me?" Kalara's voice held excitement, but Shana detected signs of it being forced.

The expression on Maligon's face did not instill confidence. "You, my daughter, will send your Watchers into this army and learn what secrets they hold. I've heard rumors of deserters running to support the imposters at the keep. We must know how many of their men are gone, and how to locate them and shift their loyalties back to me."

"With honor, Father." Kalara flushed with pleasure at her task, the only one in the room pleased with her duties. Had she not noticed Maligon's emphasis on loyalty to only him?

Maligon excused them, ordering them to begin their tasks at once.

Honest led Shana and Pultarch from the chambers, a distant look on his face. He failed to notice Shana speaking his name until she grabbed his arm to stop him.

"Yes?" His eyes still looked vacant even though he turned to the two of them.

"Brother Honest." Pultarch's voice came out gravelly as if he had been choking on something.

Maybe the tone brought Honest back, but he snapped back to the moment. "Yes, Pultarch?"

To Shana's shock, Pultarch's chin quivered. A tear tumbled from one eye. He fought to control it; she could see that. "I can't marry her."

Even though she felt the same way, his declaration stung.

Laying a compassionate hand on Pultarch's shoulder, Honest said, "I don't believe he means to marry you two." He looked between them. "He wants you to act that way, though. But be aware—" he raised a warning finger, "—Quilla is no fool. I doubt Sarx is either, though I have never met the man."

"Be thankful," Shana and Pultarch said at the same time.

Surprised, she stared at him. Why would Pultarch resent Sarx?

Before she could ask, Honest continued. "We will work on presenting two lovebirds intent on each other. I believe, if I understand his directions, we shall focus on your attraction and leave the others to focus on the coming battle."

"That's ludicrous." Pultarch squared his shoulders. "I'm a trained swordsman, a warrior. I'm sure he expects me to fight."

Honest shook his head. "Let's hope he doesn't. I fear this war will destroy many. Plus, as the presumed Husband King, you are precious to the continuation of Moniah's noble line."

The idea of continuing Moniah's line of succession through the two of them made Shana retch. She slapped her hand over her mouth and raced to the nearest window, throwing the shutters open despite the rain blowing into her face. She gripped the ledge and vomited into the courtyard below. The downpour dissipated her stomach's contents across the paving stones in mere moments. Lifting her face to the rain, Shana relished the cool air with relief.

A hand came to rest on her elbow. Pultarch gaped down at her, his brown eyes concerned. "Are you ok, my lady?"

She wiped her mouth with the back of her hand, nodded, and stepped back from the window. Taking her hand in his, Pultarch led her away from the driving rain while Honest resecured the shutters.

"I know how to do this—" Pultarch hesitated, "—Shana."

It had been some time since he'd called her by her real name, always using a jibe at her position instead.

"I will help you. And I promise to never marry you or help you continue the line of succession for Moniah's throne."

"Let's hope you can keep that promise, my lord."

Without another word, the two followed Honest to the temple, Shana taking Pultarch's arm as she had seen Adana do with Kiffen. Maybe Pultarch promised, but if she were back in the tavern running the gaming bets, she'd place her money on Maligon's plans, not Pultarch's.

46

Quilla, self-proclaimed queen of Elwar, sneered at the rain that deigned to saturate her gloved hands and cloak. Beside her, Sarx had been grumbling about the pace she insisted they keep in order to reach Adana's View. If she had her way, Maligon would change the name of the fortress to something more respectable, the sooner the better.

"Quilla, please, listen to reason," Sarx shouted in a most uncivilized manner over the pounding rain.

"I have listened," she said. "I choose not to accept your thoughts. We'd be inside, dry and warm, if I'd done that sooner."

Why in the world had Sarx waited so long to take this journey to Moniah? She never wanted to travel to this savage place anyway. Maligon insisted he needed this kingdom over the other three. An idiotic notion, but Maligon made the decisions. For now.

"Stop for a moment and look behind you." Sarx's voice turned to that wheedling tone he used to persuade her to his way of thinking.

With a sigh, she turned and looked.

She hated weak men. Donel had been weak, much to her surprise. His son Serrin's body was so weak he couldn't fight off the disease that killed him. Most of her higher-ranking officers had deserted her, the cowards. The only man she knew who was not weak was just a boy. It galled her to admit it, but Kiffen showed remarkable strength and courage. Too bad he fell for the savage Adana and her uncivilized way of life. Together, they could have conquered all four kingdoms and sent Maligon to certain death.

Sarx pointed in the distance. "Our ranks fall behind. They can't keep up. We leave them to the ravages of the weather and open to attack."

"You want me to wait for them?"

"Yes. We need them."

"But if I wait, aren't we subject to the same ravages threatening them—weather and attack?"

Rather than answer, Sarx stared at her. She enjoyed having that effect on him. Speechless, he could not defy her or try to sway others to do so.

"I thought so," she said. "We've wasted enough time." She turned her horse south. Again. Although she hated the land before her, she breathed a sigh of relief to be moving in the correct direction.

A nice warm fire, a bath, some soup, a little wine, and she might forgive Sarx and Maligon for dragging her here. As she dreamed of these things, a rider raced up, his horse's hooves throwing mud all over her sodden clothing.

Without waiting for acknowledgement, he announced, "We're under attack."

Sarx cursed and wheeled his horse around. "Where? How many?"

Aware she must pretend concern, Quilla reined her horse around and stared over the rainy landscape. "I see nothing."

"The rear lines," the man said. "They came at us from behind."

"How many?" Sarx asked.

"A small force but we're spread out too far." Casting a cautious glance at Quilla, the man added, "They wear Elwar's colors."

She sniffed in displeasure. "Deserters."

Sarx turned to Taren, who had ridden by their side, quiet and reserved, ever since they left Elwar. "Go. Gather the rear flanks. Defend them."

The words sent hot anger surging to Quilla's head. "Taren. Hold."

He yanked back on the reins, his horse skidding in the mud.

"We will not send so many. The rear lines can handle a small force. Order them to kill any deserters. Except my daughter. Bring her to me."

The sidelong glance of incredulity Sarx gave her added to her annoyance. "What?"

"We have one troop assigned to protect the supply wagons and livestock. That's not enough to stop an attack."

"They are there to protect. Let them protect."

Easing his horse closer to hers, Sarx spoke in quiet, firm words. "We need to send men, or we will lose our supplies."

Another horse thundered up, splattering more mud over Quilla. "They've cut off the last quarter of your lines."

"Cut off?" Quilla raised an eyebrow. "How?"

"They found a gap. Because we're spread out. Surrounded our rear lines."

Before Quilla could speak, Sarx barked an order to Taren. "Take ten units from this side of the fighting. We will trap their troops between them and the ones they think they trapped instead." He grinned at Quilla, his teeth mud splattered.

"We can't." The soldier looked from Sarx to Quilla. "There's a river between us, now. I barely made it across."

"Unbelievable." Sarx galloped toward the rear of their lines, Taren and the two messengers following him.

Quilla frowned after them, then shook her head. If they wanted to play battle in the rain, they could. She would take the rest of her troops to Moniah. Civilized wars should be fought indoors using wit not the lives of men. She'd tried to tell Sarx this many times, but he ignored her. Maligon ordered them to come. She came. He would pay for this order, though.

* * *

Morana watched the muddy mess of battle from a knoll. The rain poured down, adding to the confusing scene below. With only a hundred soldiers to protect the rear of Quilla's army and supplies, it had been easy to cut them off. A powerful raging torrent of water made their task easier.

She shivered in the cold and wet, but Ostreia had been correct. The rain worked for them. For now.

Shouts from the far side of the battle thundered over the steady drumming of rain. Out of the trees, another force charged. *Who was that?*

"Mother?" Navon stared at the new army.

"Stay here," she called as she kicked her horse forward, searching for Ostreia or Biaji.

Her horse galloped across the land as if it had been starved for action. Mud churned beneath them as she approached the edge of the battle. To her right, men overwhelmed a wagon and it fell over. The sight hurt to see but better destroyed supplies then supplies given to the enemy.

She slowed her horse on the edge of the melee, searching for a familiar face. The tumble of soldiers and Watchers confused her. Many of the new troops wore Elwarian uniforms. A trap or deserters like some of the men in her own forces?

The cry of a Watcher in battle howled from the far side of the mass of soldiers. Steering clear of the fighting, Morana raced around the fighting, headed toward the sound. Before she traveled a few horse lengths, she pulled her horse to a stop. Another army spilled from the trees. At the forefront ran Watchers and more Elwarian soldiers. *Who did they fight for?*

Unable to warn anyone in this mess, she wheeled her horse around and raced back to the knoll. Through the rain, she couldn't see Navon or anyone else there. She prayed only rain hid him from her sight.

* * *

Montee heard the screams and shouts of battle long before they reached the plains. She and Simeon held their army behind the tree line trying to make sense of the turmoil. Mud covered everyone. An occasional glimpse of blue revealed an Elwarian uniform, but were they Kiffen's men or Quilla's?

Simeon stood next to her, lips set in a grim line. "We might need to retreat and not engage."

By her side, the Watcher who warned them about Quilla's army studied the battle.

"Do you see Morana's troops?" Montee asked.

The warrior continued to scan the area. "There." She pointed. "Ostreia is there."

"Keep her in your sights," Montee ordered and began to search the soldiers near Ostreia. Her gaze fell on a Watcher surrounded by men who looked scruffier than some of the others. Body caked in mud like everyone else on the field, it was impossible to determine loyalties.

Agonizing moments later, Ostreia fell in side by side with this Watcher. Men gathered to them. Together, they pressed their advantage toward the rest of the battle.

It was enough. She knew who they fought with. Turning to the two glimmer makers, she said, "It's too dangerous to launch those now. Wait here."

She turned toward Simeon. "Shall we?"

He met her gaze with a rare grin. "After you."

She allowed her laughter to fuel her battle cry as they charged into the fray.

The ground oozed over Montee's boots. She fought for precarious balance and slammed into the raging soldiers. The crush of warriors held her upright. She slashed and stabbed through them, keeping an eye on Ostreia and her warriors.

A man's hoarse shout gave the only warning. A body slammed into her, his teeth and eyes bright in his mud-streaked face. She stumbled backward, stopped from her fall by warriors behind her. Her attacker's sword swung down, and she dodged, spun, and swept his feet out from under him.

The ground gave way beneath her. Montee landed on top of her attacker. They grappled in the mud. The battle continued to surge around them. Somehow, they avoided being trampled.

The soldier rolled her. He fought to pin her down, one of her wrists pinned to the ground above her head. She relaxed, aware he might not see the knife in that hand. The man sensed her release and shifted his weight. Just enough so she could take aim. She drove the knife into the soldier's eye. The man's other eye grew wide with astonishment. His mouth fell open. The full weight of his body dropped on top of her.

Suffocating from his weight, she sank deeper in the mud. It oozed over her. Gasping, she kicked and fought to get free. Harder than she'd fought the soldier.

Without warning, the weight vanished. Simeon stood above her, hand held out. She grasped it and jumped to her feet.

* * *

"The one good thing about rain," Simeon said to Montee as they scanned the aftermath of the battle, "it washes away the gore and smells faster."

She nodded, breathing too hard to respond yet. The huge mud

pit in front of them teemed with bodies. Some theirs, some Quilla's, some Morana's, and some from an unexpected source—Leera of El-war. Charissa enlightened them with that news when Montee found her searching the bodies in the field.

Now, she stood on a small knoll with Simeon, Morana, and Sariah, the Protector's face grim as she scanned the battlefield. Morana crouched over Navon's mud-covered and unconscious body. A gash across his forehead bled but wasn't serious. A mirror image of the gash oozed a stream of blood down Sariah's forehead. The fighting never reached the knoll, but when Sariah spotted Prince Navon wandering close to the combatants, she'd broken free and swooped him up, carrying him to safety.

A soldier, recognizing Navon for who he was, made the unfortunate choice to grab for him at the same time. The soldier didn't survive that encounter.

"How did Navon end up down there?" Montee squatted beside the boy.

"I don't know." Morana stroked her son's damp curls from his forehead. "When the other armies came out of the woods, I ordered him to stay here. I went to warn our forces. When I came back, he was gone. His guards never saw him leave and were searching for him."

Sariah paused to look down at Navon. "He's a strong boy. He'll be fine."

"Then why won't he wake?" Morana's voice edged on hysteria.

"He was exhausted and frightened when I reached him. Give him time. It's a lot for a child to witness."

Simeon turned a stern look on the soldiers left to protect the prince.

Before he could reprimand them, Morana rose. Her hands shook, but she'd regained control of her nerves. "No, Simeon. The extra armies confused all of us. Navon is adept at slipping away if he wants to."

At that point, Montee spotted Ostreia striding up the knoll. "We have secured most of the wagons and livestock. Those not damaged beyond use."

"Good." Montee squinted across the battlefield. The rain had settled to a steady drizzle, so she could see a fair distance. Nothing moved on the plains. Quilla's army left her men to die. Had any escaped and now hid in the trees or attempted to struggle to Adana's View? "Why didn't the rest of Quilla's army fight?"

"Cut off," Ostreia said. "Water fought the battle for us today."

"Maybe so," Montee said, "but it will fight against us if we don't move. A deluge comes. I feel it."

"What about the bodies?" Morana covered her hand over her mouth. "You'll leave them here?"

Montee shook her head. "We've checked for the injured among the dead and pulled them free. We'll use our new fire starter to honor the dead." She waved the glimmer makers forward. "Do you have enough to allow these souls to depart?"

"With the new—" one of them said, voice rising in excitement quite different from the horror she'd worn on her face moments ago.

"No. Not that. Fire starters. Do you have enough?" How many would it take to dispose of these bodies, soaked with rain and mud? She still found Adana's and Umgani's reports of the fire's capabilities hard to believe.

"Oh, yes, First Vision. We have plenty."

Directing the Watchers and soldiers nearby to assist them, Montee ordered them to burn the bodies and destroyed supplies. The two handed out the small tubes, providing a quick demonstration of flicking the wrist to release the flame.

Everyone gasped when a blue-green flame ignited at the end of the tube despite the rain. In a quick motion, the glimmer maker flicked her wrist again, sending the flame to catch on a pile of bodies. Blue and green fire flashed and took hold of the bodies, spreading with a pinkish *whoosh* Montee felt and heard even this far away. Glimmer fire burned hotter and brighter than regular fire, but this looked different. *What had Vuur discovered?* Her unease over the explosive weapon increased as she watched it burn.

The army moved farther from the piled bodies as they began to burn. The heat, even in the rain, flushed their faces. From a safe distance, everyone stopped to wonder at the remarkable fire spreading across the rain-soaked bodies.

When the glimmer makers returned from their task, Simeon asked, his voice booming above the murmuring, "How do you quench these flames?"

The question never occurred to Montee. If the glimmer makers did not object to setting this many bodies on fire, they knew how to keep it from burning out of control. All who worked with glimmer fire learned this first—do not burn what you can't put out.

It took only one Watcher, a glimmer maker also, to make that mistake. Ballene, well-known by every person in Moniah for the disastrous fire that destroyed the only forest within the kingdom's borders. Ballene's fire, a warning tale to all.

As the fire experts explained the method for putting out the blazes, Montee looked south to the horizon. She could not see it, not through the haze of rain. Somewhere, not far, rose the walls of home. Could Maligon or Quilla see these fires?

Leaving the two glimmer makers and ten of her Watchers to control the fires, the rest of the three armies started their trek to the Border Keep.

47

Shana stood in the Great Hall, a Watcher holding a large canopy over her and Maligon, as Quilla and Sarx were escorted into their presence. Standing under the canopy, but behind her, were Kalara, Samantha, Pultarch, and Brother Honest.

As the two Elwarians drew closer, Honest whispered in a low voice meant only for her, "Be strong."

Thanks to her Listening gifts, she heard him over the drum of the rain on their covering.

The two travelers looked like drenched cats pulled from a river. The way they walked forward, heads held high as if they meant to not appear bedraggled and soaked, amused her.

Rain poured down and dripped from the rim of Sarx's hat. It bore a large feather which drooped and sagged. She grinned, knowing it would infuriate Sarx to be left to the elements while the little wench he found in The Sleeping Dog lorded over him in expensive glimmer cloth and a makeshift crown of Moniah on her head.

Quilla and Sarx stopped before her, and she waited. Sarx held no title, so he should bow to her. He did not. Beside her, Maligon stiffened. Most of the fortress' Watchers and soldiers stood behind them to witness this welcome. If Quilla didn't bend, Sarx, at least should.

After a lengthy wait of wills, Maligon snarled at them. "Sarx, give proper respect to Queen Adana, the Seat of Authority in Moniah. Quilla, foreign rulers at least bow their heads when meeting a ruler within their lands."

The two grimaced but sketched the smallest of bows toward her. Neither complained that Maligon did not use Quilla's title of queen.

"Moniah welcomes you to our home," Shana said while wondering how high Quilla's eyebrows could rise. They disappeared under the remains of what must have been an elaborate hairstyle at some point. "We offer you solace from your travels and a hearth for your comfort."

She extended her hand, inviting a servant who stood by to come forward. He did, bowed, then turned to lead them away.

Neither Quilla nor Sarx moved. The servant paused and waited.

"You don't wish to refresh yourselves?" Maligon asked, his voice as pleasant as the richest innkeeper's.

"We—" Sarx stepped forward, dark eyes furious, "—were attacked. Half of our troops are missing or drowned. Our supplies are destroyed or in the hands of your enemies."

At Maligon's expectant look, Sarx added, "My Lord."

"We are aware," Maligon said. "Please, go refresh yourselves."

With a huff, Quilla grabbed Sarx's arm and marched, head still held high, after the servant who scurried ahead of them to avoid being run down.

"Such a terrible ordeal," Maligon held a gentle hand to his nose and sniffed, "having to greet those two as they reek of the road and foul weather."

For the first time since arriving in Moniah, Shana chuckled over the man's humor. He might be difficult, but he did lord over everyone, not just her. Nice to see someone as pompous as Sarx face arrogance aimed at himself for once.

As the two nobles walked away, several of the soldiers behind

Shana began to shout. She turned in surprise at the disruption. The shouts grew louder, and most of the army and Watchers stared or pointed into the distance. Many looked frightened.

No one moved to shield or protect Maligon, so they didn't perceive imminent danger. She turned to see what they pointed at and stopped breathing, eyes widening. The distant sky glowed with blue and green and pink lights flickering through the steady rain. Far, but not very far. *What was it?*

The loud jumble of voices exclaiming over the strange lights forced Shana to cover her ears. Honest saw and stepped beside her, placing a comforting hand on her back where no one would see. Who would see, anyway? No one cared what she and Honest did right now. The lights held all of them in thrall.

"A sign." Maligon raised his voice to be heard. Even with the great multitude of shouting and talking, everyone silenced. "It's a sign from the Creator. Victory is ours."

A cheer went up. People laughed and clapped each other on the back, but not everyone. Quilla and Sarx, forced to halt as their guide stared at the sight in wonder, looked more agitated, if that was possible. The people under the canopy with Shana did not relax either, casting questioning glances between them. Even Samantha and Kalara, who struggled to limit their encounters, shared frightened looks.

"Shall we?" Maligon held his arm out to Shana. If he wanted to pretend the lights meant nothing, she must follow his lead. For now. She placed her hand on the crook of his elbow, careful to not press down on the scars. Honest said Maligon didn't feel anything in that arm, but she preferred to not think about the scarred and ravaged flesh hidden beneath the sleeve of the man's purple robes.

As they promenaded—Maligon's word for their walk—across the hall toward the royal wing, he said, "You did well, my lady."

"Thank you."

Once inside, Maligon dropped the pretense, wrenching his arm from hers. He turned toward Samantha and Kalara. "Assign Watchers to their quarters. They go nowhere without an escort. Please offer them my kindest invitation to join us as we celebrate their arrival in the formal dining hall this evening."

Both women nodded, but when Kalara turned to go, Samantha stayed.

"Yes?"

"What of the lights? Shouldn't we send someone to check?"

He studied her a long time, shifting his gaze to Kalara a few times. She had stopped in her tracks when Samantha spoke.

"You do not believe it's a sign?"

"No." Samantha swallowed, her throat bobbing. "I've seen it. In my dreams before."

"A vision?"

"Possibly. I've seen it more than once."

Kalara returned, her eyes wary as her father focused on Samantha and this revelation.

Noticing her, he faced his daughter. "Have you seen anything? Visions? Dreams?"

"No, Father." She blushed, two blooms of red against the deep tan of her skin.

"Interesting. Kalara, you will tend to housing the men instead of Samantha. Make sure you stake more Watchers throughout the barracks. I want to know what they know. If one soldier sneezes, I wish to know. Understood?"

Kalara's blush drained, away leaving her pale.

"Come with me," Maligon said to Samantha and turned toward the royal wing. He waved for Shana, Pultarch, and Honest to follow him.

Pultarch stepped up and gave Shana his arm. She took it without thought, her mind whirling over the implications of shifting

Samantha's responsibilities to Kalara. She didn't dare look back at Kalara as they left her behind.

In Maligon's chambers, he eased himself into his chair and sighed, eyes closed. The four of them, not invited to sit, stood. In the quiet, Shana strained to hear the traitor's breathing. The rattle aggravated his breathing, as if he feared the outcome of Samantha's dream.

"We will forget the unpleasantness of that poor greeting this afternoon and show Quilla and her consort our gracious hospitality." Dark eyes on Shana, Maligon continued. "You will continue to behave with the decorum of a queen. Do not forget, you are besotted with Pultarch. Everyone must see it. We cannot risk discovery at this point of the game."

He tapped his fingertips together and appeared to fall deep into thought. "Honest, we should hold a service tomorrow morning, thanking the Creator for our guests' safe arrival, the sign in the sky, and praying for the souls of the men lost during their journey to Moniah."

The fingertip tapping continued a few more moments, then Maligon eyed Pultarch. "You will show every kindness to Shana. Wait on her hand and foot at dinner. Hand feed her. Watch over her. Do not let her drink too much wine. Everything one would expect Pultarch, son of the Earl of Brom, to do. Understood?"

Each one nodded at their charges while Samantha stood still, back straight, triumph lighting her eyes.

At last, he turned to her. "What can you tell me of your dream?" He reached for a carafe of wine and poured two cups, handing one to Samantha.

"It's brief. It's come several times since the day my—the day Kassa infiltrated our walls."

"Interesting."

"Each time, I see the Glimmer Isati standing before a large bowl. Blue and green light pours from the bowl. When I step closer, I see flames. Blue and green flames. The bowl holds water, but the flames still burn."

Could it really be fire? Shana knew of glimmer fire, but she'd seen it only a few times in sacred ceremonies. If the Isati found a way to burn even water, what could they do against it? Fire like that, used against Maligon, might be difficult to escape. Her loyalty to Queen Adana would not guarantee her survival of an attack with this new fire.

"Did the fire on our wall burn like this?" Maligon looked between the four of them for answers. They each had been there that night.

"No," Shana said. "It was difficult to stop, though."

The man slumped and scrubbed his face with his hands. "Dismissed. All of you. I need peace and quiet to prepare for the battle of wits Quilla will most undoubtedly attempt."

None of them spoke until they left the room. One glance at Pultarch told Shana what she suspected. He recognized the danger the fire posed for all of them, too. Honest, on the other hand, seemed pleased. She tilted her head in question. With a slight shake of his, he indicated for her to wait.

Somehow, she suspected the service tomorrow might not be what Maligon expected. A part of her thrilled at the idea while her stomach dropped to the floor. What would she do if Maligon took away her one solace among these fools?

48

After an elaborate meal from the bulk of the fortress' larder, Shana allowed Pultarch to escort her to her chambers. Her face ached from the forced smiles and laughter she bestowed on him in front of their guests. They appeared to believe it, Sarx going so far as to whisper congratulations to her on making Pultarch forget the independent chit, Adana.

Once they reached the privacy of the royal wing, Pultarch dropped his arm and rubbed his large hand over his face, then through his hair. His cowlick flopped over his forehead in the way many women found appealing. She had been one of them once, before she knew the man behind the handsome face.

When he continued to walk with her, she stopped. "You needn't stay with me. I know the way."

"I would talk with you. If you will allow me."

Curiosity compelled her to nod. "Of course."

They walked the corridor in silence, arriving at her chambers without speaking more. What could Pultarch want? She counted the weapons hidden on her body and considered the placement of others throughout her room. She doubted he meant to harm her, but no one today behaved as expected.

Her maid had lit the candles, so they entered a peaceful room bathed in soft light. Almost romantic if Pultarch wasn't the man beside her. For a brief moment, she wished for Honest. Confusion forced that thought away.

Within her flowing formal robes of glimmer cloth, she felt Bauns flutter and shift as he recognized their location. Praying the animal sensed the importance of staying out of sight, she sat on the only chair in the room. "What did you wish to speak about?"

Bauns shifted again, and she wriggled to adjust to his position.

"You can let your pet out. I know about him." Pultarch's gaze rested on her chest.

"What do y—"

"I'm not blind, Adana. You have a little pet something. It's with you all the time these days. So am I. I've seen it when you thought I wasn't looking."

Turning away from him, she hid her reaction to his using Adana's name instead of her own, much less staring at her chest where the jerboa nestled.

She clucked her tongue and Bauns emerged from the top of her bodice. He took one leap and landed on the floor in front of Pultarch.

The man squatted to peer at the jerboa. "So, this is it? Does it have a name?"

"Bauns."

After regarding Pultarch a moment, Bauns took two hops and landed on her sleeping chaise.

"What did you wish to discuss?" Shana asked.

"Adana." His voice came out ragged and full of despair.

"I'm sorry. Do you wish to discuss Adana or are you calling me Adana? Because if you didn't notice, you called me that just a moment ago."

"No...Yes, I wish to discuss her. I know what I called you. I don't wish to call you the wrong name before other people."

"Makes sense. What about her?"

"Does she really love Kiffen?" His face looked pinched and worried as he waited for her answer.

"Yes. But you knew that."

"I did." He dropped down on the chaise. "I let the Lord convince me differently. Then you came, and he decided you were good enough."

She winced at that.

"Not that you're not a good, well...um, a decent...What I mean to say is you're nice, kind. But I miss her. You look like her. You even talk like her when you have to, but you're not her. I still love her."

"Do you?"

"What? Of course."

"No. I'm serious. Do you truly believe you love her? Because I think you don't even know who she is.

"You don't want a strong woman. You frown at every Watcher who stands her ground and does her duty to this fortress. You don't like women as soldiers. You don't even like me with pretend power. I don't think you care much for Queen Quilla as a ruler, either."

He blinked back at her in surprise. "You see all that?"

Careful, she warned herself. She heard all of this through sighs and breathing and eavesdropping. Better let him think she observed it. He, at least, understood Watchers. "Yes. To anyone who wants to know or spends any time with you, it's plain as that jerboa sleeping on my pillow."

The little brown animal did not move, but it stood out, its brown fur against the pale yellow of the pillow.

"What do I do?"

"About what?"

"How do I get over her?" He looked like a small boy awakened by a nightmare.

"You find someone else." When he raised his gaze to hers, she sat back warding him off with her hands. "Not me. I'm as independent as her."

That produced a grin. "You're a pain, Adana. Don't worry. Anyone who can throw a hatchet like you is not my idea of someone I'd marry."

"Keep in mind, almost every woman inside this fortress fights and stands on her own abilities. You won't find a weak woman here."

"What about you?" He sat forward. "Is there someone here for you? Besides me, I mean."

As if he had to make that distinction. Again, Honest's face flashed in her mind, but she shoved it away. "No. It's not like anyone believes I'm available."

"You didn't notice the way Sarx's nephew stared at you over dinner?"

"Taren?" She tried to recall his face but drew a blank.

"I heard he sought Leera's hand, but since she's disappeared, maybe he's decided a queen in Moniah is just as good."

"Because he wouldn't find me attractive, is that it?"

"No."

She yanked one of her knives from her sleeve and threw it into a painting on the wall above his head.

He ducked. "What are you—"

"Come now. If I'd wanted to hit you, I would have. You said I wasn't attractive."

"I did not. You said he wouldn't find you attractive and asked if I agreed. I said no."

"Hmm." She chuckled. "You should have seen you dive for the floor."

"It was quite amusing," Brother Honest's voice came from the entry to the room.

They both whirled in surprise.

"Didn't notice me standing here, listening to your conversation?" He walked into the room, his teacher's robes swishing as he walked.

Shana swallowed. What had he heard? Thank goodness she hadn't said whose name came to mind when Pultarch asked if she was attracted to anyone.

She glanced at Pultarch. His jaw muscle worked hard, something he did when frustrated.

Honest sat down on the chaise where Pultarch had been, and Bauns popped up from the pillow and leapt to his shoulder. "Hello, Bauns." He stroked the jerboa's back. "If I hadn't seen the little queen here throw that knife, I might think these two deep in romantic conversation."

Both of them snorted.

"No?" He raised an eyebrow, glancing between them. "Good. It wouldn't do for them to fall for each other, would it, Bauns?"

Why did his remark make her want to argue with him? Pride? Embarrassment?

Pultarch saved her the problem. "Why would you say that?"

"The little queen told you why she and Adana are not suitable matches for you. Unless you change your way of thinking, I agree with her. Plus," he turned his deep brown eyes on Shana, "I believe our little queen is destined for something you can never give her."

Honest was full of flattering comments tonight. At least his words fit his name, not that Pultarch knew the origin of Honest's chosen name when he became a Teacher of the Faith. Few people knew Honest possessed Seer and Empath gifts.

"Did you seek me out for a purpose, Brother Honest?" Shana turned to her role as queen in an effort to move beyond the awkward moment.

"Yes." He slapped his hands on his knees. "I need to go over parts of the special ceremony with you if you're willing to delay your bedtime."

Pultarch rose to leave. "I'll bid the two of you good evening." He paused at the door and bowed to Shana. "Thank you for listening, my lady."

After he left, Honest turned and studied her. She looked away, focusing on Bauns. Why did she feel shy now?

Whatever his thoughts, Honest did not share them. Instead, he rose and extended his arm to her. "Will you accompany me to the temple, my queen?"

They walked through the quiet, empty corridors. After the lavish meal, most people stumbled to their beds to sleep off the heavy food and drink. She hadn't drunk anything but watered wine, her time working in the tavern a lesson on avoiding drunkenness.

Inside the temple, the glow of candles reflected off the polished wooden pews and walls. Every time she entered this sanctuary, her breath caught, and her body eased into something more fluid and content.

She looked up to find Honest watching her. "What do we need to discuss?"

"Not much. In fact, I could wait to tell you in the morning if you prefer."

Confused, she placed her hands on her hips. "Why bring me here, then?"

Laughter rolled out of him, his head tilted back. It echoed against the rafters.

"What is so funny?"

"I love it when you become Shana again. You radiate a fire unquenched by anyone, even the fools in this fortress."

The words pleased her, but she continued to stand with her hands on her hips. "Why am I here?"

The pew creaked as he sat then patted the seat beside him. After she joined him, he said, "I heard a bit more than I told you. In your chambers. Do you find Taren appealing?"

"I don't even recall his face."

Nodding, he continued. "But you hesitated when Pultarch asked if there was someone for you. You thought of someone. I sensed it."

His hand now rested on her arm. As a Seer, he'd know if she told the truth with his hand touching her. He'd done this before with her. When she needed to prove to Queen Adana she was not Sarx's spy. His hand felt warm. She licked her lips and looked away.

When she didn't answer, he spoke again. "I wanted you to say me. I wanted to hear my name from your lips."

He bent and kissed her.

She started to pull back, but his lips felt warm and soft and perfect.

She kissed him back.

49

Six Weeks Later

Shana started as if a loud noise woke her. She blinked at the sunlight streaming in from the courtyard and strained to hear what disturbed her sleep. Nothing. Not even the steady rumble of rain on the roof. Then it dawned on her; she woke to silence.

Throwing back her covers, she jumped from the bed. Bauns gave a tiny squeak of alarm and jumped to the floor, whiskers twitching.

"It's stopped raining." Shana rushed to the closed off entrance to her courtyard and pulled the heavy door open. Sunlight danced across the puddles of water, glistening like tiny jewels fallen from the sky.

From the balcony wall, she looked out over the land. A lake of water filled the landscape; animals gathered on its edge.

Malay had told her the rains will end when the animals return. Below, zebra, antelope, and lions lapped at the water, unfazed by the presence of predator and prey at the same watering hole. Flocks of birds settled on the surface, rising and settling again in a rhythm only they knew.

"If only we could convince Maligon to follow this example and put aside his anger and leave the kingdoms to their rightful rulers."

As she said this, the pride of lions continued to drink while the other animals balked and moved away, several keeping an eye on the large cats.

A knock at her door drew her back inside. Malay entered with a tray of tea and biscuits. Not all of Quilla's supplies had fallen to their attackers. They did manage to transport flour, dry no less, and sacks of sweet potatoes. The two combined made a decent breakfast, especially once she drizzled honey over them and added a huge dollop to her tea.

"The Lord wishes to see you in his chambers in the hour."

"Just me?" Shana always asked this, but he never accepted her alone.

"No." Malay sat down and took a bite of a biscuit. "Mmm. I thought I'd get tired of these, but they're so good." She dusted crumbs from her tunic. "I'll get that later. He's called for all his officials and commanders."

"The scouts returned?" Shana lost her appetite as she realized the importance of the sun's arrival. The land, now nourished, began to absorb the water. What didn't drain into the ground, the sun dried. When the rains began to taper off a week ago, Maligon sent scouts to determine when to mount their attack on the keep.

"Last night. I spoke to one of them. The land provides a way."

The few bites of biscuit she'd eaten churned her stomach like pebbles rumbling against each other. With regret, she rose and went to change.

"Should I leave your tea and biscuit?" Malay called.

"No." She didn't dare say anything else and reveal the concern in her voice.

Sooner than she desired, Shana found herself entering Maligon's chambers. The lavish furniture had been pushed to the walls and several stately chairs brought in. Pultarch and Honest rose as she entered, both sketching a formal bow even though the only other person present was Maligon.

The weight in her chest lessened as she met Honest's brown eyes. So far, they'd managed to keep their relationship a secret. If Adana and Kiffen managed to overcome and eliminate Maligon and the traitors within these walls, they could stop using lessons on Faith as an excuse to meet. Although she wished to continue the lessons, no matter what. Sometime in the last few weeks, she'd come to realize the Faith called to her. Honest assured her Father Tonch and Mother Sariah would accept her into those called.

She settled in the second nicest chair in the room, the one placed beside Maligon's. Of course, his chair spoke of the power the man wielded over all of them. The first time Quilla entered these chambers and took a seat, she'd suffered the embarrassment of Maligon commanding her to give up her seat to Queen Adana. More than one person hid their amusement at her heightened indignity as she changed seats.

After various commanders arrived as well as Quilla, Sarx, Kalara, Samantha, and Taren, Maligon began.

"The rains stopped north of here several days ago. The land thrives with growth and pathways are clearing. We can march on the keep now."

A stunned silence followed his words. Did he mean to march out this moment? Over the weeks, Shana caught fragments of conversations between most of the people in this room. Many expressed concerns over Maligon's health. It was harder to hide now. His questionable sanity resurfaced time and again in most of what she'd heard, too.

Just two nights ago, she'd heard him talking for an hour in a strange language. Once or twice, he spoke in words she understood. One line stuck out, "They will not expect us."

Either he was talking to himself, or one of his late-night visitors managed to sneak into the fortress again. It had been a while since she'd overheard them at night.

"Why aren't you smiling?" Maligon glared at all of them. "I said we can attack."

Someone to Shana's left cleared his throat. "My Lord," Sarx said, "we welcome this news. When do you wish to depart?"

"Ballene's fire, we've been waiting to move and now none of you want to go?" The man popped out of his chair and stalked toward Sarx.

"I do, Father." Kalara leapt from her chair. Ever since Maligon learned of Samantha's vision, his daughter struggled to please him at every opportunity.

"Good, daughter." His smile did not reach his eyes. "Anyone else?"

In bits and starts, each one agreed and thanked the Creator for providing them an avenue.

"What of the lights in the sky, Lord?" one of the commanders asked. "You said it was a sign of victory. Did the scouts find any evidence of the source?"

That had been Honest's brilliant move during the service the day after Sarx's arrival. He claimed the Creator left a pool of this blue and green substance to revive them before battle. It should be in the direction the lights came from.

"What? Oh, yes, yes. They saw the pool and drank from it. Refreshed them and gave them the energy to return quickly with the news."

"Where, Lord?" Sarx sat up. He scanned a large map stretched across the far wall.

When had be begun to believe? The excitement on his face implied he did.

"Show them, Samantha," Maligon ordered.

Without qualm or hesitation, the Watcher walked to the map and pointed to a position a half-day's march from the fortress.

"Here. They drained the pool of this substance so we can benefit from its power now. We have two casks of it."

An interesting twist. The truth or a ruse? No one could prove the water did not come from a special pool. Had Honest known of this subterfuge? He had not said, but she would ask him the first quiet moment they had.

After hours of rehashing their plans—the same ones they'd made every day during the rains—the commanders departed to rally their troops. As Shana rose to leave, Maligon laid his hand on her arm, restraining her. "Wait a moment, my dear."

A tingle of eagerness filled her when he only asked her to stay. She still kept a knife in her sleeve at all times. Honest, almost out the door, hesitated when she didn't join him. He knew of her plan. Although he wanted Maligon dead, he did not want her doing it.

"Do you wish me to remain?" he asked.

"You?" Maligon gestured him back into the room. "Fine. Pultarch, you, too."

And with that, the opportunity once again disappeared.

"When the army rides out of the fortress today, I will remain here. I am too weak to lead. Queen Adana and her betrothed will ride in my stead." He patted her hand in a fatherly way. "I trust you, my dear. You've grown in your position as Sarx claimed you would. I must admit, I doubted you in the beginning."

Trust bestowed on her from a mad man whom she wanted to kill. Could the Creator provide a more ironic twist of events?

Before she could speak, Pultarch objected. "Lord, you must accompany the troops. Queen Adana and I will ride with you, one on each side, but the men need to see you lead them. You're the one they've come to fight for."

"No. They must see Queen Adana ride out with an army behind her. Prove to them she is the true queen."

Within the fortress, the rumor that the woman residing in the

Border Keep was a peasant from Elwar ran rampant. All believed Shana to be the true queen. Even Malay, who knew Adana as a child, had been fooled. If she did this one thing more, would it doom her forever to the Seat of Authority with Pultarch by her side?

She could kill Maligon more easily on the battlefield. "You must go with us. They must see us riding side by side to know I stand with you."

When he sighed, the rattle in his chest sounded so loud, Shana could not believe no one else heard it. A jerk of Pultarch's head told her he'd noticed something.

"Very well. You say the same that Samantha advised earlier. I will join you children and oversee your triumph."

50

Over the last week, a pulse of energy ran through the people in the Border Keep. During the snows, many of the keep's original inhabitants moved to living above ground, freeing up space for the army brought back from the attack on Quilla's supply wagons. The extra food guaranteed no one would starve while they waited for the weather to shift. Even if Maligon attempted a siege, they could last a long time. Even then, with the secret exit from the tunnels, they could replenish their stores if food ran out.

Kiffen ran up the stairs, joining the others in the map room. From this vantage point, he turned to look south. The snow had melted over two weeks ago, and the flooding had subsided. Green grass and flowers dipped in a steady breeze as far as he could see.

Adana, Tonch, Montee, Morana, Simeon, Markel, Vuur, Nuala, and Halar stood around the map. They waited for Jerold and Leera.

The new emperor of Belwyn and Halar finally had arrived the day before with more soldiers. The early snows blocked the pass from Belwyn, preventing their travel. Not even a courier managed to make it through the pass to deliver the news of Kassa's death to her husband. Word was Halar took the news without surprise, saying only two words, "I knew."

The lack of information affected those at the keep too, only learning of Gabriella's death after Jerold arrived.

So much loss.

As Kiffen slid in beside Adana, Jerold entered the room, nodded at the others, and took a place beside Halar. Leera, and her ever-present shadows, Callan and Amar, entered moments later.

Although the two men flanked her, he felt Adana's mind pushing him to watch his sister. He did. She'd grown up; he'd noticed the night she arrived. Beyond this, he wanted to scratch his head in confusion. Adana sensed his uncertainty and pressed him to look at Leera's eyes. He hadn't told anyone, not even his sister, of the deep relationship the bond established between him and Adana. Thanks to that same connection, he knew she hadn't either. At night, sometimes, they lay in bed not speaking, just knowing.

Six weeks later, and he still couldn't explain how he understood Adana's promptings through the bond, but he followed her direction and watched his sister.

She peered up under her long eyelashes at someone. He shifted his gaze to follow her gaze. Jerold, whose eyes held Leera's with the same intense look.

"Shall we begin?" Montee said, breaking into his startled reaction.

They'd discussed alternative strategies several times over the duration of the snow and rain. The arrival of Jerold's forces gave them more to work with. It took little time to finalize their plans, though. He didn't see how they could fail.

"Our scouts spotted Maligon's men here." Kiffen pointed to the area where they had burned the bodies during the rains. "There is a pool of water near the battlefield. For some reason, they filled two casks from it."

"Two casks of water?" Vuur sat forward. "Did your scouts notice anything unusual about this pool?"

"No." Kiffen shook his head. "Why?"

Stroking his chin, Vuur considered the map. "If it looked normal, then no reason. I do wonder if any of the enduring fire remained as fuel."

They had come to call the firestarter's flames enduring fire. In a moment of agitation, Montee provided the name for the explosive weapon—Ballene's Fire. She'd said it was time the words meant something powerful instead of calling to mind a weakness from centuries ago.

"If any of the fuel remained," Adana said, "what would the water do for them?"

Vuur shrugged. "I do not know. I have not considered this. I suppose they might be able to burn it. A cask would not go far, though."

A tiny spark of concern ignited in Kiffen's chest. He exchanged a frown with Adana, but the worry dissipated as Bai'dish sent him an image of stomping on the spark. Not an important worry for now. They couldn't do anything if it was important, anyway.

"Now that Belwyn has joined us," Adana said, "I believe their forces serve us better from the tunnels. If Maligon attacks here first, we can send Belwyn's soldiers through the tunnels to surround him." She waved her hand over the broad expanse of savanna in her king-dom. "If we meet them on the plains, Jerold's forces will not be too far away to join us."

"Wouldn't it be wiser to leave his force guarding the keep from above?" Leera asked.

The shock Kiffen felt over his sister's first ever remarks about defensive plans tingled in Kiffen's mind. When had she learned strategy? "You are correct. The mistake Maligon made was leaving too few to guard Belwyn when he left. Which of us should remain here?"

"I will leave Ostreia here with half of her regiment," Montee said. "We can use Belwyn's forces better in the field."

Ostreia had received a well-deserved promotion after safely delivering Queen Morana and her troops to the keep. As a regiment leader, she commanded one thousand Watchers. At the moment, eight hundred of them camped at the keep. Four hundred might be enough to keep it from capture. He hoped they'd not need to find out.

"Since Glume maintains a connection with the giraffes, he can alert us if the keep comes under attack." Adana nodded at the plan. "I like the idea of Watchers remaining with the Giraffe Guard, and Ostreia remaining here solves that dilemma."

Halar cleared his throat. "I would propose an alternative."

Each person turned to him, many trying to mask the pity they felt for his loss.

"Why do you choose to march out of a fortified position? I know I've not been here to add to your strategizing, but I don't understand the reasoning."

"We have a secret weapon," Adana said. "One that we fear to use near the keep."

"What does it do, tear down walls?"

"Yes," several voices answered him in unison.

51

The army traveled slowly. The saturated ground, although drying out, clumped in hooves and boots. The wheels of the catapults bogged down regularly. Each time Samantha told Shana to call the troops to a stop, soldiers sought out rocks, sticks, and grass to remove as much debris as possible from their feet and their mounts' feet. If they didn't, by evening the stuff hardened to rock, difficult to remove.

Even with this hardship and the delay, Maligon's soldiers and Watchers remained in good spirits. After two months of rain, the freedom of traveling outdoors in the sunshine came as a welcome change.

On the third day, to Shana's surprise, Quilla rode up beside her, Taren following. She glanced to her left at Pultarch who gave her a wink before casting a glowering frown of jealousy at Taren. The young foreigner ignored it or failed to notice.

"Adana, as your closest neighbor and ally, I have a proposal to make." Quilla glanced around, then sidled her horse closer. "Now that our Lord can't hear us from the comfort of his chair."

The night's chillier air bothered Maligon. His curtained chair, carried by four massive soldiers, moved at a slow pace behind them. Too far away for the man to overhear. Not that Shana suspected he'd try. His health appeared to worsen each day. This morning, his lips looked faintly blue.

She glanced around. Not only was Maligon distant, but Kalara and Samantha rode off to the side, the two caught up in a discussion or argument. One never knew which. Sarx, often by Quilla's side, rode behind them in the column, deep in conversation with Honest. A distraction? She couldn't imagine Quilla kept any secrets from him.

"And what would you propose in our Lord's absence?"

"Precisely my point." Quilla's voice trilled on a high singsong note. "You and I have armies. We have warriors who will fight to protect us. Yes?"

Shana nodded.

"Maligon suffers from an illness. You can't have missed the signs. I don't believe he'll live much longer."

The woman spoke truth. All who traveled within his close company recognized it.

"We can dispose of him." The queen sniffed as if the words smelled rank. "Then unite to win this battle."

"And why would I do that?" Shana refused to look at Quilla, focusing on the woman's voice instead of her face. The day before, this avoidance of eye contact annoyed the queen. An added benefit. She enjoyed aggravating her as much as she did Pultarch, and she learned so much more this way.

The queen's voice softened to a secretive tone, the words coming out firm, nonetheless. "Pultarch can tell you; I hold much power. Donel always hesitated when I suggested strategic moves. Moves that might have prevented this war from the beginning."

"How so?"

"We both know you're not Adana, so I feel no concern sharing this. I sought to eliminate the little barbarian princess while in

Elwar. Donel, loyal as ever to her father, refused. He actually yelled at me. Can you imagine?"

She could, and from the strangled sounds she heard from Pultarch riding on Shana's left, he wanted to yell, too, and do much more.

"That would not have given you the other kingdoms though. That is what you wish, isn't it? To rule over all four?"

"Well, yes."

It had been that easy to lure her into saying the wrong thing. "So, I would give you Moniah, too? Why would I do that?"

"Oh." Quilla's mouth gaped a moment, then she spoke in a rush. "Oh no. I meant Belwyn and Teletia."

"But I said four."

"Excuse me, Your Majesty." The smooth-as-honey tenor voice of Taren interrupted them. "The fourth would be my kingdom, Lisseme."

"But Lisseme is not involved in our problems." Shana favored him with an arched eyebrow. "And you aren't royalty, are you?"

The tiny nation bordered Belwyn to the east. Maybe Quilla hoped to move the border to include them in Belwyn. Lisseme wine brought a decent price, but it didn't provide enough income to support Taren's explanation.

"All the better." Quilla's voice trilled to a high pitch. It hurt Shana's ears every time she used it, which was often.

Absorbed in thought over this absurd discussion, it took Shana a moment to notice scouts galloping toward them. She raised her hand and commanded the lines behind her to stop, "Hold."

The order echoed down the column, the army drawing to a jangling, stomping halt. Sarx and Honest trotted forward to join them, and Samantha and Kalara rushed in from their positions, appearing to compete in a foot race to see who got their first. The arriving scouts reined in and jumped from their horses, sketching a quick bow to the queens.

"Queen Adana, First Vision, the imposter queen's army marches toward us."

Pultarch pushed his horse forward. "How far?"

"An hour at most."

"Numbers?"

"Several thousand. As much as us."

Pultarch wheeled his horse about, ready to bark orders, when Shana lunged for his bridle. "You do not command," she whispered to him.

Kalara stepped forward, but Shana ignored her, turning to Samantha. "First Vision?"

Shoulders thrown back, Samantha raised her chin, bobbed it in acknowledgement of Shana, then turned to Kalara and began barking orders.

The army moved quickly, following her commands, and Samantha stood taller. Kalara, ignoring the orders, stomped to Maligon's chair. She flung back the curtains and shoved her head in the opening. In loud staccato, she engaged in heated discussion with her father.

For some time, everyone around her moved with purpose. No one wasted words or motion. They lined up in four regiments to meet whatever came over the rise on the other side of the field. Fires for flaming arrows burned near the Watchers' position and those mercenaries who had expertise with a bow. The soldiers manning the catapults lined them up to fire into the center of the field.

After assigning orders and checking in with each commander, Samantha returned to Shana's side. "Your Majesties, the hill over there will provide a good vantage point for you to observe the battle."

They hadn't chosen this field, circumstances did. It offered little shelter or barriers in trees or bushes, so the knoll provided the only point at a distance from the battle but safe enough to see the outcome. For now.

Shana headed toward the hill. As she passed Kalara, still arguing with Maligon, she noted the Watcher's hands clenched tight, the knuckles white under the pressure. From behind the curtains, she heard Maligon's tired but firm voice. "Enough."

Kalara whirled about and stomped down the hill, heading for the thick of her Watchers.

For some reason, Samantha positioned those warriors to the far right of the lines. Maybe she anticipated something Shana could not see. She would have placed their best archers front and center to pick off the front of Adana's army when they stormed the field, but Maligon's archers held that position. This could be a good thing if it worked for the other side, but Shana worried she'd missed something.

No matter how much she listened to the constant strategizing and re-strategizing over the last few weeks, the large-scale tactics of battle left her confused and missing the specifics. She was much better at Quilla's kind of war—verbal with nuance and insinuation.

Now that Kalara did not detain her adoptive father, the four dark men who had shown up on the day they left Adana's View lifted Maligon's chair to their shoulders and carried it to the top of the slope. These four stayed to themselves over the journey from the fortress and spoke in a strange guttural language. The same one she overheard coming from Maligon's rooms many nights while everyone else slept.

Huge and muscular, the men settled the palanquin on the ground and stepped back, feet planted apart, arms folded. Speculation on who these servants might be or why they showed up now occupied her thoughts on the journey. Honest wondered, too. Neither of them knew any more about these men than on the first day. The main question was how would she get through this intimidating guard to kill Maligon?

Pultarch remained below studying the formations, his arms

crossed and a frown on his face. When Samantha went to check the catapult positions, he dropped his arms and strode with brisk steps into the lines of men. He stopped at the first commander and started firing questions at him. The answers he got had him rubbing his hand over his neck as he listened.

The decision to keep him from the fighting appeared to eat at him. Would he obey the orders or rebel and fight? If he fought, it could mean one more threat to her sanity gone. Misled as he was, though, she didn't wish him harm or injury. Unlike Maligon.

At last, Pultarch returned from his fourth trip to speak with Sarx and Taren, who commanded on the front lines. Shoulders slumped, he trudged up the knoll. His presence did complicate her plans for Maligon, but the queen and her betrothed must appear together, overseeing the battle.

Quilla had trailed up the rise behind Maligon, and as Pultarch joined them his eyes narrowed in on her. Ever since Quilla admitted to her desire to kill Adana, he'd steered clear of the woman, riding as far from Elwar's queen as he could without negating his status as Shana's betrothed. *Let him take his battle frustrations out on Quilla if an opportunity presents itself.* That might distract Maligon's bodyguards long enough for her to act.

The last of their party to join them on the hill, Honest, came to stand beside her. He'd spent his time moving among the soldiers, offering prayers and blessings. Someday, when this charade was over, she might provide spiritual comfort for the people, too.

"What bedevils Pultarch?" Honest whispered so low and close to her ear that no one but a Listener would understand him or even know he spoke. "Does he still wish to fight?"

"Yes, but he's angry at Quilla, too."

"Ah." Honest nodded. "In general or something specific?"

Shana raised her eyes to check Quilla's proximity. The woman pretended to regard the ranks of men below them, but her body leaned toward them.

In a clear voice, Shana stalled her answer. "Will you guide me in prayer for our men, Brother Honest?"

Following her hesitant glance, he nodded and led Shana away from Quilla.

A teacher's prayer with an individual required privacy for its sanctity. Only a clueless stranger might interrupt such an important act.

With bowed heads, they grasped hands, the warmth of his comforting even in the day's heat. In quick whispers, she filled him in on Quilla's intriguing proposal.

"I see. Foolish woman underestimates our young lord. Will he act on it?"

"Maybe," Shana said. "And Kalara looks like a kernel of corn about to pop. She fumed when I gave Samantha the command."

Honest gave her hand a quick squeeze. "Parts of *our* plan appear to be falling into place."

They remained together, hands clasped, foreheads touching. They'd said all they wanted to the night before the army left the fortress. Riding together, unable to share their closeness, drove Shana frantic with the desire to reach out to him. She clung to his hands, unwilling to let go, and tried to forget what waited for them on this day. Her heart kept telling her this might be her last time with Honest. Desperate for more, she brushed her lips across his knuckles, not entirely appropriate but not inappropriate when praying either. Then she turned away.

From the top of the hill, the breeze below shifted into a wind, tugging strands from Shana's braid. Letting the loose hairs whip around her face unchecked, she studied her army. The soft footfalls of someone in no hurry approached. Maligon. He joined her, his disease-wracked body no more than a hands-breadth away. His strange odors of blood and infection teased her on the wind.

Everyone waited, anticipation so thick in the air, she almost tasted it.

A murmur rippled through the formations when a Soldier of the First Sight crested the ridge on the far end of the field. He carried two banners—the giraffe of Moniah and the lion of Elwar. Behind him, several lines of Watchers strode, two heavily armored giraffes walking in the middle of their ranks—Am'brosia and Bai'dish. The sight of them made Shana's heart swell with joy. They still lived.

A growl of distaste erupted from Maligon who now stood by her side. "Call Kalara to me. The giraffes must die."

Shana quailed at his words. "You can't mean it."

"I do." The ferocity of his voice and set of his jaw belonged to a man enjoying full vigor of health. Had the arrival of his enemies revived him?

Before she could forestall this action, Pultarch leapt to his horse and kicked it into motion. Whether he cared about the giraffes, she did not know. The command gave him the one act he desired—joining the ranks for the battle.

A sad worry tweaked her heart, but Shana reminded herself his absence meant one complication down.

Honest stepped forward and leaned in to whisper to Maligon. She strained to eavesdrop, but the wind whipped the words away. *Trust me,* his eyes told her as he caught her looking at him. Did the man read her thoughts? Had she opened herself too much to him in the short time they'd had together?

A drum from Adana's army began to beat in a slow, steady rhythm. It kept time with the blood pounding in her ears. The line of soldiers and Watchers marched forward, taking their formation on the far side of the field. The ground in between, lush with grasses and flowers, would soon become mired with bodies, blood, and death. She shuddered at the strength of the force preparing to attack them.

No, the army she pretended to lead wasn't hers. Her people marched toward her from the other side of the field. She could only hope they knew she fought for the true Queen Adana and not herself.

* * *

Adana sat astride her horse behind the lines of Watchers. Taking advantage of Am'brosia's better vantage point, she scanned the enemy army through the bond. They appeared well-matched for numbers. No one held the advantage in that way, but Ballene's Fire would change that. The thought of the surprise they held for Maligon brought a ferocious grin to her face. He could not win.

Her ranks marched forward, archers in front, followed by foot soldiers. The cavalry waited. If things went as planned, many of them would never enter this field.

As she scanned the enemy lines, the flash of a familiar face made her pause. She pushed Am'brosia to turn back and look at those gathered on a knoll far behind the battle lines. Quilla, haughty as ever, stood beside a woman who held the bearing of a queen. When she turned and looked their way, she felt the jolt of shock as Kiffen, through the connection, recognized Shana. Dressed as a warrior, she looked believable. Even Adana had to admit the resemblance was enough to convince anyone who had not seen her in three years. Did Shana still play a part? Or had the Listener embraced her role as queen?

To Shana's left, an elderly man in purple robes looked over the oncoming troops, excitement lighting his eyes. *Who was that?* A Teacher of the Faith stood beyond him, battle staff in hand. She blinked and focused on him harder. *Brother Honest?* Word from Roshar said he'd pursued his own designated path at the Creator's directions. *Had she placed her faith in the wrong teacher?*

The man in the purple robes turned, and she saw in profile what she'd missed straight on. This withered shell of a man was Maligon. He looked barely able to stand.

Montee signaled for the drummer to silence the marching beat. In the moments after the insistent rhythm ended, wind whipped around the gathering, snapping and cracking the flags.

The Watchers stood in a triple line at the front, arrows prepared to nock their bows, awaiting the command to raise and fire them. Now, to see if their ruse worked.

Charissa, the fleetest Watcher, trotted away from the front line and into the field between the two armies.

As she drew near the midpoint, the other side erupted in roars of excitement. Good. Many men believed that capturing a Watcher alive meant success and virility for life.

Following the plan, Charissa tripped and fell. On purpose. The grasses hid her body as she landed with a thud. Adana fought back the urge to smile over the sound, the result of heavy rocks the Watcher dropped as she went down.

A hush fell across the army on the other side. No one moved. An occasional shouted order drifted on the wind. A few in the front lines fidgeted, the temptation great. Would they react or hold? A lot depended on who led them and how well.

Adana flicked her hand to Montee's line of archers. The First Vision and ten Watchers ran into the field toward Charissa who had not gotten up.

Roars erupted up and down the enemy lines, this time frantic with the urge to act. Their lines vibrated with anticipation. The men began pounding swords on shields.

Would this work or would the Watchers-turned-traitors see the trap? For now, those soldiers waited, shoved to the sides of the lines of infantry. None appeared to recognize the truth behind this feint.

As Montee and the others drew closer to Charissa's location, one of Maligon's Watchers, hair the same color as Mammetta's, dashed toward the front lines. Kalara. She saw the ruse.

From this distance, any Watcher could see her shouting at one of the commanders—Sarx possibly. The building tumult of noise from his men either drowned her out or he ignored her.

Another Watcher raced to join Kalara, the others jerking to awareness and following. Each ran with an arrow ready to nock to their bows. They would fire on Montee's group soon if no one stopped them.

Adana held her breath. The noise continued to build on the other side of the field.

Montee's small band reached Charissa. Two bent to lift her, draping her arms across their shoulders. They turned and assisted her as she pretended to limp back toward Adana. The rest crouched and prepared to fire at any soldier brave enough to come after them.

The rumbling line of warriors, frantic for battle, grew louder, more agitated.

Charissa and her helpers hobbled slower as if she couldn't put either foot down.

Montee and her Watchers cast wary glances at the limping trio, feigning anxious concern.

The enemy line broke like a dam bursting.

The Watchers with Montee sent their arrows flying into the mob. Seven men dropped as the arrows hit their mark.

Chaos exploded from the enemy lines as the second volley of arrows took out more men. A surge in Am'brosia's link directed her to look toward the catapults where soldiers scrambled to fire. More men poured out into the field, screaming war cries.

The two Watchers and Charissa broke apart and spun in one swift motion and crouched low to the ground.

Adana counted. Three. Two. One.

Montee and her Watchers turned and ran for the safety of their lines.

Three arrows, burning with Enduring Fire, flew from Charissa's position, soaring into the oncoming soldiers. The blue-green light dazzled Adana's eyes as it streaked into the mass of soldiers. Each one hit a mark, and fire broke out in a circle at least four men deep.

Screams of pain were cut off in the men's throats as the fire engulfed them.

Maligon's catapults sent their first volley. One landed close to Montee, but the women flew across the land, fast as only a Watcher can be, escaping the craters of earth exploding upward, raining debris across the land.

Now, all twelve Watchers stopped and lined up just beyong the catapult's reach. In synchronous rhythm, they fired more arrows lit with Enduring Fire into the midst of Maligon's army.

Adana shared the image with Kiffen who waited by their catapults. With a *whoosh*, those four catapults propelled balls of Enduring Fire into Maligon's army. Under this cover, Montee and her Watchers returned to Adana's line.

* * *

The disintegration of Samantha's command over the regiments appalled Shana. Yes, she wanted Adana's army to win the battle, but the way they taunted her army with easy targets amazed her. These men shared Pultarch's attitude toward women; Adana had counted on that.

Now that Adana had made her move, she suspected it would take a powerful leader to pull the frenzied men back. Maligon could have done that at one time. Not now, sick as he was.

A roar went up as more men plowed into the open grassland. Arrows rained down on them. So many arrows and from such a small force of Watchers.

Instead of falling back, the next line of men raced after them. A flurry of motion caught Shana's eye, and she saw Kalara plunging into the fraying lines. Some of the soldiers began to straighten, but Sarx still ignored her warnings.

A hesitation spread silence over them, leaving the last of Kalara's shouts for all to hear. "Fall back! Fall back!"

Three arrows streaming a blue-green light flew from behind the front line of Watchers. The arrows landed in the midst of the hyped-up men, taking out several in one quick stroke. Shana heard the *thud* and *whoosh*, followed by the brief cut-off screams from the soldiers killed on the spot.

Maligon hadn't lied. The blue-green light was a sign for victory. Just not theirs.

The whistle and thunk of Maligon's catapults resounded in her ears. Her men managed one volley before the tantalizing Watchers escaped beyond their range. Their own men tread too close to that line, negating the chance to use the catapults.

A distant whistle and thunk sounded from somewhere in Adana's line. Balls of the blue-green fire flew into the sky. They flew apart as they descended, showering the men in deadly fire.

Below, her army scrambled over itself, retreating back to their lines. The casks Maligon bragged about had been wheeled down to the front lines and men surged around them cupping their hands into the barrel to drink.

If these barrels held the remains of fires set by this new element, what would it do to them?

They began to reform into a semblance of order as Kalara marched back and forth before them, at times shoving them into place. They listened and obeyed her command better than Samantha's. It showed in the set of her shoulders. Wherever she went, she drew the men's attention. Samantha never managed such bearing.

As if summoned, Samantha sprinted through the crowd and

leapt on Kalara's back, knocking her to the ground. The soldiers around them jumped back as the two fought like lions.

Kalara's Watchers swarmed into the fight.

On the field, the strange green-blue fires ate up the fresh grass and what was left of the bodies. None of her army noticed; their attention riveted on the ball of Watchers on the ground.

Over the screams, Shana heard a few heavy thuds. She shuddered at the sound of them, recognizing them as killing blows.

Shouts of victory burst forth from the Watchers. Kalara emerged and tossed Samantha's inert body onto the field.

Without a pause, Kalara returned to her command. Ranks re-formed, not as smooth and neat as before, but in formation. The Watchers stood front and center, Kalara at their head. Only the remains of the dead remained in the field.

No one moved.

To her left, Quilla raged. "Do not give her command. Take control. Kill the Watchers."

Far below, Sarx didn't hear. Maybe the vindictive screaming made Quilla feel better.

Shana turned toward Honest and Maligon, humor over Quilla's tantrum fading. The palanquin, the bodyguards, Maligon, and Honest were gone.

* * *

The field between Adana's army and Maligon's lay empty except for the fire raging in the grass. On the far side of the field, Kalara took command. Pulling the soldiers back in line, she strutted back and forth, shouting at them. Definitely a more dangerous enemy. The body tossed on the field belonged to Samantha. Adana felt no pang of regret for the traitor, only sadness for Halar. Maybe in death the misguided Watcher might make amends to her mother.

As this thought coursed into her mind, Adana gasped. "No."

Montee turned to look at her, but she focused on the link with Am'brosia and Bai'dish, instead. The giraffes must not share Samantha's death with Glume. Halar did not need to know of it yet. This battle wasn't over, and she needed him focused. With Kalara in charge, they might need to call him and Jerold's troops from the tunnels.

During the cessation of action, Kiffen, Simeon, Sariah, and Montee gathered around her.

"Do we seek to speak with them?" Montee asked. "Kalara will not make the next move, now that she's seen Enduring Fire."

Kalara might have been First Vision, given different loyalties. Unlike Samantha, she understood how to persuade others to follow her.

Adana's thoughts turned to Leera, who waited in front of her own men on the right flank. "Speak with whom? They have Maligon, Sarx, Quilla, and Kalara. Do we dare reveal who stands with us?"

"They no longer have Maligon." Montee turned toward the opposing side.

"What?" Adana searched the knoll. Only Shana and Quilla remained. What happened to Pultarch, Maligon, and Honest? "They could be anywhere in those lines."

"I'm inclined to agree," Kiffen said. She'd felt his presence through the link as he checked the soldiers on the other side. He had paused at certain soldiers, a sadness of betrayal wafting through to her each time. Soldiers who should fight for him, fighting for Quilla. By choice or forced, it no longer mattered.

"Leera approaches," Montee said.

Adana turned to find the young princess gliding through the ranks of Watchers and soldiers. She wore her special Watcher's uniform but still managed to look like a queen on an enjoyable walk through her gardens. In her wake, Callan and Amar followed.

One day, Adana hoped to hear how Leera managed to gather such loyal men.

Leera dimpled at them, a gesture so familiar it sent a pang into Adana's heart. "I suppose we wait."

It wasn't a question, but Kiffen answered, "Yes."

"For what?" When Leera wanted to put others at ease, she widened her eyes and looked at them in innocence. She did this now.

"That's what we're discussing," Kiffen said, a slight brotherly edge sharpening his words.

"And?" She raised an eyebrow. "What are our options?"

A tiny chuckle came from Adana's left. She slid her gaze sideways to catch Sariah, the Protector of the Faith, not even bothering to hide the grin that pinkened her cheeks. The Protector of the Faith bowed to Leera before answering her. "We could ask to meet with their leaders in the middle of the field."

Leera wrinkled her nose at this.

"We could wait to see what they do," Sariah added.

Leera tilted her head then met each person's gaze. "You don't wish to do either of those, do you?"

"We have little choice," Adana said. "They know our reach and the effect of Enduring Fire."

"What of Ballene's Fire? Why not use it?"

Kiffen crossed his arms and spread his legs in a wide stance. "We're out of range,"

The scorn he focused on his sister disturbed Adana. No matter what she did or said about this war, he met her ideas with derision. That must stop. She sent a soothing caress across their connections. They both knew Leera enjoyed her new position as leader of an army and couldn't resist bantering with them before sharing her ideas. Still, he must stop treating her like a child.

Kiffen's neck flushed red. The color spread to his cheeks. He turned away from Adana's stare for a moment. When he turned back, his face held a sheepish grin.

Unaware of the hidden conversation between her brother and Adana, Leera swiveled a little on her feet, a childhood habit used when seeking a favor. "Callan and Amar and I have been discussing the situation. We must remember we have another army. One that Maligon knows nothing of. Jerold." She dimpled at Callan, then said, "Go on. Tell them."

"You can send word to Glume through the giraffes, correct?" Callan said.

"Yes." Adana drew the word out, trying to guess their intentions.

"What if Jerold and Halar lead their forces through the tunnels and circle around behind Maligon's men? They can rain Ballene's Fire on them without warning."

"But we don't know about the flooding through that area. It might take them a week to reach us."

"It won't." Leera almost bounced with enthusiasm. "I received a message from Jerold this morning. Teletia still has an army, and they arrived at the keep two days ago. Jerold's scouts sent word that the passage was clear, so he and Halar followed us."

"Followed us?" Irritation returned to Kiffen's voice. "How many did Teletia bring to guard the keep?"

"Dear brother, don't underestimate Jerold." She laid a hand on his arm. "He left half of his men there, the Giraffe Guard is in place, and Ostreia's Watchers remained, too. And, of course, Queen Morana is there to command her men. The keep is well-protected."

Even though Adana knew Leera had withheld the news of the arrival of more soldiers, the information did fly through her veins like a racing gazelle.

Simeon, unfazed by the princess' guile and tactics, frowned in thought. "Where are they?"

Amar cleared his throat. "Almost in position."

"And they brought Ballene's Fire with them?" Adana's pulse jumped with excitement.

"Three flasks and the launching equipment." Amar stood with his shoulders back, a satisfied set to his face.

"Where is this messenger?"

After a quick restrategizing discussion, Kiffen followed Callan and Amar to join Jerold's troops, Adana and Montee remained on the battlefield focused on Maligon's disappearance from the knoll. He could be anywhere, and they needed knowledge of that location before he discovered Jerold's suprise moving into place behind him.

They ordered each Watcher to select a division in the enemy ranks to search. A Watcher's sight, powerful as it was in noting small details, might succeed in locating him, but hunting through line upon line of soldiers complicated things.

Leaving this task to others, Adana remounted her horse and focused her vision on Shana's presence on the knoll. The imposter managed a stoic face for someone not gifted as a Watcher, but little signs—back and neck rigid, shifting her feet every few moments—hinted at annoyance. Quilla talked beside her, lips moving non-stop. The queen might be the cause of Shana's attitude, but Adana doubted it. Shana kept searching the ranks of men before her, then she'd shift and check behind her, over and over. Each time, she turned back to the men below, a frown tightened her face. Did Maligon's absence bother Shana?

A fluctuation in the bond with Am'brosia told her Kiffen had reached Jerold and Halar. From what he showed her, a rolling hillside hid them from sight. With Maligon's perimeter guards silenced and bound, Jerold's men stood by the launchers ready to fire.

"They are ready." Adana turned to Montee. "Start the count."

On Montee's command, a soldier beat the drum. *Thump. Thump. Thump.*

The army across the field straightened into even lines. Kalara marched in front of them calling out orders. A cheer rang out as her soldiers welcomed the end of waiting.

No one from the other side noticed the small projectiles until they exploded over the middle ranks of men. The concussion of sound barreled over Adana. Her horse shied and whinnied in fright.

Men howled and shrieked as bodies flew into the air.

* * *

"What in blazes?" The ground shook, knocking Shana to the ground. A discordant ringing echoed in her head. Deafening, it cut off all other sound. Just like before. When they destroyed the wall.

She rolled onto her hands and knees, curled in on herself.

Another powerful concussion shook the ground. She cried out in pain as the noise pounded her head. On the ground again, she struggled to right herself. On her side, she blinked at the mass of scrambling soldiers below her. Dirt and debris rained down over the field. Bodies. It was bodies, not debris. Huge gaps separated their regiments. Vanished. Their men were gone. The rest stumbled around on unsteady feet, holding their heads. The rear ranks swarmed in retreat.

Struggling to her feet, she covered her hands over her ears. The ringing in her ears drove nails into her skull.

She leapt sideways as something collided with her, pushing her back. Jumping to her feet, she yanked a knife from her belt and spun to face the assailant.

Quilla crouched at her feet, groaning. Hands grappling at Shana, she dragged her off balance. "Help me."

The panicked way the woman crawled up Shana's arm rippled waves of fear over her. Not her own fear, Quilla's. It skittered across her skin.

Bits and pieces of sound penetrated her ears. Shana shoved Quilla away, unbothered by the woman's screech of fury. Where was

Honest? Or Maligon? She stumbled down the hill, searching the faces of soldiers running past her. Hoping to find one man alive and the other dead.

A blood-streaked face loomed up before her, the man's mouth moving, but the turmoil on the battlefield blocked the little hearing ability she had regained. He lunged past her.

The teeming mass of soldiers lurched around her, eyes wide with shock and confusion. Even those beyond the blast areas mirrored this behavior. Only a few tried to help their comrades.

Another soldier stumbled into her. Taren, his green eyes wide with fright. He grabbed her arm. "Have you seen my uncle?"

She shook her head. Taren faltered. "Can't find. Fire. Near him."

Shana looked out over the field. Fires burned everywhere. Nothing moved within the flames. "Are you hurt?"

Taren shook his head and turned away. "Must find him."

Gut clenching in horror, Shana stared at Taren's ravaged back. His uniform had melted to his skin. Clods of dirt and stone stuck out from bare skin. His left arm hung at an odd angle.

She moved to help him when Pultarch ran up to her. "Shana, thank the Creator. Where is Maligon?"

Unharmed. Pultarch did not have a scratch.

He held her arms, staring into her face. "Maligon? Is he safe?"

"He's gone."

The young lord's face crumpled in distress. "Gone?"

"Not dead. Disappeared. During the fire arrows. He and Honest. His chair. Guards. All gone."

"He left us?" He stiffened and backed away a step, eyes raking over their surroundings. "Why?"

A growing roar headed for them. Across the field, Adana's army ran into the field. Jolted out of their shock, many of her soldiers turned to run but halted, running into each other. Another army roared down on them from behind. They were surrounded.

"Come, Pultarch," Shana said, pulling free the white cloth she'd tucked into her uniform. "Let's put an end to today's death."

She took his sword, tied the cloth to it, and waved it in the air as she walked toward the wave of yelling soldiers crossing between the raging fires and craters in the field. Relief her pretense could end weakened her legs for a moment, but she stopped, straightened her shoulders, raised her chin, and marched forward.

As she picked her way through the dead and dying, her hearing returned in full. Cries of pain and loss tore at her. What had Adana done? Had this form of warfare been worth winning the victory? Fiery anger burned in her. Anger at Maligon. Anger at Kalara. Anger at Samantha, Pultarch, Sarx, and Quilla. Anger for driving these people to rebellion.

She stood at the edge of the field, Maligon's army behind her, crowded by the attackers in the rear. She held up the white cloth tied to a sword and waited.

To her left a voice shrieked at her. "Don't you dare surrender!" Kalara charged toward her, face screwed up in anger. "Put that down."

Shana held it even higher, gaze holding Kalara's in challenge.

She saw Kalara draw the knife; it happened in slow motion as she pulled her own free. Hers hit Kalara in the chest. Somehow the knife sank in to the hilt. She wondered how she managed to miss the ribs as the world went black.

52

Adana surveyed the carnage before her, the piles of fallen bodies, some already burned beyond recognition, waiting for final fires to release their souls. The part of the field where Ballene's Fire hit had no bodies at all. Disintegrated. Tears streaked down her face, for once unchecked. So many dead.

The area set aside for the injured sat at the foot of the hill where Quilla and Shana had watched the battle. Dosata, Sariah, and, surprisingly, Leera and Amar moved among the injured doing what they could.

A sudden jerk of motion drew her attention to Leera. The girl stepped back, her head snapping up as if she'd been hit. She stood frozen to the spot, skin turning ashen. The young man they'd found stumbling in a circle, unaware his body should not work, lay at her feet.

Adana took a step toward Leera, but Sariah called to her. As she turned to answer Sariah, Leera found the ability to move again, averting her gaze and turning away from the man.

"Yes?" Adana squatted beside Sariah, placing a comforting hand on the arm of the young soldier the Protector tended to.

"I sought to stop you." Sariah wrapped a bandage around the

390

man's arm. He winced but clenched his teeth, jaw muscles bulging with the strain.

"Stop me? From what?" What had she been doing that the Protector of the Faith found fault with?

"Interrupting Leera. She needed a moment. You can see, she's moved on, now."

Adana didn't need to look. "Who was that man?"

"Taren, Lord Sarx's nephew."

Understanding pricked her heart. One night, sitting by the hearth while snow fell outside, Leera told Adana about her mother's plans and the handsome man chosen for her to wed. The man created confusing feelings in Leera. At times, she had swooned from his attention. Other times, she had run from it, frightened by her mother's plan.

He would not live. The fire melted his clothes to his back, something no one had ever seen before. Debris and stones thrown by the blast were embedded deep into his back. When they attempted to remove the worst of them, he'd screamed and passed out. Many of the fragments cut to the bone.

Adana fought down the urge to vomit then and now at the memory. The desire to stumble into the bushes and lose everything she'd eaten in the last month overcame her as she moved from one casualty to the next. What had they done?

"Should we tell him about his uncle?" Adana asked.

"No. We'd only cause him more grief. He's in enough pain."

They'd found Sarx's body, identifiable by his ring and sword. The fires of the explosions left little else, but he must have crawled away from the burning ground.

Quilla found him first, the domineering woman reduced to a hysterical bundle of nerves. Now secured as a prisoner, she swung between grieving for Sarx and yelling for her daughter. So far, Leera gave the captives a wide berth.

At some point, Adana would need to decide what to do with those culpable for their actions—Pultarch and Quilla among them. She now understood her mother's reluctance to kill Maligon when she'd had the chance. His sentence should have ended him, but it kept her free from striking the blow herself. That weakness gave him a minuscule chance of survival. Minuscule but possible. And survive he had.

That one decision gave him time to rebuild and take more lives. The losses burned in her throat as much as the smoke still swirling in the air. So many gone before their time.

Except for one. A woman whose life fell to the whims of so many other people. A woman she would never have known if her mother chose differently. Shana now lay in Adana's tent. She'd doubted the woman's loyalty before, but her last act eliminated any doubt. Shana had remained true.

The scene on the edge of the battlefield remained anchored in her memory. The young decoy standing beside Pultarch surrendering to the inevitable while everyone around her ran or moaned on the ground. Then the shout from Kalara. The Watcher racing toward her, drawing her knife. Shana's quick reflexes, killing Kalara, her aim impeccable and amazing. Kalara, known for her own accuracy, fell prey to the emotions Kassa always warned them to control. That anger disrupted Kalara's aim and left a slim chance that Shana might live.

Adana approached the entrance to the tent where Shana lay. She drew back the flap and ducked into the dark interior. Biaji and Father Tonch sat on either side of the cot. A tiny jerboa perched on the pillow beside Shana, so motionless it might be stuffed. The jerboa had launched itself from Shana's tunic as the knife plunged into her neck. It had not left her side since. No one knew why she had it, but Biaji discovered a small pouch sewn into the tunic where the animal must have ridden.

Biaji and Tonch started to rise when Adana entered, but she waved them back. "How is she?"

"Lucky," Biaji said.

"Blessed," Father Tonch said.

Adana inched closer. The knife caught Shana in the throat but missed hitting anything life-threatening. She'd lost a lot of blood, though.

"She will live?" Adana turned to Tonch, the question sticking in her throat.

"Time will tell. I believe the Creator has use of her yet." Father Tonch held out an object. "I found this in her sleeve."

Adana reached out and picked up a circle of jade. A ring given to every initiate for the Teachers of the Faith. "She's training to be a Teacher?"

"Pultarch says she spent a lot of time with Honest. He must have been training her. He would have been the only one who knew she served you."

"Did Pultarch say why Honest was with Maligon? Or where they are now?"

Tonch shook his head. "I left his questioning to Jerold and Kiffen. Once I knew this child belonged to the Faith, I knew I must stay by her side until she wakes."

"If she wakes or...find me." Adana ducked out of the tent and headed to where Kiffen was interrogating the prisoners. The realization this lost woman had found a purpose in life boiled more frustration in her heart. Maligon should never have lived to destroy so many lives.

She found Kiffen and Jerold assembling a squad to pursue the traitor. Disappointment flooded her heart at the idea they might steal her revenge. The more death and despair she saw, the more the urge to carry out Kassa's orders burned in her heart. She could not leave with them. Not now. Not with Shana and so many others on the edge of death.

Sariah swept in past her, the woman's forward momentum pushing through the soldiers rushing to saddle horses and strap on weapons. "Your Majesties." Her voice, accustomed to speaking in the presence of many, stopped everyone in their tasks. Not just the men, but most of those gathered near this clearing.

With all eyes turned toward her, she continued. "A word with you, please."

When the two men nodded and drew closer to Sariah, she dropped her voice to an insistent but private tone. Everyone watched, anyway, fascinated that she'd pulled rank on them. In theory, all rulers accepted the Protector's or the Keeper's guidance, but it was not a rule enforced often.

"I beg of you to look around this field of suffering. Suffering caused by horrors we unleashed today. Maligon is ill. He can't go far. We will find him. Your duty remains here for now, serving the people who fought for you."

Adana wanted to throw her arms around Sariah in thanks. No one knew Kassa had charged her with killing Maligon. Her fingers itched to finish the job her mother failed to do. For a very different reason, Sariah's delay served her purpose.

Kiffen's head jerked up and his gaze met hers, a frown of concern creasing his forehead. She'd slipped and let those thoughts ooze into the bond. Now he knew. The wave of displeasure washing back toward her told her how he felt about it.

53

Sunlight flickered between the leaves of the trees shading the lake. Shana floated on her back, enjoying a respite from caring for her brothers while her mother did the laundry for the lady of Glenhaven. The water ebbed around her, cool and refreshing, unlike the boiling water her mother hunched over every laundry day.

Ignoring the puckering of her skin from too long on the water, Shana sighed and gave a little flutter-kick, propelling her farther from the shore. She hadn't heard her mother's step on the hard-packed ground yet, the grass swishing around her skirts, but she would call for her soon. The farther she floated, the longer she avoided the inevitable return to work.

The warmth of the day faded as clouds rolled over the sun, turning everything gray. A chill wind brushed across her skin. She hadn't heard her mother's step, but now a woman's voice called to her.

"Shana. Oma Shana, come to me." Not her mother's voice. Her grandmother's.

The water turned to ice on her skin at the memory of this long-forgotten voice. Heart pounding, she floundered to her feet. On the water's edge, her grandmother stood, a gray nightgown whipping around her feet, white hair spilling down her back. She held beseeching hands out to Shana.

Joy chased by fear wrestled with Shana's emotions. The urge to tumble into those arms stuttered. Grandmother was dead. She died when Shana was ten.

"My dear, Oma Shana," Grandmother called to her. Oma meant beautiful. The only person to ever call her beautiful stood a short distance away.

"I'm coming, Grandmother." She gave into the temptation and slogged through the water. Underwater vines tripped her, and a sudden undercurrent pushed her back. She could not move. "Grandmother."

Her grandmother smiled, body fading as she pointed to the opposite shore. Then she was gone.

"Grandmother. Wait." Huge tears streamed down Shana's face.

"My queen," a kind and familiar voice called from behind her. "You are not meant to go to her yet."

Afraid at what she might see, Shana turned slowly. Honest stood in the shallows on the opposite shore. He held his hand out to her.

"Are you real?" He could have died in those horrid explosions. So many had.

"Come to me, my queen. It's not time."

With one last look over her shoulder, she turned and swam across the water, now warm and free of vines or slush. When she touched his hand, she cried out. Silent cries. Her voice didn't work. Pain lanced through her body.

Hands stroked her forehead. A kind, fatherly voice spoke nearby. "Lie still, Shana. You are safe."

Where was Honest?

She slitted her eyes open. Shadows in the dark. She swallowed, and fire burned her throat.

A tiny flame came to life on her right, and she strained toward it, surprised at the difficulty in turning her head.

The flickering candle shone on the face of a Watcher. Whose?

The almost familiar voice spoke again from her left. "Alert the queen. She's awake."

Shana shifted in his direction and squinted at the man. He wore the robes of a teacher. "Who?" she croaked.

"Be still, child. You've endured much. The Creator favors you, I believe."

Something landed on her arm, and she shuddered, unable to pull away. The tiny weight popped along her arm and thudded onto her chest.

"I believe your friend is glad to see you awake," the teacher said.

Bauns sat on her chest, little yellow eyes studying her. Tears stuck in her throat like shards of glass. He had survived, again. The jerboa bounded off her chest to sit beside her head on the pillow.

The tent's flap snapped open. Two Watchers entered. She braced herself, pulse pounding in her head. The step of the two sounded different than Kalara's or Samantha's.

Then she remembered. Kalara killed Samantha. Kalara throwing a knife. She reached a hesitant hand toward her throat. Thick bandages swathed her throat from shoulder to chin.

She closed her eyes, choosing to listen instead of watch. She needed answers to questions she couldn't ask. Not with the angry burning in her throat.

The candle's tiny flame shone red against her eyelids. Something hovered in front of it, shielding the light. She opened her eyes and stared into eyes much like her own.

The woman smiled. "I'm pleased to see you, Lady Shana."

"No." That word came out as a tiny, painful croak. She wasn't a lady. She played at it.

Long, tapering fingers wrapped over her own. "You honored Moniah with your life. Thank the Creator, he did not take you from us."

He almost did. Her grandmother would have welcomed her, but another brought her back. "Honest?"

"We hoped you knew where he is," Queen Adana said.

54

Leera paused in the never-ending task of tending to the injured. Guilt filled her to the brim. She'd caused this, suggesting they use Ballene's Fire. With each soldier she tended, she forced herself to look deep into their eyes if open, into their face if not, and tell the Creator of her folly. She was a spoiled princess, wanting to prove to her brother her self-worth.

Amar hovered behind her, ready to hand her wet cloths or bandages. He cleared his throat. She turned as he stepped away. Following his gaze, she saw the reason for his alert. Jerold approached. His face reflected how she felt, ravaged with guilt. Without a word, he took her in his arms. Forward, inappropriate, but she let him.

The dam she'd forced into place burst. Shoulders shaking, she clung to him, gasping with the force of her sorrow.

"Shhh. Sweet one." He stroked her hair.

He took her by the arm and led her away from the injured. Far from the prisoners, far from the others, he sat her down on a rock and joined her, his arms cradling her to his chest.

"We did this." Leera's words tumbled out between gasps of crying.

"No. Not you."

His solid chest felt so good, heartbeat pounding against her temples, but she pulled away and looked into his eyes. "The message came from me."

"You did not make the decision, did you?"

The words sounded like something her mother might say to her when her conscience emerged at an inconvenient moment. She pushed out of his arms and stood before him, hands on her hips. "You will not placate me."

He stood as fast as she had. His body loomed so close she saw the growth of stubble on his face. Serious dark brown eyes searched hers. He took a step back, and she shivered at the sudden loss of his warm body. "Forgive me, Princess Leera. I don't want you experiencing pain."

"Why?" The temptation to step back into his embrace pushed at her. She fought it with every muscle in her body.

He ran his hand through his thick brown hair, the sweat of battle clumping it into defined ridges across his head. "I don't want you to associate this pain with me."

"What?" She sounded like a fool, asking one-word questions.

"If the sight of me reminds you of this tragic day, you will wish to never see me again."

That butterfly feeling deep in her abdomen awoke. The signs Kassa once told her and Adana about, the ones that pulled a woman toward a man. "I won't." She leaned in and kissed his cheek, then stepped into his arms.

Her mother would be horrified. Maybe they should go visit her among the prisoners.

55

Honest rushed to keep Maligon's palanquin in sight. The body-guards carrying it moved at a brisk pace. Maligon's sudden disappearance during the first horrible volleys of flaming arrows caught him unprepared. This man, the traitor who terrorized the kingdoms with his cruel and ruthless ambition, ran at the first sign of the green-blue fire he'd proclaimed promised them victory. He abandoned all those who fought for him by choice or force.

If not for the bodyguards, Shana might have attempted to rid the world of this man. The idea made his insides curdle like milk left out in the desert heat. It went against everything he knew and believed. Raised to serve those who kept the faith, he didn't want her to live with that choice as a teacher. Even he didn't have the stomach to serve the final justice of a protector.

Ahead, the ground rose into a steep hill. At the foot of this hill, the bodyguards stopped and lowered the chair to the ground. The two supporting the rear poles turned to face Honest, their arms crossed in defiance. Their hard eyes looked right at the tree where Honest ducked to hide moments before.

The other two bodyguards assisted Maligon from the curtained chair. He moved slower than this morning, his body bent and frail.

Pushing the guards' hands away, Maligon straightened and called out to Honest in a strong voice. "I know you're there, Teacher. Come join me."

As far from the field as they had traveled, he had no choice but to comply,

A smugness transformed the man's weary face into the pompous visage most knew.

Folding his arms so his hands fell into the sleeves of his robes, and close to his knife, Honest took a few steps forward, then stopped. "Why did you run?"

A bark of laughter startled a flock of birds out of the trees. They flapped into the sky, squawking their complaints.

"You think I ran. Like a coward. How rich." The man's shoulders shook with mirth. "I'm not needed during the battle. I can't hold a sword or fight. I'm more useful garnering my men to protect the fortress."

"Your men?" A sparse crew remained at the fortress. Not enough to support the man's claim.

Maligon gestured him forward. "Come. I will show you."

Honest crossed the space, his hands still tucked in his sleeves. The four servants followed as he joined Maligon to climb the hill. The traitor's apparent poor health disappeared with each step they took. The rattle Shana claimed she heard was faint, almost gone. This was not a man close to death. He moved with ease, back straight, black eyes bright with anticipation.

At the top of the hill, Honest fought to hide the visceral upheaval in his stomach as he saw what lay beyond. An army, not as large as the one fighting Queen Adana, but a significant one.

Maligon's smile, so evil that Honest wanted to wipe his hands on his robes to clean them, shifted into a frightening mask of vindication. "These are my true men." He stepped forward.

When Honest didn't follow, he looked over his shoulder at him.

"Come. Meet them. These men serve only me. They aren't Monian, Elwarian, Teletian, or Belwyn."

"Where do they come from?" Honest found enough voice to ask as he forced his feet forward.

One of the sentries spotted them and a shout went up in a guttural tongue that Honest didn't recognize. Shana's reports of unintelligible guttural conversations in Maligon's chambers made frightening sense now.

The chant echoed from one soldier to the next in an odd cheer. It made the hair on Honest's arms stir and straighten like the searching antenna of a bug scenting the air for danger.

"You are surprised." Maligon continued forward, his smug smile a permanent fixture on his face. "These are the sons of those deposed in the first war, the one they called Maligon's Rebellion." He breathed in deep and released his breath in the manner a man might do when he's discovered a delicious smell and knows it hints of a feast waiting for him to enjoy.

"How did you find them?" Honest tried to count the men, but his shock made it impossible.

"I didn't. They found me."

Many of the men ran toward him, and the first of them fell to his knees as Maligon drew closer. The worshipful pose repeated as row upon row of them reached Maligon. It disturbed Honest more than anything he had seen before.

They walked between the men; Maligon placing his hand on their bowed heads as if he blessed them.

In the midst of this vast force of kneeling men, a large tent stood, guarded by a man larger and more intimidating than the ones who had carried Maligon's chair. He bowed and pulled back the flap. "All is prepared, Lord."

With a nod, Maligon ducked inside.

Aware he might never survive this day, Honest followed, unsure what else he could do. As the flap closed behind him, Shana's face flashed in his mind. The sweetness of her smile when she attended to Bauns, unaware he watched her, dripped sorrow in his heart. He'd left her. If the two of them survived, he hoped she'd forgive him.

Inside, three servants waited beside a table laden with food and drink. The Monian army had rationed their meager food stores as they prepared for battle while Maligon withheld a bountiful feast large enough to feed many.

Maligon sat and Honest took the only other chair. One of the servants rushed forward with a tray carrying a decanter and two goblets. He bowed before Maligon, offering the wine, then turned to Honest.

When Honest hesitated, Maligon clucked his tongue in reproval. "It's the best of Lisseme's wines, sent to me as a promise of support by Sarx last year. Please drink." He took a large swallow of his own goblet.

If Maligon wanted to kill him, he could have done it at any point, so Honest drank. The intense mix of flavors known to give body to the small kingdom's one and only export, tumbled over his tongue, awakening flavors he'd forgotten he knew. The charm of it died in his throat as he considered what this gift represented.

"Yes. Yes. It's excellent." Maligon smacked his lips and placed his goblet on a tray held by the servant who stood by his side. The servant refilled it.

"But you asked about the origins of my secret army." Maligon settled back in the large chair made of heavy mahogany and carved with flowers and leaves. "My supporters fled when Chiora exiled me. They feared for their lives. She promised them mercy, but none believed her.

"Many found homes in the desert or the tiny villages on the edge of Moniah and Teletia. Until one day, they heard of the powerful chieftain found riding a donkey with an ox head stuck to his head, suffocating him in the heat."

Maligon grimaced at the memory. "My men struck out to find me and did. By then, the Tunngu embraced me as their god and ruler. My survival amazed them, and they feared me." He winked at Honest. "As they should.

"I brought my men into the tribe, no problem with me in the lead, and they married into the families, securing generations of supporters. They taught their children about the indignities foisted upon me by Micah."

With a wave of his hand, a different servant whisked up a tray of fruit and held it before Maligon. He plucked a small berry from a bowl and bit into it, the juices flowing over his lips. "Chiora loved me, once. That foreigner took it all. These men grew up hating Micah."

"And what of Micah's daughter? Do they hate her?" Honest forced himself to look only at Maligon while trying to sense the emotions of the three servants in the room. Their waves of satisfaction rolled over him in sickening layers. Somehow, Maligon had found a tribe willing to succumb to his rule.

Maligon shrugged. "Some do. Some don't. One can't blame them. She has tainted blood."

The heat inside the tent turned cold, sending groping hands of chill down Honest's back. "Tainted?"

"My dear Teacher, you can't believe the weak, pale blood of Micah gives her much valor or honor? She's tainted by it. As is that young son of Donel's." He shuddered. "To think, they planned to marry the two and dilute the royal blood even more."

Honest tried not to react as he asked, "You will lead these men into the battle today?"

Maligon's eyebrows rose to the top of his forehead. "No. Of course not. We shall wait. Adana will come to me if she defeats Kalara and

Sarx. If Kalara wins, then we will rise to greet and congratulate my closest friends among the kingdoms."

Honest sat back in his chair and fixed his gaze on the man, trying to discern the intricacies of his plan. "Why not join these men to your army before today? You would improve the chances of your triumph then."

"Quite right." Maligon sucked on another berry, then chewed it with relish. "I have greedy allies. It seemed best to let them go to battle against the brat queen. If she's half as strategic as her mother, then she'll kill or capture them. She does *my* will today." He plucked an olive from a bowl and popped it into his mouth. "Brilliant, don't you think?"

"To be sure. I would expect nothing less." Honest sat back, running his fingers through his beard.

"Something bothers you." Maligon leaned over and poured more wine into Honest's goblet.

"Your illness."

He huffed a laugh. "One of my more clever ruses. The Tunggu healers know many secrets of plants. A simple root created the rattle in my chest. It makes anyone who takes it look pale and unwell. Did you notice the rattle got louder?"

"Yes. Just after the rains."

"Yet, you said nothing. The only person brave enough to speak up was the tavern maid. She possesses great awareness. Too bad she'll not live to see the next day."

Honest gripped his goblet and held it to his lips, hiding the gulp of worry over Maligon's words. "Why is that?"

"Kalara will kill her. I've ordered it so. We can't have people following a decoy queen in Moniah, not if I'm going to rule. No, that position belongs to Adana. If she survives."

Mind racing, Honest tried to keep his confusion from his voice. "You mean to keep Adana as queen?"

"Of course. The day Chiora made me her champion, I promised to protect her family's line for as long as I live."

"But why go to all of this effort if you don't plan to rule?"

Maligon chuckled over the rim of his goblet. "You, my dear Brother, disappoint me. I've been ruling Moniah since the day I walked through the fortress gates. Shana is for show. Adana will be, too."

Aghast over the man's assumption that the strong Adana would submit to such a life, Honest shifted in his seat, pretending to peruse the many food options offered by the servants. He plucked a grape and chewed it in thought, forcing himself to swallow it, though his soul rebelled at the idea of food.

"I may be unaware of all of your intentions, but I must admit amazement at your in-depth plans. You have a secret army." He popped another grape in his mouth. "You plan to place Adana on the throne, but only to appease a promise to her mother." Another grape followed the last two. He choked it down. "You faked your illness. You are not going to die."

"Not today. Not tomorrow. Not any time soon. I stopped taking the root two days ago."

The pounding of a runner's feet sounded outside, snapping Maligon's chin up in anticipation. The runner stopped outside the tent, spoke to the guards, and a moment later, a woman entered the tent.

"My Lord. Brother Honest." She fell to her knees, eyes downcast.

It took Honest a moment to recognize her. No longer in Watcher's leathers, her hair fell down her back, unbound from its normal braid. Malay. She wore a simple overshirt and cotton pants. Her feet were bare.

The shock of her presence tightened the fist in Honest's stomach even more. If he received any more shocks, it might explode from the pressure. To his right, he saw the man with the wine decanter straighten, his mouth pressed into a straight line as he gazed down on the kneeling woman.

"My darling child, what news do you bring?" Maligon waved her to stand.

"The false queen surrendered."

Honest jerked his attention back to Malay. Shana surrendered?

"My daughter did not prevent this?"

"Kalara tried to stop her. She killed Kalara."

Pride in his little queen flooded warmth through Honest's chest and threatened to unveil his true loyalties. It took him a moment to realize the small sound, something like a choked sob, came from Maligon, who fell back in his chair, face ashen.

The man had loved his adopted daughter, then. Father Tonch claimed everyone had capacity for love. Somewhere deep inside Maligon, a kernel of humanity must reside. For some reason, seeing the proof of it comforted Honest and made what he realized he must do easier.

Malay frowned at Maligon's reaction. "My Lord, praise your daughter's warrior spirit. The false queen is dead, too. Kalara killed her."

Honest froze, his heart thudded in a frantic rhythm. Turning hot and cold, he groped for the knife in his sleeve. His little queen dead. All qualms of violence dissipated. He'd kill Maligon for taking her from him.

Through his anguish, he realized Maligon spoke, his voice trembling. "My daughter died honorably, then." He gestured to the servant with the decanters. "Do you hear? She left this world but took another with her. A true warrior."

He raised his goblet and turned to Honest.

In the fog of his loss, Honest heard him say, "Drink to her glorious battle with me."

Fingers clutching the goblet, Honest fumbled it to his mouth and choked down a swallow. Tears edged in his throat and scraped at the inside of his chest. He put the goblet down and reached for his knife again.

Maligon drained his cup, threw it across the room, and collapsed in grief again.

Pushing his own grief to the back of his mind, an effort all Empaths learned in order to survive the flood of emotions they experienced from others each day, Honest went to the man, his words as ironic as they felt. "Do not hold back your grief, Lord. You're among friends, here. You can allow yourself this moment before you take your revenge."

Honest wrapped his arm around Maligon's shaking shoulders and looked up at Malay and the servants. "Would you give us a moment?"

Eyes wide with concern, Malay backed out of the tent. Two of the servants scurried out behind her.

The servant who served them wine did not move.

It didn't matter. Without Shana he didn't care. Honest pulled the knife from his sleeve, keeping a close eye on the remaining man.

The servant's eyes widened. He set the tray down with careful precision, arranging it on the table to meet some obsessive need.

When he turned back around, Honest braced himself. Nearly a head taller than Honest, the man could easily stop him.

They stared at each other for a long time. Neither moved. Maligon sat hunched over, his face buried in his hands. The only sound in the room came from his sobs. They didn't even sound real. Shana deserved better, but he could do this for her. Take the life of the one man she'd sought to eliminate. Stop his killing spree and then join her in the afterlife.

At last, the servant nodded. He took a large napkin from the table, folded it, and handed it to Honest.

The fabric felt cool in his hands, and he stared at it unsure of its purpose.

The servant tapped two fingers on his temple and nodded again.

While Maligon wept, Honest covered his hand with the cloth, gripping the knife with it. He expected his hands to shake, but they didn't.

Before the servant might stop him, he drove the knife into Maligon's temple. The act felt right, a man of the Temple taking a life through the temple.

Maligon slumped against the arm of the chair.

Honest waited for the servant to speak or shout an alarm.

Instead, the man walked at a sedate pace to the tent flap and shouted something in the guttural language that Honest didn't recognize. A loud murmuring sounded from outside and grew louder. It swarmed closer.

Bracing for the death blow, Honest held out the knife to the servant. "You may do the honor. I do not need to live any longer."

The servant held both hands out, and Honest laid the weapon across them. Instead of taking Honest's life, the man turned and placed the knife in the center of the table with great reverence, then he crossed to a trunk and withdrew a clean robe. Not brown like the one Honest wore but black. Without speaking, the man returned and removed Honest's robe. He pointed him to a basin of water. "Cleanse yourself," he said.

The noise of the army outside grew louder. Was this a ritual before killing him? An effort to let him remove the sins of murder before death?

Heart pounding with fear over how they might kill him, Honest obeyed, cleaning the evidence of assassination off his body. When he turned, the man stood behind him, holding out the black robe. He assisted him in donning it. "You may leave. My men know of the prophecy for this man's death. You have fulfilled it. They will not harm you."

Honest stared at the man, convinced he'd misheard.

With little effort, the man lifted Maligon's body from the heavy chair and tossed it to the side. It landed with a pleasing thump.

A triumphant smile lighting his eyes, the servant sat in the chair, his back straight, arms resting on the heavy wooden sides. "This man you call Lord came to my village many suns ago. I was a child destined to lead my people after my father. He killed my father and gathered many men to him."

"What of his men? Won't they kill me?"

"No." The servant poured out the remainder of Maligon's wine. "They married our women. Became ours. Gave up their need for revenge."

Honest dropped back into the other chair. "You mentioned a prophecy. What was that?"

"Our woman of the giraffe, the Zirafe. She sees through them and knows the coming of events. The Zirafe told our tribe this man's time with us would end when the bearded and robed man arrived. We must succumb to his tyranny until that man saved us." He turned his dark brown eyes on Honest. "They bowed to you, not him. They welcomed you to your duty."

For a long time, Honest stared at the man. "You are their leader?"

"Yes."

"What will you do, now?"

"Return to our home. Leave this place of confusion and death."

Honest felt lightheaded with the man's explanation. The stories of Queen Moniah told of her finding an injured giraffe calf and bringing it to a small village to nurse it to health. In the process, she had bonded to the animal. The women of the village possessed Watcher gifts and recognized them in her. Could this tribe be descendants of those women?

"What became of your Zirafe? I would like to speak with her."

The man shook his head in sorrow. "Your Lord attacked her after she shared the prophecy. This is forbidden, but we could do nothing. She'd instructed us not to kill him or disasters would plague our tribe. He slashed her with a knife, making her bleed but not killing her. Then dragged her to a canyon where a pride of lions dwelled. He threw her in and forced us to watch as they mauled and ate her. He did the same to her giraffe and any other giraffe his men captured."

The horror of the story, told in this man's deep voice with little emotion, staggered Honest. He sank back into his seat and stared into nothing. The prophecy identified him as the man to rid the Tunggu of their overlord. So many suffered at the hands of the shell of the man dead on the floor.

"What will you do with him?" He nodded to the body.

"We will take his body and do worse."

<h1 style="text-align:center">56</h1>

"What do you mean, he's dead?" Adana scowled at Brother Honest, not bothering to hide her skepticism. "How do I know you didn't aid his escape?"

Brother Honest stood in the courtyard of Adana's View facing her, his face as impassive as a Watcher's. Malay, a Watcher who had been assigned to Shana's honor guard stood beside him, eyes wide with confusion over the words of her actual queen.

The sun bore down on Adana increasing her agitation. After living farther north for so long, the heat felt unbearable. The news that Honest had robbed her of her duty did not improve it.

To her right, Kiffen sat in deep contemplation. She could feel him searching the root of her anger. Let him find the full story, she decided, and opened the memory of Kassa's last words to her.

He didn't react outwardly, but she felt his effort to persuade Am'brosia to calm her. She slammed the connection shut before the animal had a chance.

Malay stepped forward and bobbed her head at Adana. "If I may, Your Majesty, I will speak for him. It is true. Maligon is dead by Brother Honest's hand."

"You remained in the fortress serving Maligon. Why should I trust you?"

Shoulders squared, Malay answered, "Because I protected Lady Shana from death and humiliation. I remained inside as an informant to my father, letting him know what occurred and who surrounded the man who kills with lions."

"And who is your father?"

"Anayetawala. The rightful ruler of my people."

"I need further proof." Adana avoided making eye contact with Malay or Honest. Too many people had lied to her. How many more must she suffer?

"Send for a Seer. They will vouch for me." Honest stood before her in his black robe, not white, brown, or green as a teacher should wear, offering the one solution she couldn't employ.

"Convenient, seeing as you're the only Seer we have at the moment. Last I heard, Helmyra remains in Elwar."

As she fumed in silence, the hurried steps of others approached. Sparing a moment to relieve herself of the sight of the man who stole her right to revenge, she turned. Jerold, Leera, Tonch, and Sariah rushed into the courtyard. Behind them, two of Leera's soldiers carried Shana in a sedan chair. Weakened by blood loss, she could not stand, yet.

Good. Reinforcements.

Adana returned her attention to Honest to find he'd turned pale. He pushed past the others. No one moved a finger to stop him as he rushed toward Shana. She opened her mouth to order him stopped, but Kiffen touched her mind with one word. "Wait."

How had he done that? She'd cut him off. Gloating humor rippled like laughter in her mind. He'd advanced further in his bond than she knew.

Honest waited as the soldiers carrying Shana's chair set it down. Shana blinked up at Honest, eyes brimming with tears.

With a choked cry, Honest dropped to his knees before her, his hands engulfing hers. "Forgive me for leaving you."

She reached out and caressed his face. "True?" So far, her full voice had not returned, so the question came out in a whispery croak.

Honest straightened, his gaze going to her bandages. "What?"

She shook her head. "Killed. Him."

"Yes."

"Good."

Adana could see the two in profile. To her surprise, Honest looked at Shana the way Kiffen looked at her.

When questioned, Shana spoke well of Honest, but she'd forgotten this in the heat of the day. The news of Maligon's death should be a cause for rejoicing. Instead, she fumed over not killing him herself.

The man who had tormented their lives and their parents' lives no longer lived. That should be enough.

She turned to find Sariah and Tonch watching her with concern, twin creases in their brows. Neither spoke.

After several breaths, Leera stepped forward. "Is it true? Maligon is dead?"

"Yes." With the admission, it felt like all the air left Adana's lungs.

Instead of the shouts of joy she expected, Leera reached for Jerold who started to lunge toward Honest.

Leera held him back. "No. This is best."

To Adana's surprise, the emperor of Belwyn relented, turning his tortured gaze on Leera. After he looked into her eyes for a moment, his face softened, and he nodded. "You may be right. We've done enough on our own, haven't we?"

What that meant, Adana could not fathom, but it pleased Leera whose smile shone brighter than the sun baking them where they stood.

"Are you well, child?" Sariah placed a gentle hand on Adana's cheek. Her hand was cool and comforting.

"I—" How could she admit she wanted to kill Maligon?

Kiffen took her hand in his. "She will be. It's a shock, knowing it's over."

"How did he die?" Jerold asked, his gaze wandering between Honest sitting with Shana and Leera by his side.

"Honest claims to have killed him." Kiffen said the words, sending a shiver of astonishment through Adana.

"Why would you doubt him?" Tonch flicked his gaze toward Kiffen, the wrinkle of confusion in his forehead deepening.

"I don't. Adana does."

A garbled sound interrupted them. Shana gesticulated wildly, sounds still difficult for her to manage. Of course, a Listener, even one involved in a surprising reunion, would not miss the importance of their conversation.

Honest tried to hush her, his actions so gentle it made Adana soften a bit toward him.

Tonch bent over Shana, their heads together like close friends sharing secrets.

Left with no other option, Adana waited.

Tonch stepped back and surveyed them, his face stern. "You must be silent and listen closely. Shana wishes to speak."

Licking her lips, Shana's gaze darted between Adana, Kiffen, and Jerold. She opened her mouth and concentrated, her eyes screwing up tight. "H-est goo-d. Truth."

"We can send for Helmyra," Tonch said, "or you can take the word of the woman who killed Kalara and almost lost her life doing so."

Honest turned to look at her, eyes wide with surprise.

Unaware of their audience, Shana nodded, tears forming in her eyes. He used his thumb to wipe them dry, and the others turned away in accord without speaking, and left them to their privacy.

"What do we do now?" Adana said.

"Restore the kingdoms," Kiffen said, "and live."

Epilogue

Kneeling before Father Tonch, Adana breathed in relief as the Keeper of the Faith looked across the gathering of people in the Great Hall of Adana's View and began the ceremony. The wall rebuilt and parts of the aqueducts restored, the fountain behind her gurgled, its happy song matching the mood of those gathered here. After six months of rebuilding and planning, they finally came to an accord of how to rule this much larger kingdom.

To Tonch's left, Sariah and Shana stood. To his right, Honest waited.

Adana knelt beside Kiffen, both wearing the new crowns of their rule as the queen and king of New Yarada. Their combined kingdoms stretched from the mountains north of Elwar to the desert south of Moniah, to the borders of Belwyn and Teletia to the east, and to the tribal lands and seas beyond the border to the west.

Representatives of each of these lands, including Chief Anayetawala of the people Maligon tortured for so long, stood behind them to witness the ceremony.

A nod from Tonch gave her and Kiffen permission to rise and face the crowd. Silence, as they had requested, met them. Then Tonch spoke again.

"Loyal citizens of Moniah and Elwar, today your divided kingdom is no more. Today, you stand under the protection of both Moniah's Seat of Authority and the Throne of Elwar. Your lands spread far and wide and encompass a vast array of people and gifts. We lift our hands to the Creator in thanks and recognize these two who persevered to bring you this day. They stand before you now, victorious and worthy of our honor."

A cheer went up, and, across the crowds, Adana met smiles. No frowns or whispers of concern rippled through the witnesses. A weight dropped from her chest at the sight.

Adana and Kiffen stepped down and took their places in the front row of witnesses.

Tonch gestured to Shana, who stepped forward, a mantle of silver glimmer cloth in her hands. Then he gestured to Honest, who stepped forward, a mantle of gold glimmer cloth in his. This shift in power made Adana dizzy with joy and relief. Her shoulder hummed pleasantly.

"As the rulers of this kingdom," Tonch continued, "you will continue to rule from the Border Keep, and it shall be known from this day forward as the Queen's Seat."

"Yes," Adana and Kiffen said.

This decision created more concern and negotiations than any other, but Kiffen refused to accept a different title. The two kingdoms had divided centuries ago between the two daughters. In Moniah, women always ruled, and over half of Elwar's rulers were women.

Tonch turned to her. "Who, Queen Adana, will you place in command of the southern fortress known as Adana's View? To protect it and ensure the safety and loyalty of your people in the south?"

Adana took a deep breath and released it. With that breath, she turned her home over to the person most able and willing to keep order this close to the desert. "The honor of maintaining our lands in the south goes to Talia of Roshar, who served our kingdom in its darkest days, protecting armies, creating a spy network, and sheltering our allies. She's proven her loyalty beyond expectation."

Talia, dressed in royal robes of blue glimmer cloth, stepped forward.

Shana draped the silver cloak over her shoulders. "Will you protect these lands as you protected so many, giving them hospitality and shelter when it was needed most?"

"Yes." The woman's usually booming voice came out in a bare whisper.

"Who will stand by Talia's side and assist her?" Shana continued.

This decision brought Adana much joy. No one else ever occurred to her or Kiffen when time for this decision came. "The Keeper of the Giraffe, Glume."

Through the shared bond, Glume's continued surprise at this honor swelled. He stepped forward, head dipped in reverence to those who stood before him. Unlike Talia, he wore fine black leathers with strips of silver glimmer cloth threaded through the sleeves. He hadn't wanted to wear anything formal, but Adana overrode him, just like she overrode his first refusal of this position. No other choice made sense with the Giraffe Guard continuing to remain a part of the fortress.

The decision about Talia took longer to decide. She'd tried to give it to Montee. Her advisor declined, insistent she must remain with Adana. Although she considered several other Watchers—Nuala, Umgani, and Charissa were high on that list—all offered to serve wherever Queen Adana sent them but not as commander of the fortress. In the end, Ostreia reminded Adana of Talia's continued support, whether an army camped on her doorstep or not.

Tonch now turned to Kiffen. "Who, King Kiffen, will you place in command of the lands known as Elwar? To protect them and ensure the safety and loyalty of your people in the north?"

Pride thrust Kiffen's shoulders back. She felt it swell through the link as he called forth his new commander. "The honor of maintaining our lands in the north goes to Princess Leera, who proved her loyalty to the true rulers of this kingdom and rallied a great army behind her to ensure traitors did not take away our birthright."

Gone was the little girl that flounced around laughing at Adana those first days in Elwar. A young lady, graceful and calm, stepped forward. She'd chosen to wear a simple green dress with little embellishment. Ever since she'd witnessed the power behind Ballene's Fire, she'd become a different person. Mother Sariah assured Adana and Kiffen that she'd become this woman of grace and power much sooner than that day.

Honest draped the golden cloak over her shoulders. "Will you protect these lands as you protected so many, drawing men and women together under the banner of your home?"

"I will." Her voice rang clear and confident across the crowd.

"Who will stand by Leera's side and assist her when her duties call her elsewhere?"

This decision had worried Kiffen for a long time. Leera finally suggested the right man for the important position. Important because in a year's time, Leera would marry Emperor Jerold and divide her time between the two kingdoms.

"Catch, the adopted son of the Earl of Brom."

The young boy, who used to run messages to the nobility in Elwar's castle, had grown in stature. A young man on the threshold of manhood stepped forward. Behind him, Conrad, the Earl of Brom, beamed. Beside Conrad, Catch's younger sister bounced up and down with excitement.

The sight of these three cast a momentary shadow of regret over Adana's soul. Conrad's son, Pultarch, should have been given this honor, but his inability to accept his position in life destined him to life as a prisoner. Before she sent him to his penance, she'd expressed this thought. He'd told her no, he did not deserve such an honor, even if he had not followed Maligon.

Along with Quilla and the Watchers who supported Maligon, Pultarch now served the tribe of Tunggu, a penance for the years and lives Maligon stole from them.

When word came to them of Catch's parents dying in an attack on their home during Maligon's march to Moniah, Adana thought of the gentle man who deserved a son worthy of his name and a daughter to bring him joy and laughter.

As these four representatives knelt before Adana and Kiffen, the crowd began to cheer. Kiffen slipped his hand in hers, and she felt the connection draw them closer. Each day, she discovered something new about their connection through the giraffes, and each day she loved Kiffen more.

When the crowd quietened, Father Tonch and Mother Sariah stepped forward. Sariah spoke for them, and although Adana knew what came next, her heart hurt when she heard the official words spoken.

"After serving the Faith for over forty years, Tonch and Sariah seek permission to retire from Keeper and Protector of the Faith. Will the people permit it?"

A gasp rippled across the gathering. Permission must come willingly, so they were not forewarned of this request.

Talia and Leera had been tutored in how to respond at this time. They stepped forward.

Talia said, "The people have heard your request and consider it."

Leera said, "Who will keep our faith and protect it if we accept your request?"

Sariah said, "The Protector of the Faith must be willing to act for the best of the people, including protecting our people from those who would do them harm. Brother Honest offers this quality and commitment."

Father Tonch followed her, saying, "The Keeper of the Faith must ensure that all understand their lives as given by the Creator and uphold the teachings of the faith to make sure none changes them. Lady Shana has proven herself faithful and determined to keep our faith and guide all who follow it."

Talia turned to Adana. "Do you accept this proposal?"

"Yes. I honor it."

Leera turned to Kiffen. "Do you accept this proposal?"

"Yes. I honor it."

The two women faced the gathered crowd and spoke together. "Those who accept this request and the names put forth, raise your hands to the Creator."

A sea of hands reached to the sky.

Later, everyone gathered in the Great Hall feasting until dawn.

Adana sat beside Kiffen, gazing over those they loved and cared for. Queen Morana sat with Prince Navon, the young boy nodding in exhaustion and jerking awake every few moments. Thanks to Ostreia's dedication to her role as envoy to Teletia, the rebuilding of their kingdom went well, and many refugees returned to serve their queen and prince.

Leera's bright laughter rang out, and Adana turned a fond gaze on her dearest friend. The night before they had giggled over how Leera used to complain at the lack of eligible princes for her to marry. A secret prince was the kind of story Leera might have concocted in desperation.

"Are you happy, my love?" Kiffen whispered in her ear.

She leaned into him. "Very."

Tomorrow, she'd tell him of the child she now carried and the vision she'd had of their daughter's future.

* * * * *

Map of the Four Kingdoms

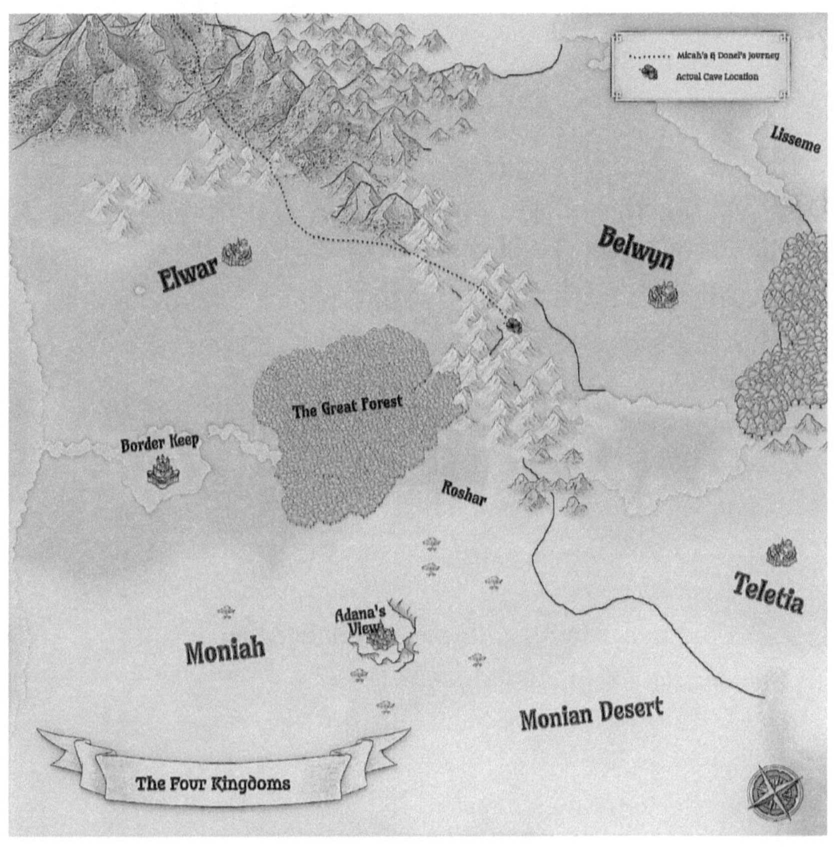

Characters

Adana: Queen of Moniah

Amar: Elwarian refugee soldier

Am'brosia: Giraffe bonded to Adana

Anayetawala: Leader of the Tunggu

Ariff: King of Teletia

Bai'dish: Giraffe bonded to Serrin, later to Kiffen

Bellu: Cook in border keep, sister to Marletta

Biaji: Watcher from the Border Keep

Callan: Elwarian refugee soldier

Catch: Page in Elwar

Charissa: Watcher

Chiora: Adana's mother, former queen of Moniah

Conrad: Earl of Brom, Pultarch's father

Donel: King of Elwar, Kiffen's father

Dosata: Watcher

Ebuli: Ancient Monian queen

Eno: Water Watcher

Father Tonch: Keeper of the Faith

Gabriella: Empress of Belwyn

Gerguld: Elwarian merchant

Glume: Giraffe keeper

Greti: Watcher

Halar: Kassa's husband, Commander, Soldiers of the First Sight

Helmyra: Seamstress in Elwar, Seer

Honest: Teacher of the Faith

Jerold: Prince of Belwyn

Joannu: Watcher killed during the battle at Adana's View

Kalara: Watcher, adopted daughter of Maligon

Karyah: Watcher envoy to Belwyn

Kassa: Former First Vision

Kiffen: Heir to the throne of Elwar, son of King Donel and Queen Roassa

Lady Elayne: False name for Shana

Leera: Kiffen's half-sister, daughter of King Donel and Queen Quilla

Linus: Former Commander of the Soldiers of the First Sight

Malay: Watcher

Maligon: Traitor to the Four Kingdoms

Markel: Sergeant of Elwar's castle guard

Marletta: Keeper of livestock, sister by marriage to Bellu

Memory Keeper: Storyteller

Micah: Adana's father

Miri: Water Maji, leader of the Watcher Watchers

Montee: Adana's First Vision

Morana: Queen of Teletia

Mother Sariah: Protector of the Faith

Navon: Prince of Teletia

Nnochi: First Vision to Ebuli who became queen when Ebuli died without heir

Nuala: Watcher

Ostreia: Watcher envoy to Teletia

Pultarch: Son of the Earl of Brom

Quilla: Queen in Elwar, 2nd wife to King Donel, mother to Leera

Ramil: Stable hand in Adana's View

Roassa: Queen in Elwar, 1st wife to King Donel, mother to Kiffen and Serrin

Ruslan: Elwarian refugee soldier

Salora: Gabriella's attendant and sometimes governess to Jerold

Samanatha: Watcher, Kassa's daughter

Sarx: Elwarian noble

Serrin: 2nd son of King Donel and Queen Roassa

Shana: Tavern maid, resembles Adana, acting as Queen of Moniah

Simeon: Advisor to Kiffen

Sinti: Watcher

Suru: Watcher

Talia: Innkeeper in Roshar

Taren: Sarx's nephew from Lisseme

Umgani: Watcher

Vuur: The Glimmer Isati, head of the glimmer makers

Watcher Ranks

PROMOTION CRITERIA

Candidate: Build fire, accurately throw a knife, use focused breathing

Archery Trainee: Display simple archery & sword fighting skills

Archer: Display advanced archery accuracy and sword control

Tracker: Able to track a quarry over rough terrain, can run 4 hours without becoming winded, skilled in knife fighting

Phantom: Evade trackers, able to fire arrow into crowd or at target without looking and still hit their mark; must complete the 10 arrow interval

Watcher (Basic troops): Can identify specific but minor changes in a crowd or busy landscape, use vision for perception of danger in unfamiliar surroundings, might experience prophetic visions

Unit Leader: Leads a unit of 5 Watchers, must have prophetic visions

Squad Leader: Leads 4 Units (20 Watchers, 4 Unit leaders)

Strategist: Trained in hazardous espionage and military strategy

Troop Leader: Leads 5 squads (100 Watchers, 5 Squad Leaders, 20 Unit leaders)

Strategist Unit Leader: Commands 5 Strategists

Regiment Leader: Commands 10 troops

Tactical Command: Commands 3 Special Forces Units

WATCHER BADGES

Candidate: Flame

Archery Trainee: Sword crossed over a bow

Archer: Bullseye target in yellow & brown

Tracker: Runner with a knife

Phantom: A closed eye/An open eye

Watcher (Basic troops): A single giraffe

Unit Leader: A herd of giraffes

Squad Leader: Brown giraffe under a tree

Strategist: Brown giraffe surrounded by bushes

Troop Leader: Giraffe on a yellow background

Strategists Unit Leader: Giraffe on a field of green

Regiment Leader: Giraffe head in profile on brown glimmer background

Tactical Command: Giraffe head in profile on black glimmer background

Also by Barbara V. Evers

The Watchers of Moniah Trilogy
The Watchers of Moniah
The Watchers in Exile
The Watchers at War

Short Story Collections
Pieces of Her: Being a Woman Is Not For the Faint of Heart
The Nature of the Beast (coming soon)

Join the Watchers' Tribe newsletter!!

Don't get caught with your eyes closed!

https://www.BarbaraVEvers.com

As a welcome gift, you'll receive a short story from the world of Moniah. Subscribers, also, get early notice on new releases and book news, access to subscriber-only contests, free short stories, updates on Barbara's appearances, giraffe news, and more.

Author's Note

While the giraffes in this story are fictional and exist in my imagination, and hopefully in yours now, I hope you'll take the time to find out more about the plight of real giraffes and the efforts the Giraffe Conservation Foundation (GCF) is taking to save them.

Giraffes suffer from a silent extinction because they do not receive the publicity other endangered animals receive. According to GCF's website, giraffe numbers have declined by almost 30% in the last three decades to approximately 117,000 in the wild. It is likely that giraffe numbered ten times as many only a century ago. Please check out https://giraffeconservation.org and help if you can. By purchasing this book, you've already helped because I donate a portion of my royalties from this series to GCF.

"Just Me" explores looking for love in the wrong place. It's a tad funny and a bit stalkerish, so it's set during the mid-1980s when people saw the pursuit of love a bit differently. This story was a semi-finalist in the prestigious Faulkner-Wisdom writing competition.

I slunk down in the seat and peered out at the parking lot, twisting around to check it from all angles. Nothing moved. Inhaling like I was about to dive into the deep end, I shoved the heavy car door open, crouched down low, and scurried to the VW.

"Pieces" is also set in the early 1980s and takes a look at suspicions of domestic violence. This one had to be set in that time period for the responses to be realistic. Also, it's the oldest story in this collection, written in 2004.

He lies. I know it. She knows it. She looks at me, her mouth dropping open in that peculiar way it does when she suspects something but is afraid to speak of it.

"John-E-Mail" tells a story through emails sent between a young woman and her military boyfriend serving in Iraq, with a few added emails from two other people. This one came from a writing prompt, and I hope you find it as amusing as I do.

I felt so left out, today. I rented Cold Mountain because Nicole Kidman knows how I feel. You know how she writes her boyfriend and tells him to come home to her and he does? I wish you could do that.

I wrote "The Wall" in response to an invite to submit a story with a political theme. On a whim, I placed a husband and wife on opposite sides of the controversy.

She'd crept up on him like one of the snakes slithering in the underbrush, a frown creasing her forehead, turning her older and less attractive in his eyes.

"The Devil's Wife" takes a look at an old wive's tale I heard a long time ago. The shortest story in this collection, the last lines require careful attention to what the character says. I think it's clever, but hey, I wrote it. LOL!

The wariness in her gaze gave Isaac pause. He knew the calculated look, the searching for a decision, trying to determine whether to share or not. What confession might spill out in his office today?

"Gentle Snow" remains one of my favorites. It looks at whether or not you'll let your past catch up to you. Interesting side note: A few years ago, an author friend, Barbara Claypole White, commented on Facebook about the tension in this story. The other author she mentioned in the same post? Stephen King! Definitely made my day!

Sarah and Gloria had explored the large house during its construction, long before she knew it would become his lair.

"Books, Brandys, and Blue-Hairs" is another of my favorites. I wrote it not long after "Pieces" but, due to its length, never found a journal to submit it to. It's been updated numerous times, so the original had different references than this version. An exploration of past mistakes, this time we dig into the family dynamics of a grown daughter forced to come home and live with her parents while recovering from a divorce. This story was a semi-finalist in the prestigious Faulkner-Wisdom writing competition.

Quiet settled over the dining room table like the night we'd learned of Uncle Joe's death. The heater ticked as it kicked on and the blowers, shifting the hair on my head, pressed hot air down on me like it had on those dark days after the book banishment.

"The Magic of the Mountain" takes another look at mothers and daughters but at a later point in life. This haunting story with elements of magical realism, never found a home in a journal due to its length. I love it for very different reasons than the others in this collection, but explaining why would take too much time.

In the last few years, only Mom and I went, content to sit on the mountain, enjoying the peace of its green embrace. This year, I prepared to return alone one last time to say goodbye.

Scan to get your copy of **Pieces of Her**

Scan Me

Barbara V. Evers is the author of THE WATCHERS OF MONIAH epic fantasy trilogy as well as several short stories and essays. From the mysterious Dark Corner of South Carolina, she crafts fantasy stories with strong women matriarchies and unusually gifted and clever animals. A two-time Imadjinn Best Fantasy Novelist, she's won several awards for her writing over the years including a Pushcart Prize nomination.

Barbara is a supporter and advocate for animal conservation and seeks to educate others about endangered species. The giraffes in THE WATCHERS OF MONIAH are no longer endangered, but giraffes in our world are suffering a silent extinction. As an advocate, Barbara contributes a portion of her royalties to support the work of The Giraffe Conservation Foundation. When she's not writing, Barbara uses her degrees in Zoology and Communication to conduct training workshops for businesses. Maybe she really can speak to animals!

Any other time, she can be found herding her husband, two grandchildren, and her rescue dog, Roxy (but don't tell them).

www.ingramcontent.com/pod-product-compliance
Lightning Source LLC
Chambersburg PA
CBHW032106310726
48972CB00001B/124